A DUTY OF CARE

About the Author

Gerald Seymour spent fifteen years as an international television news reporter with ITN, covering Vietnam and the Middle East, and specialising in the subject of terrorism across the world. Seymour was on the streets of Londonderry on the afternoon of Bloody Sunday, and was a witness to the massacre of Israeli athletes at the Munich Olympics.

Gerald Seymour exploded onto the literary scene with the massive bestseller *Harry's Game*, that has since been picked by the *Sunday Times* as one of the 100 best thrillers written since 1945. He has been a full-time writer since 1978, and six of his novels have been filmed for television in the UK and US. *A Duty of Care* is his forty-first novel.

Also by Gerald Seymour

Harry's Game	Traitor's Kiss
The Glory Boys	The Unknown Soldier
Kingfisher	Rat Run
Red Fox	The Walking Dead
The Contract	Timebomb
Archangel	The Collaborator
In Honour Bound	The Dealer and the Dead
Field of Blood	A Deniable Death
A Song in the Morning	The Outsiders
At Close Quarters	The Corporal's Wife
Home Run	Vagabond
Condition Black	No Mortal Thing
The Journeyman Tailor	Jericho's War
The Fighting Man	A Damned Serious Business
The Heart of Danger	Battle Sight Zero
Killing Ground	Beyond Recall
The Waiting Time	The Crocodile Hunter
A Line in the Sand	The Foot Soldiers
Holding the Zero	In At The Kill
The Untouchable	The Best Revenge

A
DUTY
OF
CARE

Gerald Seymour

**HODDER &
STOUGHTON**

First published in Great Britain in 2025 by Hodder & Stoughton
An Hachette UK company

1

Copyright © Gerald Seymour 2025

A CIP catalogue record for this title is available from the British Library

Hardback ISBN 978 1 399 72203 2
Trade Paperback ISBN 978 1 399 72206 3
ebook ISBN 978 1 399 72204 9

Typeset in Plantin Light by Hewer Text UK Ltd, Edinburgh
Printed and bound in Great Britain by Clays Ltd, Elcograf S.p.A.

Hodder & Stoughton policy is to use papers that are natural, renewable
and recyclable products and made from wood grown in sustainable forests.
The logging and manufacturing processes are expected to conform
to the environmental regulations of the country of origin.

Hodder & Stoughton Ltd
Carmelite House
50 Victoria Embankment
London EC4Y 0DZ

The authorised representative in the EEA is Hachette Ireland, 8 Castlecourt
Centre, Castleknock Road, Castleknock, Dublin 15, D15 YF6A, Ireland

www.hodder.co.uk

For Gillian

PROLOGUE

He would not, absolutely not, have told her to kill the noise, shut the fuck up.

Would not have hissed at her, or snapped, because she was the granddaughter of the *shef* in the village and Bresnik was merely a *mik*, the lowest rank in the clan, subservient and with no authority to criticise her, let alone swear at her. From her mouth came the tuneless words of an Abba song, like it was stuck, repeated every few seconds. Perhaps she did not know any other verses. He loathed the song and hated it more each time she droned it, but he did not complain because he was bottom of the heap and all his loyalty was directed at her grandfather.

The singing was bad but the sound from the garden shears she held was worse. She was eleven years old. She was in a routine, not varying her pace, and her face was split with a broad smile as if she had found true happiness. For her to smile was rare, so infrequent that it would be worth telling his wife of it, but only in a hushed voice because to talk of the child was dangerous for a man at the basement level of the clan. She grinned, showing a glimpse of pleasure each time she came to the end of a phase of the routine . . . The shame was that she had not been killed in the explosion.

Because the shears were rusted at the fastening that held the blades together, the child had to use all her undeveloped strength to open them. There was then the scratching sound of metal forced against metal, until she sucked more breath into her lungs, steeled herself to slam the handles together, uniting the blades with a crack like a gun being fired. All her power was directed at the effort, and the noise echoed inside the cellar and bounced off the dark walls. Then she would lay the shears on her lap while she sat, cross-legged and resumed her singing; she liked to massage her lips with skinny fingers, sometimes kissing them or dripping one access into her mouth. Then, as if responding to the closing of the blades, she would crook the finger that had been in her mouth and the gesture would seem to demonstrate that the finger had been taken off at the second knuckle down from her dirt-encrusted nails.

She was Klea. The name given to girls at birth, acknowledging Cleopatra, the ruler of ancient Egypt, altered to fit with the dialect of the Gheg tribes in the northern mountainous part of the country. Other than its link to the woman of great power and beauty *Klea* was also their word for glory. Klea's face was usually covered with a mask of expressionless withdrawal, eyes empty of emotion, like those of a slaughtered sheep or goat or a wild creature from up on the crags and cliff faces that were the boundaries, east and west, of the village. Her skin was pale and she wore a white dress, printed with sprigs of wild lavender and the wings of brightly coloured butterflies. It was said that the dress was washed each night by her grandfather's housekeeper and then dried in front of a fire, whatever the summer temperature or whether snow was on the ground, then ironed ready for her to wear when she rose – at five or six in the morning. Then, shivering or perspiring, she would take her dog and her goats out from the corral where they were kept overnight. Sometimes she would walk to the meadow or climb the trails among the rocks, and sometimes prowl where only the most sure-footed could reach . . . They laughed at her, some of the village people, but only when sure of their privacy, and used the bastardisation of a phrase brought back from England – she was "not the full lek", the lek being the official state currency, near worthless in comparison to the great American dollar. They laughed behind her back and where they were not overheard, but accepted that she possessed "gifts".

The shears in her hands had not been oiled for as long as any of the older men in the community could remember, certainly not in the time since they had been put to new use. It was said that similar shears, with blunt and dirty sharpened blades, had been used by the father of the present *shef* during the interrogation of captured Italian or German soldiers during the years of occupation. Years later, a villa had been built for the chief man, and a landscaper had been called in to design a garden to equal those belonging to the *capi* of any of the Italian clans. But there had been no interest in looking after the garden, and the plants and sapling trees had either died in the winter snowfall, or been washed away when the spring thaw came, or had been scorched to their roots in the summer heat when the power of the sun was magnified inside the steep-sided walls of the valley. The shears abandoned by the landscape company had been forgotten until they had been found and new use given them. No oil and no stone to make the blades keener, and no scrubbing brush used to remove the stains of the last occasion that the blades had been put to use.

The singing, the obscene grin, the squealing as the blades were opened and the impact, sudden and terrifying as they were rammed shut, and the fingers flickering at the child's mouth, were not aimed at the *mik*, but at the prisoner.

He was probably aged about 40. The cellar was dark but a light bulb from a hanging cable dangled above him. The throw of the light was sufficient for him to see the child who grinned each time she added to his torment but the *mik* was further back and to the side of her, sitting with his back against the door, a cushion under his backside, but uncomfortable because a Luger pistol was in his belt and the fore-sight pinched his groin. The slight degree of pain kept him alert which was important. There was no way the prisoner could free himself from the handcuffs fastening his wrists behind his back, and attached to a looped chain that was threaded into a ring on the wall and padlocked. The key to the padlock was in the *mik's* trouser pocket. Both the child and he were beyond the length of the chain holding the prisoner to the wall. The *mik's* duty was to guard the prisoner, to prevent any possibility of escape. He understood why the child was allowed to share the cellar space with himself and the prisoner, why at the age of eleven she was so indulged . . . She was responsible for the prisoner's capture.

A brave man, the *mik* acknowledged. A man of dignity.

Anyone who worked for the *shef* of the village and for the network he ran that stretched far outside the valley, beyond Albania's frontiers, into Europe and across oceans, would appreciate that inside the areas of organised crime there were times of great success and also those when the heavens caved in upon them. In such times it was possible that even a figure in the clan as insignificant as a *mik*, a friend – not a *kryetar* who was an under-boss, not a *krye* who was a boss, not sitting on the *bajrak* which was the leadership council, not top man of the clan which was the *shef* – could still be in the line of fire. A feud, a vendetta between clans and he, Bresnik, might have become target and been carted off to a similar cellar, knowing that he would be mutilated so that a message was sent to everyone in the village, then put to death. Might well happen. He was rewarded with a decent house in the village, a fridge and a freezer in the kitchen, and an electric cooker and a washing machine, dishwasher and widescreen TV, but if those heavens fell and flattened him then he would have to hope that those who had taken him would do the job fast, minimise the torture, would get it fucking done . . .

She made a dirge of the song and continued to open the blades and slam them shut and to gesture that when she was given permission the shears could lop off his fingers. Bresnik, confused and twisted, imagined the terror that their prisoner was feeling.

The child was there because her grandfather had rewarded her. Her pleading had been accepted. Without her, the man's cover would have held.

The name in the prisoner's travel documents was Jean-Claude Michel. Three weeks before, he had hiked into the village, carrying the identity of a lecturer in the language from the Illyrian period – before the Greeks and Romans had arrived and the tribes had a tongue of their own. They had been skilled masters in creating jewellery from the silver they mined. Michel had hoped to study the dialect in this remote corner of the country, accessible only by a single gravel road. He was plausible . . . he was even liked . . . because of the warmth of his praise and gratitude, his ability to flatter. He was due to move on in a couple of days and a party was planned under the culture of *besa* – was trust – and a sheep would be slaughtered, disembowelled and skinned and roasted on a turning spit . . . the men and women of the village had grown fond of him, and so had the *shef* in his villa. He had possessed little money but had insisted on paying for his lodging over by the Orthodox church, and for the meals some of the families had prepared for him . . . He had duped them, deceived all of them, except the child who was the granddaughter of the man who mattered. Under the *kanun* by which they lived they were obliged to provide hospitality to a stranger, and were also obliged to exact ferocious revenge if their tradition was abused. It was the child who had denounced him.

The man now chained against the wall, unable to reach his persecutor, nor the *mik* and his Luger and the key in his pocket, would have heard each off-tune note in the child's voice and each opening and closing of the blades, might have been spared a clear view of the fingers at her mouth, but probably had the intelligence to imagine. He had been beaten and his eyes were both near closed, and his cheeks were bruised and scars covered his head and blood had congealed in his long hair. The documents said he was from Rouen, in France. He had admitted what the papers and passport did not declare: that he was an officer of the Central Directorate of the Judicial Police, that he worked from an anonymous office block in the 6th *arrondissement*, in Paris, that he had been chosen for this surveillance operation because of his slight knowledge of the Albanian language which had been helped along by a two-month intensive course. He had been close to being accepted in the village, the hub of a major organised crime group – one of the more successful ones in this corner of the Balkans – and had been "outed" by a child whose intelligence he had most likely not considered.

The *mik* knew the basis of the accusations made.

She was a child that no one would regard as a symbol of danger, more likely the subject of pity. She seemed to move outside the villa gates with the innocence of a leaf blown along by a light wind.

Only a child. A simple child. A child who drifted on to the rough
ground at the edge of the village and walked across the football
pitch, and then came to meadows that were either frozen
depending on the season, or rich in wild flowers. She would have
her dog with her, one-eyed from a fight with a cat, and her goats
would be close behind her. Her routine did not change if a gale
blew, a blizzard of hail battered her, or the sun came low on her
face, and she wore the same bright and modest dress every day . . .
The French surveillance officer, chained to the wall, heard each
note of her song and the squeal of the shears' blades opening and
the clatter of them closing, and maybe he did not care to watch the
way she put her fingers to her mouth.

In the weeks that he had been in the village and had spoken
with courtesy and respect, and had been fed as a guest in people's
homes and had taken the hospitality offered him under the terms
of their *kanun*, he had not aroused suspicion. A fine party had
been planned, and the morning after he was due to be driven to
Shkodra and there would catch a bus to Tirana and the airport.
He had told those who had cared to listen that he would remember
with great affection, back in his office in the college at Rouen, the
warmth and kindness extended to him.

The *mik* had seen the man's last moments of freedom playing
out. Had been close to the villa's gates, hosing down the big
Mercedes saloon used by the *shef*, and the child, Klea, had arrived
at the gate, had seen her grandfather deep in conversation with
two nervous boys from the village who were about to take the long
journey across Europe. The child had gone to her grandfather,
had tugged at his sleeve, had cut him mid-sentence, had led him
away. No one else in the village, not even the *shef's* grandson who
was eleven years older than Klea, would have dared to snatch him
away. She had spoken in his ear, standing on tiptoe. At first his
expression had been of disbelief. Next, at his mouth and in his
eyes, had been doubt and rare confusion. Then, still listening, his
lips had narrowed and his chin had jutted, and his clenched fist
had thwacked in anger into the palm of his free hand. He had
called the *mik* to him, and others of the same rank, and a *kryetar*,

and had phoned for his favoured *krye* . . . Those already with him were told to watch the stranger, no phones to be used and no radio activated. The old man had walked away with the child, who held his hand, and the goats trudged behind and her dog was at her heel . . .

A good haul – two mobiles, a transmitter, three bugs the size of matchboxes with magnets attached, a diary of handwritten notes. Beyond the football pitch and the meadows was a line of pine trees that hid the lower cliffs of the rock faces that towered over the village. The items – including military standard binoculars and a camera with a quality lens – had been wrapped in sacking and secreted in a tiny cave, hidden beyond an entrance no wider than the mouth of a household bucket. After an hour, grandfather and granddaughter returned, the child skipping beside the old man and the goats dutifully following, and the old man's face was a thunder of anger. Instructions given . . . a beating started . . . protestations of innocence . . . a minimal confession easily gained . . . much more to be learned . . . a prisoner shackled in a cellar . . . bluster about being a French police officer and the retribution if he were harmed, and the words he would utter of gratitude in high places if he were freed without further injury. And he had spluttered out descriptions of his wife who ran a *patisserie* and his children who were approaching the age for important examinations, and his old father and his old mother, and . . .

Now he was silent, his head bowed, unable to block the sound of the shears in her hands.

The *mik*, unlike others in the village, took no pleasure in dishing out pain for the sake of demonstrating his superiority. Often enough he had reflected that his own time might come, and then he would pray for it to be quick. He knew the child had demanded of her grandfather that she be allowed into the cellar when the Frenchman had been chained against the far wall. Had seen her relish when she had first prised open the shears and struggled to whip the blades together, sometimes with a little giggle and more often the dirge of the Abba song. The *mik* had heard that the song had been playing in her parents' car when it was hit, destroyed, killing them but not her. She had been allowed by her grandfather to sit in the cellar and he did not doubt that she would demand of the old man to be allowed to use the shears: he needed to know the codes, what information had been passed, the specifics of the targeting.

If Klea had not been present, the *mik* would have edged closer to the prisoner and put a lit cigarette between his broken, swollen, bloody lips. A little gesture – not one of mercy but one of . . . he did not have the language to describe why it would have been necessary. But the child was there and he did not dare to.

The drone of her voice and the squeal of the blades, then the crack as they came together. The man seemed to throw back his head and a cough came into his throat, seemed to be plugged there, and another hacked behind it, and then a convulsion and the chain rattled as the man writhed. His legs came up and thrashed at emptiness. The sounds of the child quickened as if she were now provided with more amusement. The legs came up again and kicked high and the shoulders shook and must have been near to dislocation, and more frantic, as if the picture of the opened blades selecting which finger or thumb would go first was sharp in his battered mind.

And he would not tell her, absolutely not, to shut the fuck up.

But he did not need to. Another cough and a retching from deep in the man's throat and a heave upwards of his torso and a higher kick from his legs, all done for the last time. Lucky bastard, the *mik* thought. He pushed himself up, then hesitated. The child screamed, not from hurt but from rage. A scream wrapped in a tantrum . . . he had barely heard her speak, not since they had brought her back with her parents' coffins. Now she screamed, raised her arm behind her and pitched it forward and threw the shears at the dead prisoner.

The *mik* had seen death enough times. No one existed as a "friend" of the *shef* and was not familiar with the sight of death. The man's legs were twisted and his head lolled sideways, and no breath bubbled the moisture at his lips. The shears hit him full in the chest and punctured the skin but the blood only came in a dribble. The girl lashed out with her foot and yelled at the corpse.

"You pig, you cheated me. I was promised. Grandpapa said I could, said I would be allowed."

He wondered for a moment whether she would push herself up and cross the cellar floor, retrieve the shears and work the blades over his fingers. He would not have stopped her ... Another "friend" had been outside the door and would have run with the news. She got up from the floor and left the cellar, slamming the door after her and sobbing in frustration. He sat there, waiting to be told what to do.

It would have been a quarter of an hour later that the *shef* came, and the *krye* and the *kryetar*, and by that time, the *mik* had unfastened the padlock on the chain and had freed the handcuffs and laid out the body and closed the eyes, and had already whispered into the man's ears that he was lucky and that his God had smiled on him.

The old man who ran an empire of narcotics and girls and weapons said, "My little sweetheart is disappointed at how it ended, but I think now she feels better. I tell you very frankly that this rat deceived all of us except her. She can smell it, smell what is wrong ... He should be taken down the Shkodra road and at the bridge and the waterfall he should be put in the river, and his clothing in his rucksack and the camera with all the images cleared and his phones, everything he brought with him. When questions are asked, then he came to us and we entertained him, and he left us, and he had aroused no suspicion. And all his papers – except for the diary ... I tell you, the French agencies can do nothing because this man is here without the permission of the Albanian state. I say that with certainty because I would have heard of it had it been granted. They cannot send their troops, their security police, or complain because they are not able to say why their man was here – by whose authority? – In a week or two, the body of an academic will be found, and repatriated. I say it again, without my little sweetheart we would not have known of the presence of the vermin among us."

When a truck had been backed up to the outer door of the steps leading down to the cellar, and when all the Frenchman's papers and possessions had been packed away as instructed, the *mik* and the *kryetar* carried the body, with difficulty, up the narrow steps and out into the late afternoon light. The village would have seemed at peace and there was a threat of more rain later in the evening. Which was good. Rain would help to raise the level of the water in the river close to Shkodra and there would be a good chance of the body being carried out into the lake, and a fair chance of subterranean currents taking it beyond the border between Albanian and the neighbouring state of Montenegro.

A heart attack had come as a blessing to the man – and the *mik* regretted that he had not found an opportunity to put a cigarette between his lips. It was a struggle to bring his body up the steps and out into the light and they dropped it and heaved breath back into their lungs, and he mopped his forehead – and saw her.

Saw her with her dog, her goats following, and she was again a figure of innocence, and harmless. She was above the football pitch and had crossed the meadows and would have come through the tree line, and was now alone on a trail path made by livestock. She climbed and scrambled and was lost in her own world and her scream at being denied the chance to cut off a man's fingers with a rusted pair of garden shears was silenced.

I

The lord was Jonas Merrick, his manor was the Post Room.

He was there for disciplinary reasons. And because an argument had been forcefully made that his powers of analysis were too great for him to be dumped in a retirement bucket. It had been suggested by the senior kangaroo – the name given his accusers who presided over that sort of court – that the Post Room would act both as a punishment posting and an example to any others who freelanced beyond the strict procedures demanded of Thames House. A fitting banishment from matters of importance to the Security Service's smooth running. It also suggested that there might come a time in the future when his talents, under close supervision, might be called upon . . . but not now, not anytime soon. A case had also been made by his lone supporter in the building that to chuck out Jonas Merrick, Queen's Gallantry Medal and Bar, that an abrupt dismissal of an individual so devoted to the Service could, possibly, lead to a disintegration of his mental wellbeing . . . So, it was to the Post Room where he had been sent eleven months before.

On his arrival in this corner of the basement, there had been ructions among the staff. The idea that their work was so unimportant, so irrelevant, that they were suitable hosts to a man from the third floor who had crossed red lines in working practices had irritated, then annoyed. Vernon, who ran the unit, had made a formal complaint to Human Resources and had spat the word *insulting*, and a sub-committee had been tasked to examine options. A week after the cuckoo's arrival, a conversation had been overheard between the newly appointed DepDG, Brian, and the longstanding AssDepDG, the sole champion of Jonas who had lied frequently and forcefully in his defence.

"For God's sake, isn't this an area of financial waste? Who, today, needs a Post Room?"

"Difficult to make a copper-bottomed defence of the unit, Brian, but it's cheap to run. Wages bottom of the grading. You might be surprised at the numbers of Suspicious of Sevenoaks who write in with accusations of their neighbours, Russian spies or Chinese spies or Irish spies or . . . And they have other uses."

"Can't imagine what they would be. Thought letters and second class stamps had gone out with the Ark."

Sarah had heard it. She had been at the coffee dispenser beside the open door, was filling a beaker for Vernon. There had been a warning that the recently clocked-in DepDG would be touring all areas of the building, familiarisation with an edge towards winning greater efficiency and culling wasted resources. The angle of the door had hidden her. The voices were clear. Sarah was the Post Room's dogsbody.

"A sort of glue for the place, actually. Circulars on the Pride marches, concert groups and choir practice, the sailing club and golf and tennis. Actually more secure than everyone having everyone else's mobile number. Our version of Alcatraz . . ."

She had heard the chuckle.

"The infamous Jonas Merrick. I think I am, as Deputy Director General, allowed a briefing. Haven't been given it yet. Shoot, please."

"Unexpurgated or redacted?"

"Warts and all if you don't mind."

Vernon's coffee had gone cold. She could remember when the small, rather overweight man had come in through the door sharp at eight o'clock one Monday morning, carrying a briefcase, old and frayed and with *EIIR*'s gold inlay barely visible on the flap. Dressed as if he had bought a job lot from a charity shop: brogues, flannels, checked shirt and tie, tweed jacket that was stained, and a scarf and a raincoat and a trilby hat. Colour in his face but a nose slightly rearranged to the right, and spectacles that had adhesive tape on one side strengthening the arm's hold on the main frame. He had looked around, been greeted without grace by forewarned Vernon, had shaken hands but not with any enthusiasm.

The Post Room over recent years had shrunk both in influence and size. Its extent was now some fifty feet by forty, and the last loss of space had come with the expansion of the rest area allocated to the firearms police guarding the building, and their armoury. There were desks, filing cabinets, trolleys for parcels and mail, and one corner was cut off for toilets because the police had taken ownership of the former ones. On the walls were a portrait of the king, a montage of clocks showing different times across the world, and noticeboards with leave charts and dates for the LGBTQ events and the ballroom dancing and long-distance cycling and details of a dating app, a display of holiday postcards, and . . . no windows, no natural source of light.

He had looked around him, had selected a corner, then had begun laboriously to manoeuvre a filing cabinet towards it, grunting, sweating a bit, pushing it where he wanted it, then another, and another after that. The cabinets each had three drawers and when placed together they formed a solid wall. He had found a desk that seemed empty, and had lifted it at one end and let its metal legs scrape the vinyl floor and dragged it behind the screen of cabinets, then a chair. He had not been helped nor seemed to have expected to be. He had sat down, had opened his briefcase and taken out a thermos flask and a plastic box of the right size for sandwiches. Then the intruder was asked what he wanted, a question put with sarcasm. A soft voice, without enmity, hostility or apology, had said he would need a secure phone, a quality and protected computer, a comfortable desk chair. In the meantime a gross of paperclips would be a good start, and he could begin to count them – said without a flicker of a smile. And he had arrived in the mornings, and left in the evenings at the same times and his schedule had not deviated. Little to nothing had been known of him except that he had flaunted a rule of internal discipline and he was here as a punishment, and Sarah had eavesdropped a conversation between the Deputy Director General and the Assistant Deputy Director General, and had shivered with the excitement of being able to colour in a blank canvas.

"We don't care to shout this history around the building, as you'll understand. He was due to be put out to grass having worked here three decades as an analyst. His stuff was seldom read, and he had funked a low-key, the lowest possible, leaving do. Was down the road by the Burghers of Calais statue and found himself next to a shivering wretch of a youth whose body bulged in a vest. On his way to the Houses of Parliament. Never reached it, Jonas disarmed him. Should have waited for the cavalry, his critics said; in fact, gave us a useful insight into the suiciders' recruitment. I spent an hour on his files, realised their quality, drove in the small hours to his home, and put him back on the payroll. That was one ... Two. Tracked an ISIS boy returning home with a backpack of hate and a target of where the Penguin boys flew the drones from, some RAF base in eastern England. Merrick located where he would be, his mum's home, the night before the target would be hit. Played the simpleton, until the moment after he'd slapped a handcuff on him, joined to his own wrist, and received a savage beating for his pains, but saved a shoot-out or a possible escape. Now three. We sent him over to the Sixers and he does a job of work they were squeamish about. Identifies an internal leak there and two Russian boys are supposed to take down a defector who has come to us, and their boys end up as fatals, and the leak should have gone to internal security except that Jonas is grandstanding and ends up in the Thames. Long story and messy. Could have been drowned, the critics said, so he was put in a backwater, Organised Crime, and becomes the Americans' friend, and winds up a submarine importation of four tonnes of uncut cocaine in northwest Spain. Identifies a Liverpool-based matriarch and the whole family is now put away, and will be for many years. Wants an eyeball on the arrests there and is early, while the H&Ks of the local force turn up late, and good old Jonas is damn near shot to death. I'm going on ... Now five. Kept it to himself, runs a private war against Chinese espionage, an irregular in the West Midlands is turned by him and the Agency is grovelling gratitude for access to him. You are getting an impression of a man on a treadmill who needs to succeed, and Vladdy the Evil wants his head on a plate, and damn near gets it, but that's another story and a long one again."

"*Remarkable.*"

"*Naughty . . . but well worth his gongs – which few here have earned. So the Post Room is a slap on the wrist and a place to bury him, for flagrant breaking of rules.*"

"*In the future, on my watch, should I be wary of him?*"

"*Not at all. I rate him now as nervous as a church mouse of his own safety, and monitored. Out of harm's way.*"

"*Your guarantee?*"

"*Scouts' honour, if you know what I mean.*"

"*Do I get to see him?*"

"*Better not. Sleeping quietly, figuratively. No trouble to anyone, has dug out a spot similar to a badger sett. Returns here each dawn, leaves again at dusk . . . Best left to himself. Anyway, that's the Post Room, and next door to them is the police rest area. Shall we go and cast an eye over their territory?*"

And they were gone. Sarah had scurried over to Vernon, had crouched beside him, and relayed all she had heard. He had grimaced. A reputation had been forged, and to his face he was now Mr Merrick, and beyond his earshot he was the "guv'nor". Not that anyone who worked in that part of the Security Service HQ, in their basement, looked less like a football manager or a career criminal. But, that was eleven months ago . . .

Stretching high above the Post Room were five more floors of Thames House, and other than the AssDepDG none would have realised the scale of the fiefdom in the basement, not noticed how papers and documents now seemed to take an extra day, or two days, to reach their desks, barely noticed because they liked to keep their eyes on their screens. It was a state within a state, a matter on which the AssDepDG had assured his superior the Service was protected against – guaranteed it.

Jonas Merrick was meticulous in his timekeeping. Always such a crush on the 5.37 train out of Waterloo which would deliver him in less than half an hour to Raynes Park. If he had not been on the platform before the train came in, there would have been a high chance he would not get a seat.

Almost, not quite, a sad day. The end of a week in which the pieces had *almost* come together. Not quite, *nearly*. He stood, yawned . . . Little now remained for him in the matter that carried the codename of Safety Deposit. There would come a confirmation, he would not respond to it, then the business end of five months' work would be in others' hands. It was assumed that all the permanent Post Room staffers knew that a critical hour was near, and they had played some part in reaching that moment, and he recognised the loyalty shown him. There had been no stampede into the basement by the *gauleiter* muscle of the kangeroo team. It was complex, damnably so, and there were several trigger points that could fail: if one tripped then the likelihood of success dropped away like the light of a winter afternoon. Worthwhile? *Probably*. Make a difference? *Perhaps*. Sanctioned by government? A silly question.

He had finished his sandwiches, cold pork with relish, drained his thermos, crunched on his chocolate bar, brushed crumbs from his shirt and jacket. The work area had gone quiet. He was watched. Each of them gazed at him. He bent and unplugged the computer's cable, pocketed his work mobile, loaded his briefcase. The raincoat was off the peg that had been attached to the wall for him, his hat placed on to his head. Nothing celebratory, emotional. Such gestures were foreign to him . . . He nodded briskly towards Vernon, was wished a good weekend. Nodded again at Sarah and was rewarded with a blush, he had noticed the ring on her finger and the small diamond that sparkled under the strip lights on the ceiling. Much depended on the boy who had given it her . . . too much depended on him.

In his soft voice, quietly, and each of them straining to hear him better, he murmured something about "thanks" and about "gratitude" for a job well done. No rallying speech, and no suggestion that he would be gone from the Post Room by Monday morning. He left them and his stride had lengthened before he was at the door because, on a Friday, the schedule was always tight, and his heavy footwear sounded on the floor and he went past the police rest area towards the back door and the ramp up into the street.

He thought it hung on a knife edge, Safety Deposit; was more complex than he would have liked, and was without certainty.

It would have been classified as a "soft rain" except that it was carried from the north, from over the mountains that were part Albanian and part Montenegran, and Croppy's hide was due south of the target area. The rain turned to sleet, and was layering on the scrim netting that he used to protect the 'scope lens, and that of his camera. It had been raining all day and the cold nestled in him, and the tiredness – and hunger. He thought the sleet would not last and then the netting would clear, and the forecast for the early evening was that sunshine would break through: sunlight coming low and arcing into the valley was always liable, dawn or dusk, to catch the polished, precision-cut glass of the lenses.

A car with Serbian plates had arrived at the outer gates of the villa, and they had opened and it had driven in fast. He had been in his hide for the best part of ten days: only four times had he wriggled backwards on his stomach and cleared the cleft in the rocks at the back, his entry and exit point, and taken out the plastic bags that contained the empty Meals Ready to Eat carton, and the heavy duty tin foil that held his body waste. In the place he had selected, his Covert Rural Observation Post, he had the wider opening behind him and it led after four or five paces on hard rock to a goat path where he had to take care not to fall. He was satisfied with the hide and reckoned the view was the best he could have hoped for and gave him the best security that, on his own, he could have. Inside the hide was a sleeping bag, his rucksack of supplies including a jar of Kilchoan wild honey he allowed himself a small teaspoonful each evening. His own territory was of less violent and sharp-edged rock, with the high spot of Ben Hiant and one cliff face falling sheer to the channel that was the Sound of Mull: familiar ground and easy for him. Not this place. It was as he had been told it would be . . .

He was 26 years old. He was far from home, the western extremity of the UK mainland, the district of Ardnamurchan. In the village where his parents lived he would not have been recognised. His outer clothing was the messy shape of a ghillie suit, what old trackers and stalkers had worn for more than a century when getting close to a red deer, or worn in combat by snipers or by those who hid themselves, hour by hour, day by day, in a CROP. It was his trade, his expertise was acknowledged, and the name given him was Croppy, and he answered to it. Time wasted if the name on his passport was used because the documentation was bogus. For his age, his skill was legendary, remarkable, which was why a man with a quiet voice, little more than a whisper, had called him three months before and asked for his services – not demanded them and not pleaded for them, but suggested he accepted a "job of work". It would have been possible, simple in fact, to have dismissed the invitation, claimed lack of availability or said that his world had moved on, that his days working for the Special Reconnaissance Regiment were over. He had accepted, had not asked for a night to sleep on it – and two days later he had come down from the Ben Hiant slopes and a small hire car had been parked in the chip seal driveway to the family bungalow and as he had walked towards the back door his father had appeared: a young woman was waiting for him, a stranger, had come from London, called Sarah. No one other than his parents in the village, Kilchoan, would have known him in the ghillie suit, and the balaclava and the smears of cam-cream on any snatch of flesh that showed. He and Sarah had gone for a walk, up towards the new cemetery, and she had said a little bit about what would be asked of him, not much: after an hour she was gone and had a long drive ahead, hoped to get the last flight of the evening south from Glasgow. Before she would have landed, the phone had rung in the bungalow and the soft voice spoke, nothing gushing, just the simple message that it was good he was joining the team, and appreciated.

In the hide he had time to think, hours of it. Took a special mind to be satisfied with thinking, lying on his stomach, moving his toes inside his boots to keep his circulation moving, not dozing and not sleeping, staying alert until the lights in the village were doused, and the windows in the villa darkened. He knew the patterns of the patrols around the villa walls and the guards with guns, dogs, torches. One thought always supreme . . . the girl, Sarah . . . and time to think of a schedule falling into place.

He had been told the car with the Serb plates would come, and that would likely be the trigger.

The child came out of a side door in the villa garden wall.

Nothing would happen until the car with the Serb plates came. His camera lens picked up two men emerging from the back seat; a chauffeur had opened the door for one and a goon for the other, and the main door of the villa was opened and an old man stood there. A greeting that was peremptory: the business was money, no cheek kissing and no drawn-out handshakes.

He knew the girl well. Over a dress that was white and patterned with flowers and butterflies, she wore a plastic poncho. The hem was an inch below her knees, and she wore white ankle socks and trainers. There was a small fenced compound close to the door in the wall and a dog was leaping at the sight of her and a half-dozen goats had started to bleat for her attention. Croppy knew the girl and her dog and her herd. Every day that he had been here, at this time as the sky darkened, she came out and walked them – and wore the same dress.

He logged the men into the villa. He reckoned this was the start of the process for which he had been recruited, but only the start . . . and realised that the sleet had stopped and the rain pattered with less intensity. Another car approached, one with a rumble in its engine, pure power, and coming at speed.

He had seen enough of the girl to feel pity for her. There was a sadness in her face when she was full-on in the magnification of the 'scope. There had been a child like this at the school in Strontian down the road from his home. One who did not speak, never smiled, occasionally screamed and who was beyond the reach of strangers. His mother said the child's affliction was likely "autism spectrum disorder". This girl was like that kid; she had lost the ability to respond to anything or anyone, other than her dog and her goats. Another vehicle approached which stirred him. He would use the camera and the 'scope on it, and had his notepad and stubby pencil ready, and wanted a piss which was a distraction. The sleet had gone, and the rain seemed about to follow it. The girl was coming up the hill, the dog beside her and the goats trailing, and she seemed to be searching for the first flowers to appear after the long winter. He felt a strong sympathy, a surge of pity . . . Once she looked straight into the lens, then the dog took her attention.

A sports car came through the village, a Lamborghini. Massive engine, massive tyres and massively unsuitable for the road. The bodywork was sprayed lemon yellow. That also had been predicted to follow the arrival of the Serbian plates. The car arrived at the villa gates, was admitted and accelerated, and there was a cheerful wave from the driver and the guards waved back . . . that too had been scheduled. Croppy had now forgotten the girl and concentrated on the Italian car, and its driver who was his principal target. It had all been laid out for him in the messages that Sarah relayed to him from the man she called the guv'nor and then she would giggle, then give him some more. The rain had eased, the sleet blown away, and the first sunlight came over the far mountains to the north and blew towards the village and the football pitch and then would start to creep up the hillside and over the tree line, and would reach him in his hide.

"Pass to me, Skender . . . Please, Skender, me . . . I'm free, Skender, yes – me."

There was a babble of noise around him. Most of the kids wore the shirts of the great European teams – the colours of Real Madrid and Barca and Juve, Arsenal and Bayern. Skender, at 22 was the oldest on the pitch. Because he had decided to play football, work off his annoyance, the pitch was floodlit. Only when he wanted to play was the instruction given to throw the switch and allow the pylons to expand out of their tunnels, the banks of lights extended, and the power turned on. The village had no team of its own, because no other side was prepared to join any league in which they would figure. It was remarkable that the village could boast a well-kept field, lights, a clubhouse with hot water for showers, suite for referees and linesmen. They wanted nothing except a team to play against.

Skender was wearing the national shirt of his country. It was blood red and on the left side was the image of the twin-headed eagle. He rarely wore the shirt and afterwards the housekeeper at the villa would wash it in warm water, carefully and slowly, trying to protect the autographs signed by the team's players two seasons before.

The cries for him to pass the ball to kids nominally on his side, and attacking the goal in the direction of the line of pine trees went unheeded. He had no need to pass the ball, give it away. Behind him was his grandfather's villa, where his grandmother also lived, seldom seen. Because he was the grandson of the man who ruled the village, and whose empire stretched far beyond all horizons visible even from the top of the mountains, it was not necessary for him to pass the ball. However long he kept the ball, better with his right foot than his left, he would never be tackled, never kicked, never barged into. When he was bored he would hoof the ball into a mêlée of players, and many – on either side – would be looking for him to determine whether he wanted it back from either of the teams because in that village, in that community, it was of the utmost importance to be be well thought of by the grandson. He was never flattened and if he booted the ball towards the goal there was a good chance that the kid designated as keeper would manage to permit it to snake under his body and into the net . . . then would follow a chorus of congratulation, and Skender would be hugged until he shook himself clear.

Since the deaths of his parents, Skender had been untouchable in the village, and it bored him . . . but he played football that evening and wore the national shirt with its two-headed eagle that was always vigilant, could see front and back, because of his irritation. Skender would not have openly argued with his grandfather, disputed the old man's judgement. His grandfather was worth, probably, in excess of 500,000,000 American dollars. A trust fund existed for Skender, well hidden by layers of disguise, that likely topped 200,000,000 dollars, and that afternoon he had again been treated like dirt, like dog shit that he might step on and that would cling in the tread of his trainers.

A chauffeur had driven the car with the Serbian plates, and a Russian with diplomatic cover had been his passenger. The Russian had brought the messages and the codes and the confirmation of the contacts in the finance world of the Swiss lakeside city. Skender had been regarded with contempt; his grandfather had attempted to introduce him into the meeting as if he were almost an equal. But the Russian had refused . . . it was about money. Money ruled. Money sent the diplomat slipping over frontiers, using roads not covered by cameras, without a hint of a customs check. Money meant that his grandfather was prepared to do business for a 1.5% fee of the value of what was handled. The diplomat had not even shaken Skender's hand and this was the fourth time they had met in the lounge of the villa. There had been no backward glance after Skender had been made to recite the memorised codenames, code numbers, contact details. He was told when he would be leaving, and when the meetings would take place; his convenience was not considered. The car had left. In Skender's room, in an annexe of the villa, his day clothes were scattered on the floor as he had dragged on his sports gear.

He had never been criticised for being lazy by the teachers at the school in the village. He achieved top marks in examinations he did not attend. There had been glowing reports of his enthusiasm and contributions in class; he had never failed at anything he had attempted. When he was beyond the immediate territory of his grandfather – he had spent nine months in South America, had been in Rotterdam, and in the sand-dunes leading to the beaches west of the French port of Calais, and had spent time in the town of Braintree on the south coast of England – men had been assigned to walk beside him, in front of him and behind him, and to ensure that he faced neither arrest nor humiliation . . . If he felt the need to batter a man's skull – for real or imaginary insult or disrespect – gloves were produced for him, a lump hammer produced. Once bone had been crushed, the gloves and the hammer were taken and he was stripped, his clothing thrown into a furnace. He was protected, always had been.

He was the future.

Skender eyed where he might kick the ball. His grandfather, seven years before when his parents had come back to the village in coffins, had told him that he was now the future of the family. Told him there was no stepping back and that weakness inside the clan would bring a baying pack down on them that would seek to strip to bare bones everything that they had accumulated, and that a terrible vengeance would follow. There was no walking away from it, his grandfather had said. No possibility of stepping aside.

The screams were louder. "Please, Skender . . . Me, Skender . . . I am free, Skender . . ."

The pretence of a game stopped.

His sister had appeared. Beside her was her dog, foul faced, with a grin that displayed its teeth, its ears flattened. Behind them were her goats. She had come out of the darkness and had arrived at the side of the pitch. The ridiculous child's dress she wore, much altered as she had grown because she insisted on wearing only that one, was smudged with dirt and stains from the lichen on the rocks she had clambered over. She walked straight through the players, not acknowledging her brother, older than her by eleven years, nor any of the other boys. He would not criticise her, certainly would not shout at her – she would have ignored him and then whispered a denunciation into her grandfather's ear. He stood, foot on the ball, and waited for her to clear the pitch. Nor was there any reaction when one of the goats squatted low on its haunches and shat there . . . None of the kids giggled, would not have dared.

Lying on the back seat of a Range Rover, not armoured but that would not have affected the outcome. Her mother driving and her father dozing beside her in the front, and her brother far away, organising brothels in Britain. An RPG-7 launcher had been used. If Klea had not been sleeping on the back seat she would not have lived, and a third, smaller, coffin would also have been needed. The attack had been at the coastal city of Durresi. Control of the docks was an issue. The weapon had been fired on the road between the partisan memorial and the archaeological museum. Skender's sister was not known to have publicly smiled since, and had withdrawn from the world and harboured feelings only for her dog and her goats, and spent her days on the slopes of the mountains around her home, and spoke to her grandfather and to no one else . . . He regarded her as a burden. When she was off the pitch, he kicked the ball far into the darkness of the distance – and went back to the annexe of the villa. It had been his parents' home, was now his. The game had not helped him obliterate the anger he had felt when meeting the Russian, like he was their fucking servant, hired staff of the Moscow people, and guardian of their money.

It was cold that night, and the skies had cleared and a wind came down the valley, and he tugged at his shirt with the emblem of the two-headed eagle . . . He had, himself, killed the three men who had handled the launcher that had blown up his parents, and more names remained on a list, which was why security was important to him, such as the vision of a two-headed eagle that watched his back.

To catch the train each evening, Jonas relied on the speed of his walk, the absence of unforeseen hold-ups – like a road and pavement diversion because the tarmac was up for gas or water repairs – but it was known that anyone who could keep pace with him had an opportunity to bend his ear on the bridge over the Thames. A discreet few understood the value of the "Lambeth Bridge opportunity". Denys Montgomery, a veteran Six, knew of it.

Jonas had left Thames House by the back exit and crossed the pavement and been about to step into the path of the oncoming traffic, when Kev and Leroy from the armed police had stepped out. The sight of their H&Ks and Glocks and tasers and gas canisters was sufficient to cause a howl of brakes and muttering of curses, and a clear path was made for him. He had been halfway across the road when he had noticed that a black Jaguar, low on its wheels with the weight of bomb-proof bodywork, was among the vehicles waiting – and knew that was the transport used by the DepDG, Brian. Jonas Merrick had never met the man . . . A smile sparkled round his mouth. A pleasant start to the weekend and he believed that what would play out in the next few hours or days had the potential to rank on the highest leg of the ladder that measured his successes. It had started here, on the bridge, months earlier at a time when he was beginning to itch for a degree of action to entertain him in the Post Room.

Denys Montgomery had been above a central span waiting for him, knowing a watch could be set on his appearance.

Evening, Jonas . . . Montgomery, Denys Montgomery, from the other side of the river. I'm hoping you'll remember me.

Probably, but I have a train to catch.

I want to push something your way. Whether you like it or not is immaterial. Seems you have built a reputation. Your praises are sung by the Agency.

They gossip too much.

You want to hear it?

If I have to . . .

Of course Jonas remembered Denys Montgomery. Could have reeled off verbatim a transcript of his interview, a Fiver interrogating a Sixer, on their territory, in search of a leak, and clearing this man of any responsibility for an act of wanton treachery. And being told that the Yankees had a line – unconfirmed – that Russian money was being hidden from sight through the cut-off filter of a courier carrying messages from those fearful of their wealth and the launderers, who kept cash in the offshore havens – and knew where the bottleneck was, location and identity, but not more. Also, the filter and personalities were in territory that was as foreign to the Agency as the moon's backside.

What they said to me, that guy we heard of, Merrick, that's the name, Jonas Merrick, is powerfully well spoken of. We'd be grateful if . . .

If I'd take a look at it? If I've time on my hands? Am actually on a punishment posting, breaking rules, ignoring disciplines. Am in the Post Room, like it's a gulag punishment.

Thank you, I'll send it round.

A month later, Jonas had organised the workings of the Post Room to his satisfaction, had a broad picture of a problem that had started to intrigue him. He had found a village, found a family, found a young man who fitted the messenger role – had listened, had learned. And Denys Montgomery had again been on the bridge.

There was a young woman who called herself Frank.

The source of the leak. Identified by me. Tried to drown me, changed her mind. Went to Russia. Blew her chance of getting a comfortable billet there by trying to warn the Embassy people of an operation to put my head on a plate and serve it up to the Great Man.

And went to Corrective Colony No 2, in a part of their country that God forgot, Mordovia. Shorthand for it is IK-2. They say, those that know, "If you haven't done time in Mordovia, then you haven't done time at all."

Do they? No harm telling you, I rather liked her.

And I, forgive the confidence, Jonas, rather loved her.

The point of this?

Just that, should you be in a position to exercise leverage, I'd be grateful if Frank were on the table as a bargaining chip.

My train won't wait, good day.

And that Friday evening with the cars and vans and taxis jamming the bridge and the charge of pedestrians on the pavements, scurrying for the start of their weekend, Jonas had again been intercepted by Denys Montgomery who was tall and bespectacled and wore a crumpled suit and scuffed shoes, and looked like a stereotypical Mr Chips, the prematurely aging schoolmaster. Jonas had been abrupt, his habit when asked to share information, and report progress.

If it happens it will be kicking off this coming week. There may be a very short window of opportunity. If the chance comes, it will come fast. You will then be advised to make your pitch along whatever route you believe might find the bargain acceptable . . . Myself, I'm off on holiday with the caravan and hoping the weather will hold up.

He had caught his train. Had left behind the bridge that she had dragged him off because, in his vanity, he had slipped handcuffs on to his wrist and hers, and she had near drowned him before changing her mind – which Vera would have said was every woman's privilege. Also behind him was the jetty where she, Frank, had left him hitched to a rope and where the lifeboat had found him ... She would be secondary to the priorities of the business of Safety Deposit, not on the first page.

Was off the train at Raynes Park with a swell of homecoming commuters and up the road to his home. Three bedrooms, mock Tudor, pebble dash, semi-detached, and the caravan already packed and Olaf was protesting from his cage. He did not have to waste time upstairs and changing because Jonas wore the same clothes for holidays as he did for work. A peck on the cheek from his wife of whom he was truly fond ... And Frank? It was true what he had said, a few weeks before, *had* rather liked her.

In the dormitory which contained sleeping places for 100 women there were that night four empty bunks. There was the sound of crying in the darkened area of this barracks block in IK-2 in a prison described by a sociologist at the University of Helsinki as "notoriously terrible, even by Russian standards". Some shrieked their tears, some sobbed quietly.

That week, in the workplace where military and police uniforms were sewn fifteen hours a day, a prisoner had slumped from exhaustion and her leg had snaked out, and a supervisor had tripped over it. The supervisor had fallen forward and had hit her head and cut it open. The incident had not been seen by the official in charge of the factory area, nor by any of the other staff. It had appeared to them that the supervisor had been assaulted, was on the floor in an aisle between work tables, was bleeding, semi-conscious, the victim of an attack.

In the detention block adjacent to the main administration offices, four of the isolation cells were occupied. In short they were *shizo* cells. Each cell, a *shtrafnoy izolyator*, was occupied by a single prisoner. At the end was Apricot. Next in the line was Currant. Beyond her was Blueberry. The last *shizo* in the line was taken by Apple. Apricot was the foreigner; she had taught them during their lessons in English, and her lessons in Russian. Apricot had explained to them that they were "jams" which was "*just about managing*", and jams were *confiture* which was what the girls dreamed of, as if it had the same value as chocolate. This small group had coalesced around her, and the names of the jam had been taken as a code of privacy, and each one of them had the traits of obstinacy, awkwardness and mischief. The English woman was Apricot; a minor rock star was Currant and a medical student, regarded as gifted in cardiology, was Blueberry and a banking and investment manager who had called out a scam was Apple … There had also been Pear but she was the daughter of a prominent Foreign Ministry chief and her father had arranged her release and she had been carried out shouting her final protest … The women in the punishment cells had lodged a protest at the hours worked, had denied the official had been tripped or attacked, and were in isolation while an investigation was conducted.

They talked through the evening along pipes linking the cells. They were committed to keeping each other strong and to breaking the routine discipline of the prison, and Apricot and Currant and Blueberry and Apple carried old scars and new ones from the fists and truncheons of the staff.

Visitors? Of course not.

Freedom? Sleep in IK-2 was rare, so dreaming was difficult.

And struggle? Constant.

Memories of a life beyond the walls and the wire and the watch-tower? Fading, almost gone.

At home, Denys Montgomery brooded. He had eaten – a meal of tinned tomatoes and heated beans slopped over two butter-smeared slices of toast – and wolfed it down. He had had to cook for himself since his mother's death. He was 44 years old, a seasoned intelligence officer, respected at his workplace, VBX on the Thames' south side, had most recently run a department dealing with that most sensitive area of secrecy, the location in which defectors from Russia – with something to tell – were housed. No blame had attached to him when the PA in the team – typist, stenographer, paper and electronic filer, and organiser

– turned out to be a traitor, now inside the Russian system and had attempted to erase her past with a plucky attempt to warn of acute danger facing the dogged little man who had identified her . . . More humiliation, a Fiver. His mother had always prepared an evening meal for him – and there was implicit criticism of him if he was late home or rang from the office and announced he would not be eating at home. He brooded because the previous week he had made what was, by his standards, a momentous decision. The next morning, Saturday, and early, a four-yard skip was due for delivery on his front drive. His weekend work was to fill it. He had been like a lodger in his own home since leaving university, going to VBX, succeeding there but stagnating as a human being. Due for the skip were every ornament, every picture off the walls, every piece of clothing from her wardrobe, her widow's collection of paste jewellery, her photograph albums and her chair . . . everything connected to her.

The reason he would erase her from his life was simple. He had felt true affection, probably a mutation of "love", for one person only. He had never summoned up the courage to tell his mother, *I have found someone I want to spend my life with, and if that person agrees to be my wife – or my partner, not fussed – either you move out or I do.* Could have said it seven years ago, or three, but not any time in the last two years when Frank was beyond reach. Had bottled it and had imagined what his mother's answer would have been. *That's gratitude! I look after you because you are so wretchedly helpless. Incapable of changing a light bulb. Running off upstairs and playing with your toys like some indulged child. All I've sacrificed for you, and the reward is being put out of my own front door, surplus to requirements. Is that the payback for all my love and kindness? Anyway, can't imagine what sort of young woman would want to fetch and carry for you* . . . He had not told Frank of his feelings. Had harboured them, left them unspoken, had always been correct – when half the Sixer personnel were going at it like bunnies in a burrow – and distant in her presence.

He knew where Frank was. Knew that months before she had received one brief consular visit, had spoken with a girl who had been with her in the Corrective Colony in Mordovia, IK-2, had passed to Jonas Merrick the snippet of US-supplied intelligence, a courier and dirty money . . . Had entertained a ridiculous thought: that miserable little man who worked north of the river might be devious enough and sufficiently bold in ignoring protocols to prise her free. Could not think of anyone else. There were in VBX, known because of the "eccentric" architecture as Ceaușescu Towers (a tribute to an East European dictator shot to death with his wife by "grateful" serfs) many young people with academically brilliant minds. There were also a legion of former "elite forces" ex-military, and a few who snorted and then could believe in the impossible . . . None as accomplished as that unpopular and friendless man. He had been told . . . *kicking off this coming week, a very short window of opportunity* . . . The skip was arriving in the morning, and its delivery was about the only gesture Denys Montgomery could make.

He went up the stairs, past a picture of the Italian lakes, past the line of china ducks in flight, past the closed door to her room at the front. In the back, his room, he changed into his railway work-er's boilersuit, and then climbed up to the attic conversion where his train set was laid out, and the artificial landscaping and the tiny buildings. What if she was brought out and would not accept him? What if his silence had hung too heavily? What if he were rejected? No one at VBX had ever seen Denys Montgomery, high flier and dedicated to his work on Russia Desk, in tears. What if it were to succeed, *if*, only Jonas Merrick – the silly man in his silly clothes with the silly idea of what was possible – could have achieved it.

A couple stayed on in the Post Room for the night shift. Sarah could have left hours before but had loitered.

There had not been a love in her life before the trek to the Scottish peninsula where the trees were scorched by the winter winds, and heather flourished and the crags were scraped clean of lichen, and where small lakes had breaking waves. At his home she had been treated, same as the first visit, with quiet courtesy but not with warmth, nor would Sarah have known what overture to make to his family.

It was well known inside the Post Room that Sarah – their "plain Jane" – had met a boy when she had travelled north for Jonas Merrick, who they called Guv'nor, and well known also that a critical moment had been reached in the developing strands of Safety Deposit. Known also that the young man and their girl were now what they called "an item" and she wore a ring . . . and all who worked in the Post Room and fuelled the trays and pigeon-holes and racks had never before during their employment at Thames House been involved with what they sensed was a major operation. Down there, they would have regarded themselves as below the level of the "foot soldiers", on a par with the Pioneers who dug the drains and latrines in a field of war. They were inside the loop and felt a fear of it, and a pride. She had seen Mr Merrick put on his coat, fasten the clasps of his briefcase, and ram down his hat because he would be crossing the bridge on the way to his train. There had been nothing on his face that showed elation, excitement, nerves as the matter had reached crisis point. Expressionless, dour, his shoulders hunched as if bearing a burden, and the colour of his cheeks paler than usual, he had passed her.

Sarah would like to have said, *He's going to be all right, Croppy? Can you tell me that, Mr Merrick, that he'll be all right?* And would like to have heard, and seen a rare smile, *Of course he will. A very sharp young man, best of the best. Knows how to look after himself. I have absolute confidence . . .*

The Post Room door had slapped shut behind him.

They had begun to talk plans, she and Croppy, when they had last walked up the road from his home, towards Ben Hiant and the stream where he was checking the health of a kit otter that eagles had bombed, tried to kill, but then had retreated when the mother had come back over the rocks, snarling and vicious. Holding hands, and walking slowly into the wind that buffeted them, and he had shown her a "crofter" shell, walls two feet thick, no windows, no door and no roof, with a carpet of sheep shit and sheep wool, and surrounded by land strewn with rocks and bog. He had said that with his own graft, and his family's and that of their friends, it could be made habitable, and spoke about what they might do to pay for it, and have food on the table, had talked of it and had joked of it, and had known that each spoke with a desperate sincerity.

She headed out of the room and went past the police rest area. There were three of them in there, all huge because they were wearing their vests, and the sofas were littered with weapons and kit and the magazines which absorbed them when not on the street. They looked powerful to her, and responsible, but none of them were close to where Croppy had made his hide: none of them could have helped him. She went out into the cold evening wind, bent under it. She supposed it was all about trust. Necessary for her to trust Jonas Merrick, no option but to keep faith.

Croppy could see all of the village, it was well lit, to modern city standards – as he had seen when he had been through central London, or at the big camps in Cyprus before deployment into Syria . . . Except this was a village, far up a valley, reached by a stone-strewn road: better surfaces on Ardnamurchan and going out towards the lighthouse and the Point. The villa was floodlit, the church's onion dome was bright. Lights burned in the houses and were left on in the small school building, and in the telephone box, painted bright red, which had been carried off as a souvenir from England and was now standing outside the bar that doubled as a café. The lights showed the cars outside the houses, made by Audi and BMW and Mercedes – yet nobody was on the move to go on a night shift, and no one was coming back late from a day shift. The community that Croppy watched had signs of wealth and comfort, yet no man or woman seemed to him to possess employ-ment . . . obvious, or Croppy would not have been there. The young men were absent. Women were there, teenagers and the twenty-somethings and the older married ones who bulged pregnancies and dressed fashionably, and the grandmothers who still wore the clothes of past generations – and male children and older men. The young had gone, and there was a signpost facing the square in front of the villa that directed traffic to the A13 into the Barking district of east London, another souvenir, and where a proportion of the young men from the village would be.

He might allow himself to doze but not to sleep. He had not left the hide now for four days. At the back were the bags for his Meals Ready to Eat carton, and also for the crumpled tin foil shapes that carried his waste, and the bottles of his urine. It might be another day, not more, and he struggled to stay alert. Had he still been with the Regiment there would have been a pair of them in place and the back-up would have been at the nearest base from which an attack chopper and a Merlin could take off and arrive well within the time needed to chase down the "golden hour." What he did now broke every rule, each last procedure demanded by Special Forces: it had been his decision to walk away and senior men had pleaded with him in an army way to "hang on in there", and told him he was admired, respected, was the best and . . . He had packed up, slipped away without fanfare, gone home to Kilchoan.

He thought he could do without the back-up and the companionship of another trooper because he had believed in the calm, thorough preparations told by the man on the telephone, and Sarah spoke well of him . . . He blinked, saw movement beside the gate out of the garden area behind the villa, a wasteground overgrown with weeds. The girl came out – poor kid, demented and isolated, with only her dog and the half dozen goats in her hern for company. She was carrying something but he could not at first identify it. She was a diversion. She led the goats and the dog to the small compound and pushed them through the barrier then fastened it. The animals were put away every night and let out every morning. A sack of food was shaken over the fence into a metal trough, and the dog had a bone to gnaw on. She turned away . . . Croppy saw then that she carried a pair of garden shears. She walked away and he heard faintly the sound of the blades snapping together and there was a distant shrill squeal as she drew the handles open before they clattered again, blade on blade. She went inside and the gate flapped in the wind until a man came, a Klash hooked on his shoulder, and closed it.

The quiet returned. Likely it would happen the next day. Likely the movement would begin within 24 hours of the visit by the passenger in the car with the Serbian registration plates . . . Likely then he would use his phone and send the message, and start tidying and clearing his camp and begin to head for home – where Sarah was. And Croppy believed very soon he could allow himself to dream.

He thought himself in good shape, and imagined where his girl was – and remembered the voice of the man whom he had never met, whom he had listened to on the phone and who had told him that what he was asked to do was "worthwhile". Good enough? Of course, and a soft voice and one demanding trust.

"Tank, school governors' chair, sending you the agenda for Wednesday's meeting, the parents' one. May clash with the bar committee of the British Legion treasurer's report. I said you'd manage," his wife called up the stairs.

"Thanks, love, you didn't say . . .?"

"Didn't. You nearly done?"

"Bit more, then tidying up."

He was Tank. There were three of them who were referred to in the limited briefings they'd been given as the team. He was Tank because his army service – before he had come out and had scraped enough together to buy a home in Swindon, going cheap when the Honda factory shut down – had been as a sergeant in the Royal Tank Regiment. He was a devoted family man, wife and two kids, and was also what the vicar had called "a pillar of the community". When he was at home, sometimes sporadically and sometimes for weeks at a time, he was on the parents' liaison with the junior school the kids went to, and also managed the books of the bar committee of the British Legion where a few veterans met along with anyone who wanted a cheaper pint than the local poured, and there was the committee charged with maintaining the grounds of the cemetery on the north side of the town where his father was, and his mother would soon be if she didn't lay off the fags. His reputation was for "getting things done". He could drive a Challenger 2 main battle tank, also the Scimitar fast recce vehicle, and was good with his hands and good as a makeshift engineer. He was also good at sanding down the woodwork in the spare room ready for a new coat of paint. It would be finished by the next weekend, if he were not called away. In the master bedroom, in the wardrobe and behind his shoes, was a packed rucksack: if he were called away it would go with him. He had worked through the rest of the house, bought with the help of a bonus from his last Afghan posting as a private military contractor, all pristine and newly decorated except this back bedroom. Tank had a big smile, was everybody's friend, which was useful because his bulk could be intimidating.

Who knew him? His wife? The kids? The neighbours either side of the back garden? Not really . . . Another member of the team was Sword. Sword knew him.

A wounded tribesman had been taken into an interrogation centre in Helmand late at night and the intelligence officer on duty was Sword. A bit of a beating handed out, and information obtained, and a coordinate submitted where a Taliban assault squad were lying up and waiting for dawn to attack an outlying compound. Quality information, and a strike by the Apaches. Twenty plus killed and probably another fifteen carted off with injuries – and no attack launched. All regarded as a bit of a success – and the tribesman had died. Few questions on methodology asked, and Tank and Sword had been the heroes of the hour.

A man with a soft and gentle voice had called from an untraceable number, and had been persuasive . . . The reconnaissance had been done, just needed the green to flash which was why the rucksack was in the wardrobe. Legal? Hardly, but the voice had been necessarily convincing about the mission's value – good enough for Tank. Might get the undercoat on over the weekend, might get the topcoat done on Monday – if the call didn't come.

Quite a straightforward journey. But he had sensed his wife was gearing up for a statement of intent, little sharp increases of breath as if she rehearsed what she'd say.

"I am not expecting any silliness, Jonas."

Away from home and a bit of traffic before Jonas was on to the motorway circling London, a junction, and then the M3 took him and Vera, and Olaf in his cage in the caravan, off towards the west. He did not enjoy driving at night, into the glare of oncoming lights, but needs must. Then the A303, and finally some minor roads, then the Picket Post roundabout and the one at Nunney Catch, and Vera was navigating him . . . About two and three-quarter hours and down a hill towards the cathedral city of Wells and along a darkened High Street of shuttered charity shops, and into the countryside – and the caravan park. He had sighed, felt the tiredness.

Jonas answered her, "You'll not get it, any silliness."

"It is just, Jonas, that you have not always been entirely honest with me."

A fair point . . . not *entirely* honest – not *at all* honest. Just going into work on a Saturday morning "to get some paperwork done", or some such lie, and ending up in the Thames and near to drowning because of his overarching requirement personally to handcuff himself to Frank, the Sixer leak, and give her up to the Special Branch detectives who could have done the job perfectly well without his interference . . . ending up with a shoulder almost dislocated at the hands of an ISIS fighter when armed police were on hand . . . rubbernecking an arrest operation in Liverpool when he had told her that his car's clutch needed fixing and him at risk of having his throat slit before armed police had shot a young woman dead, double tap . . . and a matter of a close encounter on the Devon coast when a contract was out on his head . . . No, he had not been entirely honest.

"Matters are in hand. I do not believe they require me on the end of a phone. Even if I should be required, the issues will be settled far from here. I am completely safe from the prospect of personal injury . . . and there, Vera, the matter can be left."

He drove through the open gate and on to the site. Beside the clubhouse, dark at this time of the year before the caravanning season was underway, two pitches were taken. He defiantly drove in the opposite direction and found a concrete surface, a tap installed and a post for power, against a boundary hedge – and beyond the hedge his headlights raked over empty fields.

"Perfect," he muttered. "Ideal for you and for Olaf, and for me."

Truth be told, Jonas had a feeling of relief that the question had been put and his answer given and with honesty. They unpacked the car and Vera was inside the caravan and sorting out their bedding, then would be shoving their dinner into a microwave . . . The plan was ambitious, had many working parts . . . What could possibly go wrong? Plenty. The cat was out of the cage and in the hedgerow and he gave it time to work the ground. Jonas supposed himself on a treadmill and through his own actions had pressed the speed button and success had moved the belt to an ever greater speed and . . . Sufficient introspection, boring, tedious, stale and indulgent. He was promised history and nature on this holiday. With a snorted cough, he tried to put the mission from his mind: whether Croppy called in, did the trigger, whether the team were put on the move, whether a courier with a code book and memor- ised account numbers was heading away from the heart of a gangster's empire towards a bankers' haven, whether Denys Montgomery was delivered the belated love of his life, whether oligarchs were left ranting at empty screens because their wealth had vanished . . . Olaf obliged. A field mouse was his prey. It kicked its back legs limply while the Norwegian Forest cat's jaws held the "wee timorous cowerin' beastie" by the fold of skin at its neck. It was laid at Jonas' feet. Little bright eyes stared up at Jonas as if he could save it. It was eaten, head first and noisily – and Vera called that supper was ready.

The story of Jonas Merrick's life was acted out at his feet – never far from life nor far from death.

2

Eyes closed, Jonas shifted his head. Water splattered on his forehead.

And remembered . . . Vera had said that he must ensure the suspected leak in the caravan roof was dealt with, and had explained that driven rain, as against the variety that came down in stair-rods, was likely to get under the roof. She had put out the canister of sealant for him. He had put it back in the utility room. Could have been 40 years they had lived in the house, their first home after their marriage, and he could seldom recall what year that event had happened. The pillow beside his ear was saturated. A good start to the day.

Jonas opened his eyes and blinked. And remembered . . . A matter as yet unsettled in a village in a valley in the Albanian mountains. Had not moved on last weekend, no word yet had reached him of action this weekend, and it might be for the weekend after, or the one after that, or . . . He scratched his forehead, and was shouted at and Olaf had started to stomp over him which meant sleep, damp or dry, would not be resumed. And remembered . . . A young man, Sarah's significant item, was parked in a hide with a view over the village and was supposed to report unscripted action; he had seemed capable and came with a pedigree of enthusiastic references, and where he was it was likely to be raining or snowing, or about to be raining or snowing. But his phone had stayed still throughout the night. In deference to Vera, and the supposed sanctity of a holiday, he had switched off the bell tune it played but would have been alerted by its wriggle. And remembered . . . Promises had been extracted. No "silliness" tolerated, nothing "idiotic" or he would be in trouble. A holiday in central Somerset, out of season and cheap rates at the caravan park had led to his guarantee that the office was behind him, beyond his reach. Vera stirred. She might raise the matter of the leak in the caravan ceiling and might not, he might go unchastised and might not. He made a huge decision, out of loyalty to her, and reached up for his phone, checked the screen, pressed the button, killed the beast. Vera might humour him on the leak but little chance that Olaf, the Norwegian Forest cat, would oblige. It rubbed its jaws against his face. And remembered . . . A small creature, devoid of hostility, no threat and barely even a meal for his well fed and pampered animal, had been crunched to death by those same jaws that now pressed against his. He gulped and stepped off the bed and his right foot careered away from him and he realised he had slipped on that small creature's tail and intestines.

He went to the door, opened it. Had to grip the handle to stop the wind slamming it back in his face. Vera had told him that the forecast said the day would start poorly but weather was coming in from the west, and he was not to grumble. And remembered . . . He thought the planning he was responsible for was the most complex he had attempted since his career had veered off into what one idiot had called "sunlit uplands". And remembered what Brutus, the assassin of Caesar, had said: *There is a tide in the affairs of men, Which, taken at the flood, leads on to fortune: Omitted, all the voyage of their life Is bound in shallows and in miseries.* He had moved on, perhaps too high and too fast, and was lauded in the corridors of the Americans' spy centre, home of the Agency, and at home his "eccentricities" were permitted and punishments were mild. Wise to recall those words of a murderer? Himself, he had never killed anyone – not with his own hands, only by proxy. Used others to do the bloodletting. Was experienced in the matter of hiring men who would do the "necessary" while his own fingers remained unstained.

The cat scampered out, heading for the hedgerow and some shelter.

It was far from foolproof. It represented a gamble. If he succeeded there was a better than fair chance that fizz would be served on the fifth floor of Thames House. If it failed, he doubted that even the support of the AssDepDG would save him from a public hanging, and the opportunity of a version of house arrest on parole in the Post Room would not be on offer.

The legs of his pyjamas were spattered.

The cat, hair plastered down on its body, made a charge for the door, came inside, then shook vigorously.

He supposed himself now addicted to taking a gamble.

Behind him, Vera spoke from the caravan bed. "Well done, Jonas, so well done. No incoming calls and you leaving it there and not checking it – I think I am going to believe that you'll do nothing silly."

After he had towelled the cat, he put the kettle on to make a pot of tea. He supposed he had chosen the right people to kick an opponent's shins, hard enough to make a difference in their lives – which would make it worthwhile.

There was a rattle under the bonnet of his car.

It had been irritating him the whole of that week. His driver had twice taken the vehicle to the garage to have mechanics crawl over the working parts and attempt to discover the source of the annoyance. The driver said, with a certain impertinence, that it was no longer possible to strip down various sections of the Mercedes and use the warranty to demand spares from the German factory. Because of the war, because of the sanctions, because they were not available. Nor was it possible to sell it and replace it with a newer model because of the war, because of the sanctions . . . There was the noise of metal grating on metal. The driver's face, the explanation given, was impassive, and so was that of the bodyguard sitting in the front beside him. They were travelling from his apartment in the Arbat district to his office in central Moscow; a police car was leading them with a blue light and a siren, and more of his protection team followed in a second car. The Mercedes, with its inbuilt rattle, had a basic price of a quarter of a million American dollars but added to its west would have been the armour-plating in the doors, the special tyres, the reinforced windscreen and side windows, and other money-drinking modifications that would supposedly take him through a landmine explosion and possibly an anti-tank missile attack.

The irritation at the rattle under the bonnet was a minor factor in his stress levels.

It was about money.

His own money, and other people's money. He was Viktor. His wife was Natalya. Viktor and Natalya had two daughters both studying at university in Moscow. Viktor was wealthy, extra-ordinarily wealthy, and he and Natalya lived inside a bubble of elite couples in the capital. Being wealthy had become a way of life. Prestige addresses, transport with escorts smoothing the way, private jets, servants and secretaries all came their way – and useful friendships. He could not imagine a return to the old life of being a mid-ranking manager in St Petersburg's local government and the days of brown envelopes being passed from hand to hip pocket and a blind eye turned if reward were offered. To stand in a queue for a tram, not to be able to afford even a glance at a department store window display, to fail in an argument with a junior bureaucrat – any of them were a nightmare. He sought to safeguard his money. Before the war he had valued himself in excess of a billion dollars. All his money was offshore, and he was careful and believed he had built firewalls to protect it. Then came the war, and with the war came sanctions . . . And many of those in the highest ranks of the administration, and the Leader himself, had smiled on him, had flattered him, had chosen to accept his advice on the hiding of assets. Even the Leader had . . . Small wonder that a colonel in what had been KGB, and was now SVR or FSB, understood the practice of the extortion of money but was not equipped to handle the hidden loot so successfully extracted from the nation's economy. Half a dozen principal fami-lies had come to him and had lodged assets with him, and the Leader had too. His own money and others' money was far from Russian territory. He was trusted. Trust was a burden, a crushing weight.

Despite the rattle, the Mercedes powered smoothly along the multi-lane highway and ordinary citizens were forced to swerve into slower lanes to permit its passage.

It was about money and therefore about trust. Simple? Not at all. Other than his wife, he trusted no one in his gilded circle. Their trust in him would be based on a basic principle ... if he broke trust he was dead. Might be shot by his own guards, might be poisoned by his own chef, might be pushed from a high hotel balcony.

His theory, what they had all bought into, and the basis of the trust, was the principle of cut-out. The money of his family, and other families, and of the Leader's family, was handled by expensive but supposedly reliable men and women based in a European lakeside haven of tranquillity. He had no direct contact with them; he depended on that cut-out principle. Those with cash invested in stocks, property, whatever, put their instructions to the cabal of managers, accountants and lawyers based in that paradise city, and a courier left the capital and travelled the relatively safe route to the Serbian capital, Belgrade. From there the courier was driven to a place where it was assumed civilisation still lagged, a primitive mountain lair for a patriarch of organised crime. And on again, carried by a member of that peasant family across more borders, and into the hands of the sophisticates in that place of apparent decency, honesty and privileged reputation. Balance sheets would come back and the cut-out was expected to preserve the integrity of the money ... And sanctions grew tighter each month, each season, each year, and the rallying enemies attempted to sequester and block and freeze the accounts.

It was all about money. Money mattered to him and to all those who trusted him. Of course, Viktor did not sit, sprawled and relaxed in his million dollar car, with the rattle nagging in his ear because he was trusted. Fuck trust, it was the burden he carried and stumbled under.

His phone trilled.

A message that increased the load of stress he already bore. A courier had arrived. A transfer had taken place. A slim package of papers would be moved on later that day. On his phone screen he could find a village in a valley, sheltered from extreme mountains, could even enlarge the image so that individual figures would be near to identifiable, certainly could see the buildings and one garish oversized villa. His own money and that of others, and an amount of the Leader's money, was in the hands of the barbarians who inhabited the place.

He noted as he was driven in the fast lane reserved for those of importance, such as himself, that citizens turned to look at the car overtaking their own and were without expression – were weighted down, were without hope . . . fuck them.

Had his principal aide, a man in whom he had his total confidence, asked him, *Have you ever heard, Viktor, of a particular analyst at a building on the north side of the river in London that is the headquarters of the UK's Security Service.* No, why would he?

A man who dresses in the clothes of half a century before? No, he had not.

An intelligence officer who takes rare holidays pulling a caravan to primitive facility campsites? Had never heard of such a man.

Had never been asked such questions. He checked his calls again and wondered when the next courier would leave that village where value was based on the coca plant and its powdered form. It was what that fucking war had done, reduce him to the level of those bedfellows . . . He looked again at his screen. Nothing there for Viktor to see now because the cloud had settled on the village trapped in the valley. Saw nothing, could only put his trust in the courier.

It was an almost craven exhibition of escapism. Denys Montgomery should, by that time on this Saturday morning, have been busy with the demolition of his mother's life, dumping her furniture, possessions, and the memory of her in the skip that now filled the front drive to her old home.

He said it out loud, "Frank, don't hate, because that will kill you . . ."

He was in the attic and had the plans out for the old Somerset and Dorset line, killed by the Beeching axe 59 years before, and was imagining the station, from sepia photographs, at Shoscombe & Single Hill Halt. He often, now that his mother was no longer there to eavesdrop on him, spoke to his former personal assistant on the Defector (Relocation) team, branded as a traitor, as an embarrassment, even as a bit of a heroine.

"Have hope, because that will keep you alive."

If it had been known inside Vauxhall Cross, home of the Secret Intelligence Service, that a senior officer was in clandestine contact with "them across the river" – the Security Service, considered inferior – with no clearance granted, his future would have been shaky at best. If it had been known that the contact was with Jonas Merrick, who had identified treachery within the SIS family, then his future would have been worse than rocky. He knew of nobody else who might, just, possibly, bring Frank home.

She was the unspoken love of his life. Like a bloody fool he had never shown his feelings. Twice, that morning, he tried to call Jonas Merrick, and twice the phone was not answered.

In a hide, Croppy would never move suddenly. He took his time even to tilt his head. Would not have jerked it if he had been in undergrowth and watching a villa outside the Syrian city of Aleppo, nor if he had been on Ardnamurchan, the lower slopes of Ben Hiant, lying on his stomach and watching a wary Royal stag, or on rocks, low on the seaweed, with the tide out and an otter crunching through the shell of a good sized crab right in front of him. Slowly, deliberately, he moved his head so that he could look up the road that led into and out of the village. At first he could not see the vehicle as it approached, just hear it.

He wore a ghillie suit, the same gear that did service for him on Ben Hiant and on the hills along the one-lane track out to the Point where the Atlantic waves broke. The suit softened every sharp angle of his body and disguised the shape of his head, and short strips of different coloured materials were woven into the fabric, and looked like dead leaves, and across his face was a screen

of scrim netting; more of it across the lenses of his binoculars, and
still more laid with precision on the far side of the opening between
the two rocks and his chosen vantage point. It was a good hide,
selected with care, and it had an entrance at the rear that led to a
track good enough for agile creatures, sufficient for goats or for
Croppy, and then in the space by his feet was an area less than
three metres in length and something more than a metre in height,
and less than a metre in width. He would have liked to have told
Sarah about his hide, rather shyly boast of it, but had not because
it would perhaps have frightened her. He had been in the hide
four days and three nights on this trip, and a few hours more a
month earlier, and again a month before that. Neatly stacked
behind him, were three plastic water bottles, tops screwed tight to
prevent the urine they held from leaking, and one more that was
still empty, and along with them were the packets of closely folded
tinfoil that held his own waste ... Time at a weekly boarding
school down the peninsula in Strontian or doing basic training at
Catterick or with the Regiment had not coarsened Croppy's
language: he was almost prim, so it was urine and waste.

The vehicle emerged from the cloud wall. It was a foul morning
in the valley, low cloud and blustering winds and rain falling at an
angle, straight at the netting camouflaging his hide. The village
would have been warned of the arrival of the vehicle. Men
appeared, shrugged into anoraks and overcoats, and gathered
outside an old building that had steps leading down to a cellar.
The vehicle was a pick-up and it had the wipers going hard in the
front cab but the back part of it was uncovered, open to the
elements. When it came to a halt a crowd of men pushed close.
Croppy had good hearing but sometimes used audio aids, mixed
in with the sounds of the wind and the water dripping off the
nearby rocks, he could hear shouts of abuse and hatred, and he
saw fists raised and imagined they pummelled a victim. Croppy
saw the top man come out from the villa gate, the girl beside him.
With one hand she held on to her grandfather and from the other
dangled the garden shears: half a dozen paces behind them was
Skender, hanging back.

A man was lifted from the back of the pick-up.

His wrists were tied with rope and pressed close to his spine. He wore nightclothes, flannel pyjamas. Would have been dragged from his bed when darkness still pressed over his home. He was hooded, a hessian sack pulled over his head, and had no chance to ride the blows that were aimed at him. His feet were not tied together but a length of rope was knotted at his right ankle, and when he tried to lash out with a barefoot kick at his tormentors the rope was jerked tight and he fell into a puddle. He was hustled forward, part lifted and part dragged towards the cellar steps.

Croppy had seen it before. A captive had been brought to the villa outside Aleppo. He had watched from a mile away. Some of the snipers that he had known in Syria worked for the Hereford crowd. He had marked targets for them ahead of their movement forward, part of the work of the Special Reconnaissance Regiment. They could drop a target a full 1700 yards away ... on Ardnamurchan a client was encouraged to bring down a stag at a distance not more than 400 yards. It would have been a kindness to have shot that man being taken into the villa outside the Syrian city occupied by Islamic State, would have been as great a kindness to have ended the misery of this man in his pyjamas who was pitched down the steps into a cellar in an Albanian village – and would not happen, and had not happened ... and wondered how he would have been.

A handicap of the job, whether working in Syria or here in the north-west mountains of Albania, was the inability to intervene when torture was predictable, when death was inevitable. His job was to watch – maybe scribble a note.

He had lost sight of the prisoner. With the sound turned full up on the hearing aid, he might hear what would follow – was certain to follow. But he was distracted.

Three cars came. Like they were part of a fleet, all Mercedes. Black, tinted privacy windows, and they parked in a line in front of the villa's gates. He saw that Skender turned, but the magnification of the binocular lenses gave no clue to his mood. He wondered what offence the prisoner was accused of, as if it mattered . . . Croppy had told one of the I Corps team about the man brought to that building outside Aleppo, and the sergeant had dryly told him, *It's always about treachery. They spend their waking hours sniffing for men who have taken our shilling – which is not a role for which a guy can expect to live long enough to draw a pension – assuming we'd pay it. They are paranoid about betrayal, and they like to make a show of it. Might dissuade another idiot from letting that shilling slip into the palm of his hand. Don't be squeamish, Croppy. That's the way the world is – well, your world and mine.*

He eased his field of vision from the cellar steps and kept it locked on the three cars at the villa gates.

Skender looked away, did not meet his grandfather's glance. Rare for him to disregard an instruction given him by the old man . . . he was the heir, the future. Behind him were the three cars, same plates, all with their tanks filled. Inside the building where his grandfather lived, two boys would by now have been putting on the clothing left for them in the hallway. In his grandfather's safe, inside a room with a bulletproof door, was the packet Skender would take when he left the village that afternoon. He understood why his grandfather greeted his refusal with a narrowing of the lips over which a tongue ran fast. He was expected to go down into the cellar and to observe the pain of the traitor, as if his presence would give the business of torture greater purpose. The man had welshed on a deal. A small sum of money, perhaps a million American dollars. A million dollars creamed off: unimportant, irrelevant, but if power were to be maintained it was necessary to show the result of treachery. He thought Klea would be allowed to run like a hunting dog for the cellar steps, clutching her shears. He would eat a light lunch, drink a Coke, then the subterfuge would be acted out – and a girl waited for him. The sleet settled on his suit jacket but he would not shiver because that would imply weakness, and he was the grandson and authority would pass seamlessly to him.

Croppy watched.

The old man held the hand of his granddaughter, and laughed because the child dragged at him, wanted to get to the cellar. Not a tug-of-war for fun, not a game. Croppy sensed the increasing frustration of the child, but her hand was held tight . . . He thought that down in the cellar it would be a hard time for the prisoner.

In Syria, Croppy had worked alongside Lofty, another trooper from the Regiment. Lofty was a runt . . . one of a litter that seemed half the size of the rest and might struggle to survive. That was Lofty, barely five feet and a couple of inches in height, and weighing less than seven and a half stone. He came from a street of West Midlands terraced homes, with no mountains and no caves and no undergrowth except that at the edges of an Industrial Revolution canal. He had talent, an ability to learn, and a sense of optimism.

Croppy remembered him, but should not have. Should not have given little Lofty space in his memory.

Croppy was alone. No back-up close by. Had been told: *You come most highly recommended. I hear only the best things of you. I appreciate, believe me, this is difficult work, and dangerous work – but I am entirely confident in your ability to stay well clear of threat. You have the skill to avoid detection. Your instructions are very clear. Faced with a problem, you pull out. Up sticks and away . . . I hope that puts any nervousness to rest. We are all very confident you will deliver.* The call had been cut, leaving the phone purring in his ear. He had thought the voice was that of a tired man, an older man, and likely one who had never slept in a ditch, climbed a mountain, hacked a track in torrential rain, done his stuff into tin foil or a bottle. The morning after, he had flown out for the first time and gone to hunt for a hide, and taken up "lodging" there. Big words, brave words, but he did not have Lofty beside him.

Lofty had the optimism that came as a blind faith, talked it incessantly. A murmur in Croppy's ear, "Never forget it, don't ever. Back there at that feckin' crap hole there's a big bad chopper waiting and serviced and fuelled up, and its crew sat in a shed, night or day, and waiting for the call. Who does the call? We do,

Croppy, me and you. No matter what the weather, storm, blizzard, visibility nil, they'll come out for us. I press the button and they're on their way, the pilots don't back off. And what's in the Chinook, Croppy? A whole gang of bad bastards who the opposition would be unwise to argue with. They are there for us, don't doubt it. All they've got in their lives is the job of getting to us and lifting us clear if it gets unpleasant. They're like a cab on the rank, except we are the only fare they're waiting for if it goes tits up for us . . . Makes you feel good, doesn't it, Croppy? You're never alone, not with the Chinook and the bad boys waiting to come out and get you, take you home . . ."

It was what Lofty used to say when he was out with Croppy. And the chance was that Lofty was now in Tipton or Dudley or Wolverhampton, and on his way to his allotment and later would sink a few pints with mates in the Legion and bore the backsides off them with tales about close support and rescue and casevac procedures . . . and some of it would have been true and some of it likely not. When Croppy was out on his own or when he was with Lofty, and the little chap was curled up against him for warmth or for comfort, he had no opportunity to find out, never had occasion to press a panic button. It was a pity that Croppy remembered what Lofty used to say, because this time out there was no cab on the rank, and the reassurance was from the quiet voice 1500 miles away.

He watched the cars. He saw Skender scratch his left armpit, and the girl was still tugging at her grandfather, and the old man held her hand and men came to him from the cellar and reported what progress, if any, they had made, and the weather showed no sign of lifting.

And wondered where Sarah was and what she was doing. Which was dumb of him and caused as much pain, or more, than thinking of Lofty and the back-up that did not exist.

And thought of the prisoner, and reckoned it would be little different for him than for the man taken into the compound, behind the big wall of the building outside Aleppo, and that also was a bad thought and unsettling. Watched it all, and waited . . . and almost missed the moment.

The girl was free of her grandfather. Croppy did not know whether she had broken free of him or he had dropped her hand, but she was running to the cellar steps, still clutching the shears.

It was not a talent of Jonas Merrick but he supposed he humoured her and after a fashion he made the effort to seem interested ... he owed it to her.

The Romans had been here. The feet of their legions had tramped in step where he now stood, in the nave of the cathedral in the city of Wells. It was his habit shamelessly to implant himself and Vera into a guided party and ignore the sour stares. He was bored, as bored as he could remember. But was under obligation.

In the debit column was his arrival home after being a hero for an hour, having talked down a suicide and defused his explosive vest, and having been beaten to pulp by an ISIS fighter, and near drowned, and totally stone deaf for a week after police had discharged firearms beside his head and saved him from a multiple stabbing, and when a contract guy had felled him and was about to sever his head from his shoulders. He was in debt. Credit was harder to evaluate, by her and by him: a steady salary with civil service benefits, a Queen's Gallantry medal with Bar that was hidden at the back of her knickers drawer, no indication of impending retirement that would have dumped him under her feet all day, a minimum of interference in her social diary on days when she wasn't working at the gallantry, and good holidays, when not interrupted, in their caravan ... He fancied debit outweighed credit so his phone was switched off, left behind with the cat in the caravan. The first time he had ever done that, and it rankled, itched as bad as any addict's withdrawal.

They had done the outside, him sheltered under his trilby and in his raincoat, and her with a pocket umbrella opened. Had seen the statues of seraphim on the front facade, and been told of the Priests' Gate and the Vicars' Close, and the Hall where the clergy ate that was linked by an enclosed corridor that prevented contact with "ladies of the night". Inside the rain had dripped off his hat and his coat on to 900-year-old flagstones. He had twice yawned with true weariness and had ignored Vera's murmured criticism.

So much depended on that boy. An accident, of course it was, that had produced him. An army man had called Jonas. Had never met the one-time soldier, but the phone was better than face to face. *I am not really in the business of talent spotting, but I was told about you by a cousin, and thought it right to put you on the track of a rather remarkable young fellow. Education? Probably nil. Talent? Not for banking or legal stuff, but for crawling on his stomach close to a large red deer, one with seriously honed survival instincts. My cousin was taken out by him to drop a stag on a grim day in some ghastly God-forgotten corner of western Scotland ... Because of his understanding of terrain and cover, and wind and scent, they were damn near enough to this chap to have tickled its ears. They'd gone to shoot it, but didn't bother, would have seemed rather pointless. And, from talk on the estate where they were, my cousin gathered his experience was not abnormal. He was in Reconnaissance, that new outfit, and talked the boy into applying for the military, fast-tracked him through basic training which the boy loathed, and worked damn hard to get him picked up by the Recce Regiment, and opposition came in wheelbarrow loads − had to do his time square-bashing and guard duty on a Friday night at Catterick. My cousin backed him, had Commando connections. Big concession. The boy was put in with a final exam class of snipers and was taken out to Woodbury Common up from the Commando base. I don't want to bore the pants off you, sir, but these young Marines and the boy had to advance across the Common towards two sergeants with massive magnification binoculars. The ground was heather, gorse, dead bracken, bramble, and the sergeants were there to call them out. Of nine marines, three made it far enough forward to have managed a decent shot. Where was the boy? Not a sign of him. They waited another 45 minutes but he never showed. They shouted and bawled and whistled, no sight nor sound of him. I imagine plenty of expletives and they abandoned him and went back to their transport. Problem was that he was sat in the front seat of the sergeants' vehicle. What they respected, there was no hint of a "What kept you?" Asked what his route was, he told them − every gully, every hole where the badgers had been, every ditch, and they could trace his route and it was perfection. He got the fast track, but did not seem fussed. Someone,* *sir, you might one day have a use for.* Thinking of the boy in some primitive hide and using skills that had been around for centuries, was a salvation for Jonas, though he yearned to have his hand in the pocket of his tweed jacket and clamped on his phone.

There were scissor arches propping up the main cathedral tower. The piles into the wetland soil were of alders and they still soaked up water which caused expansion and contraction, but the guide said the arches were able to withstand and correct the movement, and Vera's attention was rapt . . . His interest perked when hearing that Monmouth rebels from 1685, after defeat in a shambles of a battle, were held here after sentence of death passed and would be hanged in the morning, seventeen of them in the market place outside. Probably raining, and a Royalist intelligence spook would have been congratulating himself on a job well done – except that three years later he would be on the wrong side and running for his own life . . . that was something for him to chew on.

Vera said, close to him, "You're missing it, aren't you?"

"Missing what?"

"A bar of chocolate, a tub of ice cream, a guide book? No. No. No. Your phone, Jonas."

"I feel a bit naked."

"Might liven things up if you were . . . Did you hear that bit about the bishop six hundred years back who felt a bit peaky, thought he was about to peg out and immediately ordered the masons to prepare his own grave, back there on the left side, and lived another fifteen years and could see it was all there and ready for him every day for the rest of his life . . . What are you thinking about, or who? How are you surviving?"

He grimaced. "Just a few folks who happened to have strayed across my path. Silly of them . . . How am I surviving? Quite well, probably better than them."

Do you not ever pick up your phone? Four times I call you, and you *don't pick up. Don't respond to my last message. Why not? Have you* *lost interest with us now?*

That was the fifth message left on the phone. Nine weeks now since she had been called. A soft voice, and seeming so caring, concerned, asking for news of their condition, the situation, regarding a British woman, held in a gulag camp. She had told him that she had been Pear, and the one he asked after was Apricot, and about the other women, had told him all she knew of the camp in the days before her own release.

Have you given up on us? When we spoke first, when I told you about the life in that camp – in IK-2 – you seemed interested then, now you do not respond, why?

Something of her regretted she had allowed herself to be driven away from the main gate, tears on her face. Most hours and every day she thought of the women left behind. She had shouted her message into her phone, and been out on a beach and the breakers, and the yelps of the gulls, had dispersed her words.

I hear from Blueberry's lawyer. God knows how he heard, but he did. They are now in isolation cells, in the shatrafnoy izolyator. *I promise you, sir, it is not a holiday there – but where now is your interest or do you just wring your hands – and do nothing, nothing . . . I thought you would help, had that ability – whoever you are, fuck you.*

The skin on her cheeks was drawn tight over the bones. She was pale, gaunt, and every glance in a mirror showed Pear that she was, always would be, a former inmate of IK-2, Mordovia. She had believed the sincerity of this man who now did not answer her, and felt dashed that he did not come back to her.

Yes, I understand, it is the weekend. She told us about your week-ends, Apricot did, how you all stop work for two days or three. May I tell you, two days or three in the shizo *cells is a long time – or forget it if you no longer care.*

Her crime had been good. A can of black paint and a brush, and the outline of a cannon smeared on the cobbles in front of the Kremlin walls. Then a second can with scarlet paint and a daubed swastika above the cannon. She had been running, not fast enough, when the police had caught her. It was good paint she had used, the best that Russia manufactured. So good the symbol could not be scrubbed out, so the cobbles had needed lifting, then replacing.

No answer came back to her – she believed it proof that words were empty, that nothing could be done for Currant, Blueberry, Apple or Apricot, and reckoned she had shamed herself by leaving them.

Lying on his back, her fingers tangling the hairs on his chest, and gazing at the ceiling through the haze of his cigarette smoke, he reflected that the name given him some twenty years before was still apt, still relevant, still deserved. Sword . . . given him by a warrant officer at the Royal Military Academy after arriving late for a lecture on "maintaining physical fitness in the field", then slumping over his desk and falling asleep: *You bloody swordsmen are just a bloody nuisance, sir, and it might be important for you to keep your bloody pecker zipped away and out of use.*

He was on the team. Across the room was a mahogany wardrobe, ludicrously big for the few clothes he possessed. On the floor of it with his shoes and boots and placed beneath his two suits, and a khaki camouflage outfit, and a few shirts, was a holdall, filled and buckled shut, no name tag. Beside him, within easy reach, was his mobile which had not rung. It was the third time she had come over, driving a Range Rover from the big house which she shared occasionally with her hedge funder husband, and that was pretty much the number of times he'd see her . . . He chased women, enjoyed it, and believed in his ability to please and had had no complaints and doubted the experience of sleeping with him was regretted by those who had stripped off, wriggled up beside him, over him, sweated, gasped or grunted or squealed, then dressed and gone on their way: he usually supplied a cigarette and sometimes a coffee. The cottage was in mid-Wales, near to Llangadfan. It suited. When the phone did ring he could be gone in ten minutes, door locked behind him, and driving at speed for Manchester's or Birmingham's airport, or for the motorway and London if it was only a briefing and not deployment.

He had done well, he thought, had performed twice: harder now to manage than in the early days when his reputation was established. She took the cigarette from his lips, stubbed it in the

ashtray beside the phone, pecked a kiss on his cheek, then rolled
away – yawned and smiled, and stumbled off to the bathroom. He
had been educated – a polite description – at a small independent
in Devon and had kicked off his trophy hunt with the daughter of
the science teacher. Another high spot had been the visiting niece
of the Academy's second in command . . . There had been a junior
diplomat from the US embassy in Kabul and that had damaged
his UK military career following a State Department complaint in
rosy language. Might have been a couple of abortions on the way,
might have been a divorce or two and likely some separations. The
military no longer wanted him . . . had been drummed out of his
regiment and had drifted into the arms of a firm of private military contractors who were happy enough to hire him out – and the
money was good and the pension was non-existent. In the latter
days of the Afghan conflict and Iraq and in Syria, his bank balance
had prospered but now the work was scarce and the cash was
more than useful.

She was scrubbing herself in the shower, would not want to
smell of him when the hedge funder came home. He supposed he
had been good-looking when younger but now his hair was thin-
ning, and a slight paunch enhanced his belly and he had colour in
his face; he was well endowed where it mattered, but the wrinkles
were starting to appear on his face. Not particularly tall but not
short, and difficult for him to realise where his reputation came
from. When she came out of the shower, dropped the towel and
picked up her clothing from the carpet, she gave him a quick grin,
one of satisfaction: most of them were satisfied. The phone stayed
silent. He didn't do much talk, and a glass of wine was usually
sufficient foreplay – supermarket stuff – and did what was
expected . . . As a PMC and loaned back to the military he'd had
a chirpy evening in Helmand when he had met up with a man
called Tank, and a business of a prisoner and "pressure" that was
applied, and a successful result . . . The woman from the big house,
and at least ten years older than Sword, was dressed and routled
in her handbag for her purse, then took out a couple of £50 notes
and put them on the dressing-table, then picked up his shirt and

gestured to the frayed collar, and was on her way. He heard her car drive off.

The call might come that weekend, or might come the weekend after, so his bag stayed packed and the money went into his account like clockwork each first of the month.

Why Sword? Good question. Why had he been "volunteered" for this assignment? Explained to him by his boss at the company. *It's about as confidential as confidential gets, it's the Secrets Act and powerful damage could be done to you if you blab it. Why you, Sword? Because I was asked to produce a man who is amoral, without conscience, a signed up member of the shit brigade – what I would describe as a proper pig of an individual. You seemed a natural for it ... By the by, there's a cut-out. You won't meet the man who's running this show. There's a girl from Five who'll do the liaison. Just a word of warning, touch her and there will be people looking for you and only too happy to slice off your testicles and pop them in your mouth and then hang you upside down from the stanchions of Lambeth Bridge ... Don't be a silly boy, don't.* He rolled off the bed. After a session in the bathroom, he dressed, pocketed the notes, and made a point of putting on the shirt with the frayed collar.

He would go outside and get the rake out of the shed and clear up the last of the leaves that had blown in from the other side of his hedge. Now she'd gone, Sword needed to be active, and wished that the bloody phone would ring ... He reckoned it almost a badge of pride that he should wear the description given by his boss – *amoral, without conscience, a shit* – like it was a compliment. He knew little of what the job involved beyond the need of a safe house in a pretty "goody two shoes" city in Europe, and the kit that was required and what would be asked of the team when push came to shove ... Just as it had been in Afghan, where the Intelligence Corps had holding cells and interrogation rooms, but hired contract people for the heavy lifting, when Tank had brought in the wounded prisoner, and questioning had taken priority over medical treatment, and a success ... The phone stayed quiet but it would be in his windcheater pocket when he did the raking. He thought it was a big one, thought it mattered, thought himself right for the job – and ready for it.

Croppy had been outside Aleppo, watching a building into which a prisoner had been taken. Few high buildings remained – proof of the relentless programme of bombing, high explosive, by the allies. Those that had stood were mostly minarets, and Croppy had become accustomed to checking his wristwatch against the timing of the various calls to prayer. Little that was tall and built to last was left to filter the pitch of the scream. Then, a couple of minutes later, the prisoner of the ISIS people had been dragged outside and hauled away from the compound gate. Then dropped, so that he knelt, and he went quiet. All of it, the noise and then the silence, Croppy remembered. And Lofty had covered his eyes with his arm and had muttered "Feckin' barbarians".

This time the scream was muffled in the mist and softened by the sleet, but it was clear and amplified by the kit in Croppy's ears. He thought it less a cry of pain, more one of despair. The body was brought up the steps from the cellar. The grandfather watched. Skender was behind the old man and Croppy could not read his face, but his armpit clearly still itched. The girl, child bulges growing in her body and the dress tight and stretched on her, buttons straining, and wearing no protection against the weather, came up the steps holding the shears with both hands. Through the binoculars Croppy saw no sense of triumph on her face, but did see blood smearing the blades . . .

The man was taken from the cellar and dragged across the street, and over the square in front of the villa, and the girl's dog howled in its pen but was ignored. As Croppy expected, it would play out whether in the hands of the ISIS people or of an organised crime gang. Fear needing to be created, respect needing to be built, and maintained, and blood proving to be power, their currency.

On wasteground, and over the road leading to the building outside Aleppo, in the high sunlight that threw small shadows, there had been a gleam, bright and intense – a knife produced from deep in the folds of a robe – and a video camera was aimed and a man pushed down to his knees . . . Some of the Regiment boys had watched videos of beheadings of western aid workers, defenceless and gentle people, as rated by Croppy. He had not seen the tapes and had walked out of the TV room in their camp rather than ogle, and he had held Lofty's arm in place so that his eyes stayed covered. The man's head had been severed. He had not fought or struggled in the moments before death, and his body and his head had been wrapped in farmers' fertiliser bags, then driven off. This would be similar.

It would be what they did to him if he were taken.

He thought that no one down in the square stared up at the cliff face and searched the rocks, through the drift of the sleet, to check if the scene was being watched. They looked into the mist, but not at the steep sides of the valley. Croppy knew enough of the capabilities of military drones to understand the power of cameras, operating as infra-red or the heat-seeker type, to follow movement on the ground when circling high above the cloud ceiling. They looked for evidence of an unmanned aerial vehicle, perhaps flown from the other side of the world by a pilot in a portable shed who sat in an office chair in front of a computer screen . . . They had called it HumInt, what Croppy did, and said that eyes, ears and a presence outweighed the importance of a drone, a lens in the sky . . . except that a UAV could not be dragged up the steps from a cellar, followed by a child carrying bloodstained shears, could not then be kicked, punched, still hooded, and be finished with a single shot in the back of the neck. The cord on his pyjama trousers had already slipped and they were down by his knees, and he rolled over. There was applause, like a goal had been scored for the home team on the football pitch, enthusiastic clapping and jeering shouts, and men drifted away and if they passed the grandfather they ducked their heads to him in acknowledgement of his authority. The child again held his hand but had wiped the blades of the shears on her dress.

He watched. The performance was over, a curtain had come down. He thought his work almost finished, maybe an hour, perhaps two, and he would make the call and be on his way. He had seen what they would do to him if he had showed out – would be gone, would not return.

A layer of white covered the roofs of the three Mercedes saloon cars, and slow of Croppy not to have realised it before, but all carried identical registration plates which confused him, and all three were being loaded with identical cases. An eddy of cold travelled down his neck and over his spine, and he shivered.

Jonas trailed behind his wife.

They walked round the moat of the Bishop's Palace. The rain had eased, and the legacy of the cloudburst was a thin shower that pattered down from the bare branches of the trees. A few visitors were ignoring instruction and feeding the swans, and ducks squawked at small kids in buggies. He regretted that he had conformed with Vera's understated demand and had left his phone in the caravan. There were times when he was decisive and others when his willpower failed him. Decisions involved his work; failure to argue his corner was in the area of domesticity. She may have realised that he faced something of a crisis because every few minutes he saw the rather baleful challenge aimed at him, as if she dared him to say that their holiday was, again, secondary to his work.

A line of faces clicked though his mind. Denys Montgomery on that Saturday morning would be wearing his boilersuit and have climbed up into the shallow space of his attic and was perhaps working out the signal system for an upline and a downline, and would be relying on him – on Jonas Merrick. The woman he knew as Frank, who could have drowned him but instead had suffered to save him, had endured months in a labour camp, and he might have the power to win her freedom. The team he had fashioned, their photographs in the files showing cold features and the complacency bred from freedom of principles, who were sitting on their hands and waiting for his direction, which might come and might not. There were the oligarchs, the *siloviki* of the regime, who hoarded their money, and whose greatest fear was that the loot be denied them – a succulent target. The men and women in the Post Room who had joined a conspiracy and silently cheered on their guv'nor . . . Sarah among them who had found a boy and a future. The boy was at the heart of it. Jonas thought of him . . .

Did it matter? Would his plan make a difference? Would the lives of the mothers and aunts and grandmothers of the kids watching the ducks and wary of the swans be affected by what he hoped to achieve? That weekend, or the next one, or the one after, would their lives be altered? All down to the boy in his hide and with a perfect view, like it was the bar seat in the theatre, of a village in a steep-sided valley. . . . The boy was a brick in a wall. If the brick were taken out then the wall would collapse. Wondered if the boy realised it, rather hoped he did not.

Jonas had chosen well. Confirmation had been in a call from a number that he did not recognise. He had taken it, usually did. Sometimes it was a scammer, sometimes it was an attempt to flog health insurance, sometimes it was gold dust. *Thank you for picking up, sir. You don't need my name and I don't need yours. What you do need to know is that I commanded a unit of SRR on a Syrian tour. We had a young trooper with us who came with shedloads of praise after a bit in Afghan, and easy to see why. Very skilled at tracking, very able at the covert stuff, of being out and away and at the far edge of safety, and we were dinning into him the need for concise and accurate reporting, nothing hysterical and nothing that was surmise. All going well, though his stoicism tended to isolate him from the rest of the unit. Usually they worked in pairs, but I had to accept there were times when he was alone because he was shunned. Stayed out too long, chose a CROP that was too close. Had an abundance of personal confidence in his own ability to survive, which some did not buy into.*

Anyway, I hear, sir, that you were asking after him. I want to tell you the circumstances of him leaving us, which may or not be relevant to you. He was tasked to watch a house behind a wall. Near to Mosul, and our belief that the family of an IS commander was there, and that he would – at some stage – visit. Our boy was there for days, snug in his hide, and would come out only to meet up with Special Forces and get a resupply of food and lose his waste to them, but we could not get him to accept it was time to hand it over to others. He had come to know the wives and kids and servants, and their guards. Finally we had the call from him, and the Tango arrived, the boy had an eyeball, was definite on identification. We accepted that the Tango might be there an hour, perhaps two or three, but unlikely to stay a whole night. It was considered justifiable to scramble a pair of Typhoons from Akrotiri and they came in and dumped a load of ordnance on the house. It was a big success because the confirmed kill was a commander of that IS-controlled area. High fives all round, and the bit of collateral was well inside what we considered acceptable. He would have been an eyewitness to the devastation and was very quiet, very sombre, when the Chinook brought him back to us . . . And he went to his quarters and wrote his resignation letter and brought it me. Tried to talk him out of it, and knew from the start I had no chance. He was talking to me, soft voice and hard to understand, about the dignity that should be given to a target, and about Royals and Imperials and Monarchs. There was a rigid line behind which he sheltered and he would not stray over it. He was gone a couple of days later. We thought him quite special . . . It is impertinent of me to say it, but I'm sure you won't mess him around, sir, will look after him. Thank you for hearing me out.

His arm was tapped "Are you all right, Jonas?"

"Of course I am."

"You sure?"

"Why do you ask?"

"Jonas, I have asked you four times if we can go and get a coffee and a cake before we go on to the wetlands. You've not answered."

"Probably a bit preoccupied. Yes, coffee and a cake would be excellent, Vera."

Croppy would not have coffee from a Costa, nor cake. He sighed, followed his wife from the Bishop's Palace. He depended on the boy.

3

Clearly unhappy at playing the role of support twitcher to Vera's enthusiasm, nevertheless Jonas dutifully followed her.

They were in the middle of a bog, on a raised pathway, probably once a railway track, and on either side were expanses of water broken by tight clumps of reeds: the Ham Wall Nature Reserve. She had quickened her step and he could see, when she turned to beckon him to walk faster, bright enthusiasm in her eyes and excitement at her mouth: went faster because ahead was a viewpoint where a group had gathered. A quarter of an hour before, while watching a great egret, big and white, with spindly legs and a long beak, and poised for a kill, she had addressed his problem, but without sympathy.

"You've no cause to sulk, Jonas. Your phone is in the caravan, the best place for it while you are on holiday. You're like a man trying to quit cigarettes, all the classic withdrawal symptoms. Come on, for heaven's sake, jump out of it . . . This is a world famous site so I would be grateful if you showed it – and me – some respect. You'll have the wretched thing when we've finished for the day, and you'll just have to wait until then."

"Yes, dear, of course, dear."

She might as well have wrenched his right arm off, but he soldiered on. She had binoculars, he did not . . . she had her phone in her pocket, he did not have his in the inside of his Harris tweed jacket . . . dangling from a strap on her wrist was her small "point and shoot" camera, he did not own one . . . She had marvelled a couple of hundred yards back, on a bridge, when a kingfisher had been pointed out to her by a fellow with a camera lens bigger than a bazooka tube, and he had sourly thought its colour was ostentatious. And realised his condition, and pinched himself, hard enough for pain to flare in his arm, and realised the scale of his debt to her, wife to him for most of his adult life and a bit of a rock, and looked to head on a bit faster so that the group ahead were caught ... He remembered when the AssDepDG, his protector in Thames House and the only man to whom he gave trust, albeit limited, had tried to give up the weed and had been so foul tempered that it was a relief when he had gone back to clandestine smoking on the street outside the main door, the side door, the back door, any door. They were eyed with suspicion, as if they intruded on a private party in the hope that, from grudging good manners, they would be offered a glass of wine, but Vera had a winning smile and had insinuated herself close to the guide. Jonas hung at the back but within earshot.

He was ignored. Men and women in front of him soon broke the mood and shuffled to the side to give Vera more space: he was not acknowledged. Stretching away from them was a waterscape that was quiet, peaceful, and ducks of many varieties paddled and quacked and occasionally had little territorial spats, and herons stood motionless waiting for an itinerant frog to pass close enough for a strike, and probably there was another kingfisher, out of sight but ready to dive. Rather a good place, actually, and his coffee at the Costa and his Danish pastry had been satisfactory, and the emptiness of the inside pocket of his jacket seemed less significant – and all hell broke loose.

Little gasps and squeals in front of him and like a platoon of Guards doing drill with precision, the binoculars of the group were raised. Chaos on the water as the ducks and geese and moorhens and coots, about the limit of Jonas' bird names, and the herons and a couple of egrets, thrashed their wings to get airborne. Made waves and made a din, and panic had set in as if these inhabitants of the wetland had no defence against attack other than flight. The guide pointed out the intruder. A single bird, an estimated wingspan of four feet, had broken the calm. A marsh harrier, and everybody's enemy if the bird was hungry or wanted some amusement. A huge wave of birds that lacked the talons or beaks that could provide any form of defence were now streaming in every direction and the sounds were raucous. The harrier had perhaps a hundred targets to choose from and some small and brightly coloured unfortunates were still on the water, might have been sick and had lost the ability to manage instant and near vertical takeoff, and were easy pickings.

The guide said to his group, "That's the male bird. He's beating them up."

What did he mean?

"It's what we call it. Beating them up."

For its amusement?

"Something like that. So much food here, and so easy to get. More about having fun creating distress and panic. Give it a couple of minutes and they'll all be back and he'll be off and sat somewhere, preening himself, and they'll be feeding and waiting for the next time the air raid siren goes off. I suppose it's a way of life."

The group moved on and Jonas and Vera now seemed to have won a degree of acceptance. Jonas assumed they were probably paying a thousand a head – with accommodation and meals – for three or four days of the guide's expertise, and he and Vera had it for free. The experience of the harrier over the water had cheered him, brought a smile to his face . . . almost saw himself in that role. He "distressed" scores of men and women in the great buildings of the Russian military intelligence headquarters in Moscow, and his actions would have, anonymously, panicked many more in the vast office block used by the Ministry of State Security in the capital city of the People's Republic of China. He and Vera followed. Rather liked the concept of himself as the creator of confusion by "beating them up" and no one able to lay a claw on him.

Vera stabbed a glance at him because he chuckled out loud. Something spectacular for his group was promised that evening by the guide, and Vera had a winning smile and they had been included.

It was what Jonas did: "beat them up". Vera had taken his arm, and she grinned at him, and his mood had become good.

Slumped in an easy chair, one that had come from a shop that wobbled between junk and second-hand and covered with worn and faded material, Cress held an open book. The problem for her was that she had read the page five times, and her eyes ached and the throbbing inside her head was lessening but still there and she imagined that her breath still stank of last night's beer. She had a hangover, a condition she was familiar with, and by a mercy the phone had not rung and she had not been called out.

It was rare for her to have slipped up to that degree. Should have been sober, alert. She knew a number of hair-of-the-dog remedies, but reckoned from experience that the best way of getting through the slow-death feeling of too much booze in the system was a hard run, five miles or six, and at a pace that would exhaust her and sweat the bloody stuff out . . . would be doing the run as soon as she had managed to comprehend that page of that book; it had more relevance to her than any other bible: *The Unwritten Law in Albania* by Margaret Hasluck, who had died in 1948 but had written the definitive work on a country few cared about. Cress knew it almost page by page, line by line – was an acknowledged expert, fluent in the Gheg dialect, was a part-time lecturer at the School of Slavonic and East European Studies, a semi-detached part of London University, and much else . . .

She was 27 years old, named Cressida at birth, which she'd shortened. Was close, as her Nana would have said, to being "left on the shelf", had ears too large for her head, a jutting jaw which spoke of her character, irregular teeth, was of skinny build and had a brain in her skull that was rated as razor sharp by those she worked alongside – she was favoured by the Met Police's SCD7, Specialist Crime Directorate.

No regular partner but a habit of one-night stands, her place or his, or up on the Common if it were summer, and names only occasionally and phone numbers never. Home was a ground-floor apartment, one bedroom, near to the wide open spaces above Wimbledon in south-west London.

She was on the team. Three of them, and she was enrolled because of her language ability. There was Tank, "a tankie and thumb up his arse and his brain in neutral" – and there was Sword, "a lighthouse in the desert and looks pretty and is fuck-all use to anyone". They would travel together when the call came – had been twice before to the location and had, after a fashion, found the property that would do the job and rented it, hellish expensive, and done the transport and put the kit in place. All open-ended but the message reaching them seemed to indicate that cost was not a factor. They had been on standby for two months, and the call had not come, had not heard that quiet and calm voice that had recruited her.

Two paragraphs and the lines were making sense – and recalling that the lady who had written it would have been in her late 50s when she was the expert on Albania and given the job of teaching the young British army officers what to expect when they were parachuted into that wild, mountain-strewn country where an abnormal culture of oath-taking, vendettas, feuds, and murder existed. She valued being on this team.

The page was absorbed – about bloody time. Up from her chair, shorts on and a skimpy running vest and her trainers, smooth-soled from the number of times she had needed to pound the alcohol out of her body, and strapped her phone on to her arm. Her life might have been considered messy, and her parents despaired of her future, but she valued the control of her own destiny, such as it was, and bowed the knee to no man, no organisation, no cult – and ate junk food and watched junk TV and read voraciously on Albania, and went with the "filth" on their raids and could interpret the dialect slang that the gangsters used when lifted. Was rather happy with her life in fact.

Wished the bloody phone would ring, so that she could grab the filled rucksack by the door and sprint for the car, but it did not.

Cress ran, started on the Ridgway, then hit the big wide spaces and let the wind and the rain clear her guts and her head.

Through a veil of snow and sleet and sometimes sharp rain, Croppy watched the cars and began to understand the game that

was played out down and below . . . The body had been taken
away, the crowd had dispersed, the villagers scurrying home in
their heavy coats, and the line of cars remained in position.

Three young men were on the step by the front door of the
villa. Each wearing a dark suit, a white shirt, and a dark tie, and
even his powerful binoculars could not tell Croppy whether
they were identical in colour or pattern. The girl was still
wearing her white dress to fit and sometimes her singing carried
faintly to him. Her dog was with her and equally uninterested
in the foulness of the weather. Crucial, Croppy knew, was to
know which of the three boys was his target, the grandson . . .
and the problem of how to respond churned in him, was beyond
his experience.

It was clear that they feared a drone watched them. Up on the
peninsula of Ardnamurchan he had no difficulties mastering the
intricacies of the remote-controlled "eyes in the sky" airborne
machines that could circle a given area, spend hours high above a
house, a compound, a village, could locate a vehicle, even a single
individual, then track it. He had experienced their powers in the
Syrian deployment: some in the sergeants' mess claimed that it
was no longer necessary to put HumInt on the ground, that the
men who did what Croppy was tasked with were redundant – that
machines did a better job. Others, and the arguments were fierce,
protracted, and never resolved, claimed that only a human eye
could make the necessary evaluation of a target. One of the boys
scratched at his armpit. The target revealed himself. Three
scratches, and noted. Croppy's skill was in remembering each tiny
detail of a target, whether it was the movement of a prime stag, a
Royal, or a hunting otter, or an eagle on the cliff above Maclean's
Nose, everything that mattered was in small detail. Three annoyed
movements of a boy in a suit . . . but what to do.

There was a phone with a signal in a pouch beneath his ghillie
suit. The phone was an option. *Just wondering how far my brief
runs. Looks like they are trying to beat a UAV link that has the
capability to watch him move out and go with him to the airport . . .
except that he is going to offer three alternatives. Could be Tirana,*

could be Podgorica, could be out through Kosovo territory and up to Belgrade and then onward, and he won't be monitored, and you won't know what he looks like, what he's wearing. I don't know what I am supposed to do other than tell you three vehicles, the same, same registrations, are moving and will split. Could have sent it. Would have been the right reaction in SRR: pass it on and let an officer take the fall position. Done his job, and could dismantle the interior of the hide, gather up his gear and his rubbish, and slip away – make the hut that was a mile or so behind him, and be gone as the light failed. Not his problem, not Croppy's.

Except . . . he winced, then bit at his lower lip.

Not his culture. Passing the parcel was acceptable in the Regiment, might be acceptable in the crowd for whom Sarah worked, was *not* acceptable on the peninsula. A man needed a plumber, or an electrician, damn near anything except help with a severe accident or illness, and he did it himself. Went as far as a neighbour, but didn't shout for the 7th Cavalry. Watched a YouTube video on his phone, was talked through that was needed, did it. Was out on a hillside, the light going and the weather indifferent, and a client was readied for a shot, and should have been calmer, should have been warmer, drier, and his breathing was poor and his mood worse, and the opportunity for a decent shot was passed over. Squeezed on the trigger. A client who'd travelled from near the Harz mountains that divided the old Germanys. Fired. The stag leaping, then running. Might be on three legs, one broken, might have been shot in the gut. And had disappeared before a cartridge was ejected and a new bullet in the breech. Croppy would not pass comment, but would take the client back down to the hotel where booze and dinner waited, and would collect his dog and go back out. Could have waited until morning . . . but an animal was wounded, in pain. Left the client to have a bath, change his clothing, have a drink or three, and eat his dinner, and had gone out into the night with the dog and his rifle and had tracked the winged deer for four hours and had apologised to it, and had ended its pain, and had left it out on the hillside for the eagles and ravens to strip, had not brought its antlers down for the client to carry away . . . What he had been taught was that a difficult job was best done by himself. Taught by his parents, taught by old stalkers, taught by the best of them in the Regiment, learned by himself.

He wriggled out of the ghillie suit, folded it, stashed it in a corner of the hide. Shoved his bag over his shoulder – money, documents, but no weapon. Left his gear in place but hidden in the cave's recesses, and his waste bottles and tinfoil heaps, and the big binoculars and the camera with the lens, and crawled out backwards. Waited, and was rewarded. Could see the old man emerge from the villa and hug each of the young men, like the game was played for a UAV lens. Croppy had seen a killing and had seen real care taken, and did not doubt that he watched a "class act", as the Regiment would have called it. He rang the number he had been given – the man who had recruited him – but had no time to hang about and he waited for an answer. He went into the snow, or the sleet or the rain, and was on a goat track, leaping over the stones.

If he fell he might break a bone. He might still be too late, and needed luck. His breath was sobbing in his lungs.

One thing was different about them, the two other boys who had also been hugged, briefly kissed like they were family, by his grandfather.

"You do it or they will kill us," his grandfather murmured in his ear.

Inside Skender's jacket, and only his, was the package. They were boys from the village, of Skender's age, had been in England with him, watching his back, and would have known that he was the future for the clan, and for themselves. If there had been a camera above them, its lens would not have been able to distinguish between them. It was the Russian courier who had demanded, on an earlier visit, that such a procedure be followed. Skender would have said that only the Russians built fear in his grandfather's mind.

The car's headlights came simultaneously.

The Russians said that the technology of the drones, which the Europeans used and the American agencies, had the capability to see through this degree of weather . . . He would not criticise the plan, thought it sensible, reckoned it an additional and worthwhile safeguard. And taking the package gave him a reason to travel for which he was grateful . . . Felt a woman's warmth and was smiling as the village slipped behind him.

Choice of a drinking hole on a Saturday evening in Podgorica was good. The gang selected on a rota. An Irish pub or a Scots-themed pub or the Engleski pub. It was the Guinness' turn to be hammered. They were the embassy crowd, and did not have to flog economics or arts or UK culture at a weekend. A phone ringing cut the banter short: Matt groped in his pocket. He did visas but was loosely attached to the Station and, under the direction of a London-based man called Montgomery – weird fish – had been put in touch three months before with a kid who spoke in a Scottish brogue, and it was hard at times to follow his drift. Difficult that evening with the music from the west of Ireland bands hammering. The message as he interpreted it, and sounded like the kid was on the move, was at the limits of his pace and he was on rough ground, was short, sharp. *The airport, be looking for me. But first be looking for a Mercedes* . . . Given a registration number, a description, a likely destination for the flight out, what he needed to achieve, and the call was cut. Matt lurched out into the night, a pig of an evening, the streets glistening from the weather.

Luck, plenty of it, had shone down on Croppy.

Had not fallen, had not over slipped. Had been stripped down to his bare arms when out of the camouflage suit, and had only the document bag slung over a shoulder. Had reached the hut, a ruin with a lopsided tin roof, had groped under the rotten wood at the back . . . and manhandled the powered scooter from under the pile, then had hooked a rucksack on to his other shoulder, and near froze in the cold but had not time to moan. Had called the half-cooked spook and heard the clatter of glasses and laughter and music as if a ceilidh was in full flow. There was a track leading away from the hut. With the Regiment the back-up was a Chinook, Special Forces, and communications handled by a team that would never have been any the worse for drink . . . The hut was his back-up and he left behind his supply of Meals Ready to Eat and empty bottles. There was water, and tinfoil and clothing in the rucksack.

Lucky that the cold had not killed the engine.

Lucky that he negotiated the track and was on the road and saw lights ahead of him only two or three miles in the distance.

A junction ahead. Straight ahead was the Shkodra road, south to Tirana. Pointing left was the sign, askew and used by youngsters for target practice, to the meandering mountain pass for Kosovo and then into Serbia and the road to Belgrade. Off to the right was the Montenegro frontier and the link to Podgorica . . . Three airport opportunities. He strained to see better. Snow had given way to a mix of sleet and rain. All three boys were out of their cars, and their body language confirmed his target. Respect from the other two, and brief brush kisses, and another scratch at that nagging armpit. Five or six seconds, and all back in their cars; one going straight over the junction and one going left, and then the final car swung right on the wheel scattering grit and stones.

Too much luck to use up at one road junction.

More luck required. He drove without lights, using the vehicle ahead to guide him. An hour later he called Matt again, and told him where he should be and what he would want from him . . . In Syria they would have needed half a troop of the Special guys and a Chinook to lift them, and likely an Apache to fly close support, and back in Thames House where Sarah worked they would have had twenty in a surveillance team with unmarked cars and some on their feet. It was against Croppy's principles to wipe his hands of the business. What he did that evening was in defiance of everything the military had attempted and failed to batter into him.

He tracked Skender's Mercedes. They were on the road he had used when he had come to the Albanian village for his recce, and when he had gone back to the airport on the far side of the border – and had used it for his two stints in the hide – and used it four days before when his gear had been piled on to panniers either side of the back wheel of the Piaggio Vespa GTS300. Great machine. And could, just about, but swerving and sliding, hit the phone keys for the number given him, but no answer, again . . . and called Sarah. Reached her in her studio apartment, one room with a kitchenette and . . . and blurted where he was, what he was doing, what he'd need, and the border was coming up and the Mercedes ahead was slowing. Extracted a US dollar bill, a hundred, from his bag and had it in his hip pocket, and was cold and wet and, as yet, had, he believed, achieved nothing.

"You're not supposed to be doing this."

Matt faced Croppy, snapped at him. Short-tempered at having been hauled out of his downtime in the bar, with his mates, visa matters on the back-burner.

"Someone has to."

Seemed to Croppy a poor response, but he had neither the energy nor the time for a fight. Or the mood. He had come fast through border control. Late in the evening and the rain was hard, and his T-shirt and jeans were heavy and clinging, and he offered his British passport to a guy sheltering in his booth, and it was opened and the US $100 bill was checked – and a work of art as it was palmed to a hip pocket. And a gesture from Croppy that indicated *Please, fast as you can, please* and the stamp cracking down. No chance of the next leg without a valid passport that had been stamped, and he had been waved on, and the road ahead was empty but for trucks. He had reached the airport – looking like the proverbial drowned rat – and Matt was waiting for him.

"Don't they have other people? This is so cheapskate. You are supposed to be . . ."

"Do as I am asking, and that'll be a good start," Croppy hissed. He could control his temper. He knew how to suck in a deep breath, hold it, then exhale and let anger slide.

"Supposed to be a surveillance guy – where this dumb name you have comes from. Supposed to be in a ditch and . . . I don't have to ask, but assume you went through the *proper* procedures and brought out your pee and your shit." And then he lost the sarcasm and his eyes squeezed shut and guilt won through. "I'm sorry, Croppy. Out of turn and out of order."

"Have you a track on him? Actually, that's a fair question. Actually, it's still there plus a camera and a big lens, and my suit, and pretty much everything that says I was there, which I am aware of and will deal with . . . Have you got a track on him?"

And Matt, who wanted to be a spook and was treading water in the visa section, grimaced. "No, I have not . . . Two flights came in just before I pitched up, stag parties mostly, one from Birmingham and another from Frankfurt, and all pissed . . . I think I saw your man going into the toilets, but not coming out and there was a crowd of Germans and Brits – anyway, no one in a suit . . ."

Unusual for Croppy to swear. He was numbed from the ride, chilled through, and was told that the target was lost. He could see it in his mind easily enough: two noisy cheerful groups of young men coming out of the toilets, the target amongst them, using them as cover, as nature would have done.

Matt churned on. "Only one more flight out tonight. One of the bucket lines, stops for an hour in Vienna then on to Geneva, same plane, different number. Should have been off in half an hour and the ticket line closed down, but it's delayed by three hours."

"Thank you."

"Does that count as good news?"

Inside a crowded concrete and glass area was not Croppy's place of choice. Time in the Regiment had taught him that surveillance was usually consigned to hillsides, ditches, thick overgrown bramble and heather. He had done limited work on the tradecraft of urban surveillance. He nodded, had gone a couple of paces, then realised he looked, felt, a sodden wreck. He went for the toilets. Fished from his rucksack clean jeans and a T-shirt and a dark fleece, and shoved the wet clothing in his bag. He came out. Like a faithful dog, Matt had waited for him.

"What can I do?"

"Go back to your bar, maybe you missed your shout." Croppy grinned. "Collect my bike out there, the Viaggio, in the taxi rank. Just wait for my call, when I'm coming back to clear the place up."

"The bleeding obvious, Croppy. This is work for a team."

He was staring into the middle distance, and the grin gave way to a smile, and a shrug. He nodded towards a cafeteria section where the lights were dimmed and the staff would have wanted to get off home, except there were passengers still waiting to fly. "They wouldn't recognise him. He's over there with a coffee. Got him? Jeans, sweatshirt, anorak and a grip bag – with his suit inside. Tinted glasses and the cap, the one with eagles on it. See him? He could be on a different travel document, wearing different clothes and they'll be in difficulties, those watching for him . . . That's why I have to go."

"I can't help?"

"You can't. Nice of you to ask. Got this far so I'm going all the way. Matt, please, ring this number, it's a girl who works for the boss man. I can't raise him. Need some urgency in the system. Do that, please. Matt. This is near to being a shambles because of an unanswered phone, but this might do the job. Please . . ."

Matt hugged him. Croppy supposed that was what other people did, hug each other. Not in Kilchoan.

"Stay safe, you daft bugger."

"Course I will. Get that girl and tell her the team needs shifting. And where I am."

He was gone. To buy a ticket, then get himself a coffee if they'd still serve him and to sit behind a guy in a baseball cap. He would need more luck, and knew it.

They had seen two more kingfishers, and a foraging badger. Jonas had been many times aware of his absent phone, but – just for that day – he believed the sacrifice was permissible. It would definitely not happen again. He reckoned that a debt was being paid. The last stop as the dusk closed on them was another raised track. He was aware that Vera was now accepted in the group so he did not cramp her, hung back, and had several times glanced at his watch and thought the amount of time the cat had been shut inside the caravan was becoming excessive ... They were to watch a murmuration.

He did not know about murmurations. Vera told him to open his eyes and watch. He believed she thought the day worthwhile if, for nothing else, he had been exposed to the interests and pleasures of people such as herself, "ordinary" people. When it happened he would have said, honestly, that the murmuration was a remarkable spectacle.

Starlings came in thousands. Little dark birds flying in tight groups. They made dark clouds as they formed up, achieved an extraordinary density and swirled above and in front of the group, and all along the path other spectators had assembled. The guide said the birds would gather each evening and find a big communal resting site for the night. There would be a "chief" amongst them who dictated where the meeting should be, and where food might be found. Little was understood of the command structure, whether they had intelligence officers to scout ahead. Thousands of starlings, tens of thousands, and the guide suggested, as the light slipped away, that some hundreds of thousands could be flying in close formation and homing in on a small copse of ash trees. He was impressed, could not have failed to be. The birds stayed close both for warmth and for protection: only one stampede to escape – a marauding peregrine falcon caused it with a chilling dive but made no kill and came only once ... And then the skies were empty and the birds had settled and the darkness edged above them.

They walked away, Vera's hand at his elbow. A few smiles from the group, to Vera. The guide led them to a parked coach.

Jonas settled behind the wheel of their car, and fastened his seatbelt, and noted his wife's contentment; he would not be chastised, back at the caravan, for grabbing his phone and checking his messages, and now felt guilty because memories of a "beating up" and a murmuration and a kingfisher were fading fast.

Their headlights lit the darkened caravan. He imagined that, beaming through the caravan windows, they would have alerted Olaf to their return: he thought they might get sworn at for being out so long.

He parked. Vera was out first, the key in her hand. He had his seatbelt off and the caravan door was opened and he expected to see the cat thread past her and bolt towards the hedgerow. Saw instead a hand come to her mouth, and heard his name shouted.

He was out of the car and bounded, fast as he could manage, to the caravan and saw their cat laid out on its side, a heap of vomit close to its mouth, its breathing laboured. He dragged a blanket from a drawer, tossed it to Vera.

"You hold him, I'll drive. We'll find a vet. Must be one in the town," and his voice quavered.

All for one, one for all.

The musketeers' creed had been a favourite in the bookcase at the home of the uncle and aunt who had brought up Frank in Oxfordshire. They had lived alongside an imagined world of honour, and loyalty and courage, and a bit must have stuck with the teenager. The block of isolation cells was in uproar. Led by Apple, who had then been beaten. Apple's protest, and Apple's reaction, and now with the frontline support of Blueberry and Currant, and of Apricot, the Englishwoman. It would have been for convenience that they had been put in adjacent cells. A mistake by the administration.

It had started with a blocked toilet.

Apple's pan was overflowing, and the water and what it held came over the rim, and her response to the absence of a plumber, anyone who might have had the skill to clear it, was to encourage the protest now underway. All for one ... The staff had arrived and had not fixed the toilet but had given Apple a beating for the noise she made: a futile reaction.

The others had blocked their own toilets, had then used their tin food bowls and had scooped out the water and the shit and the urine and had chucked the mess at the bottom of their cell doors.

Apple's initiative, but directed Apricot, telling them with a reedy shout of a "Dirty Protest" that was in the folklore of Irish resistance. Use the shit and the urine against them. In Vauxhall Cross, PA to the Defector (Relocation) Team, she had always been impeccable in appearance but that was before a stretch in IK-2, Mordovia, of almost a year.

She had been punctilious, reliable, polite, intelligent enough to write minutes of meetings and make sense of hurried interventions in discussion. Now she yelled with the others, and used the metal bowl for two purposes – to lift out the contents of the pan and pour them into the gap under the cell's door; then she used her fingers to press the stuff under the door and out into the corridor, the territory of the patrolling staff – and then beat the bowl against the door, in unison with the others, hammering out a drumbeat. It was likely that on a bitterly cold winter morning in that corner of the country, the noise they made would have been heard across the camp, would have bounced back from faraway walls, reached into the watchtowers – and with certainty would have penetrated the carpeted office space of the commandant where a fine fire burned in the grate.

It was the protest of Frank and of a once significant rock star, of a potentially outstanding cardiologist, of a woman rising inside the ranks of banking – until she blew a piercing whistle and complained of financial irregularity. The mess had spilled into the corridor and one staff member, a rank above the bottom rung, had stomped towards the centre of the disturbance, Apple's cell door, and had slipped. Lace-up shoes gone from under her. A wrist gone down to break her fall, and turned. Might be broken, or severely sprained . . . and shrieks of pain which also would have been heard between the compounds. In the trapped space of the corridor, no windows opened; there was no ventilation, and more shit and more piss was being shovelled under four cell doors. The block had started to stink.

Frank had been Apricot long enough to realise what the response would be to a staff member falling, perhaps breaking a wrist, howling in pain, and rivers of putrid brown water swirling down the length of the corridor with tributaries joining them from four reinforced doorways. Inevitable that a riot squad would gather, as inevitable as the tactic, of handling one prisoner and one cell at a time. Also inevitable would be the punishment meted out to them . . . and inevitable the reaction of the commandant who would vent fury, but would also be apprehensive about word reaching the Interior Ministry of her inability to control four wretched women.

Voices coming closer from outside the block. The shouting of orders. The noise of batons striking heavy-duty plastic shields, and the rhythm of their intent growing.

In English, their language of deception, Frank shouted, "Don't show them your fear, don't let them taste it."

"Hold strong and together," yelled Apple, whose father had held the rank of colonel in SVR and who had committed suicide by pistol shot rather than face the disgrace of a daughter who ridiculed the regime's corruption. "Shoulder to fucking shoulder."

"Unless they kill us they cannot silence us," screamed Blueberry as the squad moved into the outer corridor and retched at the smell confronting them. Her father had not visited her since her arrest for kneeing a cop's groin in a demonstration and, told by her mother, had moaned that his career was damaged by her. "They cannot touch us."

"I'm fucking scared – we have no one but each other." This was the failing voice of Current, little more than a whimper and hard to hear above the truncheons on the shields. She had sung at gigs to a thousand leaping fans, and had spat in the face of an interrogator when arrested for helping the support team of the dead dissident Alexei Navalny, and whose nose was forever crooked. "Tell me that we have each other . . ."

All the women in the squad had the aim of quickly restoring, discipline, all huge in their protective gear. Cell doors crashed open, and their work started.

At the turn of a key in her own door, a bolt scraping back and the cell filling, Apricot, cried out, "One for all. All for . . ."

She was struck and kicked to the tiled floor and lay in the filth. Who heard her shout? She did not know what they would do to her, if she would survive the night, if any of them would.

"What did you say your name was?"

"Sarah, sir."

"And where do you work, Sarah?"

"In the Post Room, sir."

"And you can't raise him?"

"He's not answering his phone. We call him the guv'nor, that's Mr Merrick. Or the battery's gone. The guv'nor's not very good with technical stuff, and there's people in the Post Room that sort his problems out, but he's not asked for help. There's a team that's ready to go – but you'll know that, sir – except that I can't raise him to give the instruction – it's what it hinges on. He calls it Safety Deposit, but he'll have briefed you on that. My supervisor said I was to call you, said he – the guv'nor – reported direct to you, sir. What should I do now?"

She could picture the man. Had seen him hovering at the Post Room door. Knew he was the Assistant Deputy Director General. He overhead conversation with the DDG. A hawkish face, and pale complexion, and bright beady eyes, and a clean, ironed shirt and a tie, but a suit that needed pressing and was the same one each time she had seen him.

"This team, get it on the move, and with a boot up the backside."

"I'm very junior, sir."

"You have the authority, Sarah, and you tell anyone who double guesses you, if there is hesitation, that they will answer to me, and it will be a whole deal worse than my boot they will be facing." And thought she heard, would actually have sworn on oath that she heard, a mutter under his breath, *One day, Merrick, I will strangle you.* "And it's your boy who is tracking the target?"

"Yes, sir, I suppose he is my boy."

"Get on with it, Sarah – and he's done well, your boy."

"He'll be all right, sir, Croppy will?"

"Of course he will. Be fine. I'll be in first thing, and you will too. Get those calls made and shift the team."

Jonas kept vigil.

There was a veterinary practice in the town, but it had closed ten minutes before they reached it. They were directed to Castle Cary. The cat had shown neither deterioration nor improvement, its breathing seemed slow, irregular and probably painful. Olaf was the light of their lives, usually showed enmity to strangers but ran their household, and was their treasure – and, though not confirmed at any coroner's court, had inflicted wounds on an escaped prisoner who had been given the task of decapitating Jonas, by order of that wretched czar, and so – ultimately – saving Jonas' life. He worshipped the cat . . . The vet's practice in Castle Cary was open.

There would have been a tremor in Jonas's voice so best that Vera had done the talking. They had waited in an outer area while Olaf was in the surgery. Had been there more than two hours and they were both aware that the vet and his nurse had stayed on far beyond their regular time. A first bulletin spoke of a small dose of poison, rat or smaller vermin, but luckily sicked up early. The nurse had come out with cups of tea for them and reported that their cat was on the mend but had shown a ferocious temper and she had blood lines on her right wrist to prove it. Finally, the vet emerged: "It's been a close call but I'm confident he'll pull through. He'll need some rest, plenty of quiet, and if he's good in the morning then I am confident that he's put the crisis behind him." A bill had been prepared, had been paid, and they had driven back to the caravan park.

Late at night, Vera in the bed, and a shared sandwich for their dinner, and Jonas on a stool, his bare feet inside the cat's cage, and Olaf slept.

Jonas had discarded his shoes and socks, his jacket and tie. He had forgotten the agents of Russia and China, couriers from Albania, and the team and the Covert Rural Observation Post. Vera had said earlier to him that she did not know how they would have survived, either of them, if the cat had gone and had had a choke in her voice and he had not trusted himself to respond and had rather feebly tried to keep the stern gaze in his eyes.

He couldn't assess how long he'd be able to stay awake but expected to spend the night there . . . was glad that his fragility when faced with the loss of the cat had not been more widely viewed . . . and had not thought of his phone, nor would he have been able to get to it without disturbing Olaf. The wind blew around the caravan, and an owl hooted, and twice rain pattered on the roof.

Might have been carried back to that great cathedral in Wells with the towering vaulted roof and the simple altar, and realised how protected he was, how blessed with fortune. Then shut out those images, and the world outside the caravan had become irrelevant to him, and his head nodded, dropped to his chest and his spectacles slipped from his nose.

4

"Jonas, for heaven's sake, wake up. Come on, Jonas, we're late . . ."

And that had been the start of Jonas Merrick's day.

"They were so welcoming about us joining them. I let you sleep in, never seen you as knocked out."

Much to remember. Vera's fast friendship with the bird-watching group and a hazy recall that they were doing Glastonbury Abbey that morning. Also to remember was the crisis with the cat, the vomit, the collapse, the vet visit, and Olaf's recovery. Jonas was still sitting feet in the cat's cage, dressed except for shoes and socks.

"I left you as long as I could, Jonas, and I've done a sandwich. You have to shave and give yourself a wash. He's fine. Stalked off into the hedge an hour ago, probably killed something and now feels right as rain. Come on, please."

Not a request, an instruction. His mind was a shambles of confusion but he registered that the cat which had provided such grief the evening before was now sitting on the upholstered bench seat and eyeing him, and had yawned, wide-mouthed, showing a fierce set of teeth. There was a bowl of hot water in the sink and his shaving kit was on the draining board, and she had put out clean socks, and the sandwich was wrapped in cellophane, and the flask filled and he pushed himself up and went to the toilet cubicle, and sunlight flooded in. He had been in a dreamless sleep and was trying to make a map of where he was and why he was there and . . .

"And your phone was dead, battery flat. It's on charge . . . No, Jonas. We are already late."

He was scraping the growth off his face at the sink, and the caravan door was open and Olaf's food was in a bowl on the floor and there was his tray of litter and some water. He saw the charger cable snaking from the socket on the wall into the drawer and was about to reach for it and realised she gazed at him, gave him the "look" that prohibited discussion. Jonas permitted himself to be bundled from the caravan. It was only when he reached the car and had opened the driver's door that a great truth burst in his mind . . . it was what retirement would be.

He hesitated, awake enough now to know for how many hours he had been without his phone, and his mind was further clearing, but Vera had reached across him and had pulled his door shut.

The group were at the entrance to the Abbey. Vera was greeted. Jonas was ignored. He was now awake enough to realise that his phone was six miles back up the road and in a caravan drawer. Awake enough to consider where he stood, for what he was responsible, why Safety Deposit was set up and whether it might now be playing out. He felt like one of the back-bleeding zealots who stripped off their shirts and vests and flagellated their spines with knotted whips. If it had not been for the cat's sickness he would have checked his phone, would have slept his normal hours and woken at the usual time . . . Of course he would not tell his wife about Safety Deposit, nor anyone, because the detail was stored out of sight from intruders in the "larder" where he always put the choicer bits of his plans hidden between plastic trays in the fridge tolerated – just – by his wife. Important? He thought it was. Make a difference? Would hurt them, upset them, annoy and anger them.

Worth the effort? Most definitely . . . His reputation remained high in obscure corridors of the Agency's offices at Langley in Fairfax County. Americans who had never met him, never would, please God, spoke his name with a degree of awe. Their analysts had picked up on a rumour mill that oligarchs in the Kremlin, the kleptocrats' who had ravished Russia's wealth and shipped its precious assets abroad, were now concerned with sanctions, with confiscations, and with the worst fate of all, of "losing the dosh": not savings book deposits but cash that ran to billions in any currency, in investments, in property. His contact "across the pond" – fatuous phrase much loved by the Whitehall bureaucrats – was Solly Kravnic from a CIA task force supposed to trawl through the Russian elite's cash heaps, and they spoke by secure phone, the American with his camera on his own face and Jonas showing him a portrait of Olaf. To answer the concerns, these senior citizens at the new czar's court were using a "cut-out", a courier run from an OCG in a village high in the northern mountains of Albanian. The organised crime group was reckoned to have a contract to shift instructions from the cash rich Russians to the experts who handled their loot, were well paid for their services, in the Swiss city of Geneva where traditions of private handling of anonymous funds ran deep. The Americans had turned to Jonas Merrick because their own knowledge of Albania was weak . . . Why was Jonas Merrick rated as a high-level player in the world of counter-espionage, counter-criminality, counter . . .? He had achieved a reputation, was now on a treadmill, and it went ever faster. There was a gym in Thames House and men and women went there before going to their desks, or in their lunch hour, or at the end of their working day, and emerged sweating, frail and stumbling, from self-induced exhaustion. God forbid that Jonas would ever strip down and go into that torture area, but he understood addiction and the curse of reputation . . . Vera beckoned him. They were in the ruins of the abbey. The guide was in full flow.

". . . It was a place that soaked up money. Wealth was power. The church must have power, must have wealth – needed attractions. The cathedral at Canterbury had the killing of the archbishop, Thomas à Becket. They needed to match it at Glastonbury and came up with 'relics' and after 'relics' the next best bet was 'martyrs'. That's powerful stuff. Relics are excellent for bringing in the visitors, so a vial of blood from Jesus Christ, from the day of crucifixion and brought here by Joseph of Arimathea, was a bit of a masterstroke – and it needed to improve on that. So, snap of the fingers and what appeared was the grave of King Arthur and his Queen Guinevere. Religion, noble legend and a tragic death in

battle when fighting back Saxon hordes, all very positive. If we
can move on . . ."

Clever people in those days, Jonas thought, cleverer than those
for whom he worked. He felt minimally undressed, the pocket
where his phone should have been empty. Vera told him they
would be going to a museum, then he would have to climb a tor,
500 feet, for the view.

"Which will do your waistline some good, Jonas. And don't sulk
– and don't mutter at me that actually there are better things you
should be doing."

"No, dear, of course not."

"How you doing, kid?" Currant's call down the pipe on the back
wall that ran through the isolation cells.

Blueberry had to lie in four or five centimetres of faeces, urine
and water from the blocked toilet to get her head low enough.
"I'm doing well."

Currant wriggled through the shit and the piss and the overflowing water and used the other end of the connecting pipe, and
echoed the message. "Apple, how you doing?"

She was the smallest among them, but Apple burned with a
hatred of the system of government inflicted on her country. She
had been arrested in the merchant bank where she had worked,
had made a show and kicked and bit and tongue lashed. "I am
strong. Together we are stronger. If they don't . . . Not thinking
about it. I am doing well . . . and Apricot?"

It was Blueberry's job to call up Apricot. "How you doing?
How is the Englishwoman while taking a bath in shit and piss?"

"I am surviving. Not saying this is how I used to spend most
Sunday mornings, but managing. Have to show solidarity. That's
it. 'One for all, all for one.' Hold firm. Want to know how I am?
Just About Managing. Good enough? Just About Managing. All
of us, come on . . ."

The shout echoed down the corridor . . . "Just About Managing"
. . . yelled like it was their anthem.

The email was personally typed by the newly appointed command-ant of the camp designated as IK-2. She had a friend at the Ministry of Justice, also a ranking colonel, and this was personal and to him, the way that things were managed.

They are disruptive and difficult and are a hindrance to the smooth running of the establishment. They have become, together, a weather-vane for complaint. I am already, as you may have seen, deluged with handwritten letters demanding changes of rules and procedures. I recommend that, at the earliest possible opportunity, these four women be removed from the camp. There are, of course, excellent facilities for female detainees throughout the state. Where I was previously posted, Murmansk, would be suitable for one, another to Moscow, another to Siberia, and the last one to the Far East. They should be individually lost in the system, deposited where they can no longer act as catalysts against good order and discipline – lost and forgotten and unable collectively to breed an atmosphere of confrontation and rebellion. Your help, as soon as is possible, would be appreciated.

It was an admission of failure. That afternoon, the Special Services squad would enter the block with pressure hoses and would clear the cells and flush these animal women from one end of the connecting corridor to another, and they would regret their bravado. She, herself, might well wield a baton.

It was what the troopers in the Regiment would have called a "heavy" landing, or a "bone breaker".

They hit the tarmac, then bounced, and one wing was almost on the concrete and the other faced a thin moon . . . Engines went into reverse, slowing the bird, and a cabin full of passengers swore or made religious gestures, or clutched their seat rests with white knuckles. The pilot was possibly running short of air time, or had already gone past it – and there had been severe turbulence out of Vienna. Not a happy flight. Croppy was a stranger to aviation travel, had never been on an aircraft before joining part of the military.

But they levelled up, the wheels taking the load on the end of the next bounce, and the engines went to reverse thrust and they slowed fast. Croppy had managed a short sleep, and was satisfied when he could see the top of the head, thick dark hair, five rows in front of him. It had bobbed furiously when they had come down . . . Croppy realised that there was pressure on his hand and a woman's fist covered his, and she blushed when their eyes caught and muttered an apology, and the contact was removed . . . It was a sort of silly moment, he realised, when his concentration might have been broken and he could have lost his target.

Croppy was familiar enough with his man. He had followed him at a distance of several hundreds of yards, and when the view was magnified by his 'scope and messed by the scrim net. He had seen him walking around the village and observed the deference shown him by the older people and by the kids who showed him no cheek, no impertinence. Different now. He had stood up twice on the flight's first leg. Just another guy – not an integral part of a dynasty and not part of a highly ranked and resourceful organised crime group. None of the stereotypes: no tattoos, no shaven head, no scars from knife fights, no glossy rings on the fingers, and no "arm candy" – as the troopers called the girls who clung to guys as if fearful the loot might slip away from them. A decent looking kid, passing Croppy to get to the toilet and having to squeeze back because the girl was manoeuvring the trolley down the aisle, and he had given her a smile. Confident but not arrogant . . .

He remembered how it had been when he watched properties in Syria, sometimes with Lofty and sometimes, as he preferred it, on his own, and had become familiar with them. Recognised the kids, the women and the staff who came and went, and was a voyeur. Might as well have walked out of his home in Kilchoan and gone up the one street when it was dark and walked into every bungalow because what was the reason to draw the curtains and seek privacy. And noted that the target kept one arm across his chest, and could assume that a packet was pinioned under his clothing, against his skin, of sufficient importance to be carried that way and . . . A call from the crew for their patience while the aircraft was still moving.

Phones were out. Passengers babbled, would have been calling horror stories about the weather out of Vienna and the landing at Geneva. He joined the clamour but with a murmur: failed, again, to reach Jonas Merrick, contacted Sarah who was breathless and stressed – and he just felt knackered and hungry and wanted a bed. Was it all rolling? It was.

"All in hand. I spoke to a top man – actually, ever so nice. No one has any idea where Mr Merrick is. Disappeared, gone to ground, no one knows. His team, the guv'nor's team – Mr Merrick's team – are on their way but not there till a bit later. Croppy, you go careful, won't you? Go careful and . . ."

All he needed to hear so he rang off.

The aircraft came to a stop. Engines were shut down. Doors opening . . . and he realised that pretty much everyone he could see on the flight had made a call, himself included, but not his target. Assumed that a phone was carried but was switched off . . . They were allowed off. The airport was near shut down and they went towards the immigration people, bored and unwellcoming.

He was three places behind his target. He went through and immediately his arm was tugged. A guy was blinking tiredness out of his eyes, a name was given and a card flashed that carried the legend and logo of the UK's place in Berne.

"I'm not used to this sort of caper."

"Then do as I tell you, and you'll be fine,"

"Bloody awful hour of the day, not used to this."

Seldom that Croppy felt his temper rise. He said, "I'm working and I don't do chat. Follow me and do what I tell you."

"No need to get stroppy, friend."

But Croppy was tailing his target. Heard the man behind him snort, then fall into line as they went to the Hertz desk.

Croppy whispered, "A car now, your name, your details, your credit card – don't argue it. Do it. And fast."

Must have been something about his voice, or his smell, or the shape of his hands that could hold a knife and disembowel a shot stag and clean a carcass and any argument suspended. His target was at the Budget dark, asking for his pre-booked car, first trade of the day, a similar small Japanese vehicle was being ordered from Hertz.

Exhaustion rolled over him.

His hands still shook. Despite all his travel, Skender still hated flying.

He used an Albanian passport in an assumed name, good quality from people in Viera in the south of the country, and the card he offered was provided by a bank in the Italian city of Brindisi. He had difficulty filling in the form because of the tremors in his fingers and needed to clamp his fists.

But he was a changed man and his grandfather would not have recognised him. He had beaten men to the point of death, using a baseball bat or a rock. Had stabbed men with a short-blade knife to the extent that the chance of surviving trauma surgery and blood loss was small. Men who had invoked the anger of his family had been pitched out of their homes on his orders, women screaming, children huddled in fear, men hooded and bundled into the backs of vans – but he was afraid of flying.

Now, for a window of several hours he was free of the world for which he had been bred.

A pretty girl took his details and she smiled and his response was polite. At another desk, a man was talking in nervous English, was flustered and had filled in a form incorrectly and it needed to be done again. He supposed it was a display of tiredness and maybe a similar level of reaction to the bad weather that had plagued them . . . And then the girl told him that the car he had booked had not been cleaned after its previous hire so, he, too, needed new forms and another bout of her fingers flitting on a keyboard . . . And he had no way of knowing that the few minutes taken up by him having to choose a new car was one more act of "luck" for a man he had never seen or heard of but who stood nearby.

He launched his chest, checked the packet was secure.

The keys were given him, he was thanked. Through a plate glass window and a doorway he would see the sign for hire car collection.

But he went in another direction, and to the back of the departure lounge and to a bank of small locked boxes. It was an irony of which he had no knowledge: that an expensive international mission was codenamed Safety Deposit and had the specific task of bringing him down, destroying his family's enterprise and breaking into the finances of the family's major clientele. Always when he left from the village, a feeling of freedom engulfed him, of happiness. He tapped the numbers, opened his box, took out a phone, checked that it was charged, and rang a stored number.

His face lit up with pleasure when it was answered.

Sarah said, "It's just so unlike him, sir."

She was at her desk but stood because, in front of her, was one of the deities of the building, the Assistant Deputy Director General. Vernon, who ran the Post Room, said with the dropped voice of an "insider", "If anything happens inside this bloody place then he'll have his fingers in it. Key man, know what I mean." And Vernon tapped the side of his nose as if it was important that the "secret" travelled no further than the Post Room, the canteen, and likely the pub round the corner where the shift usually retired for sustenance.

"Called age. Comes up on some of us quicker than others, but we all get it."

His hair was not brushed. The suit was the one he wore every weekday, and the shirt was probably retrieved from the laundry basket, and his tie was not straight and his shoes were not polished. The only fresh thing in his appearance was the fleck of dried blood on his shirt collar that said he had shaved but carelessly.

"I wouldn't have thought that he . . ."

"Usually a mistake to do too much thinking – more important, where's the team?"

She thought that a reprimand and flushed. He did not disabuse her. She sensed the anger mounting inside him. Her dad, in the housing association flat in Peckham, south of the river, would have grimaced and muttered "About to blow a bloody gasket."

"Took off fifteen minutes ago. Should be in Geneva in an hour."

"The lad that was recruited, did he get as far as the airport?"

It could have been the assumption that Croppy would have lost his man en route, or not had the skills, or was short of the necessary commitment.

"Actually he's done rather well, or better, done very well. Don't you call it an eyeball? He has an eyeball on the target man and is following him and they're out of Switzerland and in France. That's all I know – except he's done amazingly. I won't have anyone say he hasn't. It's not his fault that the guv'nor won't pick up his phone."

She flared her answer back at him and sensed movement at the door, and heard a snort or a chuckle. A pair of the armed police who guarded Thames House were hovering as if anticipating that they might be called upon – for what? She had no idea. Sarah was without knowledge of firearms – had seen those lying on the tables in the police rest area, had also seen the collection of rifles padlocked behind a reinforced grille in Croppy's home, and there had been a cardboard box of bullets on the dining room table that might have come Special Delivery. She'd not take rubbish thrown at Croppy.

"Very capable, I'm sure."

"If it isn't impertinent to ask, where do we go from here?"

"Not impertinent and you have every right to ask. You go nowhere. Stay put, that's what I'm asking of you. Who you call the guv'nor, Sarah, who I call a stubborn and obstinate and awkward old bugger – who I value highly – will be in later today, and his back will be a bit sore because I will have bent the rod across it and given him a bit of a slapping . . . A simple little bit of kit locates a telephone. His is in a caravan park, his wife's is in a pocket or a handbag. I have not rung hers because I am rather enjoying the prospect of creating surprise. And because of your endeavours, Sarah, and the boy's, we are still in the game despite your guv'nor. You'll see him later. Hopefully he'll wear the expression of a whipped cur, but don't bet on it."

· He turned and was ambushed by the policemen.

She overheard the AssDepDG being asked, "You needing us, sir? Rescue and Recovery, anything like that? Nice little spin into the countryside?"

"No. Absolutely, no. If any of us need armed protection it will be from the hands of Mrs Merrick. When it happens it won't be pretty."

"You only have to ask, sir," and another chuckle.

And the footsteps receded. She could see those wind-scarred mountains and hills, and smoke that blew horizontally from chimneys, and waves crashing on to indestructible rocks, and a croft where the walls were built from stone and where a roof was needed and windows – and a door that could be closed to keep out fear, danger – what faced him.

The AssDepDG's driver was Harry. Harry was using satnav to Vera Merrick's location.

"Are we going fast or is that asking the obvious?"

"The bleeding obvious answer, Harry, is faster than fast."

"There's bikes up ahead – that'll help us along. And Sunday morning should be a decent run."

Harry had a talent for getting police bikers to clear a way for him along any crowded road and the AssDepDG doubted their speed would often drop below a ton. Ignoring the printed sign in front of him, and lighting a fag, he said, "There's a rather sweet girl in there. She blazed defiance at me because Jonas Merrick is the guv'nor in the Post Room, has won that degree of loyalty. What worries me is all that duty of care crap that we live with today, looking after people. Pretty obvious that she is an item with a young man who is in a place of risk. No back-up that I know of. Playing games around a hornet's nest. Tough old world, Harry."

"Tough old world, sir – and can't always have the resources you'd like."

"What my mother used to say: make do and mend. Which is hard on the people who are making and the ones doing the mending . . ."

The first bike was visible.

". . . but I doubt Jonas knows that."

Jonas felt almost happy. Those who sat near him on his commuter train, or lived in the same road, or checked him in and out of Thames House, would have been surprised had they seen him as he parked the car at the base of the tor. The group had travelled in a bus, and Jonas was required to let Vera out and then work his own vehicle hard up against a hedgerow. Almost a jauntiness in his step . . . and he had even chuckled out loud in the museum. There was a word for someone like Jonas in these parts: a *pinchfart*, meaning a miserly man.

He started up a narrow winding path. Vera had promised that straight after the climb they would return to Olaf and the caravan and he could retrieve his blessed phone. By way of encouragement, the guide had told them as they began the climb that an abbot and two of his monks had been dragged up that same route by horses – on the order of their king, Henry VIII – and at the summit had suffered death by hanging, then drawing, then quartering. No doubt on the word of an intelligence officer, Jonas had thought. It was hard going for him, close to eighty years of age and his exercise extended no further than his walk to from the station five days a week. What also pleased him was that he could congratulate himself on the tidiness of his parking, in the lee of the bus, and it would be the bus driver who would take responsibility for blocking this country lane – and laughed some more . . . and felt as free as he had in years. Vera was ahead of him, had been co-opted by the group, and he cared not. Would he reach the top? Would have a stab at it and struggled upward and sometimes reached out and found an arm to steady him, then would shake it off and would climb again unaided. Brisk sunshine was wrapped around him and he saw no dark clouds, no lowering rain storm, and the wind blustered against him.

He thought the tor had the shape of an inverted plant pot, a massive pimple rising from the level ground of the wetlands. Saints and sinners would have been here, kings and humble people, and Alfred, the great man of his time, and it was possible – why not? – that Joseph had brought the cup that was the Holy Grail up this same path and had buried it at the top. He managed one foot in front of another and wheezed, and had no thought of a car swerving on narrow country lanes, barely negotiating the bends, and reckoned a degree of peace in his life had been found.

Vera called down to him, "Come on, Jonas, you can do it. Just keep going."

Tank's job was transport, having the right wheels in place. The balloon had gone up and a phone call had come through and he'd been out of the house and heading fast for London's Heathrow. Problem was that the vehicles, ready and fuelled up and chosen with care for the work, were all in Geneva. And Tank was still at Heathrow – and cursing.

Cress was behind him, propped on a bollard and playing a card game on her phone. They were waiting for Sword, and there was a good chance, bloody well had to be, they'd manage the next flight to Geneva.

Along with the wheels, Tank was on the team to offer muscle. His size and the tattoos on his arms and his close-cropped scalp gave him a ferocious appearance. Which was why he had "done well" with the wounded Afghan. It was said by a staff officer that the necessary intelligence had been given them: more than twenty bad guys put away because of it and no one in the command echelon seemed concerned at what had driven this Talib fighter to cough up where his muckers were bivouacked while waiting to launch their attack on the UK guys. Rank was softer now but the hard man image was useful when the freelance stuff of the private military contractors was on the dip. Truth to tell, he needed the money that this job for the spooks paid. Without his wife's earnings, the family would have struggled. Took what was offered so the mortgage was paid, and the extras would pay for a van and gardening gear, and that work seemed to pay good money in the Wiltshire villages.

He heard the siren from way off, and the car came into sight up a ramp. Had to hand it to Sword: he knew how to pull rank, that sort of officer nonsense. Somewhere between the Welsh wilderness and outer London, he must have been on his phone and talked some guy at a duty desk on a Sunday morning into laying on a car, would have dumped his own in some prearranged rendezvous in suburbia ... With the Afghan, Sword had done the soft-spoken encouragement and Tank had been responsible for the finger poking round the entry wound – and Cress had done the translation. A good team, but late for duty that morning. The police car pulled up, blocked oncoming traffic, had the light going and eventually killed the siren.

Cress kept at her game, showed no sign of interest. Sword was always everyone's best friend, big pumped handshakes with the cops and it would have been a good story that they'd been spun by their passenger. "Good luck, sir. Hope it goes well, sir." Sword ambled towards Tank.

"What the fuck's going on?"

"What I gathered, we should have been up and running last night – certainly on the first flight this morning, not the third. Seems they couldn't raise the boss man. Gone on holiday, and not picking up. I was called by a girl who seemed to know little about anything."

"It's a clusterfuck shambles."

Sword took his hand out of his pocket and smacked Cress's backside. She kept her eyes on her screen but managed an accurate kick at Sword's shin which would have hurt. They went through the airport doors and Cress showed their tickets, and they kept walking – and the talk was of a girl who had rung her late at night, hesitant and stumbling and poorly briefed and making apologies, and her guv'nor had gone off the track. Each member of the team had spoken to him, but didn't know his name or what he looked like, but had the impression that detail figured big with him, and he was competent. But the girl, obviously a junior had let them know that she had the backing of an Assistant Deputy Director General, whoever that was, to stiffen her spine, and get them out of their beds.

"Is that it?"

"Yes, that's it."

Croppy was in the driver's seat. The man from the embassy in Berne stood, towering over him outside the car. His hands were on the wheel but his attention was on the rear view mirror which was adjusted not for the road but to cover the other car of interest, one in the Budget parking bay. He listened but his replies were staccato: it was not that Croppy was being rude but it was usual for him to show his lack of interest, and brutally. In the glove compartment was wedged a slip of paper which carried the make of the car that his target had hired and its registration . . . He had no idea how far Berne was from Geneva, nor any idea of what time the embassy man had been roused, nor by whom – nor was he interested.

"I come all this way, a hell of a journey."

His target was walking towards the Budget compound. Looked cheerful. Like Croppy, he'd not have slept, not showered, but might have managed a sandwich. But Croppy had ridden the Piaggio Vespa through a storm, had been soaked and chilled, and had been stuck outside, and sat in his car.

"This car, in my name, my card. What's going to happen to it? I'm responsible. I'm a bloody diplomat not some hairy-arsed action man. I've put my career on the line."

What Croppy had learned was that challenging people's time-tables, doing frequent calls for catch-up on locations, seldom won anything other than irritation. He knew the team had beem alerted, were already travelling but had not been given an arrival time. He thought he had little option but to continue his lone surveillance, or the effort he had put in was wasted. That was the culture of the peninsula where he had been reared, a job was only complete when seen through to the finale. The target waved to the girl in the Budget booth, opened the driver's door, and chucked a bag on to the back seat. Like Croppy's, it was a modern car, a city car, a convenience car, a low-priced and mass-produced model. The car was backing out of the bay, and the girl had come to the door bathed in that winter sunshine and gave a little flick of her hand

and was given one back, then Croppy lost the target's face. He started his own engine and fiddled with the mirror angle.

"What I'm saying, if anything happens to this vehicle then I have to answer for it. What is it being used for – where are you going? I don't even have a name for you. Everything has come from the dirty raincoat crowd in the embassy and they're a gang of tossers. I should have refused . . ."

Croppy closed the window. He saw the mouth of the man from Berne moving but could no longer near him. He reversed clumsily and he yearned to sleep. Two cars, bottom of the range, unremarkable, going south then crossing the river and, following the signs for the French frontier and the A40 highway. Twice he had eased out of his lane and horns had shrieked and his eyes were watering and he blinked to try to clear them.

He followed his target and did not know where he was led. He wished he had talked longer to Sarah, and had received the benefit of her optimism. They were out of the city and into countryside, and mountains loomed. It would have been unimportant, but appreciated, if his phone had tinkled and a voice had told him he had done well. Not that Croppy was a medal seeker, but it would have been appreciated. The target held the speed limit, and always two cars back, or three, was Croppy.

Very few, if any, who had a long-term concern for his well-being would have given the *shef* an explanation that was a blatant untruth.

Skender had. He drove out of Geneva, away from the lake with its soaring fountain – described in tourist brochures as "iconic" – towards the frontier and the east. It was unlikely that a man would survive if the untruth were discovered, and if the man was the grandson of the clan leader it would make little difference to his fate. The lies had been spun three months before.

He drove steadily, kept in his lane and did not exceed the speed restrictions. A succession of top-of-the-range vehicles pulled out from behind him and swept past – Mercedes, BMWs and Audis. It was only on these journeys that he drove anything as basic as this hire car where comfort, speed and status were limited. His life was about privilege and entitlement and as long as he could remember Skender had been marked out as special, expecting a future laden with responsibilities. The lie had started on his return from his first visit to Geneva as the courier. It was simple, easily told.

He had returned to the village. Had gone to his grandfather's office, had been welcomed, been hugged and given a brusque kiss, and had felt the new frailty of the old man's shoulders, like age was chasing him. It had been accepted. The trust was total. He had prepared what he would say on the flight back to Albania, and gone over it again in his mind while driving in the village. He had noted that his popularity was endorsed on his return and that the *miks* greeted him with warmth and respect. The women had kissed him and cackled laughter into his face, and the girls had hung back shyly as if acknowledging that he was far beyond their reach, and he had gone to see his grandfather and had reported that the mission to Geneva had been successful in all aspects, and that he carried sealed envelopes containing responses to the matters detailed. The next day, the car would come from the Serbian capital, and would collect an envelope and he would see again, the contempt of the passenger for someone so young, a peasant boy who had got lucky, born into a village doing well from the cocaine explosion, with heroin thrown in, and the 'phets doing business, and the tarts from Moldova and Bulgaria and Ukraine who were in demand in western Europe, and the migrants with the dinghies. Not hiding their contempt, not then and not this latest time ... His sister, Klea, had gazed at him, he remembered that, but had said nothing.

He had told his grandfather who he had met, where he had met them, and given his assessment of the sort of men they were – investment managers, accountants, lawyers. Had told his grandfather they had treated him like the postman who brought their mail, the gardener who raked the leaves off their lawns, and had spoken of their greed, his assessment, and had given his opinion that their loyalty existed only while money flowed into their hidden accounts. Under pressure – lights in their faces, two or three nights in the holding cells of a police station, enduring the noise and the bad food and the dirt – they would cough up their secrets. Conclusion; the less they knew, the more advantageous to the clan run by his grandfather. He was heard out, not interrupted – then he had told the lie and given a reason for his new schedule, what he thought necessary, and the old man had nodded his agreement, a small matter but detail was important.

His life was fashioned by his grandfather, who had personally solidified the power, the authority and the statures of the clan.

How Skender reacted to the death of his father and mother, was laid down by the old man. He had been fifteen years old when the coffins were brought back to the village, and with them – just released from the hospital – was his kid sister, physically unhurt so the doctors said, but traumatised.

His grandfather had decided when he should travel to the UK, who should accompany him, given him targets for business achievement. Had decided when he should first kill . . . Not the man who had ordered his parents' killing because he was behind a wall of protection and given a form of sanctuary by the *Sacra Corona Unita* in Apulia, down the eastern Italian coast. Like a pegged-out and trussed-up goat provided for a tiger to kill in front of tourists, the driver had been located and made available to Skender – six months past his fifteenth birthday – to kill. A man had been brought hooded and bound to the village and taken down to the cellar. Young and lacking in muscle, Skender had been given a baseball bat and told by his grandfather that this would be the start of the campaign to find all those responsible and kill them.

He drove through the frontier without being stopped and the mountains were snow crested, and the river ran in spate because the ski season was coming to an end and the high slopes were thawing. He passed the small industrial parks of warehouses and factories and past the chalets that were empty now but would soon fill with hikers anxious to trek in the high passes.

Even in his teenage years, Skender had presumed it important that a man should "die well". The man in the cellar, roped to a heavy metal ring, was no longer hooded and a light was aimed into his face. By dying well, Skender assumed that a prisoner would go to his God with dignity and be spoken of well by those who beat the life out of him. Others, later in his life and past his twentieth birthday, would whimper as he approached them with a bat, a sledge hammer, a close-range pistol, or a can of petrol, and would shriek about their wives and their children, or would cower on the floor and try to protect themselves. Not this man, not the first ... no insults mouthed, but he had lifted his chin and had worked phlegm up his throat and into his mouth and then had spat it on Skender's trainers then had seemed to laugh at him. Skender had hit him, but his aim was poor and the blow fell on his shoulder and the man had gasped but had not ducked away. The cellar had been crowded but his grandfather was not there. He had aimed a mass of strikes on the man and blood had spurted and his breathing had faded, and Skender had been overtaken by violence and had struck him again and again until Bresnik had taken the baseball bat from him, and had led him out of the cellar. Only later had he realised that his sister had been there and had followed him back up the steps and out into the fresh air, rain sweeping the length of the valley.

A week later his grandfather had decided that another stage in his education had been reached, and a village girl, three years older then Skender, had been sent to his room ... and that too was celebrated.

It was about trust and loyalty, and his grandfather increasingly confided in him regarding the strategy for the development of the clan, and its business and what level of negotiation was possible with rivals, and on what scale violence was permissible in the maintenance of power. But now Skender had lied, and lived the lie.

The sign on the highway, the A40 into France, led to the ski resort of Chamonix, where Skender had fuck all reason go.

Excitement coursed in him.

All of the group were staring at him.

Jonas, inside the chapel that topped the tor, had found a stone buttress on which to lower his weight.

The guide had broken off from his gory description of the death of the abbot five centuries before and gazed at Jonas.

He was panting and had an ache in his chest. He reached up to loosen his tie but his fingers were shaking . . . actually he had expected mild congratulation on having made it to the summit. The faces peering at him were wrapped in interest – he could not see Vera – and others who had independently climbed the narrow, awkward path. He gasped some more, and then there was a titter.

A little ripple of laughter was contagious. It was started by a woman, small and chirpy, grey hair tied into a messy bun, and her face had cracked open, and then a man joined her, and the sound moved over the group like a wave, even engulfing the guide who had, earlier, seemed irritated that his talk was interrupted and his clients' attention wandered.

Difficult for Jonas to comprehend. He heard a distant shout, could not make out a word of it, then linked them. Eyes beaded on him and he realised he was the subject of their mirth. He strained to hear better and held his breath to quieten the wheeze in his chest and the laughter slowly died. He recognised the voice.

He pushed himself up but his legs were weak and he tottered.

"Is he there, Vera? You hiding him up there? Well, get him down and sharpish. Show yourself, you stupid old bugger."

The group parted. Jonas stepped out of the shelter of the chapel's thick walls. He had much to be grateful for, owed plenty to the AssDepDG. In times past this was the man who had stood Jonas' corner when those wretched disciplinary sub-committees were sharpening pencils and seeking to sentence him to the purgatory of Organised Crime, or the China Desk, and the slow death of the Post Room . . . except that the alternative was worse: retirement and an invitation to an annual lunch and an address from the DG on current play, but with a Need To Know warning attached. From somewhere close to his thumping heartbeat he was aware again of the significant absence of his phone.

"Come on, Jonas, I'm not waiting all bloody day. Time to go back to fucking work . . . If I have to come up and get you, then you'll be going down bloody fast and arse over tit. Get a move on."

He went out into the bright light, and did not pause as he headed for the first steps of the descent. He had to pass Vera. She stood with her hands on her hips, teapot style, and her look was of thunder. He had promised her that work would not intrude on this weekend away, guaranteed that the time on the wetlands was theirs, not shared with the office. She would have felt humiliated . . . The guide had already resumed his talk and was into the geology of the tor and what stone had fashioned it and where prehistory water levels had been. He took the first shaky step down. It seemed almost sheer and his hand was out in the hope that Vera would come close and steady him, but his wrist flapped and his hand was not grasped.

"Come on, Jonas, we have work to do. Haven't got all day for you to act the bloody invalid."

He looked down. At the bottom of the path he saw a track crossing a field, then a small gate, then a narrow country lane. In the lane was the group's bus, and close behind it was his own car, rather well parked he thought, then a sleek black saloon. The car was known to him. One of the fleet that came from the garage under Thames House, beside the armed police rest area, and within a spit of the Post Room. Sitting on the bonnet, cigarette in his mouth, was Harry. He only saw Harry when he was called back from a mission or when wreckage needed clearing up at the end. Harry was the driver the AssDepDG always used in a crisis. Better that he did not look back and see Vera's face, better to spare himself. He took the first steps. Waiting at the bottom, where the path and the track joined was the AssDepDG.

"Come on, Jonas, stop fucking about and get down here."

He made a fast decision. Would not grovel, would not apologise, would not run a reel of excuses. Promises to Vera were their own business and did not excuse him from his commitments to Safety Deposit. The cat's sudden illness was between himself and Vera and the anxiety it had caused was not for mitigation. The phone being placed in a drawer and then its battery going flat would not be mentioned. Twice he thought he would topple but no helping hand was available. He supposed that by now the group would have exited the chapel and started to come down themselves, and hoped that Vera was with then but did not turn to check. He believed an elderly member of the Royal Family had said, *Never complain, never explain,* and thought that wise counsel.

The voice from below beat in his ears, "Hope you have some bloody good answers, Jonas. Absent without leave, never thought it would be you, Jonas. Not making much of a fist of getting down, are you?"

He concentrated on his slow descent and rated a fall would be both painful and humiliating, and saw that Harry had lit another cigarette ... He arrowed at the bottom, and the AssDepDG's anger was a fraud, and there was a trace of a smile on his face.

Jonas said, "A pleasure to see you."

Relief at having achieved the ascent – and the descent – rolled over him.

"Time to go to work."

"As long as we're not expected to get too pompous. Do you know the fate of Richard Whiting, the last abbot, up at the top? Strung up till nearly dead, then losing his guts and chopped into four parts for display to the local citizenry. A bit over the top for stepping out of line, don't you think?"

He was told that the AssDepDG would drive the car back into London. Harry would collect the caravan with Vera and tow it home to Raynes Park. That they had located Vera's phone signal, so knew where he was . . . had her phone number from the previous occasions that it had been necessary to dig him out – pathetic bugger who needed strangling – because of his inevitable stubbornness and obstinacy, and . . .

He had broken off his cold rant, and did the winning smile, and greeted Vera who had joined them. "Don't you worry, Mrs Merrick, we'll take good care of him. I have no idea why we should, nor any idea why you didn't give him a healthy shove from the top. Just need him for a few days, the chance to administer a solid kicking. I gather it's full of unanswered messages, so we'll collect his phone before we cart him off."

He sat in the passenger seat beside his mentor and his senior, and fastened the seatbelt. At the top of the hill the group were waving farewells, and might be wondering who he was, what he did, why he was called away, and might not . . . Settled back in the seat, and closed his eyes and hoped to doze – would get some sleep once his phone was collected. He didn't ask what had brought the AssDepDG driving at speed early on a Sunday, but did not doubt he would be told. Had one question.

"Is it manageable?"

"Yes, going really well."

5

Sitting bolt upright in the passenger seat, expecting at any moment collision and the explosion of the airbag into his face, Jonas had his hands locked together and his knees shook.

He should have been thankful for the silence in the car but was not, and grateful that he was not quizzed about the switched off phone and his inadequate response but, again, was not. The journey from Somerset was consumed by quiet except for the trapped fly buzzing on the inside of the windscreen, and his phone, charged and functioning, spewing texts. The AssDepDG held his own phone while keeping a precarious one-handed grip on the wheel.

Jonas was not grateful that he was not subjected to an inquest. *So what the f**k did you think you were doing?* He had reported nothing of the cat's bilious attack, nor had to defend Vera's loathing of him bringing his professional life on holiday . . . He felt that he had cheapened himself both to his wife and to the AssDepDG, and supposed his inadequacy was further exposed by that clinging silence. His mind was easily diverted by the proximity of tailgates and fenders and bumpers as the car's bonnet pushed up against any vehicle that strayed into their path. It had been a reckless charge up from the west and now they were in the empty streets of the capital.

In between clasping his hands and hissing breath through almost closed lips, Jonas had reflected on why he was given the protection and indulgence of a man so senior in the hierarchy of Thames House. Approaching the Embankment he had pretty much cracked the problem. He was a mule. A beast of burden. Two weeks earlier he had spoken to an old fellow with a clapped out voice but a retained sense of language. As a nineteen-year-old he had been parachuted into some ghastly mountain stronghold of a warlord in Albania to better understand the moods and motivations of that country's clan leaders. Young then and a second lieutenant, now with almost a century of years behind him, he had given Jonas an insight into the grind of daily life, and had said: *They are lazy buggers – excuse my French – and like to leave the heavy lifting to others. Brutal in every aspect of their lives, enjoy handing out pain and humiliation but, to quote a worthwhile phrase:* They don't like it up 'em – *good at dishing but not so happy at taking. Devious as sin, never to be trusted and they'll never be your friend. I couldn't stand them ... The only friends my little band of brothers had there were the mules. They were exploited, kept on the move with massive loads of munitions piled on their backs. One of them broke a leg, stumbled through the rocks, obviously in pain. We would have unloaded the creature and put it out of its misery with a mercy shot in the head. Not them. They cut some branches, made a splint of sorts, fastened the lengths of wood to the leg where the bone was done for, gave its haunches a whack and off we went. As long as it was useful, the mule was kept at work. Got me, sir? Curtains for the mule if it could no longer perform ... apologies for going off track and you were talking about their young men. Treacherous blighters and ...*

He supposed himself to be the mule and, whatever the increase in his stress levels, he would be kept at work: imagined those makeshift splints, and imagined the rod on his back. He was a hybrid creature: the result of a coupling between a jack and a mare and belonged to the whims of the AssDepDG.

Jonas supposed himself, and Vera confirmed it, an individual with a limited reservoir of humour. Would have reckoned laughter absent from his psychology. But he was effective and dogged, and had all the attributes of that wretched mule and so was used.

It would have been his driver, the Assistant Deputy Director General, who had the talents of fun and laughter and humour, and Jonas reckoned they showed themselves in the guise of mischief. Jonas assumed that he was exploited because he fed that streak of anarchy in which his protector indulged ... The alternative? What of him when he could no longer carry the load, when the agonies grew too great? Where would the "bullet in the back of the head" put him? Retirement in a semi-detached three-bedroom house and no march to and from Raynes Park station, no walk over Lambeth Bridge twice a day. The day after he knew he was no longer fit for work would be the start of an enduring hell which he could imagine but would not be able to survive.

They reached the roundabout, took the turning away from the river and passed the shuttered café where on a weekday he would have his coffee and his pastry. The AssDepDG braked in front of the lowered barrier – Jonas facilitated it for him . . . The mischief and anarchy were given the oxygen they needed because of Jonas Merrick's ability to weave plots and carry out plans that would have been flatly refused by the myriad of sub-committees in front of which they'd have been placed. The man was off message, a rogue element, and Jonas carried the burden for him, and dreaded the day he might hear the cocking of a service revolver . . . Not that he had ever handled one. A pass was flashed, an official nodded to the driver, and they went inside.

"Come on, Jonas, time to go to work."

Out of the car. Past the police rest area, and Kevin and Leroy were off shift and not there to wonder what brought Jonas back on a Sunday afternoon.

"That rather decent girl is managing the show, Jonas, but it is high time your knees were under your desk . . . and when you are up to speed it will be time for you to return to the third floor. See you in a couple of hours. Get it moving and sharpish."

He imagined, behind him, that wolfish smile. He tapped in the code for the Post Room, his workplace for close to a year. It was supposed to have been a punishment for Jonas to have been sent there but it was where the detail of Safety Deposit had been knitted together. He went inside. Vernon, expressionless, was at the supervisor's table and glanced up, acknowledged him, but said nothing. Jonas shrugged out of his coat and headed for the wall of filing cabinets that hid his private territory. And thought he might regret leaving this safe territory and going back up to the third floor when his punishment concluded.

Sarah had pulled up a chair on the far side of his desk.

Her head was down on her arms, her hair spread over her wrists. Under her arms was a lined writing pad with Croppy's name in capitals. But her forehead obscured what was written in handwriting beneath his name. Jonas settled at his desk. With a gentleness that few would have thought he possessed, he moved her hair and slid the pad from under her arm and checked what she had achieved.

Little was left for him to do, but he had the reins back in his hands, doubted he would let them go again – no longer felt that he was merely a mule, had flushed the pain out of his mind, and started to move Safety Deposit forward.

The turning snaked off the highway. Croppy was finding it hard to keep his eyes open. There had been moments when he thought he had lost the car ahead, and he had driven faster, and once he had accelerated in the overtaking lane, and passed two of those double-sized heavy lorries that dragged outsize trailers – and realised that he had actually passed the car he was tracking and needed to brake and drop back. He had seen the Albanian kid, had stolen a sideways glance at a face that seemed relaxed, calm. He drove down a hill, took the bend past a hotel and bus park, crossed the bridge over a tumbling river, and kept following.

They were in Chamonix. Winter was skiing and summer was hiking – except that it was too cold and too wet to hike, and the rain was too heavy and the temperature too high to ski except on the very top slopes. He had to go slowly because of a press of pedestrians in a street flanked by cafés and sports gear outlets. Croppy didn't ski. Little enough snow came to Ardnamurchan, and leisure was in short supply. He imagined the equipment would have cost far more than he had ever earned in a year. More cafés and more shops and the young milling round and reckoning the road was their territory.

Why were they here? No.

What had Chamonix, playground for the affluent, have to do with his target? They were almost clear of the cafés and the ski gear shops when a voice bellowed at him, an entitled man: ski boots, over-trousers, anorak, a beanie, big gloves hanging from arm clips, and skis on his shoulder and poles in his fists, and girls with blonde ponytails, and more guys like him close by. Anger, might have been real and might have been pseudo, dripped off the man, and a baying voice which he remembered from Guards officers in his Regiment days.

"Watch where the fuck you're going . . ." They came, with that accent and that attitude, up on to the slopes to kill a deer . . . The deer had to be killed then their teeth had gone. Without being "put down" they would have suffered a miserable death by starvation. "You bumped my pole. Keep your fucking eyes open." Croppy was hard to rouse, almost impossible to provoke. No eye contact, no response when the handle of the pole was banged against his windscreen. He had lost the car ahead, and there was a brass band coming up the street marching five abreast – would have taken more than their music to lighten the place. Croppy drove up on to the pavement and clipped a café billboard, and reckoned that was justified, and men and women scattered and a couple of kids on scooters.

A square opened out ahead of him. Saw a church against a backdrop of almost sheer mountains, draped in a film of snow. St Michel's church, the main tower dating from the 12th century, once the property of Benedictines. Which mattered not at all to Croppy . . . He had lost him. He braked hard, jerked the little car to a halt, and heard the scream of protest behind him and the blast of a horn.

His eyes travelled the square, absorbing. He had the trained eye that was believed capable of filtering out chaff, spotting only what was necessary for his work: locating a stag that was condemned, or the villa being used by a big "bad boy" and what made the compound different if "he" was at home. He searched . . . and saw a pretty girl in the middle distance who had her arms round the neck of a boy and they were kissing, and holding each other tight.

And he saw the car that he had followed since leaving Geneva airport, the driver's door open and the hatch at the back was up. The boy eased back from her – just for a moment – and scratched at his armpit, then held her again. Croppy saw the target's face and noted the happiness.

Tiredness washed over him, mesmeric, and he heard the sea and it lulled. He shook his head viciously, and called the number. To his surprise it was picked up by Mr Merrick.

"Not moaning but I'm dead on my feet. When do the others get here?"

"Quite soon. All been a bit of a scramble at this end. Be with you as quickly as is possible. Do your best, stay awake . . . Plenty to do at my end. Let me know what changes."

The phone purred in his ear. They were still kissing, the target and the girl with the loose, soft golden hair.

He had a trust fund worth just south of 200 million dollars.

She had a first class honours in Anthropology from Heidelberg.

His grandfather, elderly but in good health, was worth more, in cash, property and investments, than 500 million American dollars.

She had an additional degree in Business Studies from Zurich.

He, Skender, had never – as a child, a teenager, an adult – needed to concern himself with the cost of anything he fancied to own.

She, Birgitte, a German national, had been taught how to save money, use it easily, and needed to work to have a roof over her head and food on her plate.

To him, she was forbidden fruit.

To her, he was an excitement that she had not known before.

Skender was infatuated.

Birgitte was in love.

His fear was that his grandfather would learn – by accident, or betrayal – of this girl and would wreak full vengeance on him. If that should happen he had no idea where he would seek refuge, and thought about it often. The reach of the family would be long

and persistent. The man who had arranged the murder of his
parents had the security of an Italian clan around him; he would
have no such fall-back position, no grouping that would close
ranks for his protection. Any marriage or permanent liaison he
might make would demand the approval of his grandfather, and
Birgitte would never achieve that blessing. He had been encouraged as a teenager, in France and Holland and the UK, to put
himself around, but then he came home and freedom was denied
him. The way his marriage would be arranged was that a father
would visit his grandfather, drinks would be served and calcula-
tors produced, a deal worked out and then hands would be
shaken ... A few weeks after the negotiations she would be
produced. She might look like the arse end of a goat, might have a
limp, might be overweight with a tyre round her. And after the
wedding service he would be expected to go at her like a rutting
deer, and children would be produced – and she was never to be
humiliated, or ridiculed. It would be an alliance, a business opportunity, and no alternatives would be offered. It he disobeyed he
would be cut off, hunted down and killed, and he knew that the
abilities of the clan led by his grandfather were superior to those
of the FBI or the French and German units and of the National
Crime Agency in London. There would be an inevitability about
a life where he was startled by a slammed door, by a shadow
following him, never free of it. Their stolen hours in Chamonix
were possible because he was the courier for the rich bastards in
Russia who were more terrified of losing their money than their
lives.

Birgitte had no criminal convictions, had never been inside a
police station or subject to investigation. Once, at a student
demonstration in Heidelberg, she had been caught by a cop's
baton while protesting about the reduction of grants for those
studying more obscure disciplines; the state reckoned there were
two many anthropologists and not enough engineers or chemists.
Ever since she had met Skender her fear was that the handsome
tanned boy with a forest of dark hair on his head, and with the
smile of a child when he was relaxed, would drift away. She

thought it would be without warning, just a meeting cancelled by text, her questions winning no response he would just disappear into the fog that enveloped Chamonix each winter. She worked in an exclusive estate agency dealing in the major properties in the town and surrounding foothills, all going for exorbitant prices. He had headed for her desk and asked if her firm had any good apartments for sale. Did he want one with a view of the mountains? They were more expensive. Actually, he had told her that he did not want *one* apartment, but a block . . . And they had both laughed, but in less than half a minute she had realised that he was not joking; he wanted to know the details of a block, twelve or more apartments, at a million euros each, minimum. He'd think about it, he'd said, and had shaken her hand and . . . a month later and they had almost collided on Chamonix's main street, she had come to know a different side to him. They were kissing like they ignored the rest of the world, and what it might throw at them, thought only of themselves.

They had landed at Geneva, a crosswind on the final approach, but insufficient to wake Sword.

He grunted, pushed up his polaroids, felt Cress's elbow in his rib cage. Once would have been enough but she gave him another jab. They had disembarked, checked their phones, and Tank had gone for their transport at an airport garage where he had a "special" arrangement, one where a manager was well greased.

The city was darkening, an early dusk coming and cloud edging up from the east, from the Mont Blanc range, and the wind had a chill on it. Sword and Cress waited for Tank and both smoked, and she did better rings than him . . . He'd wondered often enough since they'd first met in Afghanistan, if she did or didn't. He'd have said that work mattered to him and to Tank because it was survival. He wasn't sure about Cress, whether work was important to her or was just a hobby: he thought she'd a mind of her own which would make her a bit of a trophy.

Sword had brought with him spare underclothes and socks, a couple of shirts, four linen sacks with drawstrings, and a pack of the strong plastic ties the kind that gardeners used to fasten young trees to posts, and two rolls of reinforced tape, some pencils, a note pad, and a small voice recorder.

He thought the job would present a challenge . . .

He sent a text message. *Sonny Jim, You still got your eyeball? Off to buy a cuckoo clock, then'll be with you.*

Sword reflected that few trophies were gathered that did not require extra skills, and a dose of determination. The Afghan lad had been something of a challenge because they were notorious amongst the military interrogators for looking at their feet or at the ceiling, and soaking up the splashes in the buckets or a bit of slapping, and saying nothing. Quite proud of what they had achieved with the Afghan boy and the plaudits had been justified from the army brass that were in the know. A coordinated hit with the Apache bird's 30mm cannon and the 70mm rockets off the wings had given plenty of fresh food for the vultures and eagles, and an attack had been negated and some British squaddies had not made it on to the repatriation flights. And the Afghan lad had not survived long after snitching on his mates.

Had the answer. *Have it – when you joining me?*

Their target was an Albanian kid from a crime family. Likely had a spoonfed childhood. More likely had never been seriously confronted in his short life, and would have a low pain threshold. Cress had said, matter of fact, "Will just be a matter of time, question is if we have that time." Tank had said, "We'll see when we've taken him – shouldn't run before we've started to walk. I'd say, he'll think he can crap all over us, and the clock'll be against us." Sword would call the tempo. Reckoned he had what the army "Ruperts" would not have given him – cover if it went arse-up. They'd have disowned him and the team if the prisoner had corpsed on them and if the Apache strike had hit bare rocks, if the squaddies had been blasted, if it had been a failure. Sword believed he had the support of a man inside that great characterless hunk of stone, Thames House, or one of its annexes, and there had been something about the man's voice which was quiet and calm and which gave a sort of guarantee of seeing the team "right" if it were cluster fuck time. It was Sword's belief that the "good old boy" who had gone looking for them as recruits would lend full support. Good to believe that . . .

He replied, *Seven Ps, Sonny Jim. Call in if it is a major panic, otherwise we'll be with you when ready to be.*

He showed the exchange of messages to Cress.

She said, "I'm not complaining. 'Prior Proper Preparation Prevents Piss Poor Performance.' Sounds good . . . Sounds from what London are hearing as if the Tango will be busy shagging, so we've time to get things in place and do it right."

They waited, had another fag, and the evening closed on them, and low on their list was the guy, Sonny Jim, who was supposed to hold the eyeball. The "seven Ps" were something of a bible. Sword thought Cress was good-looking, would make a fine trophy, but she seemed indifferent to him and they went to get themselves a burger while they waited for Tank to arrive with the wheels, and to buy a map that showed the route to Chamonix – the town that had not been included in any part of the planning. They were playing catch-up which was always testing, but what they were paid for.

He was one of many accountancy-trained men with a residence in the city of Conches, south east of Geneva and beside the Rhone, the river not flow from the lake.

On that Sunday evening, this particular accountant – of Lebanese and white South African race – cursed in strong Anglo-Saxon, enough to raise the eyebrows of his wife in the kitchen and cause his children to gape. The reason he swore was that a meeting arranged for tomorrow, was – without explanation – postponed. There were no leaves left on the branches of the many trees surrounding his property and those that fell to the ground were supposed to be raked and bagged and taken away by the gardeners' crew who attended weekly, at notable expense. The strength of the wind was growing and sleet was mixed with the dead leaves that the wind prized out from the shrubbery and dumped on his patio and against the plate windows. The garden debris irritated him, the change of plan annoyed him.

His problem was with that fucking little Albanian.

He was supposed to meet the boy at 10.00 local time on the de la Fusterie where the secondhand book market took place, books on the stall protected from the weather by clear plastic sheeting. There he would hand over his digest of a "gentleman's" accounts as listed in a property portfolio, in cash, in investments held in the names of shell companies, and all the paraphernalia of rinsing the guy's wealth, and in return he would be given that "gentleman's" latest wish list. It happened, this transfer, once a month. Summoned to meet him in the square where the books were bought and sold. An Albanian kid whose grandfather had a franchise for the couriering of messages to and from prominent persons in Moscow. The abrupt message telling him of a new time for the exchange caused his blood pressure to notch up. His original schedule would have allowed him to meet the arrogant little sod – who could probably barely read or write and whose only talents were for breaking legs or administering a *coup de grâce* – get the exchange done, be at the station for a train, first class, that would get him to Basel in time for lunch. With an ill grace he accepted the revised timing – and had good reason to: money.

A message had also landed on the phone of another resident of Conches. An investment manager, middle-aged, owned four passports – he used the Swedish one most frequently, and should have been presenting it at 13.00 central European time the next day for a flight Frankfurt. Only a very few people, all of them important, had his number. His scheduled meeting would not be at 10.45 local, but at 13.15. In his office at home as the evening darkened, his breath hissed between his teeth and the frown deepened on his forehead. He loathed the Albanian boy. For his own children, he paid – handsomely – for an education in elite schools in Geneva that would send them to prestigious universities to study finance, wealth management, and some laundering techniques, and would then oil their way into major banking systems. However bright they were, however diligent, they would never earn the sort of money that accrued around the Albanian boy. As an investment manager, and trusted by the brat's grandfather, he knew the circumstances of the cash and the affluence – but the boy was a peasant. He showed no respect for the investment manager's talents, and what increasingly drove this expert on financial manoeuvring to near distraction was the knowledge that the family from the northern Albanian mountains – where doubtless the pigsties had gold-plated taps – could bring him down. The association with them could see him exchanging the fine 4.5 million euro home he occupied with his wife, her mother and their three children for a cell in the Poschwies Correctional Facility in the Canton or Zurich. It was regarded as the harshest in the country . . . He stayed coupled to the Albanian couriers and their Russian "friends" for one reason only: money.

And two lawyers, also from that network of private roads, houses behind high walls and dense hedges, with automatically controlled outer gates and razor wire barriers, also received adjustments to the time they were expected to meet a youthful Albanian the next morning in different cafés in the banking quarter or Geneva. These men knew of each other, but never met socially, and most certainly had never discussed the rich pickings from their Russian clients . . . In a good year any of them could pocket 10 million dollars for discreet and profitable handling of funds. In an exceptional year, when the increasing severity of sanctions bit deeper, they might clear 20 million. If it were a bad year and significant value was lost to the ledgers, then the cost could be high enough for their wives to be down in the city boutiques being fitted for widows' weeds. In a shrinking market, the Russians paid the best, had more to invest than any cocaine baron from Mexico or Peru, or Albania. Not for any of them to complain. Not for any of them to send back a curt message saying that the rearrangement of their schedule the next day was impossible.

All acknowledged the maxim, *He who pays the piper calls the tune.* The Albanian boy could call the tune, rip up his schedule, set new times for meetings, and the tune was a simple one and easily understood, especially by the wealthy accountants, investment managers and lawyers in that exclusive district of Geneva. The tune was easy to dance to, hard to forget – it was money.

Out of Geneva, over the border, the highway was raised, and below it was an encampment. The sort of living area that local authorities wanted out of sight.

Headlights bounced off the low cloud that was their ceiling.

A keen-eyed driver travelling towards Chamonix would have noticed the spread of a close collection of caravans and SUVs, might have seen the children playing in the dark and the dogs patrolling, and the older men working on their engines: the sound would have been of the speeding vehicles on the road above them and their own electricity generators. The gypsies were from Romania, were just about tolerated, kept to themselves, avoided the world beyond the slip road that led to their camp. Their own lights were minimal, but those on the highway it up the steady swirl of the sleet. They managed to survive the nascent hostility of those in nearby villages, and only one item was in short supply: money.

A primitive life and a hard one, but always eased if money was coming their way.

The bucket clattered and then bounced and then came to rest in a far corner of S/3/12. Jonas had used all his strength to hurl it through the open door of his cubicle.

It was one of those with a perforated tray near the top that was used for squeezing most of the moisture from a damp mop. In its flight, the bucket had cleared the round work area in the centre of the room where a dozen members of a surveillance unit had been listening to a briefing given by the formidable Aggie Burns. As it had careered across the space, dregs of water, dark and smelling foul, had spattered two members of the unit. It was barely a minute since he had entered the room, Aggie's place, on the south-facing side of the building, on the third floor and twelfth along the corridor from the lifts. When Jonas had come in, she had been in full flow about a target, a Person of Interest, to receive the full attention of a foot surveillance squad as he travelled from his

home in Walthamstow, east London, to a mosque across the city
the north-west. Aggie Burns had not broken off from her monologue but had raised an eyebrow as if to display her surprise that
his banishment was over. Some of her people had stared at him in
interest and she'd needed to cough hard, rap a pencil on her desk
top to regain attention: they would have known of him, the legend
attached to the identity of Jonas Merrick, and might have heard
tittle-tattle, as Vera would have called it, of his exploits. He had not
smiled at her nor had he ducked his head in any form of greeting.

He had pulled at the handle of his office door, found it
unlocked . . . the mop followed the bucket, caught a central strip
light a glancing blow, enough to fracture the strip and cause it to
short, and the shaft landed on the table and papers fluttered, and
the curses started up. Next it was a clothes rail on wheels, loaded
with skirts, blouses, shirts, trousers, anoraks. It squealed as he
launched it towards them. It hit a chair, toppled it and spilled the
woman who had been sitting in it to the floor.

"Jonas, what the hell are you playing at?"

He gave no answer, but a plastic-topped table followed, and its
load of baskets of make-up and wigs, and scarves and newspapers.
The debris of the surveillance trade flew from the door, rained
down on Aggie's people. Had he looked up, he might have grinned
ruefully at the glass-covered frame on the wall. Above her desk
was displayed a high-visibility vest seemingly issued by the pothole
section of Liverpool City Council and issued to Jonas by her at his
request, it carried liberal dark stains on the chest, his blood or that
of a young woman shot dead by armed police as she had been
about to slit his throat. There might have been a trace of a smile
before he had opened the door to his cubicle, but not once he took
in its interior. This was the space he had occupied for more than
two decades working for the Security Service, as much his own
territory – before the disciplinary kangaroo had banished him to
the Post Room – as the chair in the kitchen snug at home in Raynes
Park, where he drank his cocoa, Olaf on his lap and Vera sitting
across the fireplace from him. His home from home had become
a cupboard space for the surveillance crowd and the place where

the cleaning staff dumped their gear. In a blizzard of activity, the cubicle was cleared.

Aggie shouted, "You miserable little sod, Jonas. Don't think we've missed you. We were bloody glad to see the back of you. First time anything useful came out of that space was after you'd been sent to the basement. Don't think I'll get an apology out of you for this outrageous show of temper. Jonas, what are you doing?"

Jonas had not finished. Books were hurled, city atlases and guides, folded maps, foreign language dictionaries. Three or four pairs of handcuffs and a plastic sack of flash and bang grenades, everything he could find until the cubicle was stripped bare and the little table that had served as his desk was cleared, and the charts for annual leave that had been stuck on his wall for surveillance people were torn down, crumpled, and thrown over his shoulder. The fury vanished, his face calmed.

Jonas stood in his doorway, leaning on the jamb, and said, almost casually, "I am a mule. A bit of a donkey, a bit of a horse – a mule."

They were all gazing at him. There would have been, other than Aggie Burns, a few who remembered him but the turnover in surveillance was always quick. Among beem were those who'd have tracked Mary-Lou, the Chinese tart, the obsessed brain boy and a master agent sent from Beijing to relieve the UK of weapons secrets, and they'd have known they were part of the triumph – and known of a tribunal of judgement. He turned back into his cubicle, and was down on his hands and knees and four containers of cleaning fluids were lobbed across the room. He emerged with a portrait of the late Queen, the Annigoni, and glass showing a spider's web of cracks. He took it to Aggie Burns' desk, laid it there, turned his back on her, and gestured at the door.

A command, not a request.

Pushing a trolley, the sort used in a supermarket for shoppers at a weekend filling up, was Sarah. She looked nervous. In her trolley were his computer, his keyboard, closely packed paper files in cardboard boxes, two landline telephones with encryption capabilities, and a laptop. The trolley was brought to the cubicle door and the computer was lifted off and he showed Sarah where he wanted it, and his files. He went across the outer room, focused his attention on a small table on which a drooping pot plant had been placed. He deposited the pot on the floor and commandeered the table, and an upright chair, tipping off several coats. He carried the table and the chair into his space and positioned then against the wall opposite his desk. Sarah was crouched at a bank of sockets, and when she stood, his computer was flickering to life.

In a hushed voice Jonas said, "Sarah, I'll be grateful for your help in the next few hours."

"Of course, Mr Merrick."

"Thank you," he said quickly, as if unused to spilling confidences. "We are close to something considerable, and you have contributed."

"And Croppy has."

"Correct, and many others. It will move very fast now. So, let us go to work."

"Please, can I ask one question?"

"You may. One."

She hesitated, she twisting the chair and staring at his hunched back.

"Hurry up. I don't bite. What is your *one* question?"

"Why, Mr Merrick, did you choose Croppy?"

"He was available, was recommended, he came without baggage. Now time for some concentration, and what is relevant."

It was chilly in Thames House. Under the regime of the recently installed Deputy Director, Brian, the central heating in the building had been turned down three degrees and at weekends most officers and staff worked, if possible, from home.

And it was cold in Geneva. The wind blew sharply off the lake and the sun had set.

In the resort town of Chamonix snow came in flurries and there were also rain showers which meant the pavements would soon be gritted.

On Denys Montgomery's wristwatch – as he entertained

himself in the lagged attic of his home with the running of the replica Somerset and Dorset line – there was a dial that featured the time at what he believed was the hellhole of IK-2, Mordovia, and his phone displayed the temperature there . . . It was his determination that, while the business involving Jonas Merrick played out, the conditions of a select few of the inmates there would never be far from ranking as priority. It was late at night in the prison camp, now below freezing, no respite from the brutal intensity of a gale sweeping in off the tundra and the snow-draped forests.

They were stripped naked, their clothing, filthy and wet, heaped by the shower block door.

Fresh clothing lay in a pile nearby.

The four of them had been herded towards the most distant showers where water had cascaded over them, and batons were used to hurry them along.

They had stood together under the water. Apricot's arms round Blueberry's shoulders, and Blueberry holding tight to Apple, and Apple clinging to Currant and Currant to Apricot, and all determined not to collapse in full view of the staff . . . They had been turfed out of their cells in Isolation and a pressure hose had scoured the floor and a pump used to unblock the toilets and they had been brought to the showers.

Without warning, the water pressure reduced, turned into a miserable trickle.

Staff lined the route from the shower to the door. Not senior staff, but those from the junior ranks whose names did not figure on the employment lists in the files of the Justice Ministry. A lesson was to be taught. Lightly the batons were smacked into the palms of their hands, making a soft rhythm of menace.

Water ran off the women's thin shoulders. Apple said, with a hissed defiance, "We go, girls, go together, in our own time, and fuck them."

And more water dribbled off slack breasts hanging like punctured balloons on their chests. Currant, who would never get to be a rock star, shivered and stammered, "We don't show fear."

The water was slow to clear in the shower tray and swirled at their feet. Blueberry, who should have been a doctor and who knew the strain on their bodies, said, "We get the fuck out, and never bow the knee."

And Apricot used an elbow to wipe her thin hair from her face. Thought she might have saved a man's life, a man to whom she owed nothing, and the proof she had preserved him was the punishment of time in IK-2, and said, "We go, go like they cannot break us . . ."

The ceiling strip lights shine brigtly on them. White tiles under their feet and alongside them, level with their knees and hips and shoulders and sodden hair, the grouting loose. A place where the soul of humanity was locked out . . . They clung to each other and walked up the corridor. No quickened step, no cowering back.

Apricot had once been Frank, a smart, quiet young woman working in the heart of the British intelligence community. Had loved a man who was bogus and had entrapped her; had betrayed the location where a defector was kept anonymous and safe. Had helped to prevent the revenge killing of the man who had identified her as a traitor. But all of that life was gone, and she was Just About Managing.

They were slapped, poked and prodded, kicked in their spindly shins, spat at. Fiercer with each step they took. Blueberry's lower lip was split and blood seeped onto the white tiles, and more came from a wound on Apple's left knee. Apricot was not struck with a baton, nor punched or kicked and wondered if she had special status among them. But she would not abuse it, would never hide behind it, should it exist.

They reached the end of the corridor. Staff pushed them aside and most of them stamped off into the night. A few remained . . . the clothing was picked up. Flimsy towels were thrown at them. Frank was Apricot now, and any thoughts of the great building on the south side of the Thames were she had once worked, of her small Paddington flat, were erased. Her home was IK-2, her friends were Blueberry and Apple and Currant, and her horizons had shrunk to the corridor down which she walked and the cold that gripped her body. Outside there would be icicles hanging like daggers from the edges of the roofs. They were escorted back to their dormitory, and up an aisle through the bunk beds, and none of the women already there, caught their eye. As if the possibility existed that they could contaminate, could bring down punishment by association, as if defiance was a plague.

Currant and Apple shared a bunk and so did Blueberry and Apricot, and they clung, to each other, tried to share their body warmth – and knew of no one who cared.

Chamonix was not a town that slept early.

Hunched down in the driver's seat, engine and heater off and lights out, Croppy watched the front door of the block.

He could not know how long the target would stay inside.

Nor if the car park was patrolled and he might be turned away for trying to spend a night in a parked vehicle.

And did not know when the team would be there to take over responsibility, nor where they were, what they did, why it took them so long – why he was alone with the smell of his socks and his stomach rumbling . . . Remembered a client who had said, "I am telling you in absolute truth, young man, for a hot coffee right now I would happily kill." Would not have killed, would have welcomed . . . He fought the inevitability of sleep, and twisted his body and curled his toes, and shivered.

All through the long evening Croppy was aided – as if a conspiracy had selected his side of the argument – by the rampaging noises on the pavements and in the streets. Tourists pitched out of bars and restaurants and clubs, and people at parties in nearby apartments shouted and laughed and sometimes argued at the tops of their voices. He heard people being sick and heaving around drains, but most were simply mad with exuberance, like it had been when the troopers in the Regiment had come out of Syria and were airlifted to Cyprus and free to keep the dives of Limassol in profit. He had not joined them. He despised drunkenness, not from a puritan streak but because he did not want to be incapable of making a decision. The noise went on late.

He did not call Sarah. She would be asleep, but he did not know where. She might have gone home, or be in one of the pocket handkerchief quarters where personnel could stay overnight, or be in the Post Room in a sleeping bag on the floor . . . They would be married and together for the rest of their lives when the mission was completed. That was a comfort . . .

He had identified her apartment, the woman with the loose golden hair, had seen the lights come on seconds after they had passed through the main door. And the target had not looked behind him, not scanned for risk.

Best he could do was think of Sarah. He had his rucksack on his lap, could get no warmth from it, but it was helpful – and hours passed . . . saw them once at the apartment window. Kids went by, clutching cans and shouting at each other: one can was dropped and then kicked – remembered what a sergeant had said about kicking cans down the road: *Waste of time, problem put off, the longer it takes to pick it up and the more often it's kicked then the harder the job.* Liked that. He held on to Sarah, and the struggle was harder and his efforts to keep his eyes open became fiercer and less effective . . .

He saw the girl come to the window, wearing a man's shirt and probably nothing else; then the target came behind her, in a bath-robe that would have been hers. They looked down, saw the source of the noise, then drew the curtains.

Croppy; shivered, waited.

They were worrying times for the oligarch.

Sleep evaded him.

His wife, woken by his restless tossing and turning, had urged him to explain the problem. He had shrugged her away, which to her would have confirmed that his monthly curse was again active. Always like that when the date came round, and had been since his responsibility was acquired. He arranged the courier system. As the sanctions imposed by the Americans, and the less efficient

British, had tightened and made a wall around the monies collected by this privileged elite, so he had taken on the role of organiser, and the pressures had steadily built.

This weekend, the courier travelled. The "experts" in Geneva would file their reports, deduct their fees, present new difficulties, more problems, greater expenses – but alternatives were sparse. Cash leached from their overseas finances and options were beyond reach. The nagging throb in his mind, which he could not lose, came because of his connections . . . He had been a minor functionary in St Petersburg when he had started out, transport system. Had a decent head for figures, a good memory that enabled him to reel off timetables, and had been intelligent enough to hitch his coat-tails to the career of the coming man in the city, who now sat in a gilded throne inside the Kremlin. He had been noticed, his attitude appreciated, his efficiency valued. He now owned property in St Petersburg, and Moscow, had a *dacha* in the forests outside the main ring road, a villa outside Sochi on the Black Sea, and an apartment overlooking Piazza Navona – except that Rome was now off limits. Other leaders in the inner circle had been security policemen or had run detachments of foreign-based spies – good at what they knew but naive about the ways of consolidating wealth when the markets were in the hands of enemies. Men had come to him, had divulged the details of their wealth, and requested his help. None the sort of people, as he judged character, in whom disregard would be tolerated, nor the sort of men whose overtures it would be sensible to rebuff. He had been given portfolios, had lumped the assets together, had alerted the team of managers and lawyers and accountants and bankers in a far-away Swiss city, had agreed payment terms that were based on the successful concealment of tens of millions in dollars, sterling and the euro, or hundreds of millions, even of billions. They were the nest eggs, the pension funds for lives of potential luxury. If the regime collapsed, God forbid, retirement would have to be spent inside North Korea, or within Syria, or as a guest of the Iranian ayatollahs, or in Shanghai where he'd be regarded with serious contempt. Not a welcome thought but preferable to swinging in the wind from a lamp post overlooking the Moskva River after the mob had stripped off his Rolex and rifled through his wallet. The sums were too large, which added to the sense of fear – and more stress when the man behind that high wall had summoned him for a face to face, a one on one, and had provided the paperwork and the passwords for half a billion that he should handle . . . Escape from his commitment was now impossible. If there was a financial catastrophe and he was within Russia's territorial borders, then the outlook for himself, for his wife and daughters, with powerful enemies circling and emptied pockets hanging from their trousers, would be bleak. Not to be contemplated. It was that weekend that the courier travelled from northern Albania to cash-rich Switzerland.

He detested the Albanians. His experience of them was limited but he had heard tales of their behaviour. A sophistication rating of far below *nil*, talking interminably about their *honesty*, their *kanoun*, their treatment of brothers or neighbours or anyone idiot enough to do business with them that set standards even the Chechens could not match. Until the packets returned to Moscow, by the end of the following week, he would be nervous, on edge . . . too many of those found "wanting" in recent weeks had managed to hurl themselves from upper floor windows. The night slipped slowly past him.

His phone cavorted on his desk. Jonas was told that a pool car was waiting for him at the side door entrance on Horseferry Road.

He thought himself back in charge, matters progressing. The business of a weekend when control had briefly slipped from his grasp was not referred to, was forgotten. All in place . . . had spoken to the Scots boy, who was holding up well and could soon head off and sleep his heart out. And the team seemed competent and enthusiastic. His call to Solly Kravnic at the Agency had further emphasised that his position as the key player in the operation was confirmed: that vast flatulent building in Langley, in the state of Virginia, was now moving three of their most proficient "geeks" to a military airport that Jonas had never heard of and they would be in the air, by private aircraft, when told of the successful lift. It had not crossed Jonas' mind that he might within a few hours be ringing EssKay, as the American liked to be known, to report that the mission was in "abort mode", had gone pear-shaped. Thanks for his efforts were profuse. Denys Montgomery, from his echoing loft, had texted him. *We're all depending on you, Jonas, pulling this off, and the howls of pain in downtown Moscow will be clearly heard in Tallinn, Vilnius, Riga. Good luck, friend.* With no offering of courtesy, Jonas had responded, *Sorry, but luck plays only a small part in such matters.* And Aggie Burns had poked her head round the cubicle door and murmured something about a good theatrical show and wished him well and asked him if, again, his face would be rearranged, and an apology was not expected for the interruption to her briefing . . . And Vera was long home, and Olaf was well and Harry, who had driven her, had come into the house and repaired the catch on her collapsible ironing board, and a sandwich would be in the fridge.

The AssDepDG was loitering in the corridor.

Jonas had his coat on, and his hat, and a plastic bag had replaced his briefcase that was at home. He had gestured a wave to Sarah who had found somewhere to sleep. She had started to say something about the surveillance boy, about Croppy, then had realised that the senior man was there and had minded her tongue.

"I'm going to walk down with you, Jonas."

"Please yourself."

"Feeling cocky?"

"Not that I've noticed."

"Everything in place?"

"As much as can be."

"I always like to hear confidence," the AssDepDG murmured.

Jonas realised the power of those eyes, gimlet sharp and seeming to strip him down, could skewer him. Without the man's support he would still be the analyst hidden away, writing reports on individuals that no one in Thames House read once they had seen his name on the top page, and on situations that might develop destined only to be filed, his judgements not acted upon. Now, when he cared to go public there was grim acquiescence in upper rooms, and the gathering together of personnel for a kangaroo session, but they would make a show of punishment then come back to him for more. He felt special, appreciated at last, which was good defence against the failure that could, possibly, descend on his work.

"Have dotted the 'i's and crossed the 't's. If the subordinates do as planned then I expect a healthy outcome."

A narrow frown brushed over the AssDepDG's forehead, and his lips pursed, and a reply was considered – but not given.

"Safe home, Jonas."

"Thank you."

"And be a good boy. Don't fuck up."

For a moment Jonas rocked, and was about to spit back a reply but the AssDepDG was already on the move down the corridor, and past the coffee machine. He pressed the lift button. It might have been a boil, the confidence he had displayed, but the man had lanced it, drained it. He went down in the lift, emerged into the atrium, and saw the table on the right-hand side that was always used for drinks, the bottles of warm prosecco, and the envelope that would carry the John Lewis/Waitrose voucher – because finances were tight – for leaving occasions. Would it work out? Had to believe in his own planning, didn't he?

He went to the waiting car that would drive him to Raynes Park, and the next day matters would be decided. He walked briskly, nodded to the driver, sat in the back, was driven into the night, and wondered what sandwich filling Vera would have given him – and how that decision, the next day, would shape up.

6

Jonas felt chirpy. He regarded himself as the man in charge, and any doubts or hesitations were on the back-burner. A Monday morning, the one in the week that he appreciated the most, when he left home after a weekend of killing time, plotting further moves on a target in the refuge of the caravan while supposedly checking the electrics and plumbing, and inspecting the ceiling and windows for leaks. Had even spoken, almost in friendship, to his neighbour Derbyshire, and been greeted with astonishment.

"Going to be a good day."

"You think so, Mr Merrick?"

"Sure of it, not a shadow of doubt, an excellent day."

Perhaps Derbyshire, who worked in double-glazed conservatories, had glanced at the sky and seen lowering cloud, gathered in deeper shades of grey, and puddles on the pavement from the overnight rain. Perhaps Derbyshire had been at home the previous afternoon, dozing in an armchair, when Merrick's caravan had been towed up the road and then parked more confidently than the miserable old beggar managed. Then, later that same evening, a second car had pulled up outside Merrick's home and he had stiffly emerged from it, tottered up his pathway and had to fiddle in his pocket for his key.

As if unwilling to let the opportunity slide, Derbyshire had chiselled further.

A sly question. "And how was the West Country, Mr Merrick?"

Almost – not quite – a grin from Jonas.

"Very attractive. Quiet, did a bit of walking, a bit of twitching, worked well . . . Sorry but must get on."

He had a purposeful stride. Good reason for it. All in place and all determined by Jonas before the strangely engineered whiteout that had seen him lose control, wrestle to get it back and now have it tucked under his arm. Safety Deposit had the potential to be the finest achievement of Jonas Merrick's professional life. In the next few hours he would face the very real possibility of acclamation from the few who knew of the plan he had put together. He would almost have liked to turn, go back, pause at Derbyshire's gate and tell him that his neighbour, Jonas Merrick, was in the process of pulling off one of the great coups for which his Service was supposed to be capable. All down to him . . . the Americans were not up to it, and his own Service had not the initiative or the determination to see it through. But Jonas Merrick did. He left Derbyshire in his wake and thought the man might by now have bolted inside to tell his wife that the chances were hot that "old Merrick, the toad" was a changed man, showing the first signs of relocating to the human race. Sometimes, she had told him, Vera came out on the step after his departure – might have been carrying Olaf – and stood there, craning for a last sight of him, and might wave. He did not look back . . . a quick glance at his wristwatch and confirmation that he was on time for his train.

As he walked, his brogues with their steel toe and heel reinforcements rattling him along the pavement, he could reveal to himself what he believed were his talents. Those of a mule? Certainly not . . . Those of a miserable old beggar? Probably not. That Monday morning hurrying for the train as he always did, satisfied that he was neither early nor late, he pondered and reckoned that his appearance was more suited to that of a spider, a black laceweaver, large and dark and formidable, and sitting at the heart of a web of its own manufacture, controlling access to his heartland, luring in opponents and destroying them once the web had disabled them. He smiled.

Smiled through the journey into Waterloo. Smiled on his route towards the Palace of the Archbishop and the bridge. Saw Kev and Leroy who had come to the crown to look for him, and then would shadow him back on the north side . . . No words spoken, but the chances were that one of them would go forward, and be in place to halt the traffic on the roundabout and let him cross in safety.

He was a part of that great surging mass of workers struggling to get over Lambeth Bridge, trying not to be elbowed out of the way and into the bus lane. He held his place, and the building loomed ahead of him . . . and he was escorted by Kevin with Leroy holding up the traffic. No fuss made, but it happened. Happened also that the car bringing in the Deputy Director General was stopped, and a smart rap on the horn by its driver was ignored by the police officer, machine pistol across his chest, who obstructed their passage. Jonas saw them from a corner of his eye but kept his head ducked down, did the Nelsonian bit which he'd always considered wise and opportune.

Had his coffee and pastry from the café. Had his seat on a bench close to the sign commemorating the work of a master mason in the fashioning of the original graveyard of St John's, ate and drank and scattered crumbs for the chaffinches. And walking towards him was the man with his barrow of tools and his plastic bag for rubbish. He had two feelings for the gardener, diametric opposites. The man was spared the weight of responsibilities that Jonas carried – the man would never know, as he hoed and raked and swept, that feeling of accomplishment to which Jonas was now adjacent. He dismissed the first, rather gloried in the second. He sat upright and the songbirds gathered at his feet as if in adoration. It would be a triumph . . . Of course his mission was short-handed, inevitable but necessary. Of course the boy who acted as their spotter should have had back-up . . . Of course the team should have been more carefully vetted and better resourced and been composed of men and women with more experience . . . Of course, had the numbers been put in place, and the procedures, then there would have been leakage. Leakage would have brought one of those sub-committees scampering out of woodwork. Night following day, certainty and inevitability, a sub-committee responding to leakage would have slapped Safety Deposit down. Not conjecture. Vetoed and a chance to strike missed.

He put his beaker on the bench and the pastry wrapping and napkin, and stood up. His phone bounced in the inside pocket of his jacket of Harris tweed. He started to walk, wanted to be clear of the bench before answering. He was non-committal as he answered, then realised he had left his rubbish behind and saw the gardener closing on it and heard the squeal of his barrow's wheel: and saw a look of disappointment on the man's face. Like he had failed in his manners. The thought snapped in Jonas Merrick's head: for heaven's sake, he had work to do, was not escaping the world's actualities by hiding in a London garden and tidying up imaginary leaves, and . . . He heard a small voice on his phone and walked out of the garden.

"It is Pear . . . You, you are the one I speak with?"

"I am, actually, quite busy."

She sat on a bench, looking out over the harbour of Reykjavik. An obsessive knitter, she was halfway through a pattern for a child's bonnet, pink, and would give it to a charity when it was near to Christmas. She liked to see the sea that stretched away between promontories and linked with the ocean, and gulls circled her noisily: She thought the man she spoke with rude, dismissive, but would not be silenced.

"It is about my friends."

"Of course, your friends. Monday morning, always a busy time."

"It was your colleague, Mr Montgomery, who put us in touch."

"Indeed he did. I have a mountain of work on my desk – can we, please, be brief."

She ground her teeth, spat gum from the back of her mouth, and launched. "The lawyer called me again. He takes a risk to do so . . . Do you know about risk, Mister? In Moscow it is possible to take a risk. In London can you take a risk? In Reykjavik there is no risk unless their embassy sends men after me. The Russian embassy. But they have only a very few in the city, people who could kill me . . . My lawyer called me. My lawyer and theirs. They have been taken from the isolation cells, put back in their dormitory, and this morning will go to the benches where they will be put to work. Not for long, not in IK-2. If they are in the dormitory and at the workbench, then he says it means for a few days only. It is decided they will split them and send them far apart. Do you hear me? Send them away, scatter them like chaff. Do you hear me?"

A hesitation, then the distant answer. "Hear you, yes."

"In this country, where I am now safe, trapped like a condemned chicken, but safe, they have a separate religion. It is about spirits, what they call 'elves', little and magic people, and as many believe in them as have Christian faith. They call them 'the disappeared people'. It is what my friends will be, but without any mystery and without romance, the *disappeared people*. Do you listen to me?"

"What you say has my full consideration . . . I repeat, I am a busy man."

"You do not sound to be interested in what I tell you."

"Your opinion, which you are entitled to."

"Neither concerned nor even interested."

"It is presumptuous of you, Miss – *Miss Pear* – to believe you know what does or does not interest me."

"What do you propose to do?"

"Whether I *propose* to do anything, or nothing, is not a matter I would discuss over an open phone with you."

"You are prepared to condemn them?"

"Maybe I am and maybe I am not . . . Good day to you, Miss – *Miss Pear* – and I hope in distant Iceland it will be a pleasant one."

One last hiss as her breath was angrily drawn over her lips, and she ended the call. She supposed him a bureaucrat, a little man in stature and status. Tears welled in her eyes and a sharp wind came off the sea and burned the moisture on her cheeks.

At her sewing machine, at her usual bench, Apricot – once Frank who worked for the Secret Intelligence Service and had been condemned as a traitor – was making uniforms for the military. They would be insufficient for winter in the Ukrainian trenches . . .

but what happened in political or military or diplomatic levels was of little concern to her.

It was still snowing. It had been snowing when their dormitory was woken at six, when they were hustled into their inadequate green uniforms, and with a flimsy coat over their shoulders, taken outside into the exercise area that was ringed with razor wire. A well-coddled woman, bulging in appropriate clothing, had taken them through the compulsory daily routine of stretching and bending and arm swinging. If a woman refused to attend or stayed in her bunk bed then the whole dormitory was punished and their weekly wage of some £6 was slashed. The whole dormitory would have suffered for the "rebellion" of Blueberry and Currant and Apple and Apricot, but they would not be taken into grey corners and threatened, beaten, scratched and bitten, because it was already known that they were going to be moved on. It was still snowing when their porridge breakfast was taken, and would still be snowing when they were given their midday soup. That they were allowed to sit in a line, pressed close to each other, was further evidence that the camp regime no longer needed to hand out further punishment. They were on their way and probably would recall this time of imprisonment as a golden age in comparison to what faced them.

And it was still snowing when they were herded back to their benches. The work space hummed and squeaked with the noise from the sewing machines. They could speak if they kept their eyes on the drive of the needles, if their voices were whispers against the throb of the machines.

From Apple: "I'll not let them split us."

From Blueberry: "If they split us, they control us."

From Currant: "They control us and we are alone, weak."

From Apricot: "An answer, clear enough, so we are not separated."

She had said it, had thought it before, but had not spoken of it. A woman who was said to have defrauded a bank of millions of roubles and funded a lifestyle of luxury but had been brought down because she would not share her loot with the investigators, had run at the wire, had jumped, had started to scrabble higher, and had chosen well because a fallen branch had lowered the last strands, and had poised to jump and had been shot. One round in the chest. It had been in the second week that Apricot had been in IK-2 – and no one in the lines of workbenches had looked up, and nothing had been said, and the sirens had not sounded for more than a couple of minutes.

Apricot asked, "Would anyone care, shed a tear?"

Currant said, "The only one who might have cared, once, played drums in our band. I heard his new group plays for the military behind the fighting lines, so he farts in my face. No one would care, certainly not my family."

Apple said, "My father killed himself, my mother blames me for his suicide, my boyfriend – what I thought he was, in the bank's foreign exchange – said that I deserved to rot in hell. I know nobody who would care."

Blueberry said, "Some students at the medical school could have spoken in my defence, or some of the lecturers. None came to my trial. A boy I sometimes fucked was in another bed within a week of them holding me . . . Only us, we care for each other."

Apricot said, "And me. How did the woman do it?"

Which woman? The last woman to take her life had swallowed slivers of glass from a bag of light bulbs left by a contract worker, perhaps because his break came and he wanted to go outside and smoke. And the broken bulbs were fortified with larger shards of glass from covers used in the staff garden where their summer vegetables grew. And another had hanged herself, done it quietly in the night, and it was said that other inmates had known and had not saved her, and justified it.

Each of them busied themselves creating a different part of a soldier's cheap and ill-fitting uniform, and each agreed that their permission to sit close, sleep close, face no further punishment for blocking their lavatories, was proof, if needed, that the commandant of the camp expected them to be moved on.

"Would we do that?" Apple asked.

"Would, and should plan for it." Blueberry's answer.

"Something to swallow, or something for a noose, or something . . . anything," Currant said.

Apricot spent two or three seconds examining her own life, thought of a prim upbringing, and months without having her hand held, and the fierce passions that Pieter had aroused in her and his treachery, and of the men who walked the corridors in Vauxhall Bridge. Thought of no one who cared. It left an emptiness, and she sewed a collar to a tunic and thought of it bloody and mud-stained on a casualty in a ditch. Reckoned these women around her were the only spirits who had her trust.

"And if I am weak . . .?"

There was a nod, a shrug, a grimace. Good enough answers. If she were weak she would be helped . . . When they finished their work that evening, before their meal, the small boxes of needles that were allotted to each machine would go missing, and each of them in their own way would become scavengers.

Croppy jolted awake.

The sound of the car horn was vicious in his head, rang in his ears.

It was because the community of Chamonix was intolerant, fast to take offence, and loath to be delayed, that Croppy's sleep had been broken. A BMW car, sleek and black, entitled to free movement, was reversing out of a parking bay, but had to ram on its brakes because a clutch of youngsters in full ski uniform wandered too close to the car's rear fender. The driver of the car reckoned he was impeded. The would-be skiers reckoned the car should have waited for them to pass before backing out. A typical moment in entitled Chamonix, and exacerbated by the flow of pricey alcohol the night before. Croppy registered what had happened. He raked his glance sideways, found his target's hired car. It had mist on the windscreen – had not been used over night. If the skiers and the BMW driver had not enjoyed a brief spat he would have slept on, and likely missed his target . . . *Sorry, sir – really sorry, Sarah. Just keeled out. Could not stay awake. His car had gone, don't know where* . . . What he would have said, and thanked the Lord, and the saint in whose name the old Kilchoan church had been built, that he did not have to say it.

He sagged back in his seat. Coffee would have helped but he did not dare leave the car.

Croppy rang the number. "When you getting here?"

"You in panic mode, Sonny Jim?" A man's voice and a crisp accent, what officers had, as if they should only be disturbed when the roof was caving in.

"No, but . . ."

"Has the lady pulled up her knickers yet, best of your knowledge? Probably not . . . we'll be in Chamonix when we're ready to be. Stay patient."

There was a light on behind the lowered blinds at the wide windows leading to the apartment's balcony. He saw shadows move around the room, but they were slow and without the urgency he'd have expected if departure was immediate. His gut grumbled and the back of his mouth was rough. He dare not close his eyes. He turned on the radio which would help his concentration but would also draw attention to him. Did that compromise? Had to. It was the way of the men and women who did time in the Covert Rural Observation Posts that *compromise* was what they inflicted on themselves. How long could they last before bugging out of a position? How close could they get to a target's door? He played a mind game with himself . . . How much was the apartment worth in which the target and the golden haired girl were holed up? How many euros to buy it or rent it for a month? There was a ruin on the road out of Kilchoan, up near the new cemetery, just short of the fields where his dad's farmer friend kept the Highland bull – how much would that plot fetch? Did he have what it would cost, and would Sarah have to chip in with her savings? Wrestled with numbers and dilemmas and stayed awake, just, and did the arithmetic slowly – and saw them.

She had said she needed to open the real estate office by ten. Skender had not told her the obvious, that he could have bought the business where she worked, outright. One phone call, one message from the lawyer he had rung, and the offer would have been made and the owners would have gawped, and agreement for a deal would have come back by return – and Birgitte would not have needed to go to that office again, turn the key, switch on the lights and start the daily drudge of checking emails. He had his own business to concern him.

He held her hand when they left his car, his bag locked into the boot. The car park was full, not a bay spare. He led her towards the exit and past a small car where a man sat slumped, young and with a tanned face scattered with stubble.

Out of the carpark and past the information area and into the wide square that was lined on two sides with coffee and breakfast outlets, but he had made coffee that morning and she had whipped him a small omelette and scattered grated cheese over it: they had played a game of reproducing what they were not. They were not a couple united in a degree of love and living together, surviving in a cocoon of happiness, with all the time that was needed to whisper the sincerity of their affections. He had work to do and a package to open and individual packets to distribute to men who would barely hide their dislike for him. She had to open a business for the day, and it was likely she would have no serious clients and there would be empty chairs unless the rain came on hard later in Chamonix. When they did not want coffee and did not need to eat, there was a place they chose to go and sit, say little and think quietly.

Above them were the lower summits of the mountains on the north side of the town and, astride the sharp ridges, above the pine trees, was a ceiling of dense cloud. The rock formations were harshly grey and the gullies were filled with tumbling avenues of snow. The church was a lopsided building with a high tower on its right side, then its main body and then the lowest part, flat roofed. There was also a building where weather forecasts were pinned up, the offices of the mountain guides – the men who went out to recover the lost and the injured and the corpses – then steep steps towards a double door that was ajar. An elderly woman glanced at them from the entrance.

Skender stood back while a woman went inside and he heard the organ being played. For both, the music inside the church of St Michel was soothing.

Clear to him from their second meeting that Birgitte was aware of what he did – organised cartel crime. Also aware that his job involved extreme violence, at a calculated and horrific level ... The second time she had met him, he noticed a bruise on her right cheekbone. A man had come into the office, had demanded to see an apartment, had produced a wallet bulging with cards and folded cash, as if that proved his pedigree. A visit to the apartment and a bare bed in a back room and an expectation of her cooperation. Desperate for a sale, wasn't she? Was not, and a smack in the face for her pains and the door slammed after him. Skender had found the address the man had given Birgitte. She had waited an hour or more beside him in the cold, and the man had emerged. She had expected a row, an altercation, a slapping and a warning. Unlikely the man would ever screw a woman again after the kicking given him. Unlikely that he would ever walk properly again, certainly never run – the full weight of Skender had come down on his legs with a cold fury. The man's mother would never look proudly on him because one cheek had been slashed open with the sharp side of a door key. Not the work of an amateur and she knows it. She had not walked away but had tucked her arm in his and they had left together, the man flattened, moaning, and they had been inside the church, his hand holding hers, when the sounds of the ambulance had come muffled up the aisle to compete with the organist. She knew, and did not back off.

Confused and garbled talk about their future, but confronting the reality.

Him heading for a world of betrayal and deceit, and running – and her following him in the darkness of fear and pursuit. It was what they talked about when they came to the church, sat on the benches of stained wood, were looked down on from the altar where priests in vestments hurried at small acts of work, and while the organ played.

He would renounce his old life, she would turn her back on all that had seemed safe and certain . . . for love. It was madness and both accepted it. In front of the altar, the elderly woman had lit a candle, then spoken briefly to a young priest, and they were smiling like the church was her family, and she bent a knee at the crucifix before hurrying away, the priest following her up the aisle, and spoke to two others who sat in peace, with the stillness of the interior around them. The organ music was restful. Perhaps he was barely out of the seminary, and perhaps they taught now that clergy should make a greater effort to commune with parishioners.

Skender was unclear whether he recognised them. He paused close to them. He spoke in French and Skender understood enough to comprehend.

"I think I recognise you, I think you have been here before."

"I have, yes."

"You are most welcome . . . this your girlfriend, your fiancée? Do I know her from the Allée Recteur Payot?"

He realised that the talk was harmless, well mannered, and realised that he would have to change if he was to alter his identity, and shake off the cloak of suspicion he wore at all times . . . He saw kindness, was unused to it. His family, if he left them, if they ever again could reach him, would kill him. The rain had come on, and she had twice checked her watch.

After her breakfast, porridge with goats' milk and a glass of water, the same that she had had since she was first able to use a spoon and feed herself, Klea went in search of her grandfather. She would talk to him of her brother.

She came from the section of the villa where she lived with her grandmother, close to the corridor that led to Skender's home. She crossed a wide hall where a woman worked uselessly with a polisher to further shine the marble floor. The woman's husband – only a *mik* but devoted to the leader of the clan – stood in front of the door that led to her grandfather's office.

It was an instruction that when he occupied the office, and entertained a guest, he should *never be* interrupted. But she was

Klea, the light of his life, and had free rein. She thought herself ignored – thought Skender was given too much attention. She knew her grandfather entertained because a car was outside on the gravel, low on its wheels because of the armour-plating in the doors, and two more cars with the visitor's guards were also there, and they smoked and talked quietly to each other. The conversation between her grandfather and the visitor – squat, short, ugly and with a crudely healed scar on the right side of his forehead – would concern Skender, always Skender. Whether her brother should marry, who her brother should marry, when her brother should marry, and what financial rewards would be given him . . . and what would be his obligation to her, to his sister. Her grandfather talked of little but Skender. She thought the visitor's guards eyed her. Had heard them giggle, like kids, when she had turned away, but not loudly because they knew who she was, who her grandfather was. She strode towards the door.

She could hear their voices, heard Skender's name. She reached for the handle but was blocked. The *mik* smiled at her, helplessly, and shrugged, but did his duty. She kicked him; stood his ground and did not whimper. She kicked him again, broke free of his attempt to stop her, turned the handle and went inside. Brandy on the table, and a wintry landscape beyond the window behind her grandfather's desk, and shock spreading, and the visitor standing.

She started on her complaints, one after another, as if the garden shears were in her hands, opening and closing.

Her grandfather tried to calm her. His visitor grimaced in embarrassment. She was soothed, indulged. She spat out the accusations that she was sidelined, was ignored, was . . . and her grandfather told her she was his "sweetheart", his "angel". Her anger grew . . . her grandfather told her this conversation was "for another time". At a gesture from him, the *mik* was behind her and carried out the instruction, grabbing her around the waist and carrying her out.

Klea did not bother to collect a weatherproof coat or her transparent poncho. She went out through the main door of the villa. A layer of snow lodged on the roofs of the visitor's car, and the guards had retreated inside their vehicles. The snowflakes came in at an angle because the wind funnelled in the valley. She had no protection against the wet and the cold, and she went past the steps down into the cellar – and past the telephone box that had been brought from England and past the road sign to Barking, close to where Skender had been, 2400 kilometres away, and went to the pen and let out the goats, and her dog was almost buried in a snow drift. She crossed the football pitch, and headed for the foothills of the mountains and the possible shelter of close-growing pines – and the anger surged in her.

It was she, Klea – the name of an Egyptian queen who was the greatest beauty of her time – who had identified the spy who had come amongst them and who could have destroyed her grandfather. It was she who had been covered in the blood spattered from the bodies of her mother and her father when they were killed – and it was she who was ignored.

She stamped off through the snow, each step causing her to sink to her ankles – and walked on and the animals with her ignored the deteriorating weather.

The responsibility for the "safe house" was Cress's. The jargon used by Sword and Tank called it that, a *safe house*, but she had little sympathy with that language: it was the place where – if fortune managed a grin – they would hold the little beggar and get the business done.

The huge complex of buildings was hardly stirring when they had pitched up on the outer ring of Geneva, close to a bend in the wriggling path of the river. The car park had been full and only very few residents were up, washed and dressed and off to work. Cress had fought her corner in choosing the place. Her mind had been made up by her grandmother, Daphne. Daphne, kept mostly at arm's length, devoured "true crime" documentaries on daytime TV. The Great Train Robbery was the subject that animated her, when a mail train had been robbed some 60 years before and the "ruffians" – Daphne's words – had driven lorry loads of mailsacks, bulging with used cash, to a lonely farm in the Buckinghamshire countryside, north-west of London. They had thought that a remote rural hideaway would ensure they were not seen. "Piffle," Daphne had said. Country people would be the first to notice anything different – "nosiness is in their genes". This observation had stuck with Cress . . . she had chosen a dense estate where they would do their work, unbutton their target's tongue. In Le Lignon, built in the 1960s, were 2780 accomodation units either in tower blocks or back to back "walls". Well in excess of 6000 people, all ages and all races, lived in this satellite city. There was a school, shops and kiosks, mini-markets, pretty much everything except a police station. There was also violence, vandalism and arson attacks, but the local politicians had decided that to install a police presence would finally kill the dream that Geneva was a place of modern calm. Security gates on internal walkways made a chase more difficult and also presented a continuous fire hazard . . . A perfect place for them. Cress had thought, and with a shifting population, where neighbours came and went and silence was the better option if suspicion was aroused. She had argued it, and the little guy in London had bought it. It had been rented two months before, over the odds price, but cash had sweetened it and the let ran for another month. She had checked it over, had carried in some of their kit, and food and drinks from the all-night store. It was ready for them.

A knock at his fifth-floor door, an immediate response from Brian, Deputy Director General and next in line to God Almighty at Thames House.

"Enter."

Not said pleasantly, no hint of welcome. The DDG's tone reflected a peevish mood and the source of it had been shown him the previous Friday evening, and again this morning. His car held up, his driver blocked in traffic and an armed officer holding him back while a colleague escorted a doddery creature across the main road. It was about his status in the "family" of the building, his importance, his relevance to its smooth running. And then he had waited several hours from the time he had instructed his PA to summon the Assistant Deputy Director General.

"I thought you might have been with me sooner."

"Quite a few meetings this morning, Brian, and I had not been told by your office that it was a matter of acute urgency." A smile, rather simpering, and lacking in deference.

He rattled into his denunciation of being held up in traffic while Jonas Merrick, travelling at the speed of a care home patient, was escorted across the road, and then started on the man's appearance.

"I have to say, he looked cocky . . ."

"Only a rather junior employee here, in spite of his past form."

". . . and I am told he has vacated the Post Room, is back in his quarters on the third floor."

"Yes, I heard that also."

"What would he have to be cocky about? What sort of work is he engaged in? I was assured that only matters of minimal importance were to be given him."

"No idea, but be certain of it, Brian, I will check most thoroughly."

"I will not tolerate freelancing in the Service. And he must come under the authority of a line manager. Is that very clear?"

"Crystal clear, Brian. I will investigate."

"Thank you."

The AssDepDG exited. He returned to his work – pension grading, and further remuneration for holidays worked – and . . . he believed it dangerous when a man with Merrick's record, and his gongs, appeared as a cat with a bowl of cream – and felt he had covered his back. There would be no sub-committee disciplinary hearing and a slap of the wrist: Merrick would be out if procedures were ignored and protocols broken.

Where they might do the lift was Tank's domain.

Would be on French soil. Where a feeder road came off the Autoroute Blanche, the A40 motorway, and Tank had chosen the place from the aerial views on his phone.

There was a bonus. A caravan settlement was close where cash was likely to smooth a conversation.

Would do a deal among the caravans and their towing vehicles and their dogs and their scavenged cars and trucks from which the guts had been stripped so that identities were lost. Assumed they would be gone within a week, or a fortnight, moving on and leaving an empty site to fester before another itinerant crowd pitched up.

Tank's big hand shook those of many – had sweet fuck all of their language but the cash he carried was expert at translating requirements . . . and they were on their way to meet Sonny Jim. All in place, except that nothing yet had been achieved.

"What sort of ship are you driving, Jonas?"

He balked. Jonas was at his desk, at his screen, and had drunk one cup of coffee from his thermos and was concentrating on flight times from east coast Yankee-land to the UK's Channel Islands, and the Agency man was due to call him in fifteen minutes, and the team were on the outskirts of that French ski resort place, and he had chuckled when told they were short of snow there. He looked around at the source of the interruption, Aggie Burns.

Jonas' eventual response: "What sort of answer are you searching for?"

"Just wanted to know."

"Is that an accusation? 'What sort of ship'? Actually, I say it myself, rather a good one – and going hard for a result."

"Glad to hear it."

She was expert at killing confidence with the tone of her voice, faintly mocking or with an exaggeration of praise. He was as fond of her as anyone he knew – except for Vera, and Olaf, and would have included the AssDepDG in the most favoured list. Aggie Burns' people spent long hours on street corners or stuck in cars tracking targets round housing estates, and her work was expensive to fund and critical to the preservation of life at railway stations and concerts and busy streets. If a bomber with a vest won through and blood, guts and gore were on the streets then the blame was most easily shifted on to Aggie Burns' shoulders – not enough of her people on the ground – and the criticism would be merciless . . . She stayed in post. Jonas thought she had nothing much else in her life except for the "family" that in her world was Thames House; no partner, no cat and no solidly built house with a mock-Tudor facade in a suburban bolthole such as Raynes Park. She was capable of needling him.

"I drive a very good ship, am busy, and am grateful for your concern."

"Just making sure."

"So, now that you have made sure, permit me to go back to work."

"Jonas, just be careful that you look after those slaving away on the lower decks of your ship. Apologies for disturbing you."

She was gone . . . He had been about to tell her that all was well, as best he knew, on Safety Deposit, that it was coming to the "end of the beginning" moment in a matter of hours, that he was a juggler with balls in the air but had dropped none, so far, but she had rebuked him which irked Jonas. Of course, he looked after them . . . and wondered what the hell she had meant in her codified warning. It was said by the AssDepDG that she had squealed in pain when from an upper window she and others saw him dragged off Lambeth Bridge and plunging down into the Thames. On the morning of his last appearance before the kangeroo people, and their disciplinary court, she had managed to sidle close to him, had caught his sleeve and had murmured, "You had a great result with those Chinese beggars, a few shortcuts but worth it, two dead but not your fault. In there, give them hell and not an inch of rowing back." He had wanted to share with her a modicum of what was now in place, not detail but a flavour – and the prize at stake. Would have said, his chest puffed up and his back straight, "There is plenty at stake here, a very great deal. Won't be popular in high places, not with the Threadneedle people. The Bank of England crowd would moan that this may destabilise our economy, affect deposits, billions in cash, belonging to Russian thieves. All they care about in the City is the volume of cash they are holding, not where it came from and in whose name it is held. They will be very hurt, that supposed elite in Moscow, and when they are hurt they will turn on their leader, and pistols will be cocked and knives sharpened and food contaminated and a noose or two prepared. It is a very worthwhile mission that I have organised. Bigger, better, more influential than anything I've done before. Very complicated and pulling in many strands. Down to me, Aggie . . . I'm very confident." Might have said that, might have seen Aggie purse her lips in admiration, deserved. Had not had a chance to say it.

He did not know what she had meant, but it was beneath his dignity to march out of his cubicle and go to her desk and require an explanation . . . And the American rang, his phone vibrating, and his landline was warbling too, and he turned and looked for the girl, for Sarah, to answer the landline but she was not there.

He answered the American, but irritably, and requested that he wait, but not for long.

Sarah's chair was tucked neatly under the table he had taken from Aggie's territory for her to use. Her desk was cleared. No papers, no maps, no mug, and no laptop – not even a paper clip. He had not seen her go, had not heard her leave or close the cubicle door after her . . . He was on the verge of achieving a quite extraordinary result and the girl whom he had invited to join him, to whom he had offered a most privileged position, had – what Vera might have said – "scarpered". A minor distraction.

"Apologies, Solly, for the delay. Very soon, Solly, but not yet. When I have something to tell you then you will be told it."

He should not have been annoyed. His planning was in place and a supreme moment was close. He did not know where the girl was, nor what Aggie Burns had meant . . . *careful that you look after those slaving away* . . . no idea.

"Hi, Sonny Jim, how you doing?"

There was a man and a woman, a second man was at the wheel of a van that had privacy windows above the front doors and no windows at the back. The man spoke, casual, relaxed like there was no big drama.

"Gone to church has he? Sensible place to be."

Croppy blinked, sucked in some air, and pushed himself up
from the wall where he was sitting close to the Information Centre
that was open but doing slow trade. The rain came down steadily
and the cloud was low above the church's spire, and the town was
not yet stirring. He tried to walk towards them but felt himself
about to keel over, and had to reach down and let the wall take his
weight again.

He managed a croak, "What do you need from me?"

"Don't think we need anything. Suggest you go get a bit of
sleep, a big burger, crash for an hour and then a bar and a few
more, and then bugger off home. Job done, over and out, and we'll
get on with it."

He tried to focus on the man who called him Sonny Jim, like he
was staff, or the guy who carried the lunch up the lower slopes of
Ben Hiant, or poured the drinks when a stag was felled on
Stallachan Dubha: a thin shouldered man with a drawl in his voice
and posture that said he enjoyed being looked at, and without
blood in his lips. Croppy wanted to pee and shook with tiredness
and the man had gone over to the van that was stopped by a No
Parking sign.

The woman headed for the van too and they had their confer-
ence. He heard some of it.

"Doesn't look much. Fuck only knows why the best place to
take her, make a girl feel wanted, is the bloody church . . . Don't
know where she's from, German or Scandinavian, I'd hazard . . .
Let's hope matey doesn't keep us hanging around . . . and Sonny
Jim, doesn't he know he's out of the frame? Want a Mention in
Despatches, does he?"

She went to the church door and the prat with the officer's
voice followed her, and the one in the van was lighting a fag, the
engine idling. Croppy, best as he was able, had tried to count the
visitors into the church and out of it, and could no longer hear the
organ, and thought the couple might be alone in there now, bar a
priest or a cleaner. He had been dismissed.

Croppy had been stretched to the limit of his endurance. Had
no right to expect that he would have tracked the target from the

villa to the point in the road where the vehicle convoy had split, then to the border and the airport, with Matt's help on to the aircraft, then to the car hire. Had sat in the car with the stink of his socks for company, had dozed and nearly slept – and was not thanked. Happened on a stalk up on the hills, plenty of the punters did not bother to express gratitude – and he only remembered the one who had the military connection and had done the soft talk that was good enough to recruit him.

He went to the van. The driver flicked a fag end past Croppy's shoulder.

He asked, "What'll happen to him?"

"Not your concern, Sonny Jim, not in any way. A bit above your pay grade."

So Croppy turned away and started to trudge towards his car. Had taken a few steps and then bent and picked up the still smouldering fag end and carried it to a bin, and stubbed it out against the side and dropped it in. Had to sleep – then face up to the next kick in the guts.

He saw little but the road ahead.

Difficult driving and lakes of water were forming on the highway when he turned for the west and the signs to Geneva.

He had lied to his grandfather, had given a false itinerary, would claim if challenged that his phone was off – an additional security measure . . . The wipers made a poor job of clearing the windscreen, and a film of wet was thrown up by the lorries ahead of him. Not many drivers used the outer lane. He drove steadily, both hands on the wheel, and few cars passed past him. He was more concerned with what he saw, sometimes vaguely, through the windscreen, less concerned with what followed him, and his glances at the mirror were rare.

It was hard for Skender to concentrate on the road and on the delayed meetings ahead. He grimaced at the thought of the second hand book market and the open-air stalls draped in plastic sheeting . . . He thought of his girl, and of the feel of her hand in his and the wetness of her mouth and the silkiness of her, and all the differences between her and the tarts on offer to any man in his position. Thought of her, and the explosion that would detonate in maybe a month's time when his grandfather realised the lie he had been told. His mind was a kaleidoscope of thoughts, a few of them pleasant and a few of them about his new experience of what the magazines called "love", and a few that were near to terrifying – what would be done to him, how he could escape and where to. Enough to think about, actually too much.

He saw the blue light behind him.

Skender checked his mirror, nudged his brakes. The light was on top of the roof of a dark van. The signs said there was a slip road off the highway, a klick ahead. What had he done to be followed by a police wagon? From inside his shirt, he took the package that had been brought to him by the Serbian courier, and then he slowed some more, wedged his elbows against the wheel and with his hands was able to lose the package underneath his seat, behind the lever that changed its position. The slip road was approaching and the van with the blue light was moving up on him, and traffic was speeding past him. If he had not had so much on his mind – principally the truths he had told Birgitte about their future, and the lies he had told his grandfather about his future as head of the family with the reach of an octopus' tentacles – then he might have searched for an answer to why a police van was alongside him, and why an arm was out of the lowered window, carrying a fluorescent strip that identified the police and pointed repeatedly for him to turn off. Ought to have asked more questions, but his grandfather had always told him not to fuck with police when the stakes were miniscule. Skender raised his hand, acknowledged the message, and slowed some more.

It was Jonas' plan.

He listened, a snaking cable between his phone and a firmly lodged earpiece. The woman did the talking. "Following us, good as gold. Just another boring old routine cop-stop. On the slip road, another hundred yards and we hit the brakes. Rain's pissing down, no one in their right mind is going to be looking then wondering what to do. Stopped. Smiling at us, like we're his friends and he's going to be *polite* and *pleasant*. Should be straight and easy. Sword and Tank out, and we have the engine ticking, but the kid has switched his off. We all have police armbands. My guys will be smiling too. All chummy. His door open. Jeez, the rain is something, and . . . here we go." Jonas was rigid on his chair. "Tank has reached in, has him by the collar. Half out, and the message is dawning. Bit more than half and he's starting to wriggle. Sword whacks him. Across his nose. A plug of material in his mouth, and the hood over his head. He's thrashing around. Can't fight. Can't see. Tank has hold of him and Sword has his arms behind his back, and is taping his wrists. All done fast, and they're coming. My job now is to hit the horn. Three long blasts, get the guys out of their caravans. Done it. Back doors open and they're in. The kid is trying to yell but can't make any proper sound, just grunts. In, yes, door closed. On our way.

"Heading out. Up to a roundabout. No one following. We did a check on the way up. Didn't spot any cameras, reckon we're good for no cameras. A hell of a fracas in the back. Tank'll do the muscle. The kid may kick around a bit but they'll have him well snared. Not a bad bloke, Tank. What you see is what you get. If the kid doesn't calm, and quick, then Sword will get busy. You don't get what you see with Sword, because he'll grin, then he'll hurt. Suppose that's why you picked him. Back on the highway and up to the speed limit. Just hitting water walls. Don't they call it aquaplaning? He's gone quiet."

Why Jonas had picked them all – he was satisfied from their records and CVs and the recommendations that they all had something worse than violence, which was a fondness for it, for gaining what was required . . . And he wondered, fleetingly, how they would be at whatever passed for home in their lives, how normal, how damaged, and how far was the limit at which they'd back off? Or were they just the same as himself? Facilitators? Keeping the trains running on time? Or, the Orwell idea: *People sleep peaceably in their beds at night only because rough men stand ready to do violence on their behalf?*

Jonas heard some curses, and banging, and the echo from inside the back of the van, and the commentary resumed. "On our way now, and plenty to do, so signing off till we get to where we're going. All quiet in the back now and probably time for Sword to tell him a bedtime story."

Jonas called Solly. Jonas did his usual routine about "don't expect me to give running commentaries" but told the American that it was time to put his people into the air. An executive jet was assigned, a twin-engine Gulfstream, and should be up and gone soonest.

Jonas Merrick faced his screen and the wall, and allowed himself a unique gesture, first time in his life. Inside the strictures of his heavy tweed jacket he raised his right arm, clenched his fist, then punched the air. Would not have matched the physicality of Tank or Sword, but used his full force, and did it again . . . told himself that he deserved his own congratulation.

Then he started on his lunch. Took his plastic box from his briefcase and examined the sandwiches that Vera had prepared for him, and started to munch his way through the contents, and a wrapped chocolate biscuit was included.

7

"Authorised them to use a thumbscrew, Jonas?"

"What do you want? A videolink?"

"Steady, my friend, none of us are too bright, too beautiful not . . ."

A crisp interruption from Jonas who had not yet turned to face the looming figure of the AssDepDG in his cubicle doorway. "Have work to be getting on with as you are doubtless aware."

". . . bright and beautiful not to need the support of allies, those demented idiots who watch your back. A simple enough question: *Authorised them to use a thumbscrew, Jonas?* Taken that on your broad shoulders, have you?"

"Are you asking for chapter and verse?"

"Most certainly not. Am happiest with the least possible information being slapped in my lap. Daft of me actually, Jonas, not to have put a damper on it from the start – but I think matters were a bit far down the road when I was first put in the picture."

Which was true, but could not be faulted as a low blow. His reputation in those great organisations of American authority – Federal Bureau of Investigation, Central Intelligence Agency, Drug Enforcement Administration – was high on the cusp. He was a "go to" figure, a man capable of getting things done, a guy who achieved results, one who "flew below the radar", but he did not parade himself in search of citations. It was what they thought of him, and rated him sufficiently highly to follow the intelligence with a caveat of guaranteed cash. The Yankees did not do Albania, had neither the history nor the expertise, nor perhaps a willingness to put their own individuals into harm's way in that theatre. They had provided intelligence on the movement of couriers using the low-profile crime family as a hub, and were reaching towards bank accounts and investments held by a select few in up-town Moscow, looking for a way to "upset them" or, as Solly Kravnic had succinctly put it, *"get them annoyed enough so that they scratch their own balls so hard that they just about draw blood"*. And Denys Montgomery, supposedly singing from the same hymn sheet, had chimed in with indications of which oligarchs and klepto-thieves were involved, right up to the biggest catch of all, the new czar. Plenty had been set up and was running, well-oiled, when he had requested of the AssDep DG that they walk together from the back entrance of Thames House and along the pavement before the crossing to Lambeth Bridge and he had briefed him, but sparely.

"Depends, I suppose, whether or not you want to win – want it enough."

"For heaven's sake, Jonas, next you'll be informing me that it is all right to break open the 'spirit of the game' nonsense. We are not talking here about the behaviour of players in a cricket match. We are talking the unwritten rules of spy-craft, talking about coercion. We have standards, Jonas, which you are well aware of."

"You do not have to be here. Can push off any time you think appropriate, take a turn on your golf course."

"Not that it would interest you, my friend, but I was summoned this morning to the fifth floor, and was questioned about you. Yes, Jonas, your good self. An indication that it has been noted that your head has peeped above the sandbags again, that you have evacuated your billet in the Post Room and moved back here, that you threw a bit of a tantrum because the premises you now occupy were put to better use as a store cupboard – made something of an exhibition of yourself. I covered for you, again, cannot quite account for my singular stupidity. Look after yourself, Jonas."

"Thank you for your attention."

"My question – you're happy using thumbscrews, are you?"

Jonas shrugged, eyes never leaving his screen. "I don't second-guess my team. Their window of opportunity is open for a very short time. I accept that now we have achieved a dislocation of a particular courier system . . . of minimal importance. To gain a hold on the codes used and the placing of the investments so that they can be seriously interfered with, that has to be done fast before the window is slammed shut. My team know that, understand very well the requirement for speed . . . may I tell you something about the people on my pay-roll? In the Afghan affair they had a prisoner who was short of the medical care needed if his life was to be saved. The prisoner was privy to information concerning an ambush that might have resulted in many UK fatalities. He gave my team, three of them, the detail of where the attack would take place and where the Talib people were gathered. They were hit with an Apache strike. Some twenty-five of the Talib fighters were killed, and the next day our boys stayed hale and hearty, suffering no casualties. My team had that competence. Remarks about 'thumbscrews' are not appropriate . . . there is a wider plan."

"A wider plan for the possible return of gulag inmates, of interest to us and to our cross-pond chums . . . and while that window of opportunity is open, what strictures govern the actions of your team?" The AssDepDG's voice hardened, like gravel spat from under spinning tyres. "Don't fuck with me, Jonas, what is their red line?"

Now he turned, and faced the AssDepDG. The room behind was empty except for Aggie Burns at her desk with her head down and he knew that she would have heard most of what was said.

"They don't have one. They have a job to do. They have an end game to achieve."

"And torture justifies it?"

"It is called 'enhanced interrogation', it has a degree of legitimacy."

"Only legitimate when on the winning side. You better hope you win, Jonas, and that the thumbscrew is expertly applied. You will swing on the end of a rope attached to the girders of Lambeth Bridge and I – sad to say – will likely twist beside you, unless your team know their business."

He heard the AssDepDG's shoes slither away across the outer room, but felt the need to have the last word.

"I wouldn't have chosen them if they didn't."

The message had been sent by Cress.

To the point and no embellishment: *Done the lift.*

The thuds and bangs and grunts in the back of the van were now sporadic. There was a parking area at the frontier near the unused customs sheds. Cress turned the van into it and braked sharply. She heard the doors snap open behind her and daylight flooded the back. She looked round. The guy was bound, a turkey waiting for a Christmas oven, flat on his stomach, tape binding his ankles and wrists, and the bag was over his head but with a breathing slit, and there was a bloody mess where his mouth would have been. He was held fast by a length of rope that was hooked round his waist and lashed to a stabilising hook. The doors slammed shut again. She was joined in the front by Sword. He had that look about him, had seen it when the prisoner at the holding centre at the Helmand base had been brought in: like a school-child about to be offered some serious fun. She supposed they were all like that, the twisted folk who got things done. Sword was beside her and fastening his seatbelt, and Tank was lumbering away from them to the parked car that was waiting for him. Tank did the wheels and Sword did the kit, and both had done what was asked of them: all that remained was for Cress to put in her share and scrape the necessary out of the shape, immobile, but making noises that were indistinct because of the cloth in his mouth.

She drove away. Could see that Tank followed her in a small compact . . . needed two vehicles, and they would have expected that extra expenditure to have been rejected, but it had not: added up to a "money no object" caper and that had brought a ray of sunshine to Sword who did the expenses, mostly short on receipts, and he'd put on a twangy Scouser accent and called out something about "nice little earner" when they'd talked of it on the flight.

They were through the frontier buildings, back in Swiss terri-tory, and the rain had not eased and sprayed the windscreen.

"Find anything on him?"

"Nothing that mattered."

"Not anything?" Surprise registered.

"No notebook, no sealed envelopes, no memory sticks, a mobile phone but wouldn't expect anything on that, what we need. Anyway, switched off now. Had a rummage in his bag and didn't net anything. But it was superficial."

She nodded, kept her hands on the wheel, eyes on the road. A shrug from Sword. Asking too much to expect it delivered on a plate. They each had a self-given role to play when it came to the pressures of interrogation and a "ticking clock" that was pressure building for a result. Sword gave the impression of power and strength and of being without conscience, and Tank could inflict horrid pain and soften the will of a victim. Cress's job was to ask the questions and create the mood where the guy actually wanted to spill it . . . She would have work to do – and likely the others too.

She brought them into the western suburbs of the city, following a satnav route that pushed them off to the left and on to the Rue de Rhone and the Quai de la Poste, and over the bridge and then the signs were for Vernier, where their workplace waited for them. Together they had done the "questioning" of the wounded prisoner in Helmand: official praise had followed and then the cold shoulder. No threat of prosecution but only because a few in the hierarchy knew the background to the extraction of the information and all the time a damned clock ticking. Had been on a kidnapping in Jordan, "no holds barred", and a child returned to a family, and a day's work for a hangman. Had done a supposed drug dealer in Glasgow, no police evidence that was sufficient to prosecute and no confession of supplying below par heroin doses to the daughter of an industrialist. They'd achieved it, the confession. Had put the dealer off the street, had also put him into the Forth and Clyde Canal where he had been unable to swim because his hands were pinioned behind his back . . . Then they had gone their own ways and no work had turned up for the team for more than three years. Tank had taken on contract gardening and Sword made himself "useful" to ladies of a certain age and certain wealth, and Cress was back at the School of Slavonic and East European Studies and her speciality in habits Albanian.

Would be good to be back there again.

She had done Albanian boys – pushers and protection enforcers and pimps – out with the Flying Squad units, and then there were solicitors on hand and cameras. Few of them seemed fazed by the questioning. They rarely dignified the process with a "no comment", just picked their noses or cleaned their fingernails and seemed certain that their noses wouldn't be smacked, their nails not extracted. Confident, taking it in their stride, but different now. Had that bloody clock ticking, had stuff that she needed to know, and wondered how the boy would be . . . a pleasant looking lad. She headed for Vernier, and Tank tailed along behind . . . Couldn't say how much the boy was going to make it "difficult" for himself.

In his parked car, the meter fed, Croppy slept.

Sleep had been slow coming. Hard, when he was dead on his feet, to close his eyes, get a dose of sleep that was meaningful.

The couple, his target and the target's girl, had been a trigger. Had seen them come out of the church. Her arm in his. Going down the steps, and a kiss at the bottom. Not long and lingering like it needed to be remembered for a few weeks, but short and with a grin that was mutual, and a message that in a few days they would be back together. He saw that a priest had come out on to the steps and spent a moment looking up at the mountains, wondering if the rain were ever going to ease, and had seen them and had smiled to himself – like they were customers with potential. The girl had headed for the main drag through Chamonix. Hopeful skiers were gathering to head for the slopes, high up into the cloud where there might still be snow. Shops were open, and pedestrians milled on the pavements and delivery vans queued to get up the street. Pretty girl. Croppy thought her the type who would have put on jeans and boots and dug a vegetable plot, and taken a bale down to a barn, and knelt to unblock a drain – and would have rated her *almost* as pretty as Sarah . . .

His target had headed back to the car park. Croppy had been able to see both the target and the van. He remembered, word for word, what had been said to him, his dismissal and the casual contempt of the name awarded him, Sonny Jim. He did not seethe, did not care *that* much. The target had gone to his hire car, had extracted a packet in a reinforced envelope from under his shirt, and had bent inside the vehicle had straightened, looked around him, realised he could no longer see her, had got into the car and done a fast reverse and a turn of the wheel, had gone. And the van had tucked in, not immediately behind the car but two or three back – basic, professional. The target gone, and his girl gone, and together they had been a trigger to Croppy.

He had turned off his phone, and curled himself into his seat.

He thought of Sarah, of the rain driving across the openness of Ardnamurchan, and the two of them wrapped in supposed waterproofs that always failed, and managing their work, then sitting close to a fire in a hearth – and thought also of what he was condemned to do . . . drive to the airport at Geneva, drop off the car and book himself a one-way ticket to London – but with a diversion, taking him in the wrong direction. He had no stomach for it, but it was a law of his life, and to be obeyed.

We have a lift.

Among Sixers on the south side of the river in "Ceauşescu Towers", Denys Montgomery deserved his reputation as a steely, determined counter-intelligence officer specialising in the confusions of the day's situation inside Russia, and was regarded as both expert and efficient. The second strand of his reputation dealt with the evaluation of his character by those who worked around him. Diligent always. Calm, always. He imagined himself to be on a list, a limited one. Having received the message that confirmed the *lift*, there was no requirement for him – at that moment – to act. If he did act, was authorised to do so by a junior official with the Fivers across the water, then he would be told. He had not drawn up the operational plan, had not been consulted, had been told what *might* be his further function.

He picked up his phone. The office door behind him was closed. The radio on his desk was turned to a classical channel. No ears were prying. Glanced again at the screen message. *We have a lift.* An expression almost of diffidence, well disguised, hid his reputation for a tough and uncompromising streak.

He keyed the number.

The twin strand of his reputation was of a man who reacted well under extreme pressure, was never flustered or theatrical. He had absorbed the twin afflictions of having an outsider infiltrated into his Defector Relocation Team in search of a traitor: a job not given to their own internal security people, but to strangers, and had accepted that the instruction came from the gods and would not be reversed because his toes were stepped on, his tail tweaked. Nor had the toys been thrown out of his pram when the outsider was Jonas Merrick, a nobody from Thames House, nor when the unspoken love of his life – Frank, demure and distant, always correct, soaking up the sneers of her superiors, and working as his PA – had been named as the leak . . . Much of that plan, though not acknowledged, had come from Denys Montgomery.

A rasped voice, oozing impatience, answered.

He said, "Thank you for your message."

"You don't have to ring me to express thanks – is that all?"

"I was anxious there might be more for you to share."

"Nothing more."

"And to be certain that my requests in the matter stay as highest priority, and . . ."

"I have made no promises. Should we reach a favourable conclusion then what is possible will be evaluated and argued for. Ditched if not. It is an adjunct, not more and not less. I am busy trying to concentrate on the real areas of that priority list."

Denys Montgomery's face reddened. His fingers squeezed on the phone, damn near crushing it. "You are the rudest and most unpleasant little man I know. You are obnoxious and . . ."

Again he was brusquely interrupted, and might have heard the suspicion of laughter. "Views shared, I am most happy to confirm, by many. Join a long and hopefully orderly queue. I am not in the business of massaging your own view of your importance. When I want your contribution, I will tell you."

He thought of Frank, could not escape her. He could not estimate how great was her value as a bargaining chip in any list of priorities. He sat at his desk, his head in his hands – and might have imagined the snow falling steadily and heard the wind whine on the coils of wire.

Next to Apricot was Blueberry.

It was late in the afternoon and dark outside, the arc lights illuminating wire topping the fence, windows, and the cold eating into the prisoners' hands, and the day's shift almost complete, hunger weakening them, and a supervisor passes Blueberry and stumbles. A weakness in the damp floor, and a plank loosened, a nail head exposed, and the blow from the supervisor's boot would have shifted it as she passed.

Bending at the waist, her viewing machine stilled, Blueberry reached out into the aisle and tugged the nail. The action drew blood from the tips of her fingers, but she sucked them, then reached again, and dragged on the nail. Blueberry pulled again and the rusty nail was disloged. She secreted it in her uniform pocket, and went back to her sewing.

Apple leaned forward, would have seen what she had done and touched her shoulder in congratulation. The nail, three inches long, would do major damage to her digestive system, would puncture it and would spread poison. Slower than hanging. Less chance of a stomach pump, more lethal than broken glass, but slower than a noose fashioned from a pyjama leg. They had promised each other that they would do it; kill themselves if they were split up. Remembered saying, *And if I am weak . . . ?* The response had been clear – she would be helped. They would not be separated.

She folded the army tunic carefully so that the supervisor could not find fault. She started on the next uniform, began to sew the collar in place . . .

Jonas took the call on a secure line.

"EssKay here . . . how you doing, JayEm?" A chuckle reverberated in his ear.

"Fine, thank you for asking," said curtly. He had never met Solly Kravnic of the Agency, doubted he ever would. He was in that mood where he doubted the value of colleagues and might have forgotten that the American's organisation wrote the cheques enabling his plan to happen.

"I just wanted to say something, Jonas."

"Say it."

"A bit premature . . . what you call *the lift* is up and done, but the pips still need squeezing clear and . . ."

"I have people on the job who can usually manage some squeezing."

"Sure you have, Jonas . . . And the people who can handle the material that we are confident you will provide are on their way. Folk here speak highly of you, of your organisational abilities and your efficiency, and above all of your commitment and determination. What that means is your ability to do the work and not be suffocated by all the restrictions we seem to wade through over here – like goddamn treacle . . . we are very confident."

"Pleased to know that . . . have plenty to be getting on with."

He replaced the receive phone: Jonas would have doubted that the DG or the DDG had ever received such personal endorsement from a senior Agency man. For a moment he preened himself. Had forgotten that Sarah wasn't there, but remembered what EssKay had said, each word of it.

The rain had eased, allowing small shafts of sunlight to break the blanket of cloud.

In the Place de la Fusterie, the plastic sheeting covering the stalls glistened. Had there been clients looking for particular old volumes it would have been difficult to see through the sheeting . . . Not that the accountant had any interest in checking what was on offer, and at what price.

He had waited 20 minutes. He was not used, in his world of finance, to having a schedule broken. First, he should have been in Basel, in a restaurant, in the dry and the warm, in deep and private conversation. Instead he was among a mess of tables and the stall-holders were wrapped up well, sitting on benches at the side of the square and watching dismally in the hope of a potential sale. Had it not been for the money that was deducted from the investments he made – whether cash or on deposit, or through the shell companies – the accountant would have stomped away.

There were four entrances to the square. His eyes searched each, expecting to see the boy ambling towards him, flicking away a cigarette and smiling, reaching inside his coat and producing a package and smiling some more. Like some courting display on a natural history TV channel, he would then produce his own packet. The courier would check the figures on the one he had, and the code it carried. They would be exchanged. Barely a word would pass between them, and he doubted that he would earn an apology for being so fucked about, and they would go their own ways.

He checked around him again – and realised he was being watched.

An investment manager allowed his features to pucker in annoy-ance. Firstly, he had driven himself into the banking quarter of the city, rather than use his chauffeur, because the business on Place de la Fusterie was of such sensitivity – to his client and to himself. Then he had walked, and the hems of his trousers were soaking from the water that had been speared up by a taxi driving through puddles. His mood was deteriorating further because the Albanian boy had not shown.

He spotted the accountant. Not a man whose company he liked. Not a man with whom he shared confidences. To the best of his knowledge their client list did not cross over. The people he dealt with, who topped his list in payment for his inventiveness and discretion, had his whole attention, and paid for the service. He looked around him, and recognised a lawyer who was glancing at his wristwatch every few seconds, rain increasing irritation. He knew the man because of his expertise in the purchase of properties on the French Mediterranean coast. He had started pacing and was smoking.

Another lawyer approached the investment manager, and he knew this one because of a game of golf two months back on a rare morning when the course was dry enough. The Golf Club de Genève was the most exclusive in the city, the only one he would have patronised. This lawyer was an intelligent man, and was looking thoroughly pissed off. He charged high fees that were paid without complaint because he was good at his job; an increasingly difficult job as the sanctions targeted the clients that he supposed they shared.

They seemed drawn to each other, the investment manager and the accountant and the two lawyers, and the newly arrived sunshine lit their faces and showed growing anger. All of them had been stood up by an Albanian kid, and all carried packages that he was supposed to take from them, after giving their clients' instructions, for carrying back to Moscow, of course in total secrecy.

A muttered chorus. *So where is the little fucker?* And each of them thinking, "All that righteous shit you prattle. But you're like me. All of us are up to our necks with the scumbags . . . for the money."

Skender was pulled from the van by his ankles. When most of his body was clear, his arms and jacket collar were held so that he could stand. One of them must have crouched down because a hand steadied against his legs and the ankle tape was cut.

It had been tight enough to restrict the blood flowing to his feet and he would have toppled had he not been held. He could smell their breath: nicotine. A coat was hooked over his shoulders and he felt another hood pushed down over the sacking that hid his head. He was shoved forward, tripped on a step and would have plunged on to his knees, but hands gripped him. He heard doors swing open. He lurched and banged against a wall but they pulled him through and into a corridor. He sensed the men holding him regarded this as a vulnerable moment and the pace quickened. He heard a babble of voices muffled by doorways and a TV football commentary in French, and an argument in a language he did not know and music turned up loud. He heard a door opening with a creak and he was pushed through and his upper arms cannoned off the door's frame. He assumed he was in an apartment block. He was spun in a half turn, and pushed face first against a wall. He wanted to pee. Not a word had been spoken – which told him of discipline, which meant he was with serious people. Serious was the first evaluation that he made. Serious was important and would govern how he responded, how long he had. But not who . . . His ankles were taped together again. His wrists were freed, and his hands pulled up so that he was resting his weight on the balls of his feet and his toes, and then he was pulled some more and then the tape at his wrists was wound around a hook or inside a ring. He wanted to sag but could not and thought his upper arms would come loose from the shoulder sockets if he let his weight slide. His shoes were removed and he heard them kicked away. There was a smell in the room that came through the sack over his head and into his nostrils, one of damp and emptiness as if a window had not been opened for weeks.

Skender wanted to say "Do you know who I am?" but his mouth was plugged and his words would have been incomprehensible, and he would not have known in which language to speak.

Would have said, "Do you know who my grandfather is?"

A boot came down on his toes and he shifted them back, to the limit he was able, and the stress pulled harder in his arms and he thought soon the joints in his shoulders and elbows and wrists would begin to crack.

"Do you know that you have taken the wrong person? Put me down and I will explain who I am and who my grandfather is."

He heard the sound of scissors being opened and closed. He began to struggle. He could not believe they knew about such punishment . . . His shirt was pulled away from his trousers and the scissors cut it in a line from his waist to his neck, and it fell at his waist. Then his belt was unfastened and again he heard the opening and the closing of the scissors and his trousers dropped to his ankles. They left his pants but a hand, wearing a rubber glove, was moving inside his underwear and was at his back, between the cheeks and probing ... He heard his bag being unzipped and the contents being tipped out on to the floor: his toilet bag, his phone, his clothes. He thought he heard a curse but the words were garbled.

Could have said. "I will tell you who I am. I am Skender, heir to my grandfather's clan. I have power that you can only dream of. Can reach you wherever you hide. We operate by the code of *kanun*: the greatest hospitality and generosity to a friend, the promise of ferocious vengeance to an enemy."

The gloved hands were removed. He thought he heard his bag being ripped apart, and his shaving foam squirted till the can was empty. Earphones were looped over his head and adjusted so that they were snug on his ears.

Wanted to say, "It is a mistake, isn't it? Just a mistake. Wrong man. You have no business with me and I have none with you. For going after the wrong man and for no cause, I can pay you and so mitigate that inconvenience."

A hissing noise flooded his head, loud to the point of deafening him. It was not music, was not natural, it burst into his mind. Skender had heard of white noise and had heard of hooding and of wall standing and knew them as part of the Five Principles. A police officer, a senior man from Tirana, had come to see his grandfather to pay homage at his court, and had said that he had been on a course for Europol where the Five had been talked of, and their effectiveness. The next would be sleep deprivation, then hunger, no food, no drink.

Feet shuffled, a door closed, others closer sounds mixed with the artifical noise in his ears, made him want to scream, and he tried to think of his girl as protection against it but could not find her.

He heard her singing, out of tune and into the raging wind, the same song from those awful Swedish people. It was a penance of the *mik*, that in order to stay close to her grandfather, he had been given the thankless job of minding her, watching over what the old man called his "precious princess", his "angel of petals". He heard Klea approach and thought soon she would be within the arc of his flashlight.

She had missed her evening meal in the villa with her grandparent, and he had been called, irritably questioned. Where was she? How could she be outside and alone in such weather? He had ducked his head, shown his devotion to them because Beznik could not imagine a life without the family's patronage, was fearful of the day when Skender took over the running of the clan . . . So, in a thick anorak and with a hood over his head, and holding a flashlight, he had spent at least an hour and a half at the entrance to the pen where her dog slept and where her goats were corralled, had allowed the snow to layer him, and hail spit in his face. Now, finally, the snow had turned to rain. *If the mad little bitch wants to spend a day scrambling in the forest and among the rocks, then that is her privilege, but fucked if I am going to stand and wait for her – and be snarled at.* Would not have considered even mouthing it into the fierce wind that whined around him, but could think it. It was the mark of the level of trust that the old man, the *shef*, placed in his worn and blistered hands, rough from a lifetime of manual work, that he was given the task of watching over the girl. She was horrible, cruel, a creature of darkness, but his wife would have reminded him, had he voiced his thoughts in the safety of their bed, that a normal kid had been changed for life by being on the back seat of a vehicle that was hit by an RPG-7 grenade and been covered in blood and tissue from her mother and father. As a justification for her moods and behaviour the past mattered little to the *mik*.

He heard her coming nearer. Then he caught a shadow of glimpse of her dog on the edge of the coned beam from the flashlight. Then he saw the goats huddled close to each other.

Then he saw her.

Beznik cursed. He had been given a responsibility. The penalty for failing a duty was expulsion. Expulsion could take several forms under the code: he could be expelled and set loose on the road leading away from the village, with or without his wife. He could be taken out to the football pitch, a crowd already gathered, and among them would be the faces of those with whom he drank in the village's bar and see only coldness and rejection. Expulsion could also mean that he be taken down the steps into the cellar or thrown down, and pain inflicted; and perhaps hear the snapping of shears. Perhaps . . . if Skender were here, in the valley, he would have hoped that he would protect him, but Skender was not there.

He cursed when the flashlight found her.

Her dress hung over her arm. Klea was clothed only in her vest and pants. He dutifully turned the light away from her. He had seen her muscled legs and the width of her hips and the tight waist and then the spread of her body above. Her hair was plastered down on her scalp, and water bounced from her cheeks and her mouth was wide as she bawled the chorus of the song. He shrugged out of his own anorak, hurried towards her and tried to drape it over her shoulders, but she pushed him away. He hovered near to her, neither helping nor speaking, as she put her goats into their pen, and fed her dog from the bucket.

The responsibility weighed heavy on the *mik* . . . only Skender could have protected him. He trailed behind her as she stamped her way past the building with the steps down to a cellar, and past the telephone box, across the square and in through the villa gates where men kept impassive faces as they saw her and opened the door, and rain water cascaded off her and floated across the polished marble floor.

She had spoken not a word to him but looked cheerful and was almost smiling.

The housekeeper brought a towel and started to dry her.

He loathed her but would never dare show it. Now he heard her demanding to see her grandfather, ignoring suggestions that she wait until their meal was finished. The towel was wrapped around her, but slipping, and she went to the door to the dining-room . . .

Out over the Atlantic ocean, cruising at 520 miles per hour, with an altitude of 30,000 feet, and burning fuel like tomorrow was an unimportant day, the Gulfstream flew with five passengers, two cockpit crew and a steward who doubled as Jack of all trades.

The passengers comprised a bodyguard who carried gas canisters, a handgun, bullet proof vests and basic medical kit; a "smoother" who made sure that the cars were in place when wanted and the communications were in line and that pizzas were available when ever they wanted them; and the geeks, the reason the Agency had co-opted the Gulfstream. The three of them had been plucked from their desks and put into a degree of storage at the airfield until a signal had come from their boss that they should "get their hands off their dicks, get in a line, get moving over the apron, get up the steps and buckle in". They were considered the best available.

All three had their laptops on their trays, about as precious to them as anything they owned. One read a comic featuring a hero who kept the world safe from bad guys. One read a dog-eared copy of *Playboy* from before the Covid lockdown. One read a trade magazine and was looking for a tablet for his grandmother, not too expensive and maybe second hand, and possibly he'd program it himself.

What was common among them was the ability to break computer safety codes and the ability to hack. In malware terminology they were "Trojan Horses". They could get inside an electronically fortified area, wriggle around behind the fire wall, do the damage, and get out leaving minimal traces. They called themselves the Trojan Mustangs, and fancied themselves as free-roaring horses, out west, with a licence to summon up havoc . . . which they would if data were put their way.

It did not really matter where they worked but the island of Guernsey in the English Channel was the location chosen for them, with a put down at the airport of 1500 yards of runway. Of course they had been told it was important, what it was hoped they would do, but they rarely showed enthusiasm or interest – just another job.

It was an argument that had engulfed men of both entitlement and ego, had lasted from the time they had met, unwillingly and breaking their cover, in the Place de la Fusterie among the stall of secondhand books that were covered in plastic sheeting and attracting no buyers.

Who would make the call? Which of them would speak for all of them?

A GRU contact had been given to each of them with the specific instruction that the conduit could get a message to the oligarch in Moscow who seemed the lynchpin of their recruitment, in circumstances only of "emergency".

Was it an emergency? Fucking well was to those who had changed their plans for the day, then hung about for hours, been soaked by the rain, and a low-life courier had failed to show. The local embassy was already closed for the day but the assurance had been made that the number given them was manned day and night. Arguments, after a fashion, had been settled – a lawyer given the job.

He made the call from his home. A long time ringing out while the lawyer tapped his feet, impatient, expecting a zombie to answer, and getting one.

A code given . . . a pause while the zombie went away to find the book where the code would be listed along with who it should be passed to inside the building that was set back from the road, behind a high fence, a flood-lit perimeter.

The message, after the code had been checked, was recorded. The duty officer in the GRU section laboriously wrote it down. To whom should it be delivered in the morning? An officer in Military Intelligence. From whom was it sent? An investment manager, an accountant, two prominent lawyers based in Geneva, all with cover names. What was the message? *No show*. Simple enough for any illiterate arsehole to comprehend.

Tank said, "Nothing on him. Carrying nothing – except his phone which is dead."

Sword said, "Not in his bag and not in his clothing. Certain of it."

Cress said, "Suggest we leave him strung up there, lullabies playing in his ears, and his feet ready to crack. Miss out the food and drink and sleep. Then go for it again – around dawn."

At her desk, back in the Post Room, Sarah read her book.

Looking at the diagrams, it was obvious to her that she would have to learn how to drive a JCB digger, a tracked one. The book dealt with the challenges of restoring stone-walled crofts that had been built 200 years ago, then abandoned in what another book on her desk called the Highland Clearances, 150 years ago . . . formidable.

Vernon had not yet broached the matter of why she had left the third floor and returned to them. His own desk was cleared and his screen switched off and most of the ceiling lights had been turned off. He lived in a housing association flat close to Elephant and Castle, but spent more time in the Post Room than at home with his family. Had served 37 years there.

He would have seen her come back to the basement, pick up the daily work of the section, and seen her head in her hands and would have noted her reddened eyes. "Thinking of staying much longer, Sarah?"

"Not much longer, but thank you for asking . . . Just a few calls that might come through that I can field."

"Because I don't want to shove my nose in . . . get what I mean? Is it that bad?"

"Could be, if I'm looking on the black side – but that's making a fuss."

"About your boy?"

"Has to go back where he was, collect some equipment. It isn't a state secret, Vernon, but where he was is going to be alive, powerfully angry. What do I know? Well, it won't be a good place to be, but he's going to collect what he left behind, came away in a helterskelter. It's just bits and pieces of his trade, worth something, not much. Should have been ordered straight home, should have been praised."

Vernon said, "Because I run this little outpost of sanity in the building, Sarah, I am supposed to have a duty of care for all of you, and I take it seriously and worry about it. But I have time, and 'others' may not have the same opportunity."

"Couldn't bear it up there with him. We all respected him down here, but he's changed. Never thanked Croppy for what he'd done, way over the odds – talk about extra miles. And Croppy rang him tonight and told him he was going back for his gear. Mr Merrick's duty of care should have shown him the need to forbid it but he sanctioned it. He's on a hillside, he'd made a Covert Rural Observation Post. He's close to a community of career criminals, horrible people – drugs, girls, weapons, money laundering all over Europe, enforced by violence and, like I said, they will be angry, big time."

Vernon said, "You are our family, Sarah, you matter to us. Let's hope it all seems better in the morning."

She would not have expected Vernon to come to work the next day, smooth his hair, knot a tie, take a lift to the atrium, then up three floors and down a corridor, then get admittance to S/3/12 and read the riot act to Jonas Merrick about duty of care. To those who knew what he had done, Mr Merrick was a legend. It hurt her, how much he had changed.

On the road to the airport, Croppy reflected on where he went and why . . . and thought also about a conversation.

Hello, this is Croppy.

Yes.

I had a sleep.

Good.

I'm going back there, to my hide.

And . . .?

I left stuff behind when I had to chase after him.

Yes . . .?

Thought you should know.

Do what you think right.

Wouldn't want to leave stuff there.

And give them our footprint, very definitely not . . . We have moved on rather a long way from there, as I'm sure you understand. Make sure nothing comes back from there to bite us.

Yes.

Quite busy at this end. Have our lift completed. Really quite busy.

In the hide he had made on the hillside with the view down over the rocks, the tree line, the football pitch, the building with the steps at the side and the telephone box, and the girl's pen for her goats and her dog, and the family villa, were the tools of Croppy's trade . . . his ghillie suit of sophisticated camouflage, the precision binoculars, a plastic box of Meals Ready to Eat, his water bottles, two filled with treated water and two more into which his urine had gone, and the body waste that was in little packets of tin-foil, his gas and his flash-bang canisters, his notebook and his pencils. It had been a shambolic departure from the hide, crawling out boots first and then knowing that he must stretch his legs, and get away from there fast and along the track and hammer it all the way to the hut with the broken roof and the corrugated iron covering under which were more supplies, all prepared because that was the way the military had taught him.

The weather had eased. He had passed a gypsy camp in a cutting beneath the highway, remembered it from when he had been tailing his target towards Chamonix, saw lights among the trees, and smoke from a fire billowing over the traffic. Had spoken to Mr Merrick . . . he had hoped that Mr Merrick would have told him to forget the debris of his surveillance and jump on to the first flight to London, and had also hoped to hear just a few words of praise, perhaps an acknowledgement of what he'd achieved. Had spoken to Sarah, shouldn't have done as he'd upset her.

A sergeant, an instructor for the Special Reconnaissance Regiment had banged it into recruits. "Never leave a calling card, don't show them you were there. Best chance, if you've cleared out well enough, is that they'll bet the last dollar that the leak came from one of their own. That's when they do more work for us than we've achieved and start eating their own. Creates suspicion, paranoia, fucks them up . . . Don't leave anything."

Had tried to get Matt in Podgorica but hadn't raised him, and not left a message.

So, they had their lift completed . . . It was rare for Croppy to pass judgement on those he was supposed to be working with, or working for. Some of the other stalkers or estate managers used to spit when talking about clients, and some of the officers and senior NCOs in RSS would mimic and ridicule and swear blue about the "idiots" tasking them, especially the people from SIS. He allowed himself to consider the team he had met outside the church of St Michel in Chamonix, and thought them vile – rude, opinionated, arrogant and likely cruel . . . The signs would soon show the turn off to the airport and he would check the timetables and hunker down in a seat, and sleep some more. Should not have rung Sarah. And thought that perhaps, he read too much into Mr Merrick's responses.

At the front gate, holding the cat, was Vera. The rain had slackened but not stopped. Jonas had no idea why she was there, wonders if a crisis were about to be reported.

He had covered most of the walk from Raynes Park station along the avenues of identical houses towards his own home. He had a spring in his step and had turned over in his head all the good things that had happened that day, and had savoured what the American had said. It would be a triumph, had no doubt of it – still a few hurdles, but all manageable – and a personal triumph. Good things were bouncing around his mind, until he had seen Vera.

She had a detached expression on her face, and the cat scowled.

A problem with the central heating, a fault developed with the car, her printer malfunctioning? Would be difficult but he'd say it: "Can we please view this with perspective? A leak under the kitchen sink is not the end of Western civilisation . . ." On the train home he had rather gloried in the knowledge that all those sweaty men and women crushed around him had no idea of the scale at which he, Jonas Merrick, operated, of the weight of responsibility he carried.

"Yes, dear? I've had a long day. What is it, dear?"

She said, a distant voice as if puzzled at what she wished to express. "It is, sorry to say, about you."

"Something I need to know? Vera, for heaven's sake – what?"

"What you need to know, Jonas."

"Sounds gibberish . . ."

She took a deep breath. Softly and with obvious concern, Vera said, "You've started to strut. More's the pity but you don't even notice it. Strut, Jonas. I watched this morning when you went off down the road. Almost arrogant, like this world, our world, Jonas, is beneath you. It doesn't suit you, and strutting does not dignify you. Are you too high and mighty now, Jonas? If you are, we don't like it. I don't, Olaf doesn't. We like you as you usually are, which is dignified and humble. I expect you're going to tell me that this is the most important assignment you've ever had, that the stakes are higher than they ever were, that you're going to change the world. Don't try it, please, because I will not tolerate evasions, nor will Olaf. Right, that is what I wanted to say, and now it's off my chest we can go inside, not discuss this further, and have our tea. It is mince and mash tonight . . . If you behave like that in the office I'm surprised they haven't frog-marched you up to the top and chucked you off the roof. Or, worse, withdrawn your card, ended your employment and retired you. Given me responsibility for minding you. Are you looking after people, your people, or only looking after yourself? Jonas, I won't have you strut, and that is my last word."

She turned on her heel, rather elegantly, and Olaf clung to her shoulder.

He reeled. Thirty years and more of married life and never spoken to like that before.

He stepped forward. There was an almighty list of things he could have blurted back in a hasty defence, but he left them unsaid. Took another step, but an uneven pavement and the toecap of a brogue caught, and he lurched and had to clutch at a tree to prevent falling on his face, and the impact opened his briefcase and scattered papers and threw out his sandwich box and his thermos flask.

He collected them, went inside and closed the door and Olaf had caught her mood and ignored him. He enjoyed mince and mash but thought it likely to be a quiet meal. Even if he chose to go down that route, Jonas Merrick had never apologised for anything in his life, didn't think he would know how to.

8

He came across Lambeth Bridge, and Kevin and Leroy had
noticed him and were moving at their own sedate pace to step out
into the traffic. He did not wait for them but ploughed on. Not a
glance to right or left, felt nothing – neither valuable nor useless
– and around him was a shriek of brakes, tyres screaming, horns
blasting. He had reached a central island in the embankment by
the time the two policemen had restored order.

He went for his coffee and his pastry . . . noted that both the
policemen eyed him with a mixture of concern and puzzlement.
Noticed that the staff in the café looked him over and frowns flickered on their faces. He knew why he caused confusion . . . The
previous evening's mince and mash had been eaten in silence,
both with heads lowered, and the cat sat in a chair, distancing
itself from him. She had gone to bed early, he had stayed in the
snug and had worked at the papers that would dovetail any
possible response if the team came through with the codes or
entry sticks, whatever . . . Jonas understood little of the science of
laundering dirty money, and was ignorant of the business of
hacking and firewalls, what might be expected from the Trojan
Mustangs. He had caught the eye of the ticket inspector on the
train when he had flashed his season ticket and it had barely been
noted, but he had been peered at. He had slept in the chair, not
intending to but had dropped off, dead to the world. Vera's movements in the kitchen had finally woken him: she had been preparing
his sandwiches, as she always did, and filling his thermos. A fast
wash, a change of socks, a faster shave and his upper lip missed
through carelessness, and a nick on his chin still intermittently
bled. Those who had known him as a creature of relentless habit

on the train, in the café, in the garden and in Thames House would have been astonished to see him so disheveled. No mention of Vera's accusation of "strutting" had passed between them. He wolfed his breakfast, and had almost bolted from his home, but his calm had returned when he arrived on Lambeth Bridge, and his self-confidence had eked back.

Apologise? Of course not – nothing to apologise for.

Boastful, arrogant? He did not recognise such descriptions of himself.

Self-centred, caring only for himself? Rubbish.

He sat on his usual bench and the chaffinches at his feet squabbled over the crumbs he brushed off his trousers. He indulged himself. Was a Master and a Commander, not afraid to take control of a situation when lesser men stepped back, awed by the burden of authority. Wallowed in the image of himself standing alone and taking the heat and calling the decisions, with men and women working in the field on a plan he had concocted . . .

The gardener, a man he knew to be ravaged by traumas brought on by a previous military campaign, one now largely forgotten, had brought his barrow close, with the stiff brush and the rest of his kit. Jonas had always thought there was a rather charming philosophy about the man, and a humanity. He often talked with him, and reckoned that a kindness on his part.

"Good morning."

"Morning, sir."

No one else called him "sir". Not anyone in Raynes Park, not one of the 2000 or so people who occupied Thames House.

"I was considering the responsibility of command."

"Not something I ever went after."

"Lonely. Can't be shared."

"And safe, sir. Commanders put men and women in harm's way, don't face the dark and the danger of combat themselves. They stay safe."

He snapped back. "Someone has to make decisions, get us to the end place."

"Perhaps, sir, but not me . . . I suppose some people can accept that getting to that 'end place' will cost casualties, but as long as they are 'acceptable statistics' then what's the problem? Excuse me, sir, but can you shift your feet? Thank you, sir."

He had lifted his shoes that seemed scuffed and were without their daily polish and was no longer sure whether his socks were from yesterday or clean on.

"We can't all back off."

"Don't suppose we can . . . Let's hope it works out well for you, the decision making . . . Good luck, sir."

Jonas peered up into the masked face and thought he had been insulted but could not be sure. It was the first time that he had ever received what approached a rebuke from the gardener. It was also the first time that he had been dressed down with blunt words by Vera . . . He pondered that. The barrow still needed oil, there was a rhythm in the sweeping of the brush's stiff bristles. The gardener had unsettled Jonas. Vera had not. Olaf, taking a cue from her, had showed him no affection that morning. What irked was that he had been accused of "staying safe". What the hell was he supposed to do, hike to the mountains of Albania, tramp across the frontier fence dividing Finland and Russia, march into Geneva with a bullhorn and denounce their dealing in the thieved cash from Russia? He went to the side door of Thames House, flashed his card, and more eyes with no expression to them, examined his yesterday shirt, and crooked tie, and the nick on his chin and the part of his face the razor had missed.

He crossed the floor of S/3/12, and Aggie Burns was briefing, but stopped talking. On into his cubicle and noticed that the new desk remained empty, and dumped his case on his own desk, and switched on the computer, and Aggie sang out.

"God, what state are you in, Jonas? Been on an all-night binge?"

He ignored her.

There had been two flights for London, both taken off, and one to Frankfurt and the Paris one was boarding, but Croppy was in his seat in Departures and was going to stay there until the fog cleared at Vienna. The connection from Vienna to Podgorica was delayed. A couple of ladies sitting close to him talked a mixture of American English and German and Croppy deduced that fog in Vienna was a regular feature at this time of year.

He felt good. Had slept well in the car, had slept well in the warmth of the airport, and the the sky above Geneva was clearing, but the fog that had come down over Vienna's *flughafen* was obstinate and the feeling was it would be another hour before the crew boarded, and they might get away before the pilots ran out of time. For Croppy, who betrayed little frustration, his self-imposed deadlines were threatened, the schedule he had set himself was awry.

The way he had planned it when he had pitched up at Geneva's Cointrin airport was that he would get the flight out, get himself into Podgorica and meet with Matt from the embassy. Get the best service that Matt could provide because the guy was desperate, for a transfer out of general Foreign Office grind and into what he reckoned were the sunlit uplands of SIS, and a dream of intelligence work. He should have reached the valley in the late afternoon, done the hike from the hut in early dusk when the low sunlight, if it were there, would have been behind the mountain range. Cleared up the hide, and nestled there for a few hours until the first layers of lighter grey reached the valley and the villa and the football pitch. In the very first stages of dawn he would have left his hide and gone back to the hut, and his suit and binoculars and the weapons, and his notes would have been stowed . . . Could not try and move in the dark because out there on the hillside there was as little light in the night as there would have been on Ben Hiant. Would have been daft to risk turning an ankle, tripping and breaking an arm, and he was a stranger there and had little knowledge of cross-terrain routes.

He would have to put together another schedule. He had patience, and discipline . . . It would have been good to be back in the UK. He would have met Sarah, and hugged her and they'd have been shy with each other and she would have blushed, that was the sort of girl she was. They'd have talked for a bit and sat in a car and been driven back into London – and she'd have gone back to work to finish up the loose ends of the operation and he would have taken the long train ride that would get him up to Fort William, and late in the afternoon his dad would have come to collect him, and he reckoned before the end of the day that Sarah would have sat down at her laptop and written a letter of resignation from the Post Room. He passed the time until the fog had lifted and the plane was ready to board examining in his mind the problem of getting some degree of damp proofing under the old walls of the ruin where he and Sarah would live. It would be a grand place when it was finished, with grand views and wind and soft rain.

Discipline was a paramount part of his life so the damp-proofed foundations they would put in were mandatory, were as important to him as going back to clear the hide, removing all signs of his presence from an abandoned hut. It was the way he lived . . . and he thought some more about the stags on the hills and taking his girl up there and teaching her what he knew.

His wrists were freed and Skender sagged back and would have fallen if he had not been supported. Fists grabbed him, held him secure.

He thought he would fight them.

His own shit and piss were down his legs and had gathered in his trousers that were down at his ankles.

He *hoped* he would fight them.

He was manoeuvred a few dragging steps across the floor, then was dumped on to a hard chair. Through the material of the hood he could see that a light was beamed into his face and that darkness was around it.

He would fight them because that was in the history of his family, told again and again by his grandfather, drilled into him. Might have been true and might have been lies, but the stories were told often enough. They said that what was expected of any member of the family . . . then his grandfather had been a year old, his *great* grandfather had been questioned, tortured by the Military Intelligence of the German occupiers and had never given them a word as to where the resistance camp was in the mountains and had been tied to a tree and shot in front of the villagers. Had to be tied to the tree because he was too weak to stand and face them. His grandfather's cousin had been taken by the partisans after they had assumed power, the Hoxha people, and fingers taken off and a tongue sliced out but had refused to show on the map the location of the village's weapons cache. A dispute with people from Durresi about money, about trust, and a body of another cousin found beside the Tirana road, throat slit from ear to ear and his testicles cut off. No one in the family had ever been accused of betrayal.

He would resist them because it was a microbe that ran in his blood.

No one, at any time in his life, had threatened Skender. Not at school, not in sport, not in dealings with other clans from other villages, not with the dealers who hung around those tower blocks where he had been sent to learn the art of trading, not in his own village. It was as if he carried a plastic card that detailed his family and his connections hanging from a lanyard round his neck ... Had never been challenged, never been beaten ... He knew now, from their movements, there were two men with him and a woman. They hardly spoke, and only in whispers and as yet no question had been asked of him. He was exhausted, and hungry and desperate for water, and the gag was still in his mouth and his nostrils were raw and his shoulders were a field of pain, and he stank. He could not put together an explanation of why he had been taken, for what purpose, nor how his security had so collapsed.

They moved around him and he realised they believed they already had mastery over him. His own people would have kicked him, spat on him, belted him with a pick-axe handle and the questions would have come in a torrent and he would by now have been bleeding and a knife shown him.

The woman worked through the beam of light, sat on the floor in front of him, lit a cigarette for herself, then spoke in his own language.

"Now, Skender, we know who you are and we know the importance of your family, and we know about your girl, and we know why you were coming to Geneva."

Rather a sharp voice. Seemed that this was routine work for her, that she would be businesslike and to the point, and he thought the language she used, and the inflections, did not come from Albania but from a classroom.

"I'll not tell a lie, Skender, but your position is not a happy one, and can turn quite bad for you quite quickly . . ."

She paused. The light was blocked, a bigger body covering it and the hood was lifted. A hand in a plastic glove prised open his mouth and dragged out the gag of sodden material. He felt himself choke and bit hard. He heard a yelp, and then his face was hit with a fast repetition of blows, and the hood was dropped.

"Silly boy, Skender. Didn't rate you that low. What you should understand, Skender, is this. If you want to walk away from here, have a cuddle with that nice girl of yours, then I am your best hope. I think your only hope."

Tank was ignorant of the language, Cress delivered a short summary in English each time she spoke to Skender. He clutched his bitten hand, trying to stifle the pain.

"These are bad bastards, Skender. They'd be happy to put a poker up your arse, red-hot and straight out of the fire, if that would help loosen you up. Understand me?"

"Bad bastards" was a mild description of himself and of Sword. Tank thought Sword worse . . . She was as brutal as either of them but her voice could sometimes rumble like the sound of a contented cat.

"We have a box cutter blade, Skender, a new blade and sharp. Can take off your ears or your nose, or what your lovely girlfriend appreciates. It won't mean any more to these bad bastards than using a knife to peel an apple. They've done it before and they'll do it again. You want to be grown up, Skender? Or do you want to be the village idiot where you come from, with no ears and no fingers and no balls? We could send you back and all the kids can run round after you and see how dumb you were. Can we get down to some questions now, and some answers? You sensible enough for that?"

He would not come easy, Tank's opinion. Best hope had always been that the paperwork he was delivering, or a memory stick, was taped to his body, on his stomach or in the small of his back. But they had found nothing on him or in his trainers or his bag. Tank's mind wandered . . . this was his way of earning a living. What they would be paid for this excursion would cover the mortgage for next month and the month after. Might pay for the materials for the new dormer, and even for a bit of a holiday. And he had the gardening start-up gear to pay for. A bank manager, if such a species still existed, might ask, *And what sort of work do you do, sir?* And Tank might have to answer, *Want to put together a gardening business because my old trade is rather drying up. That's loosely based on private military contracting, a bit thuggish, can put me in line for some nasties, that's torture to get under the skin of people who decline to give up the information my employers are wanting to have. Not pleasant, but needs must.* His wife thought he drove a truck for the PMC when he was away. But he was part of a team that threatened to slice off human bits that stuck out, and the likelihood was that pretty soon they would be getting out the plastic sheeting and spreading it over the floor and sticking it on the walls. Tank could not have said how they would decide, if push came to shove, who would handle the box cutter.

"Thinking about questions, Skender, and thinking about answers. We're not too interested in time, Skender, but you should remember that time is not only money from our point of view, it is also pain from yours. Mess about and it will get, as night follows day, unpleasant."

Beyond the walls and the doors TVs were turned high, and there was an argument on the landing and youngsters screaming in the stairwell.

Tank thought that Cress had a lovely voice, a soothing one, and a shame she only did cruelty with it.

"You want to get back to your girl. I want to go home. What's holding us up, Skender, is business. That box cutter knife is a horrible little thing, and sharp, and we know where it hurts most

– nose, ears, tongue, toes and fingers and your privates – think about them, Skender. You can be a hero if you feel it necessary. A big hero to yourself, not to anyone else, because no one knows where you are, and who we are, and nobody will find you, and that nice girl, my bet, will be on her back in a month and enjoying herself and forgetting you existed. No one will recognise you wanted to be a hero. Right, questions."

If he had been a smoker, Tank would have valued having a fag to hold. Had to make do with picking up the heavy kitchen scissors that they'd used on the masking tape. Sword was at a low table, the knife in front of him. Cress eased herself a little on the floor and set a tape machine going beside her. Was the threat real? What they said they would do? Probably was, Tank reckoned.

"You are a courier, Skender. You carry messages to people in Geneva from families in Moscow. Instructions for the handling of the money is given you at your home and you travel with it. It's supposed to be a foolproof communication road. Except that you are where you are . . . Skender, I need the instructions."

The calm, soft voice told Skender that she was not angry, not in a hurry. Told him also that she would not hesitate to use the box cutter.

"Skender, playtime over. Where are the instructions?"

They had said to him in London, older men, and they would have had the instructions from his grandfather that he be taught all that they knew, and more . . . Take a point on the ceiling, fasten on it, hold to it. Say nothing . . .

"I have a feeling, Skender, that you can hand it out but cannot take it. You are not a self-made boy from an urban slum, from the gutter and toughened up. You are a spoiled and privileged lout, and already you are concerned about pain, and whether you will scream. Already you have soiled yourself and we have taken photos of it. I am asking you . . . the instructions?"

His mind was a mess, had a right to be. Who did he protect? Who did he care for? How would his pain help a reputation that would already be trashed? Finding answers, and all done at speed . . . and he knew box cutter knives and the keenness of the blades and had seen packages of cocaine, bubble-wrapped then folded in greaseproof paper, sliced open with the lightest of pressure. Protect who? Not his grandfather who would have cut his throat, done it himself had he known of Birgitte and a planned escape and long hours in her bed. Who did he care for? A German girl, and amazingly she had chosen him, not for money but for . . . no idea. Who would his pain help? Men in Russia, those close to the Leader; wealthier than his grandfather but with more greed zipped in a wallet, and always when their messengers came he, Skender, was treated as an object of contempt. But . . . *but* . . . he needed his pride – would be mute and crippled without it.

"Hold out your hands."

They were taped together at the wrist. They had lain on his lap and had covered his groin. He could not see. He did not know whether it was the woman's intention to grab them, let one of the men get to work – with the cutter, with pliers, with a cigarette lighter. He put out his hands and sensed that she came closer to him, wriggled on the floor until her knees were against his shins, above the ankles that were taped to the front chair legs. And smelled her toothpaste breath she would have had her head over the mess that was in his underpants and his trousers. She took his hands. He felt her fingers and they were small, and almost gentle, and his bladder strained . . . she stroked his hand, first with her fingers and then her nails, and then it was the cold touch of the steel. So cold and so precise, and so thin. She shifted the angle of the blade so that he felt its edge, and his bladder broke and he tried to writhe away from her but hands, heavier and muscled, were on his shoulders and he was pinioned.

He felt his head spin, thought he would faint, never had before – and remembered the pride, remembered also that they would not end his life. Kill him and he had told them nothing, and he shouted and his voice filled the room.

"I know nothing."

Yelled it at the walls and the words echoed back at him. He heard no footsteps from the corridor outside, only the dead beat of music and shouts and laughter and argument.

"That is so poor, Skender. You have to do better. Have to."

He flinched, felt the nick, a little cutting motion from the blade followed the first moment of pain, then the warmth of the dribble of blood. It came from the top of his right forefinger and flowed freely on to his stomach, and into the hair at his groin was then around his thighs. Without his pride, what was he?

"I know nothing."

He pissed again, and her voice was cold.

"You are a fucking idiot, Skender. For that you will pay, pay in pain, pay big. A dumb fucking idiot."

He was slapped across the face, then his shoulders were freed. The blood had stopped running. She had moved away from him and he sensed movement behind the light as they gathered together.

Skender called out to them, "Remember who I am. And who is my family. And what is their reach . . . Think you are safe from that, any of you?"

He had wrapped himself in his pride, and thought it enough. The idea was alive in his head that very soon they would slip away, abandon him, and he would free himself and would trip the hood off his head and go to the door and open it, and walk out with no trousers and no underpants and no shoes – and would walk away . . .

The Aquarium, with its huge glass walls, was located on the Ulitsa Grizodubovoy, given the number of 3, and the majority of its staff, at varying levels of responsibility for gaining military intelligence of use to the state, arrived for work at Khoroshyovskaya Metro station, on the Purple Line.

Two of the officers, middle-ranking, low in responsibility, were sifting incoming overnight signals, according them priorities. Andrei and Konstantin were on the second coffee of the day, and were behind schedule because of a longer than usual cigarette break in the back car park. They came to a signal from the embassy in Berne. The message was about a "no show". It carried no coded title. It did, however, indicate a five-digit and three-letter attachment for checking in another file which also had a specific entry line … Both men, using two fingers but fast, clattered their keyboards, and in turn – because at GRU only the best equipment is good enough for them – a Restricted file opened. The second file was now ransacked … not one either man had heard of. A name materialised on the screens.

"Fucking hell," mouthed Andrei.

"One of those shit faces in the inner circle," snorted Konstantin.

"It will be about money … made it fast and now sanctioned up to the throat. Somebody is a 'no show' and he has the influence to use us as his fucking telegram service. Not because his portfolio is up half a per cent, but because something has crapped on him from on high."

Konstantin lifted a phone. Dialled a number from the second file. A snappy voice answered.

"I am Konstantin, major – we only use given names on open lines – and I am Duty Officer, GRU External Services. We have received a message, part encoded, and realise that it is involving matters associated with you, and coming from our embassy GRU station in Berne, Switzerland. It just states 'no show', and no explanation. I am assuming you understand its significance, but am unable to help further since we have no records of dealings in that area currently, and …"

The receiver was put down.

Konstantin said that he felt he was talking to a man "white at the gills".

"About money."

"Not about cuckoo clocks and milk chocolate and wristwatches – about money."

And both of them, lowly ranked and lowly paid, reckoned their day improved.

The bubble in which Viktor existed was small and was sought after by those on the outside with undisguised envy. He was a man of power, and yet felt himself now reduced to the status of a street trader. In the eyes of the sanctions committees he was at the summit of influence inside the Federation of Russia. He was believed to have access to the supreme leadership. Men and women, old and young, if they had access to him, which was difficult, would have ducked their heads as if he deserved sincere respect, and would nod agreement at his insights and laugh at his jokes, and be devastated if he cut them, and they could only offer him sycophancy, not friendship.

He had been at a meeting of trustees for a new sports complex in the suburb of Vsevolozhsk, in Leningrad Oblast, close to the Road of Life which had linked the besieged Leningrad to the rest of Russia in the 900-day siege, and a historian had lectured the committee on the importance of this 60,000 population in terms of symbolism – for which Viktor cared not a fuck. He resumed his chair and another local who had been waiting to speak now piped up with the information that the town was the *first* place in Russia to have its streets lit by gas lamps – for which he cared not a flying fuck. What he did care about was that a carefully organised courier system had without explanation fallen on its arse. He had been clever as a child, a street boy. His brain power had been indispensable to the thugs who had taken over City Hall, had moved with them to the capital when they had been installed in the great ministries, and been awarded the special passes that took them in and out of the side gates of the Kremlin. He would have said to his wife, if he were confident that they were not bugged, that only half a dozen men in the state *enjoyed* – a rare description of it – as much influence as himself with the ultimate leadership. He was chairing a meeting about a fucking sports complex, and a hammer battered inside his skull.

He had been invited, refusal not an option, to administer a slice of the new czar's money and had moved it into the care of those in Geneva who were indispensable, but ludicrously expensive. He had placed other people's money inside that bubble – and the majority of his own. Because he had their trust he had charge of their money and had believed it secure, within the market's vagaries. A good plan in place, good people used, and as another expert droned on about the height of the water table on the proposed building site, he blinked and scratched and took off his spectacles to polish them unnecessarily.

The beauty of the plan, as he believed it, was that he was distanced by the cut-offs. The fucking disaster of the plan, as he now recognised, was that he was so distanced that it was not possible for him to pick up a phone and browbeat a minion for information. There were plenty of greedy bastards who soaked money off him – and it would have bust wide open all his cautions and protections were he able to do so, to speak direct to Geneva . . . and ask them what? Only a "no show", not yet a catastrophe. For a "no show" he could sit tight. For a catastrophe he must take his car to the Kremlin, have begged an appointment, mix honesty with self-preservation and confess how much he had lost, where it had gone . . . and might live and might not. He smoked furiously. There were signs forbidding it throughout the room but no one dared remind him.

Viktor, who had been a coming man, felt his status fracture, crumble. He would be back in the capital by early evening. Voices played around him but his interest in a new sports complex was long exhausted. It was Viktor's practice not to involve his wife in affairs of money or of state. She might meet others with a similar position, and the wives – or mistresses – would gossip. That evening, he thought it likely that he would tell her what a "no show" could mean for them.

Bureaucracy's cogs, poorly oiled, ground noisily in the capital where snow flurries thickened.

A decision had been taken in the cavernous square of buildings, set back from the road so that the public who struggled in the deteriorating weather, or were stuck on the Ulitsa Zhitnaya highway, would not be able to see much of it. Authorisation was given for the removal of four prisoners from a prison camp – IK-2

– 400 miles south-east of the capital. They would be taken out on Thursday of next week and dispersed. Agreement came after consultation with the SVR foreign intelligence-gathering organisation, necessary because a foreigner was involved in the transfer . . . *No problem for us, let the bitch rot wherever you put her* . . . arrangements had been made with the Federal penitentiary Service, in the same building as Justice, for secure transportation to prisons in the Arctic, in the Far East, and in Siberia.

All in place, all ready – what Jonas supposed sporty people would have called *under starter's orders* . . . except that no flag dropped or gun fired.

He was the architect of Safety Deposit, had nurtured the idea, had put a timetable in place and coordinated the movement of the players, put them into a state of readiness and now was nagged.

Had taken a call from Denys Montgomery. "Just wondered, Jonas, where we were? How is it progressing?" Had responded in poor humour. "Have been accused by my wife, no less an authority, of *strutting*. Too big for my boots, too confident in an outcome and needing to bridle in my feelings. Took it as a rap on the knuckles. What I am saying, it is a good operational plan and will deliver – I have not yet been informed by my team, *when* . . . That being the case it would help if you allowed me freedom from the distractions of acting like a railway timetable call centre. When I have something to tell you, then I will do so." And had put the phone down which was ungracious of him and lacking in dignity – of little concern to him.

The AssDepDG was hovering at the door to his cubicle. "You winning or losing, Jonas?" And snapped back, "Am waiting patiently. Ever tried it? Will hardly help to have my team ring me every ten minutes and tell me the state of play. I am not there, I cannot intervene, I depend on my professionals. They will do what is necessary and pass a message as soon as is possible. Enough? Right?" Had felt a greater weight on his shoulders, but not experienced doubt, though his face itched where his shaving had been inadequate and he yawned more often. He had received the look from the AssDepDG which meant that his reply was unsatisfactory but it was the wrong moment for them to scrap.

Then Aggie Burns. "Not my business, Jonas, but sound travels well in here, and you are behaving like a complete plonker. So bloody superior. Heard what you said: *strutting.* A fair description. People trying to help you, Jonas, so might not be the best tactic to piss on them. Remember, you have no one on the fifth floor who is going to watch your back. They'll cut you loose. My advice, Jonas, is to show some humility. Always best when no outcome is certain." He had not looked at her, could not help himself from saying, "When I want advice I will request it." She had gone and given him a smile, one without humour and laced win sadness.

Solly Kravnic from the Agency had called. Fishing for news. Called, ostensibly, to say that his geeks, the Trojan Mustangs, were on approach into Guernsey, would be taken to the location where they had accommodation, extra gear, communications that were secure – but had called to learn how the interrogation progressed. He had answered with the one word "ongoing". Thought that enough. *Ongoing.* Was uncertain what it meant, probably that nothing was yet extracted. A dry gallows joke had been made about the use of thumbscrews. Would he have accepted its value, or any other paraphernalia that was reckoned to help the process of breaking a suspect's resistance? Vera might have left him if she had known. He had to stay strong, he told himself. Silence clawed around him. Realised why the quiet was so deafening. Sarah was not behind him, shifting, breathing, typing, easing her chair forward or back – and fielding the phone calls. He did not know where she was – but he would not go looking for her, nor ring her number. The world seemed to close around him.

Skender was manacled again, his hands high above his head and fastened to the walls, his weight on the balls of his feet, and the headphones back on.

The team were huddled in a corner, not that he would have heard anything they said while the noise burrowed deep in his head.

They had done the theatre, had used the heavy scissors to cut the necessary lengths from the plastic roll bought on an earlier trip, left in the apartment. The pieces were now in place. They covered the walls, the window, the doors, the one small square table and the two stools, and were stuck in place with masking tape, floor to ceiling. The linoleum around the chair was covered. Part of the theatre involved tilting the chair on to two of its legs, sliding the plastic underneath the chair's seat, while he sat there, then lifting the other two legs. Nothing said in his hearing, nor needing to be said. Of course Skender, Albanian boy from a senior clan crime family, would know the reason plastic sheets were spread on the floor and on the walls, and over the window. Likely would have done it himself when younger and being initiated, and would have used the scissors to encourage a confession, or from the pleasure of inflicting agony. He would have a clear idea of why the surfaces were covered. Cress and Tank sat on the stools, Sword leaned against the window. A debate in progress, and frank words spoken in hushed voices, as if each of them realised that bullshit time was on the wane.

Cress cut to the quick "We piss or we get off the pot. Are we up for it, guys, or are we not?"

Tank murmured, "Used to be able, didn't have a problem, don't know about now. Got to live with yourself, haven't you?"

Sword whispered, hesitantly, "I don't feel anxious to lead, might follow if Tank or you, Cress, went first."

She said, "Easy enough in Helmand because it was our people that we were doing it for. This is harder."

Tank said, "Nice-looking kid, nice-looking girl. Can slap him about, but that knife – a bit harder."

Sword said, "Take his dick off and he bleeds, and we can't stop the bleeding, then he's dead, and fuck all use to us if he's croaked. That's a whole bucket harder."

"I thought I was up for it."

"Never doubted I was, until now."

"What the fuck are we going to do? Call up London. 'Mr Merrick, please. At lunch, is he? Pass this on, grateful if you would.

This is Sword, I am speaking for Cress and Tank, and we've had a collective dose of the yellows. Don't fancy what we said we could do, gone squeamish, lost the balls. Understand, we're cowards, took the money and shouldn't have. Sorry, for being such a pathetic failure.' And put the phone down. Have to do something."

Cress said, "Maybe 'something' is letting his brain fry a bit longer, then being aggressive, then maybe doing an ear, then maybe . . ."

Tank said, "A big breath and a big gasp, and maybe . . ."

Sword said, "Always best to kick the can down the road, let it rattle and let it roll, then maybe . . ."

Enough said. The man hung from the wall and his feet somehow still took his weight, and the noise in his head was a muffled howl. They went back to what they had done before the inquest on what they could manage, or had lost heart in. Sword had the scissors in his right hand and was opening and using then, and did it again, again and again, what he did. Cress was at the table, her notebook open at a fresh page, and did a drumbeat with his pen and was in symphony with Sword.

Nothing more to say, and the gasps of the man at the wall merged with the sounds of the scissors and the pen, in unison.

Out of sight, out of the minds of all but a few, the girls huddled.

Apricot stayed silent though it was congratulation time for Blueberry. In a growled low voice of triumph, she explained to Currant and Apple and Apricot, how she had stolen two dud light bulbs from a workman's basket when on her last toilet break. Two more bulbs would go into their collection. Success indeed . . . they would not be separated.

Pear called. She understood his impatience with her, assumed he had lifted the phone as a reflex, and had not bothered to check the incoming number and its country code. She launched.

"Do not hang up on me, I beg you. I am told that you alone have the power – God only knows how you possess it – to bring them out. We have the parish of St Nicholas in Reykjavik, and the parish of St Bartholomew, and I will go and light candles and kneel if you are as successful as I am told you might be. I have heard from my lawyer friend. He has the friendship of a personality in Justice."

She was sitting outside. Runners passed, confident and at ease, and the wind came in hard from the west, up the fjord, and gulls barked at her.

"My friend has a contact because he pays for it. Anything in that fuck-awful country is possible if you pay for it. Anybody is for sale . . . He gets the money from Currant's father who will not visit her, will not write to her, but pays for news of her. I tell you, Currant and Blueberry and Apple, and your woman who is Apricot, are inseparable. I promise you that if they are split they will kill themselves. The cross I carry is that I allowed it to happen, abandoned them. I should have refused to go. I am ashamed. They will not permit themselves being sent to different prisons, solidarity and strength broken."

A cruise liner was in the outer harbour, a white monster. Tenders made avenues of spray as they carried towards to the quayside.

"They are to be moved on Thursday. Except they will not be moved – they will be dead. Do you have a sense of urgency? Yes? No? They will be dead . . ."

"Sorry, Croppy, but it's the dumbest thing I ever heard of."

"I don't have an option."

Croppy had moved fast to make the connection. Had tracked Matt down in an Irish-themed bar where he had been hosting two local hacks, now sitting in a corner with fresh Guinness. They faced each other across a table littered with beer mats and spillage and dead glasses.

"Course you have an option. A bloody sight better option would have been to turn west, get on a flight and be into London in ninety minutes."

"Not possible."

"Anything is possible. Going back there just to lift some gear is worse than ridiculous. Dumb, stupid, idiotic – am running out of words."

"It is discipline, what I do."

"Then get disobedient. Croppy, you have done everything asked of you, and more, much more. What is so important about the gear?"

"It is unprofessional to leave stuff behind. It's called 'giving a footprint'. It shows them how it was done. It . . ."

"More rubbish, Croppy. Turn your back, go where you're wanted. Don't make a fag end out of the job. They'll have a warehouse somewhere in Aldershot with a thousand pairs of binoculars, and enough of those ghastly meals to keep the Parachute Regiment fed for a month, and . . ."

"It is part of what we do."

"Go back to that wilderness of yours, that girl you spoke of, that house you're going to renovate, forget this place. If they ever ring you again, the London people, just don't pick up. Right, I want a run with the spooks, think it might be fun, but not as a freelancer. Want the 'shaken but not stirred' bit, twice over, but where, if I ever have to cross the road, I have back-up, and am inside that 'golden hour' for preservation, which you always had. Go back to your girl."

"Regrets, Matt . . . It is about pride, and pride comes from doing a job as well as I can. I go home when it is finished . . . I sweep it all up, stay in the hide overnight and then move out just before dawn – enough light to see where I'm going, but not be spotted. A bit of help would be appreciated . . ."

"By the by, don't be fooled by the weather right now. It's due to close down – bad up there where you're going."

His glass of Irish beer drained, Matt went back to the hack, pleaded apologies, fixed a date in a couple of days. They went out into the street. Matt would drive him to where the Vespa was parked.

Getting into the car, "And something else, Matt."

"What? What else for fuck's sake?"

"I don't have a date or anything. Nor really know anyone else to ask, anyone I would want more than you. Would you be best man for Sarah and me?"

"Cursing the kettle won't make it boil faster." An aunt of Vera had said it in the early days of their marriage, before Jonas had suggested visits to their new home were not entirely welcome. He had sworn mildly because the kettle was slow . . . scowling at his phone would not encourage it to ring.

He finished his second sandwich. Was surprised she had prepared it after the previous evening's spat. Cheese and pickle and cucumber.

No further visitors had braved a crossing of the floor of S/3/12 to reach his cubicle door. Aggie didn't come, nor the AssDepDG on whose patronage he survived, nor did Sarah put her head round the door and ask if he needed help with his computer, with coffee, with his phones . . . and beckoning to him was a further night of frosted quiet in the snug of his home, even the cat shunning him . . . and the Americans were quiet. What it added to: they waited for Jonas. And there was nothing he could do to satisfy them because he had had no message from the apartment block in Le Lignon, on the outskirts of Geneva – and could reflect on that city so expert at praising the morals of its banking systems while turning the cheek to scandal.

Geneva, a pretty lakeside place with fine mountain views, and expensive ones, far beyond the price limits of Jonas, and much to boast of . . . Amongst the very top drawer of cocaine use in Europe . . . an estimated \$100 billion in assets held by their banks . . . a whistleblower had claimed *protecting financial privacy is a fig leaf covering the shameful role of Swiss banks as collaborators of the tax evaders* . . . Credit Suisse, a giant among several near equals, fined \$350 million . . . good trade for the relationship managers employed to vet clients, and little pressure applied if "due diligence material" was denied . . . Russian oligarchs spoke well of Geneva, and dictators around the world, and kept their *consiglieres* in well-paid work . . . an ability to "look the other way" and a story of a client who wished to withdraw \$109 million in *cash* which weighed 600kgs and needed two pallets to rest on and two armoured vans to carry it away – where to? Who cared? And no war memorials in Geneva, and no streets on which bombs had fallen, because this was a community far too sensible to indulge in such puerile games . . . he knew a little of the place.

A young man had visited Jonas in St John's Gardens, had sat on a bench with him, and they had shared a National Trust umbrella and the rain had pattered on it and Jonas had been brought up to speed. It is "risk averse" Jonas had been told and the greatest risk, his informant had claimed, would have come from the whistle-blower. Jonas had asked, "If the oligarchs' cash were interfered with, put at risk, what effect would that have?" The young man had shrugged: "Not going to put him and his family on the poverty line, but will dent his self-esteem, and if he is looking after, or advising on, others' wealth, then his well-being is in danger. They would be sensitive to humiliation, to any loss of prestige. As a description of violence, the image of rats in a sack is often quoted. My own impression is that would be a tea party in comparison to an oligarch fallout over *money*." Good enough for Jonas, and a final cigarette had been tossed towards the bin where the rain would extinguish it and the young man had wandered off.

No one came . . . and the phone stayed silent. Jonas knew of nothing he should be doing, and he sweated.

9

There had been a raft of calls on Jonas' landline.

The last had informed him he was late in answering an enquiry as to his proposed leave dates – did he understand they must be taken within the next two months or be forfeited. "Top of my list," he'd snapped. Had snatched up the phone each time in the hope of a front line despatch from Geneva. The second to last was a request that he complete and return information on his pension status and would he be leaving government service at the end of the financial year? "At the very top of my *must deal with* list," he'd muttered. Who knew? Who knew when Safety Deposit would wind up: might be out on his ear by the end of the day, and might be deafened by a bombardment of champagne corks.

Jonas was drained by the waiting, and the afternoon wore on and it was the time when – in the past, before his banishment to the Post Room – he would have eased his chair back, closed his eyes, and taken a nap. His phone had hardly rung in those happy days, after his sandwiches were eaten . . . Down in the Post Room, Sarah had fielded his calls, done it efficiently and allowed his light sleep to continue. He was no longer in the Post Room, and she was not sitting with him inside the cubicle in the corner of S/3/12. The third to last was from N/1/194, Housekeeping and Associated Costs, complaining that a form sent to him had not yet been returned, and could he please give an indication of the level at which his personal radiator should be set, and did he – noting his age – require, under Civil Service edicts, heating above the standard level of 69F/20C? His answer had been brief, on the edge of politeness, and he had pointed out to the caller that he wore a jacket of Harris tweed, old but very serviceable. He should have been free to concentrate but that afternoon was bombarded with irrelevance. A solution . . .? The call before that: did he wish to take advantage of a new personal fitness course available in lunchtime breaks, with a minimum payment *per diem* of . . .? He did not.

The solution yawned at him. He missed her, had need of her.

He used his screen as a mirror. Checked his tie was straight and covered the collar button. Broke with protocols and neither switched the beast off nor cleared his desk . . . and left his cubicle. Aggie Burns was at her desk and had a clutch of team leaders round her and a map spread between them of an inner city housing estate and they'd be plotting stake-outs. She had urged him to show "humility", and he had urged her to button her advice unless he requested it. No eye contact. One of the older men in the group studied him though and would doubtless know him by his *sobriquet* of Eternal Flame – "never goes out". He walked past them, opened the door, closed it after him and set off towards the bank of lifts. He might have heard his phone ring, and might not, but did not slow his step.

Others in the lift, heading down to the staff canteen or Security, or the garage – or the Post Room – failed to make eye contact. The way of the Service was to avoid recognition, to compartmentalise as proof against familiarity, leading to gossip. Arrived in the basement. Through the open door into the armed police rest area he saw his friends, Kev and Leroy, and they looked up, then down as if they did not know him . . . knew him well enough to have saved his life and tugged a knifeman off him in a Devon caravan park, and see him across the road when the traffic was difficult. The best men he knew . . . and offered them no recognition, mutual. He went into the Post Room.

A few weeks into his lodgement in there he had realised he had acquired "respect". Suspicion in the first days, but that had thawed. To his face he was *Mister* Merrick, in chat among themselves he was the guv'nor, which he relished. Because of the open plan of the Post Room, although he had fashioned a den of his own, he heard conversations – who was expecting another family addition, whose mother had died, whose boy had won a college place, who was tempted to ditch a championship season ticket, who fancied Brexit and who didn't . . . and he was the guv'nor. It was here that *the guv'nor* had fashioned the plan, sculpted it to near perfection, for Safety Deposit. Had surprised himself that he had dared to think beyond the reach of a handrail or a lifebelt – and with side bars of success a possibility – but the call had not come and instead the phone had diverted his attention again, and again . . . and again. He was not greeted.

He sensed the chill in the room where natural light failed to penetrate. No warmth, no friendship. That hard won respect absent in the new glacial quiet. Vernon did not look up. He was not asked his business, nor what could be done to help him. He waited, and the quiet clung around him. He could see Sarah's back. He went past the coffee machine, crossed the floor and stood behind her. Her screensaver showed: the boy, a shy smile, a couple of days' growth on his face, rough and unruly hair, a sort of granite composure, slight build that was not impressive but eyes that were strong and unwavering. On the wall she faced was an A4 sheet of paper showing the twin ends of a stone ruin with walls around the chimney stacks that were two feet thick, indestructible. The side walls of the building were perhaps six feet high and fashioned from rough-hewn blocks, and Jonas realised that at no stage in his adult life could he have moved one of them. The door frames were gone, and the windows were open spaces and, beyond the wreck that had once been a home, was a tumbling stream in near spate and a faint hillside and then a dark ceiling of cloud.

Jonas said, crisply, "Sarah, at rather a critical time, I am being deluged with calls. I would be grateful if you could return to the third floor and field them."

She turned to face him. Her complexion was pale, her eyes reddened. A small voice, one that tried to act out that the question was unimportant, asked, "Is Croppy back out?"

He shrugged. The world moved on. Croppy, the surveillance, was history. "I suppose so. Why not? On his way home, isn't he? I have to get up to the third floor again."

Jonas started for the door. He heard her chair scrape as it was pushed back, then her footsteps followed him.

As Jonas reached the door, Vernon chipped in: "Mr Merrick, 'Why not' is because he went back, to that village, Croppy did, because he had left his gear behind – night sight, bins, camera, defence weaponry, all that stuff that telegraphed he was there. She's not heard that he's on his way out yet. But I suppose you knew that."

He kept walking. Had to because he did not know how to reply, and she followed him.

He was near to breaking: Skender knew it.

One of the men had removed the headset, had lifted the hood and had poured water from a bottle over his face. He stood on the plastic sheeting and each time it moved, his feet slithering, Skender heard it. He was also aware of the low voices but could not hear what was being said because his ears still rang with the shrill whines and moans from the headphones and into his ears. It was what else he heard that pushed him closer to a cliff edge.

Tormented by that unnatural noise, Skender felt the presence of his sister. She was in front of him, beside and behind him. The water that had been splashed into his face had flowed in to his mouth and throat and had dribbled down his chin and across his chest and some spattered lightly on the floor where his soiled trousers and pants were at his ankles. He could see his sister because he could hear her . . . He recognised the snap as the blades of the shears closed, and the stunted screech as they were opened wide, then the clatter as they were rammed shut. Like the scissors that had been used to cut the pieces of plastic sheeting that were now in place to catch the blood that would flow when they sliced or sawed pieces from his body . . . After a fashion, perhaps and only from a sense of personal pride, Skender had believed he might hold out, lose an ear, a fingertip, the flesh at the end of his nose – but have a degree of honour intact. Could go back to his village, pack the few items that were of personal value to him, and write a note that would be left on his bed, and be gone. Into the night, his car disappearing into the mist that would shroud the valley. A sense of honour had seemed important to Skender . . . and now it flowed away as if into a gurgling drain. Why? He saw his sister and heard the scissors.

The sound of the scissors closing, sharp and brutal, was amplified because one of the them, who talked indistinctly, held an object, might have been a pen, or the upturned handle of a screwdriver, or a metal cigarette lighter, and was banging it on the table. It had been intentional to corrode his willpower, weaken his resistance: the hood and the stress posture against the wall, the hunger and thirst, and the uncertainty of when pain would be inflicted. All from a textbook, the five principles of enhanced interrogation. But this was different, accidental, not programmed. They could not have known. Whoever they were, whoever they worked for, could not have known . . . He knew – which was why he saw his sister.

The scissors opened and closed, reinforcing the sound of the rhythm banging on the table of the pen, the screwdriver, the lighter, whatever it was. The sounds merged and the greater noise seemed to match that made when his sister – troubled, deranged – opened the shears and then flexed her muscles and closed them. Klea was close to him, he could not escape from her. Might have been chained in a cellar, might have been manacled against a wall. There could be no plastic sheeting in the cellar under that building in the heart of his village, facing the square in front of the villa. He thought her best dreams were of having a trussed victim offered up to her and being able to go forward with the dirty blades opened towards fingers or toes or prodding between legs . . . and Skender found himself starting to writhe.

Klea had been a normal child. Like any other child who had parents from an influential crime clan. Would have been attractive at that age – four years old – and not yet aware of the dangers, and the privileges, awaiting her. A life mapped out, dictated by grandparents, then by parents, and involving an education and a choosing of suitors, and perhaps a spell at one of the universities in Italy, studying finance and business, and a wedding that would ally their clan to another prominent Albanian family. Any boy who had looked at her, touched her, flirted with or kissed her – let alone fucked her – before the chosen guy would have been taken out to a bit of woodland and kicked and hurt plenty and then had a bullet put in the back of his head, and likely his parents would have been charged for it. That was seven years ago, but everything changed when she had travelled with her parents to Durresi. She would have died with them had she been sittting up right and playing with her tablet or her dolls, but had been asleep. It was a miracle that she had survived, unmarked and apparently unharmed. Had said at the hospital, while her mutilated mother and father were under the pressure hose in the mortuary, that it was the clear work of St Nicholas, the country's national saint for seventeen centuries. She had come back to the village, would barely speak to anyone except their grandfather.

He knew she had used the shears, and knew that she would use them again when, *if*, he ever returned to collect what he would take, write his notes, then disappear. Would keep her shears safe, and the one-eyed dog that pitifully followed her, and her fucking goats. The noise of the blades and the beat came together and had seemed louder as his ears had been freed from the sound pouring into his brain from the headphones.

He was untied, and his weight sagged. A big man held him upright and manoeuvred him across the plastic. He saw his sister, her cold and lustreless eyes, dead like a goat's, and the snapping came closer. He was in the chair, and the tape was used to pinion him. His hood was lifted and the light shone straight on to his face. The woman was in front of him, cross-legged on the floor, and was below the light's beam, her face in deep shadow. She asked him if he was comfortable. The man who had carried him was now behind her and held the cigarette lighter. He nodded.

"That's better, Skender, much better. We have the knife, we have talked about which piece of you we will take off first, but we don't want to do that. Prepared to, but don't want to. We have no hostility towards you, personally. We're just looking for the infor-mation you can give us – and then we can all go home – in your case back to that pretty girl you left in the ski town. Don't doubt for one moment, Skender, that we will put you through the misery of huge pain. That is why we were sent because our employers know we do not give a fuck what we do to you. Make it easier for us, Skender, because then it is easier for you. Got me?"

He nodded again.

"Don't disappoint me."

He was shivering and the chair moved on the plastic and the noise was still in his ears and her sister was in his face.

A whisper from Sword, "Go for it, Cress."

And from Tank, "He's about to piss himself – all the brave stuff is down the khazi."

Tank heard the snap of Sword's scissors and could not have said why he started to match the rhythm with the handle of the box cutter knife, and could see the poor bastard's shrunken genitals and . . .

She said, soft and clear and in her own language, "We'll do this in my language now, Skender. Enough mucking about in yours. I watched and I see it in your eyes that you know what we are talking about. English, yes?"

Again, he nodded.

"I want to send you back to your girl, and I've no more argument with you . . . The instructions, Skender, what you were taking as courier from your village and into Geneva. Where are they, the instructions?"

She saw the collapse coming like rocks that teetered above a high cliff, resolve slipping.

"Where, Skender?"

The wet came down his leg, Tank saw it steam in the lamp's beam and flow to the plastic spread on the floor and make a puddle there. A final shove and the rock would plummet down.

"Last time, Skender, where? You owe nobody anything, only yourself and your girl. Where?"

A blurted answer, in his own tongue. A jumble of words and gasps, like it was an agony but, Tank felt, less of an agony than having his bollocks sliced.

She said, "When we put the lights on, guided him into that slip road, it was then that he dumped his load. Put this package and what he had to deliver in Geneva under his driving seat. It is my fault and your fault, Sword, and Tank . . . We all reckoned he would have it on him or at worse in his bag and not left in the car. A brown envelope and Skender's writing on the outside, just *Rue de Place de la Fusterie*, only that address. That is the car that we left with our new 'best friends', made an offering to them to break it up, detach and flog. It is where it is, or *was*, and can but go have a look. Tell London that we've done a clusterfuck? I don't think so. Tell them something when we know it, but right now we need to go and look."

A matter of importance? Hardly.

A member of the commandant's staff, walked into a dormitory hut inside the wire surrounding the IK-2 complex.

A matter of convenience? Certainly.

She checked her tablet for the bunk numbers. The ceiling lights were subdued and cold air wafted the length of the building. The windows were supposedly sealed but draughts broke through them, and snow piled on the sills and the lights above the coils of perimeter wire pierced the window blinds. The woman was ill-suited to the work, and wished to that faint image of a God that she acknowledged that she had never heard of the FKU Corrective Colony No.2, Mordovia, and, more importantly, had never applied for a posting here . . . must have been drunk when completing the application form.

She walked up the aisle of two-tiered bunks, checking numbers as she went. The smell hit her, the scent of hunger and cold, and she would have said, of despair.

Previously she had worked in the administration office of a youth offenders' institution and it had been put to her that a move to IK-2 would likely lead to career advancement. She hated the place, thought it brutal for its own sake, unnecessarily violent, relying on a forced labour regime and without a sense of care for inmates. She knew about the women to whom she would speak. Had seen them in the commandant's outer office when they had come, by appointment and within the regulations of the camp, to protest against living and working conditions. She had been there eight months, and knew that one among that small collective had been freed – through influence – but those remaining complained more often, and with accuracy, in relation to orders from the centre. The criticisms went to the Ministry, which was demanded by their traditions, and clogged the smooth running of the place. Always there was an inquiry running on the section of the camp, this dormitory . . . as if they had nothing better to occupy their time.

She held a torch and followed the numbers. Came to two bunks, one frame. When she came off shift she would go back to her staff quarters and would strip down then pad to the heated washroom, would shower, scrub herself and seek to erase that smell, that taste. She sympathised with this foursome who waged a conspiracy, a provocation, against the administration. Not a thing she would have dared to mention in the staff mess . . . her torch beam found the numbers, and ranged over the neatly made beds on the two levels, both empty. She stared down and then up at the next frame, saw bright eyes reflecting back. Two beds, two pairs, perhaps for warmth and perhaps for precious companionship . . . Herself, she could have entertained a man or a woman in that place, in the staff sleeping rooms and not been disappointed with either. It was bitterly cold in the dormitory, close to freezing, but she rated "companionship" as the more important for them . . . perhaps for herself.

She checked her tablet, saw the names, identified the numbers. She would not show sympathy because that would be exploited, and ruthlessly. She was watched, challenged. They could have claimed that to disturb their sleep was a violation of their rights since they were expected to work shifts, with minimal breaks, of fifteen hours . . . she could have claimed that for women prisoners it was against the rules to sleep two in a narrow bunk bed, regardless of the cold. She doubted, when her statement was absorbed, that a complaint would be lodged, nor would she report their violation of accepted practices.

She steadied herself, named them, and saw eyes blink in the light, and read four lines. They would leave on Thursday at dawn. Locations to which they would be moved, separately, would be known before they left. Shifted for "administrative convenience".

Only one of them seemed to flinch, and that was the English woman. She turned on her heel . . . realised that once they were dispersed their individual capacity for disruption would be fractured.

Brave women? Yes.

Stupid women? Certainly.

Broken women? Inevitably, she thought.

On a rock, her dog pressed against her legs as if gaining warmth, Klea sat in the darkness.

She watched, and she waited, and she knew.

She had no torch and the lights from the village did not reach this high. The cold made pimples on the skin of her arms and legs, the wind whipped across her face, and a light layer of snow rested on her hair.

Clouds were carried on the wind that came down the valley, sometimes high and thin, more often heavy and laden, and there were moments when the cloud ceiling disintegrated and the light of the moon could break through, but not at that time of the evening. If the wind was behind it, and not blowing from her and her goats and her dog, then a brown bear might edge close but would back off if it sensed her presence, and there might be a sure-footed fox prowling but that also would retreat if it was aware that she had a dog. It was possible that wolves would be attracted by the smell of her animals but her presence would frighten them . . . Once, on a foul evening and with a storm at its height, she had caught a glimpse of a lynx, perhaps less than 50 metres from her. Klea told her grandfather everything she saw, and if he did not believe her then she would punch his frail, thin arm. Most times he believed her.

A vehicle's headlights came down the road and towards the village. The lights were dimmed enough to see the road, but not broadcast the arrival. She noted it, thought it unnecessary for her to look again. She could have said where the visitor came from, what was his business . . . she settled back to watching the slope of the mountain before the cloud made a ceiling.

She would wait, and had confidence in her patience.

She had told her grandfather he would come back, knew it.

Wine was in him, and *raki*, 50% proof, and what his precious child, the lumpy creature with the changed mind and unchanged dress had told him. The *shef* had refused to eat with his wife that night. Was at a table that would have seated a dozen, on his own, his wish.

The man had been shown in, and hovering behind him was the courier who had brought an envelope from Belgrade.

He could reflect on his own mortality . . . no clan leader died happily and in the family's bosom, asking if he remembered the "good times". The clan leaders usually died in a prison hospital, or in a gutter with 38 calibre rounds in their gut or their skull, or they died with a whore in a cathouse, or with a heart explosion of pain. He faced a crisis and accepted it.

The man was GRU, came from the Belgrade station. Had been before and had not shown respect then – showed none now.

"He is fucking missing. He is a 'no show', and you say you know nothing."

Face reddening and eyes flashing. "I know nothing."

A finger jabbing in his face. "He is missing. Confidential papers are missing. Where the fuck is he?"

"I will not be spoken to as if . . ."

Interrupted, shown as respect, and a Russian junior intelligence officer standing wide-footed in his office on a carpet with a value of 100,000 euro, and behind the man was a painting of a two-headed eagle that was worth some 75,000 euro, and a machine pistol was mounted on a wall, an MP40 from the war with the Germans, captured from an officer by the clan leader's own father . . . And the alcohol ran in him and the food weighed in his belly, and the hurt was great because he had no answer.

"People believed you. People who are both powerful and fucking stupid. You are a fucking pygmy in comparison to real power. Maybe you are just as fucking stupid. Where is your boy? Is his head between a girl's thighs? Is his head blown away with coke, or heroin? Where the fuck is he?"

"I don't know."

"What communication from him?"

"None."

And they could both hear activity on the floor above, along the corridors from the annexe where his grandson lived, coming down the winding, gilded staircase and into the hallway, and through the open door of his office where he sat, humiliated, and he believed their power. They were searching Skender's rooms. He could have had the thugs thrown out, pitched from the front door, he could have had them shot, tied up and thrown into their cars, fuel caps unfastened and coiled newspaper thrown inside, could have had them taken to the cellar of the building across the square. Could have gone outside and screamed into the evening darkness for that mad child to come back and bring the rusted shears, and use them . . . but he did not dare.

"You are dead meat . . ."

The voices called down that they had found a piece of paper with the name of a car hire company at Geneva airport, also the name of a hotel where he was booked for the night before his meetings . . . and people were on their way from the station in the Berne embassy . . . He did not dare to fight them and remembered the noise he had heard as a child of a rock falling from the hills above the village, an incessant rumbling before the crash, homes destroyed and a road blocked – impossible to withstand its force. And so it seemed to him.

". . . some clever game. Every fucking bone in your body will be broken – and those of your wife, and your grandkid. Every fucking one of you. You are finished."

He believed it.

"That is better, Jonas. Much better. I'm pleased for you."

The cat was in Vera's arms. The street lights were on, the evening gloomy, and he had left Thames House with Sarah back at the desk in his cubicle . . . The matter of her boy was not referred to again. He had no idea what he would have been expected to say to her, and his mind had moved on – and his phone had stayed silent, and no report yet from the safe house in Geneva. The plan had taken weeks to think through and more weeks needed to beg for the resources from the American agency, and more weeks to assemble his team, and Croppy. He was determined that he would not play the helicopter, hovering over them, and he tried to shut from his mind the situation the Albanian boy might be in. Three times the face of Denys Montgomery had appeared on his phone screen, and each time he had switched him off – and Solly Kravnic had been on and each time ignored. Now, Jonas approached his front gate and the narrow path beside the hard shoulder where the caravan was parked, and Vera and Olaf were there to greet him.

"I am tired, am feeling my age – what is 'better'?"

"Your walk, Jonas, is better."

"Not been an easy day, not easy at all. Sort of teetering . . ." and he pushed past her, not prepared to discuss his work crises on the pavement. The door was ajar and she used her toe to open it, then put the cat down on the hall carpet, helped Jonas shrug out of his raincoat and lodged his trilby on the hook above it. He wanted to put on his slippers and sit in front of the snug fire, eyes closed and only hearing, feeling, what was familiar and comforting – not wondering, in his name, what torture a man was enduring. Could have said that the future of a tyrant was in the balance, that a despot's regime might be shaken to the depths of its foundations, might collapse, might survive intact. Might put his pipe in his mouth, not light it of course inside the house, but enjoy the taste of it. "How is my walk better?"

"Watched you all the way up the road. You were not strutting. *Strutting*, Jonas, did not look well on you. Back to earth, and you are better for it."

A smile from her, and she was in the kitchen and the kettle was on, and she started to tell him about a client and two very pleasant watercolours sold, and no haggling about the price ... The message she was sending him was clear. In his own home, with her and Olaf, his work was uninvited, the tensions it brought not wanted ... Perhaps Vernon hinted to his wife of a "difficult day" because of the stress felt by a young woman for whom he nominally had a duty of care, and Aggie Burns had no one at home to greet her and would likely share her problems with a bottle, and the AssDepDG would likely still be in his office, also waiting for a call and mulling the future and repeating a quote from a leaving party where a former Fiver had quipped, *the best kept secret at Thames House – there is a life outside*, and Brian, DDG, would doubtless be arriving at his Pall Mall club with an evening ahead of him entertaining a dreary Finn or Egyptian in the same business. He knew of no other life and it was a treadmill.

"Thank you, dear ... it would be good to strut a little. Trouble is, I have nothing right now to strut for. Convinced myself I had, but it was an illusion ..."

He had done good time, but not good enough.

There had been delays on the road into the mountains after leaving Podgorica and Matt, and letting the diplomat follow in his own car while he had battered on astride the Vespa. There had been a tree down and a swarm of men gathered with chainsaws but the road was not yet cleared, and there had been another hold-up for him because of cattle on the road and his effort to get past had drawn anger from the farmer and his sons.

The new schedule would lose him the night hours.

In darkness Croppy lay a last time in the cramped space of the hide. He wanted out but could not because all his instincts – a man trained to work from a Covert Rural Observation Post and to move safely and over rough ground – prevented him from taking that risk. He had arrived too late ... had reached the hut, had packed everything he could see without using a torch, then had made his way to the hide. Had thought he had given himself a window but lingering on the main road while the tree was cleared and the cattle corralled, had closed it. And worse . . . the moon was creeping up when he was ready to leave the hut and he'd reckoned if that light held constant he could get across the rocks and stones and gullies and into the hide, five minutes needed to stow what he had left there. But the cloud had come back, and rain with it, and what light he had needed was denied.

Easy to imagine. Dumped on the hillside, in the open and above the tree line, and an eighteen-inch tumble with boots slipping and a broken ankle. Remembered the corporal in the SRR who had left equipment in a hide when the Chinook had come to take him away, and a warrant officer, fierce even by Special Reconnaissance Regiment standards, had icily ripped him apart for his carelessness.

Some freak in the cloud formation and he saw the moon. Pure silver.

In those few seconds, Croppy saw her. On a rock, still as a statue.

It was Croppy's nature to think well of her, to harbour a genuine pity for her condition. He had seen her, her dress with the patch-work of panels that increased its length and its width, plastered against her body, and her hair flat on her head, and the dog pinioned against her, and the goats close. She had stared ahead into the darkness of the rock face.

Behind and below her, in that moment of moonlight he had noticed that, there were more cars outside the villa than usual, men lounging beside them . . . But not the business of Croppy who only needed time to clear his hide, gather what he must take, and slip away in the first grey of the dawn. He assumed, by now, the work of the thugs in Geneva was done and the curtain had lowered.

The dogs came to meet the car, a pack of them.

She asked "You ever had rabies, Sword?"

"Not for a couple of weeks, Cress. Think they'll go for our throats?"

"Better than evens chance."

They had hardly spoken on the way out from Le Lignon, down a hill and into the city, and then over the big bridge crossing the Rhone. They had driven through a couple of red lights on either side of the bridge, but on their side was the fact that the bankers' city went to bed and to work. Had hit deserted streets, and up and out and into the countryside where a shiver of moon made it through the cloud ceiling. Had not talked because there had seemed little point, and would further erode confidence in the outcome – which stayed low, bumped on the bottom. What they had spoken of briefly was the blame game and who would glad-hand them in London with the news, and the shrug, and the helpless smile. Cress had said she would, but Sword had reckoned that a man, in days of diversity – much of which mercifully avoided his billet – prevented him from avoiding a gentleman's action. He would call. Give it the soft soap. *Sorry, but we did what we could. Bust a gut trying.* That had been settled and little more left to talk of . . . she drove well, and her trousers were tight on her thighs and her anorak, grabbed as they had run from the block, was open. Only on the rarest of occasions, like a funeral, did Sword stop wondering when the next trophy might turn up, but did not think this was the time to consider positives and negatives.

There were faces at his window.

Slobbering jaws, yellow teeth, deep throats, and flopping tongues and all up on two legs and bashing the glass. He gave them a finger. Cress drove on and seemed unbothered. There were cables that crisscrossed the space at the end of the lane and occasional bulbs dangled from them. Some were bright, some were faint, and their headlights played over a mess of caravans parked without pattern . . . The kids came in a swarm. The dogs were kicked, tugged, pushed and drifted back and the kids were fearless. Cress braked.

"Onwards and upwards."

"Thinking only of Britain and the King."

He was out first, had better French than she did, insufficient to pass an exam but would do in a gypsy park. "Take me to your leader," would do it. Remembered the guy they had dealt with before, and the scar across his forehead and thinking that if this guy had won that fight then his opponent must have been in bad shape. Ioan was his name. He had his wallet in his hip pocket. She locked the car behind her, before kids engulfed it.

"Get the show on the road," he said.

"I don't have a better idea," she said. As she had killed their headlight, he had noticed the skeleton of a car close to the tree line. The doors were off, and the tyres and wheels, and the bonnet, and most of the engine had been taken.

No point him looking at her, and no point her glancing at him. They used the lights on their phones and walked towards it. What they could see of the paintwork matched what they had followed out of Chamonix, and it was the newest addition to the graveyard. The two front seats were both out.

Pushing, shoving, the kids, with their escort of dogs, took them to the edge of the camp where shadows hung long and where the trees dripped heavy rain. The seats were dumped in a heap along with those from other cars, and already mud had settled on them. She swore, and they started the trudge back towards their car.

Ioan stood there, gut bulging over his tracksuit bottom. He pointed into their car. Sword knew he had locked it when they had left it, but the driver's door was open.

An envelope was on the driver's seat. Beside it was Sword's wallet. Cress reached past him and snatched up the envelope. Sword grabbed his wallet hand and flipped it open – all the cash had gone – and he remembered the barging and pushing from the kids, and had not noticed the wallet leaving his pocket. They climbed back into the car. He supposed it a streak of luck that the wheels were still on, and the engine came to life, and the tank had not been siphoned. When he turned his head he saw that Ioan was closing his caravan door behind him: he assumed they would have found the envelope when the hire car was stripped, expected him back, kept it ready, and the bonus was that the kids had lifted his wallet, relieved it of some 1000 euros. She drove away and up on to the slip road and then the highway, and her foot stamped on the accelerator. He made the call. A young woman's voice, no excitement expressed, just formal thanks.

He had his arms around her, she had one hand on the wheel and the other holding his face, and their tongues licked each other.

"What do you call that?"

She said, "I call it satisfactory, quite satisfactory."

First they nearly went off the road, then nearly off the fast lane and into the barrier. They took the envelope back to Swiss territory, and the airport.

Clouds broke apart and light seared. Croppy glanced at his wristwatch and saw that he was now in the "small hours", the time that nurses said old people passed on. The area in front of Croppy was lit, then the wind came and blew away the light and the cloud scudded back. It had been a good time for him, whether asleep or just halfway there, and he had been thinking of his girl and that had calmed and comforted him . . . The light had come and gone. The same minimal period as before, just a few seconds. He had looked out through the slit in the rocks and had seen where the ground fell away. Had noticed the stone with a layer of pale textured lichen, where she had sat, and the layer of smaller rocks where the dog and goats had lain. . . . Croppy would not see her again, would not think of her again . . . and thought of Sarah, picturing her at the controls of the digger, with the gutting knife and a shot stag, learning to put slates on roof beams, and slow cooking venison heating on a stove. Thought of it.

Croppy slept again, or maybe dozed.

His phone wobbled on the bedside table.

Jonas snatched for it, missed it. He had lurched from sleep into a wide awake state and his body heaved. The cat was disturbed and hissed at him. He reached for the phone, missed it again and heard it clatter to the floor.

From Vera, "Oh, for heaven's sake, Jonas, put the light on, pick it up, answer it."

He swung his legs clear then went down on his knees, retrieved it from under the bed.

He was, at that moment, almost frightened to answer it. Might hear what he wanted to hear and might hear what he dreaded hearing. Too many hackneyed phrases cavorted in his mind but chief among them was *Nothing ventured, nothing gained.*

He heard an exasperated sigh beside him. Vera did not have to tell him, one more time, to get on with it, answer the phone, switch the light off, go back to sleep. . . . If it were *failure* it would be laid at his cubicle door, the load his alone, not shared and he would endure the inquest without an ally, would be alone at Thames House for the few hours before they were able to cobble together a quorum and get a kangaroo court in place . . . If it were *success* then they'd be queuing round the block to trumpet their own contribution to the triumph, and maybe he'd be called on high for a glass of sherry . . . Or it would be what the surveillance team in A Section called a "score draw", like nothing had really happened: could be that Sarah was going home, was alerting him to a hair appointment, had a session with the dentist, had a day off booked, had . . . He pressed the button, connected.

"Merrick."

He was told the Geneva end had come through.

"And . . .?"

He was breathing in, little panted spurts. She told him what Geneva had reported.

Jonas said, "I am going to repeat what you have told me and you must interrupt if I have it wrong . . . Geneva says that they persuaded their target to tell them where to locate the packet of instructions he was taking from his village to Geneva to be given to investment managers, lawyers, accountants. The packet is now retrieved and is in the hands of the team. That is a fair digest?"

"Yes."

"Sarah, it is important now that we act in haste, and I authorise you to send the Gulfstream from Guernsey to Geneva, on arrival to pick up the package and fly it with minimum delay back to the Channel Islands and there it will be delivered to . . ."

A soft voice, without emotion, no excitement or point scoring. "I have already done that, Mr Merrick. The plane is in the air."

Almost annoyed at her calm, he rasped, "And you'll have on file a number for a Mr Kravnic of Langley. Please inform him."

"That is Mr Solomon Kravnic, the Agency. I've told him of developments. What he calls the Trojan Mustangs will be ready – 'bright and bushy-tailed', he said – for the packet's arrival in St Peter Port. He'll speak with you later, when you're in."

"And there is a Mr Denys Montgomery from over the river, I'll . . ." His voice died, and he sensed the answer and was correct in the assessment.

"He'll be waiting for you at the Lambeth Palace end of the bridge."

"Thank you, Sarah."

"Goodnight, Mr Merrick. It seems to have gone well. I'm glad."

He was about to ring off, and perhaps she waited in anticipation of one more remark. He should have been leaping around the bedroom, bouncing off Vera's chest of drawers and her dressing-table and the chair on which his jacket and trousers lay. Should have been punching the air. Did not. It came to Jonas as an after thought, not important, but best said.

"Take the rest of the day off, Sarah, and be with your boy. Did well, didn't he, in that early stage?"

The voice, said, "He's not back yet. A lad from the embassy over the border is watching for him. Hasn't made the rendezvous, is delayed. Good night, Mr Merrick, and I'll be here when you get in."

Hard enough in these matters, his limited experience, of keeping to schedules. Delays were inevitable, not crises. He switched off the light. Climbed back into bed. Vera very soon would start to snore softly and the cat rumbled pleasure that peace had returned. He doubted he'd sleep: remembered the photograph of a young man's face and a ruin that had chimney stacks and no roof, and all else seemed increasingly irrelevant – and wondered what the next day would bring, and was fearful of it.

IO

"I have to say it, Jonas. It is amazing where you have put us."

Jonas Merrick hardly broke stride. He came from under the wall of Lambeth Palace and crossed the main road, and had reached the south side of the bridge, and wondered fleetingly how long Denys Montgomery had waited for him.

He answered, "A little way along the road."

"I meant it sincerely. Incredible what you have achieved."

And Jonas saw the genuine admiration, and thought the man who fell into step beside him had been awake for most of the previous night whereas Jonas had slept steadily, had shaved carefully and wore a clean shirt and clean underwear and clean socks, and had polished his brogues while Vera had made his sandwiches and filled his thermos.

"Nothing to 'strut' about," he murmured and allowed himself the liberty of a brief smile. "Perhaps the end of the beginning, not – emphasised *not* – the other way about."

"The latest news from your hackers – I have to say it, Jonas, but this operation goes back to the glory times of my lot, the fifties and sixties of the last century, and I have to say that it would not be countenanced now in my building. Anyway, the hackers, are they through the defences?"

Jonas shrugged, which meant very clearly that he was not chasing after updates and had not been sent them. They talked . . . all a matter of timing – assumed that a positive result was forthcoming from St Peter Port and the geeks flown in – and the need to synchronise, what Vera would have called crossing "i"s and dotting "t"s, and then chuckling. Except that timing was everything, and if events did not mesh then all he had planned and prepared for was wasted effort. Quite blunt in that assessment . . . and he would not dispute the judgement of Montgomery that this was old-fashioned thuggery and better suited to former times – the Cold War, the colonial unrest at End of Empire, and the final throes of the Raj campaign in the Province when bombings and assassinations had often shifted the balance of power in government's favour.

The Sixers would not contemplate such action as Safety Deposit; nor would his Fiver bosses. Had there been a committee set up to examine his proposals, and he'd outlined what he intended to do, and achieve, then there would likely have been guffaws of laughter round the table, then eyes narrowing, mouths smirking, and heads shaking at the very idea of it, and likely the meeting concluding with the suggestion that *You might consider, Jonas, either taking some leave and having a damn good rest, or getting to know your garden more thoroughly and on a permanent basis . . . Fond of caravan holidays, I hear, Jonas, perhaps an opportunity to stretch them out . . .* And they would have dismissed his thoughts before the necessary break for coffee and shortbread biscuits had come round.

Halfway across the bridge and the wind was sharp and it was necessary for Jonas to grip the brim of his trilby, and his coat flapped at his knees and, for a moment, he allowed himself to look to his right, at the dark swirl of water, at a tug with a load of barges filled with refuse, at a floating gull, and remembered . . . a hell of a splash when he, and *she*, had gone in – and under. Terrifying, and handcuffs linking them. He did not know why she had abandoned an apparent suicide effort, taking him as her persecutor with her, and reverted to survival, but making sure that she could free herself at her own wrist, and leave him where his rescue was pretty much guaranteed . . . And this man, matching his stride into that northerly wind, loved *her*. It was love that drove it . . . and damn sure that the sub-committee would have laughed if he had claimed that "love" was a potent reason for launching the business. Without Denys Montgomery's concept of love, then Safety Deposit would not have been thought of, and the elaborate meshing of timings and people would not have happened. It would kick in if those strangely talented people, the Trojan Mustangs, were able to out-think, out-perform, the men or women who dealt in firewalls . . . not that Jonas understood any of that, challenged when a light bulb needed changing. The woman, Frank, had saved his life twice over. Enough reason? Certainly . . . He stopped abruptly.

"Denys, convince me she is worth saving. Much less compli-cated if we simply cut her adrift. Without the issue involving her, we would be, I venture, at the 'beginning of the end'. Have a go at it, convince me."

His arm was gripped. The traffic nudged past them. Headlights beamed at them and the streetlamps threw a gloss on to their shoulders and Jonas' hat and Montgomery's thin, greying hair dancing in the wind. Dawn on the way on a winter morning and rain seeming to gather in the clouds.

Montgomery said, "I suppose you have a right to the answer, Jonas. Succinctly, it is an obligation. One of ours. Messed us about, but had cause. We failed her . . . missed out on duty of care. We get an impression of what has been leaked . . . after she ended up there, in Russia, she cooperated with them but at the margins. Names you at first, then rowed back on it and put her own life on the line for your protection, and is now in some bloody hellhole of a gaol. When I joined the Sixers there was a senior man who had been on the Military Attaché's staff in Saigon, early days of the American commitment. An American is wounded, needs a casevac. A section of his chums is under fire and cannot extract him, so a platoon is directed to add to the firepower, and they are pinned down so a company is deployed, and if that isn't sufficient then it will be a battalion, and up through a regiment. Getting a casualty out is not negotiable, he said, and rather admired that somewhat simplistic Yankee doctrine. I called it an obligation, Jonas, which is strong enough reason for me – and you?"

"It will do," he said.

Brave words, Jonas thought, but then talk was always cheap from behind the lines. Denys Montgomery had claimed that duty of care was "not negotiable", was an "obligation", and could not just be filed away under the heading of "collateral damage". They parted. Montgomery swung on his heel and headed off towards his own building, on the south side. Jonas went on down the slope and towards the roundabout and wondered if that particular shift of armed police were on duty or whether he would take his life in his own hands and venture into the traffic. He had his phone out and dialled his cubicle's number. It was answered immediately.

What news?

No news. That same small voice.

He was hurt, knew it. Managed it across the road and through the traffic, and bought his cappuccino and his pastry, and nibbled and sipped without enthusiasm and was ignored by the gardener. He went in through the side door, and would find her on the third floor, south facing, in Room 12 at a table in his cubicle . . . and what to say to her?

He was boxed. Croppy understood that.

There had been low cloud at first light. He might have been asleep. Difficult to judge how far his guard had been lowered, his innate caution dulled. He lay on his side in the hide and a fraction of light penetrated the slit in the rocks that served as his observation post. He had been about to start feeling around him, make an inventory of what was in the hide, what needed removing. Needed to be done fast while the light was minimal, and then he'd be gone. He had the camera, and the night vision gear, had waste in tinfoil packaging and two small bottles of his urine, and had three cartons of Meals Ready to Eat. Had just collected them when he heard breathing. Rough, and seemed scratched across a raw throat. Because of the low cloud he could see only a few feet from the hide, not as far as the villa, the village, or the football pitch, but he had seen the dog.

It had a nose that twitched as if to notify its alertness, and only one eye. He had seen it many times, always close to the girl's ankles unless she let rip a piercing whistle or a sharp cry and then it would shoot off to push one of her goats back into the little pack. The one eye was bright, the other dead, skin closed over its vacated socket. The dog lay a little lower than the opening between the rocks, might have been five yards from the gap between them. Croppy could smell himself, his own body odour, but not the dog's. It had yellowed teeth and mottled gums, and the gaze of the single eye never moved, and its breathing steady. The girl had materialised from the cloud, her white dress now filthy, her hair tangled, and she was two or three paces behind her dog.

This was bad ... worse was any reasonable evaluation of his situation. A whole further degree of worse had come when the new smell and the new sounds had intruded into the hide. A situation outside any previous experience. At home, working the hills above Kilchoan, he had not known life-threatening danger ... would have done in Syria except that when tasked forward from the base and watching ISIS homes – sometimes with Lofty beside him, and sometimes on his own he had known that he had only to press a button on his phone and guys would be running from the Ready Hut in their flying suits, and more would be on the big machine guns – and coming faster, no yelling necessary, would be guys from the Hereford deployment.

The dog and the girl were in front of him and the gap there was way too narrow for him to crawl through.

The hide opened out behind him, which had made it as good a place as he reckoned he could have found, which was where the smell was coming from – the goats as they milled around, the soft sounds of fur rubbing against fur, and stones being shifted as they moved. When he had seen her before he had assumed that bad luck, pure chance, had put this sad, afflicted girl close to him. Luck and chance playing an unpleasant trick. Croppy did not believe that now. He had been tracked, boxed.

One goat entered the hide, second and third close behind, and started tugging the gear he had collected, his camera, image intensifier, food, water, and waste, and he heard a crack. That might have been a lens fracturing. A mouth was against his ear, and a tongue slobbered into it. And a little more light was entering the hides and he could make out the items scattered around him. He had intended that the webbing bag would be the last thing he retrieved and would shift into his ruck sack. It was big enough to hold half a dozen cans of Coke, and in it were the bare minimum of what he might need in term of weaponry – three canisters of flash and bang, and three more of gas – and if he were to use them he would need to have soaked a cloth in what water was still in the hide and wrap it round his face to protect his eyes. The bag was to have been carried away with him when the light was good enough for him to risk crossing the hillside ground with no track. He had it close to his hand.

He did not know if the girl had hunted him down, or had happened on him. Little happened by chance in Croppy's world. The light grew and with it the growing certainty that the girl was busy in an act of destroying him. He felt paralysed, could not help himself. An epitaph: destroyed by a child.

He needed clarity of thought, and needed to anticipate what other surprises could ambush him. Felt the cold around him, and the clinging wetness of the air, and shivered.

"What happens to me?".

They had kept Skender tied to the chair, still hooded. He had been allowed to sleep lightly, and given a sandwich and a plastic beaker of water, but was still their prisoner.

"We haven't been told."

He had given them what was demanded of him the previous evening. Two of them had gone out and he had been left with one guy, and all the lights in the room had been switched off with the exception of the one beamed into his face, and he had been taken to the toilet. No idea how much later the two had returned and there had been low voices of elation.

He asked again; "What happens to me?"

"We don't know. When we are told we will deal with it. Perhaps you walk out of the front door after we've called a taxi for you. Perhaps you walk out of the door and we take you out of sight, off behind the bike sheds, put you down on your knees and put a bullet in the back of your skull. Perhaps we leave you here till Christmas. We don't know. What we're told to do, we do."

"I have a right to know. I cooperated."

The woman's voice; "Skender, get the message. You have no rights . . . We have no further interest in you. You are disposable. No interest in the putrid, scumbag crime clan that your family operate . . . and just so that there no mistakes in your mind, we have no regrets as to what was done to you. You got off light . . ."

"When will I know what you will do with me?"

"Sometime, maybe. Sometime, maybe not. Just sit back and enjoy the ride."

Would they have done what they had threatened? He'd no doubt they would have. He thought the threat had lifted and knew that soon he would start to feel guilty at buckling so fast.

Tank had slipped away and would be doing a brew in the kitchen, and Cress had started to strip the place down. She'd begun with the plastic sheeting and was crudely folding it, and she would swab the surfaces with bleach. Prints gone and DNA, and if the place stank that was not important. They had been careful entering and leaving and little of their faces would have shown up, and the paper trail they'd left behind at the airport was fake, and their features were deniable.

Word seeped, had that habit, thought Sword. Times had been hard and work scarce. Word was water and found a way to spread itself about. No detail, no exact scenario, but those who cared to know – private military contractors, principally – would hear that Tank, limited and honest and solid – and Cress, great girl and clever and would be a riot if ever in the mood – and himself, who of course had called the shots, had taken on a guy from the heart of a ruthless crime gang from the Albanian mountains – a "murderous gang of cut-throats and drug traffickers and girl smugglers and arms merchants" – and had bent him into such a corkscrew pose that he'd, good as gold, coughed up the information which he should have gone to his grave protecting. Would do them well, and would be able to go all coy when the matter came up for discussion. *Sorry, but details of past operations have to remain out of bounds. What I can say is that our customers were well satisfied, and further contracts will be shown the same dedicated service.*

Tank brought tea for Cress and himself, and a beaker of water for the boy. Sword and Cress behind him, and Tank at his shoulder, and lifting the hood and allowing him to sip, then tilting it so he had enough, then dropping the hood. They waited for the phone call. Good at waiting . . . and relished the thought of their reputation blossoming.

Another man, not Tank . . . another woman, not Cress . . . might have been puzzled as to how it had turned out so well and so fast, a success story with bells on it, and no idea why he'd capitulated when the box cutter had only broken his skin. What an old sergeant in his Catterick Garrison days would have called LMF, and grimaced, because Lack of Moral Fibre was about as low as a fighting man could sink. The boy was supposed to be a "fighting man", supposed to take it as well as hand it out . . . contracts would come wafting in when the word reached the people that mattered. Be a hero's welcome – among the few, very few, who'd need to know, and perhaps a stiff one from the cabinet of one of the top rankers in the hierarchy of the Service – and perhaps a bit of a cuddle from Cress if the mood took her. Plenty to look forward to. What would happen to him, to the boy? Couldn't give a flying fuck. Feel sorry for him? Not much.

What was it all about? Had been at the airport and seen the fast dropping lights of an executive jet coming in on the runway, and heard the roar of reverse thrust as it had slowed, and done a minimum of formality in handing the packet to a young cockpit guy with a poker face and a dried-out American accent, and seen him trot back across the apron and up the steps and a door easing shut and the Gulfstream was back into the night sky. Thought it had style, big time. No idea what it was about, not his business.

Apricot sat at her workbench and her right foot worked the pedal of the sewing machine. It was dark and overcast, and she worked on lightweight trousers for an infantryman, and supposed them suitable for a Ukrainian summer.

They had all been subdued at their session of compulsory physical exercise, and during breakfast – a tasteless gruel and some bread. She supposed that a dietician would have claimed that the food was sufficient to stay alive. Not worth her arguing the point because it was likely, and the four of them were committed to it, that today was the last day of her life. She worked diligently. Had she been asked, she would have been hard pressed to summon up a decent argument as to why it was necessary for her to stitch the garment pieces together with the same dedication as if the work would be repeated the following morning. If what she produced that day, that evening, was turned down by Quality Inspection then it would be flung back on that desk at dawn on Thursday . . . except that she would not be there – nor would Blueberry, nor Currant, nor Apple. Would be in the cold house, in a zip up bag, subject to a death certificate filled out in the hospital wing of IK-2. Sobering, except that she was sober. Frightening, and she was frightened. Best to concentrate on the work otherwise all that would be left for her to think about was *how* . . . That discussion was for later, when the shift was over, and they would huddle together in the dormitory and plan it – and give each other strength.

Frank's upbringing had not been challenging in any degree recognised by the prisoners held in Corrective Colony No. 2, Mordovia. Brought up by a cautious uncle and aunt, childless, stern, distant and well meaning. Education paid for out of their pensions. A job, found through contacts, in the Secret Intelligence Service. Life passing her by and men ignoring her. Until a foreigner, with a pocketful of plausible lies, targeted her at an am-dram group – and she discovered passion, what she thought was love, and little pieces of "help" were requested of her. She worked in the group in charge of defectors, had to sort through whether they were "dangles" planted by the intelligence services of Russia, whether they were high-grade traitors and worth breaking the bank for, or were merely disaffected. Worked there, unmasked there, broke out . . . Nothing that matched the cats' claw fights of Currant who had been with a group supporting Navalny; or Blueberry who had kicked a policeman's balls near out of his groin; or Apple who had taken documents that proved a bank fraud initiated by FSB to an Italian news agency, care of the embassy in Uliza Vesnina. Hard kids, tough, had taken what the state chucked at them, and now were just bored with the fight – and might want out if they were broken apart, dismembered. She thought them the finest people she had ever known, the bravest. She thought herself hardly worthy of a place in their group.

None of them spoke that morning. Did not make eye contact, nor touch each other. Frank thought they were all now afraid of breaking the solidarity. It would not be her who showed weakness – would not be, could not be. To be the one left alive would be the ultimate humiliation, unbearable. They would not talk until the food break at midday – more soup and more bread. Then the matters for discussion were simple: what method and when. It was on course and she thought it irreversible.

She sewed, thought she did well, might be praised by the supervisor for her diligence.

More coffee was brought to them, and waffles.

Three guys, all geeks, ploughed on in the boardroom of that discreet private bank above the harbour. The blinds were drawn, so no one had a view of the sea lapping in at St Peter Port. They would not have been interested in the history of the castle guarding the entrance, nor in seeing what yachts and launches packed the marina, nor in the pristine patios of pot plants surviving winter outside the banks. Private banks. Holding private wealth, discreet about who they gave office space to.

A thick fug of cigar and vape smoke filled their work area.

They ate their waffles with their fingers, and drank their coffee straight from the jugs.

In the heart of the night there had been a scream from the city, tyres turning fast on tarmacadam, and the lights of a police car with vehicle in pursuit and hugging its fender, and any islander disturbed enough to peer from a window might have believed that a transplant organ was being ferried to a hospital – beyond comprehension that a single padded envelope, size ten inches by eight, and half an inch thick, and addressed only to *Place de la*

Fusterie, and sealed with two lengths of Sellotape, was worth that noise, nor the time and cost of a Gulfstream jet at $9000 an hour, and add-ons, and fuel as extras, and the cockpit boys had been told to get their heads on pillows and try and make up the necessary rest hours because "God alone knows when you boys are up next, and where you're going." The dawn had come and the lights of the boardroom still burned. On the mahogany table were three laptops, and mouse pads that showed wild mustang horses. And heavy metal blasted the air, and fingers danced lightly on the keyboards – and occasionally, like the cheep of a small songbird, it would be made clear that one of the trio had penetrated a wall, broken it down, or wriggled below it, or induced it in its ignorance to open a gate and let in the Trojan beast. Notes would be made on A4 pads and would be gathered by their facilitator who had the patience of a suffering saint and joshed them without mercy. It was coming together . . . and one spoke out for all, yelling into the Cuban tobacco fumes.

"Fuck me, I thought they'd be better than this. They are shit."

But the big question was not yet asked, nor did their manager harry them for it. "When would they be finished and ready for the proactive strike, *when?*" Soon, not yet. Sometimes they would get up and walk around the table, and sometimes let go a blast of arse air, and sometimes scratch a scrotum and sometimes stand at a window and look up at clouds, and sometimes spill coffee on that polished table surface, and sometimes break another wall.

They were not guys who would be nagged. They all understood that big issues rested on them, possibly lives. Knew the importance of what they did, otherwise they would not have been called out. They were the best, aimed to prove it, and knew time was not their friend.

The growing light that tipped over the summits beyond the village was no ally of Croppy's.

He had nothing to occupy him in that last hour other than turning over the dilemma: when to go for the break-out.

The cloud had lifted. It was dry. A scattering of snow covered the high points far above the villa but most had cleared at the level of the hide . . . the goats had taken turns pushing inside and had rooted around his garments and his sleeping bag, and the rucksack with his gear, and wrappings of food items had been licked and worked over, and they had crapped on his ghillie suit. Which was all immaterial. What mattered to Croppy was when . . .?

It turned in his mind. Did he want to live because he yearned for the future – having a wife, having kids, having a renovated cottage in a backwater where eagles and red deer were the neighbours he and his family would know best, and growing old, and a warm bed . . . Or did he want to live because the alternative, in his situation, was likely to be extreme pain, inflicted agonies, the torture that would reduce him to screaming, death coming as the big relief. Mind made up. Decision taken. Would go for it – but always the matter of *when*. They did courses for the troopers in the reconnaissance teams on reaction to capture, and tried to create scenarios where it was almost real, and deployed Special Forces to rough them up, used darkened buildings, hurt them some . . . except that it was phoney. A line was drawn and no one wanted any of them in a hospital bed with a broken arm or a loose eyeball, or a resignation note on the boss's desk. They told the recruits that only the brave, the best of the brave, summoned up the *cojones* to go full blooded, no hesitation, for escape. Said that the longer the matter was left the weaker the degree of intent. The coward let the situation drift in the hope of something better. Big word that – *coward* – but it was one the senior instructor had used. Maybe in one minute he would go, or maybe in two minutes. If it worked out then it was a probable that they'd have him down to lecture recruits, run an Escape and Evasion session; if it didn't then he would be forgotten.

The girl, sat with her back to him, twenty yards from the front of his hide. The dog was nearer, half that distance, and his one eye never left the slit. Far below was the football pitch, and some kids had just reached it and might have a kick around before the school was opened. At the front gate of the villa stood the head man.

Croppy knew him well now, recognised that he smoked too much and was already into the first cigar of the day, and was dressed as if he was the CEO and waiting for a car to ferry him to an office tower, wore a suit and a shirt and a tie, and paced as if a torment wracked him. Each time that he paused and looked up and might have seen his granddaughter, he seemed to duck his head as if in a form of greeting, then turn away. Croppy could not see the child's face, but her shoulders never shifted and he thought she would have given her grandfather no acknowledgement. She seemed to hum a song, teenage stuff, but was tone deaf. Other kids messed in the square, and women were out of their homes and steps were brushed, and shopping bags carried, and washing lines filled. It was the dog that bothered him most because it had a meanness on its jaws, and teeth that were ragged and uneven, and he smelt its breath. There was an old tale of the special forces operating in the Province that was in his own regiment's folklore. A wild rabbit captured in a cage and taken to a hide, and if a farmer's dog came too close, was too interested, ears back and hackles up, and the farmer walking behind his dog and starting to watch it, then the cage would be opened and the rabbit pointed in the direction of the dog and let loose. It was hoped the rabbit would distract the dog, divert the farmer. Croppy had no cage, no rabbit.

Then cars came, and men piled out, and their protection hovered close and the boss, the *shef*, who was the grandfather, went to hug them but the gesture was not returned, and they went inside, and he'd looked up at the hill and the steep slopes where his granddaughter sat.

"You're only a side show," Jonas snapped into the phone.

A gasp at the far end of the line. Heard it. Would have been still dark there, and Solly Kravnic was up and about, trying not to wake his own household, only some 3650 miles away. It was a remark of rudeness and stupidity and would have still been winging its way across the ocean floor when he realised it . . . but he did not, of course not, apologise.

A terse response, "Maybe to you, Jonas, but not at our end."

The sideshow primarily involved Denys Montgomery and his efforts to tie in the freedom of his former personal assistant across the river at VX, Ceauşescu Towers, into a deal with the Russian state . . . a minefield. A sideshow because the principal concern was the hack into a meshed nest of accounts, investments, property deals belonging to the significant oligarchs feeding off the czar's table, and hopefully the czar himself. The fall-out, if the hacks penetrated deep enough, could be off whatever scale, Richter-style, measured open warfare between these good folk, and the stability of the state . . . Which was enough, Jonas could have said, to be going along with.

He took a step back, as far as he was prepared to go, a short step. Said without grace, "I'll add it to the shopping list."

"That will be two guys – one is a former paratrooper who went walkabout in Kaliningrad, strayed across the border, said he was researching battle sites from World War Two, crazy, just stupid . . . The other is some green zealot girl who cut a hole in a fence on the border with Norway and went inside to march single-handed on the town of Nikel which has a serious problem with chimney pollution from the cooking they do there of nickel ore. The two are banged up, and we'd like them back. They should be on your shopping list, aptly put, Jonas."

"Will that be all?"

"That'll do for now. Names will be with you in five minutes."

"Will do what I can, and no promise given. Had not expected that I might need a charabanc to bring them out. Please, remember, 'no promise given'."

"Which sounds strangely boring from you, Jonas. Suggest you go for it, make use of an opportunity. How are my Mustangs doing?"

"Waiting to hear. Thank you."

He rang off. Had been abrupt, had been combative, had been jolted by that description beamed at him. *Boring.* Was confused by it. A description not meeting his own assessments of himself. *Boring.* Was that how he was seen? He sat hunched over his screen.

He had balls in the air, attempted to juggle them, more balls than he had hands, and at that moment all were aloft, now more had been added. Sarah was behind him, and would have had her earphones in and would have registered the verdict of him, boring . . . Easy to realise that he had cut out for himself a role greater than he was capable of managing and he felt sweat rising under his collar and an ache in his head. Jonas, not a surprise to those who knew him, did not swim, had never been taught to swim, had never needed to swim, and was now floundering, out of his depth, and did not know from where a rescue might come. He had always thought of himself as little more than the functionary who, in a bygone age, made the trains run on time, pulled the crowded cattle wagons away from the stations and sent them off on their journey. A manager. Perhaps was just that, a "boring" little man. He poured coffee from his thermos.

From behind him, Sarah said, expressionless, "First, the Geneva team want to know what to do with the boy: I told them to wait out, keep him close. Next, in Peter Port, they're close to extracting what they call the jewels, another hour at most."

"Thank you."

"And nothing on Croppy. Still seems he's delayed."

"Again, thank you." Had no idea what else to say.

A cigarette shared in the lunch break away from their machines; outside, the temperature below freezing, and seeming not to notice the cold. The woman from Administration came outside, shivered and looked around her.

A black mood and black humour from Apple. "I thought of using a sheet, a good noose and tying it to a window bar and jumping off the bed – except the sheet would fucking tear because it's shit made, and I'd end up with a twisted ankle on the floor."

The woman saw them, wiped the sleet off her face and strode towards them, and the cigarette was passed again.

Blueberry said, "I reckoned I'd go for the perimeter, climb the wire, get shot from a watchtower – except the dozy bastards would likely miss and I'd be left up there to climb down, and they'd set a dog on me, but the dog would say, 'Come on, let's get out of this fucking place together' and the future would be lost in the bloody forest for ever and both of us eaten by a fucking bear."

A firm step, an advance and an officious posture. The fag had died and, force of habit, was pinched out and pocketed by Currant.

A simple message. A finger pointing in turn to Apple and then to Blueberry and then to Currant. They should be packed, ready to leave at 05.30 the next morning, Thursday, and so would not be required to do the physical exercise session. Frank, who was Apricot, stared at her . . .

And was told, "You are staying. Perhaps you go in a few days but maybe you do not. You stay – and attend physical exercise. That is all."

The thought lodged in Frank's mind. Did that absolve her from taking her life, as their pact had agreed? If they were to be split they would kill themselves. Agreed, confirmed with a kiss. A sisterhood's promise. Freed from it, or not? She gulped . . . they read her. They would have read her mind, her uncertainty as to whether she had escaped what was pledged. And they were three, and arms around each other, like they were a team . . . Frank's chin jutted. She was a part of them.

She joined them, hooked arms round her own shoulders, held them close to her and their breath made vapours, mixed and rising. *All for one, one for all.* Was joined to them. Was the nail rusty enough to kill with infection? Was the glass from the light bulbs strong enough to cut slivers in their guts where sepsis would breed?

The bell went. Obediently they went back into the work area to return to their machines and the quota of uniforms that must be finished before the end of the working day.

"What happens to me?"

And Skender was answered, "When I'm told, I'll tell you, but I haven't been told."

He doubted they would kill him. He was still hooded, had not seen their faces. The room had been cleaned and the plastic folded away and an hour ago it had been taken out of the apartment, and he assumed it binned. He would go home . . . would think on his feet, would discover the level of chaos, would lie and lie again, would confuse the old man who was his grandfather, have the idiot eating from his hand, hugging him, maybe kissing him, and would lie some more – and would make a reference to his girl, not load it with detail, perhaps talk of a holiday with her – would emphasise, repeat it, of his commitment to the family, but give some psycho-babble about needing "space", and more shit about love for his family and his commitment to safeguarding the future of his darling sister. Would go home, be gone within a day.

He waited.

Enough time gone? Too much time. Twisted and flexed his muscles and knew they would be cold, stiff, unresponsive after a night – and too much of a morning – motionless in the hide.

Croppy wriggled to get the rucksack on to his shoulders, and then the webbing bag with the canisters. Then more wriggling and contortions and getting the suit on but without fastening it. Ready . . . took a deep breath and knew that he was committed when he had a flash and bang in his left hand and a gas in his right.

Pulled a lever and the clasp broke and he was down to seconds and counting, used the flash and bang. Rolled it out through the slit and had that moment, frozen, when he saw the dog and the malevolence in its sole eye and saw her shoulders and saw also that the cars were still outside the villa, and the square was quiet and the kids were in school, and only a few men out and gossiping, and . . . he had counted the necessary and turned in the narrow low space where the great rocks had been dumped, and had twisted himself enough to be able to toss the gas, out of the back entrance to his hide.

The first one to go would be deafening and the light would blind anyone close to it. His head was averted. Inside the hide was as daylight, a brightest torch beam, and any noise would be held inside and magnified – and he had turned in the space and faced the wider back exit where the rocks opened – and the gas blew.

Croppy did not know what was there, if anything, anybody, was there. All of his training was about stealth of movement, and all he knew from the mountainsides where he could roam in pursuit of stags, called for caution and quiet. He was weighted down, his legs had stiffened like old branches, and his knees and ankles were clamped awkwardly, but he tried to run and could not see where he headed because of the thickness of the gas – potent stuff, military grade. Not the gas that would have done for kids in the Bogside in the old days, but stuff for serious players who needed incapacitating. He had his eyes squinted almost shut, and his nostrils squeezed tight, his mouth closed, depending on that last intake of breath to get him out, on his feet and going forward. And tripped . . . and went down, and pushed himself up and went forward again. His eyes hurt, stung like pricking needles, and nausea was in his throat. Not a time to slow, whatever the old rules had told him. He broke the clasp of a flash and bang and threw it behind him. Could see now what was ahead of him, and his ears just clearing from the first he had thrown, were wiped out by the second.

He was in a bubble of silence, and found a peace from the pain in his eyes only when they were closed. He seemed to move at the speed of an old man. For a moment Croppy reflected on the idiocy of the discipline that had sent him back to collect the gear that would have cost just a few hundred pounds to replace, and believed that its discovery would not lead to Sarah, to her guv'nor, or to him when he was safely back in Kilchoan, cleaning a rifle or digging the potato patch or . . .

Teeth stabbed the back of his shin. He turned, opened his eyes, and one gazed up at him. The single eye had that stare that he knew from a stag that was wounded by a client's bullet, could go no further. He had to steady himself while the pain ran in rivers and stood on the leg in which the dog's teeth were embedded, and kicked with his free boot. Kicked savagely, and felt the grip weaken. Perhaps the dog howled but Croppy did not know because his hearing was gone. Kicked again, and the hold was broken, and he was moving.

Half a dozen steps, in agony and slow, and Croppy believed he had broken free, and was heading in the direction of the hut and threw another of the gas canisters behind him. But there was a dragging weight on his legs and he could not break free. The girl had her arms round his legs and she clung to him with an animal ferocity.

He was puzzled, then annoyed, and it was seconds before the implication of what had happened belted Croppy.

Men were scrambling up the hillside, some with shotguns and some with staves, had come through the tree line. Even the old ones, gaunt and wizened, were sure-footed and moved quickly. Had to free himself . . . he could throw gas and flash bangs at them, but first he must be free.

Croppy looked down at the girl clinging to him.

Pure white skin at her throat and neck, a face that was weather washed and without blemish. She was looking up at him, bright eyes and an open mouth with full lips – and what he saw was her triumph; deserved it, had cause for it; she had made a fool of him. He was the stalker that the most knowledgeable of the clients requested when out on the Ardnamurchan slopes, the boy who had been reckoned as the pick of the recruits accepted that year into the Special Reconnaissance Regiment. He tried to tug at her hair but the grip on his legs held fast and he thought she laughed at him, but could not hear.

One chance left to Croppy.

Saw her neck, and the muscles knotted with her efforts. It had been the instructor's tour de force moment in unarmed combat lectures. Extend the right hand. Fingers straight, and the heel of the hand exposed. They would demonstrate it with a hapless goon, but not actually strike . . . A rabbit punch. A target point behind an ear above the collarbone, at the base of the neck. He readied himself. She was without defence. It was her or him . . .

Croppy hesitated. He had never hit a woman.

He had never quite recovered after the fast jets had flown from RAF Akrotiri on his identification of a target's presence – and

knowing the wives were there, and a servant woman, and children ... what they called "collateral". Quite soon afterwards
Croppy had quit.

The blow, done as the instructors had demonstrated, would kill;
if not done quite right would paralyse. She was a girl, still a child
– all his instincts prevented him from doing it.

The moment not been seized and a blow battered his shoulder,
and he went down, and many hands reached for him, and the
blackness come – as dark as when night fell on the strand of water
from the ferry dock and the last sailing had long gone. As dark as
that, and the fight over.

The message came from a boardroom inside a building used by a
small private bank in St Peter Port on the island of Guernsey. It
was sent to a Solomon Kravnic, resident of a condominium
convenient for the Agency and close to Washington, DC and also
to Jonas Merrick, occupying a cubicle on the third floor of Thames
House in London.

"All ready to go – await the shout for us to clear their screens."

If the message were acted upon, that decision would amount to
an act of undeclared warfare: a big-time deal, concocted by
Merrick and funded by Kravnic, and big stakes on the polished
table in the boardroom.

With a disinclination to share, Jonas was reluctant to discuss the
timetable for what he had called earlier that morning a "sideshow". Before, in his recent career, he had worked down
backwaters and been up cul-de-sacs. He thought this was different,
and the issues more toxic than anything he had tackled before. At
that moment of quiet, his phone on his desk, and gentle voices
reaching him from Aggie Burns' fiefdom outside his door, and the
gentle pattering of a keyboard as Sarah worked behind him, he
reflected that the matter now involved lying, untruths, deceptions,
and reflected also that he was well able to employ those weapons.
And his opponent was well versed in such matters, had a word for
military deception, *maskirovka,* and used the tactic often enough

for it to have become a cliché. The question in his mind ranged over the amount of time he could award to the sideshow.

He thought of the scales in a shop in the village where he had been brought up. The shopkeeper, wearing long brown coat over his shirt and tie, measured out sugar, boiled sweets, flour and rice, with tiny adjustments made possible by changing the weights. Thought of those scales. On one side would be the screens on which investments, cash and properties were listed and vulnerable to button pressing, wipe-out. On the other side, and needing to be balanced, was the sideshow and the wish that a woman be brought back from a prison camp with an errant battlefield historian and an eco-warrior. Nerves among a few of the affluent thieves in Moscow or St Petersburg would now be jangling, sounding alarm bells, because their courier had gone off the radar, and as they became more desperate they would demand that the bankers and investment managers and lawyers change the codes which had hidden their wealth – and a chance lost. How long before the codes might be re-set? A day or half a day – two days, maximum – and what benefit did the sideshow bring? Jonas could scratch his head or his backside . . . but fail to see the benefit of the sideshow. He rang Denys Montgomery across the river.

Was brusque, rude. Stress was eating at him. "Not negotiable, not for debate . . . you should meet with their people. You have half a day, until midnight, to gain their guarantee that the exchange will happen – the woman from your office along with the idiots the Americans want. And in return we will use our good offices to put, by unspecified means, their courier back in his village. Half a day for the guarantee and a day for the exchange. About a quarter of a minute after that the screens will empty . . . You tell them that one window is open, briefly. How do you explain that? You use your imagination."

He rang off.

It would now be moving at a stampede, unless – *unless* – the *maskirovka* fell on its face.

Jonas started to work his secure phone and among his calls was a demand for an ambassador to be pulled from the luncheon he was hosting, spoke quietly into the receiver. *No, not calling me back in an hour, not in half an hour, but now. Well done for understanding that. Now – who am I? I am Jonas Merrick and I would be extremely disappointed had he ever heard of me. Get him to the phone.* They did . . . and calls to a massive apartment block in the suburbs of Geneva, and to a huge office block, in Langley, in the state of Virginia, and a Kravnic hook-up, and calls to parts of the building he had never spoken to before, and to the extension number of the AssDepDG . . . Then it was time for his sandwiches. The side-show was the gamble. Without that delay the screens showing the value of accounts previously thought to be well disguised would have already gone blank.

He opened the plastic box and admired what Vera had prepared for him – and thought kindly of her now that he was deemed free from "strutting", and unscrewed his thermos, and was questioned.

"But, Mr Merrick, what are we going to do about Croppy? Still delayed and no word of him."

And answered, without sympathy, "I understand that he is still delayed. He remains, with other matters, high in my thoughts. I am considering what, if anything, I can do about it, his situation, whatever it might be."

Then he stood, went to the cubicle door and opened it and did not look at Sarah, and went through the room used by the A Section watchers and ignored Aggie Burns' questioning look. He went to the corridor, leaned on the sill and looked out through the blast-proof window, needing a clean, and down at the bridge and the river, and the weather had cleared and a golden sunlight rippled on the water – and tears ran on his cheeks and down on to the lapels of his jacket, and he let them flow.

I I

Jonas listened.

"Good of you to make yourself available so quickly, major."

"Always a pleasure, and a privilege, to meet with you, Mr Montgomery."

Jonas had taken a bench to the right of the one occupied by the officer of GRU, military intelligence, at the embassy of the Russian Federation, and Denys Montgomery, a veteran of operations against that state. To the left of them a young man with the high cheekbones that were the Slavish stereotype and close-cut blond hair occupied another bench. Like Jonas he would be wearing a discreet earpiece and somewhere under a jacket would be the receiver that had the capacity to record the nearby conversation.

"To the point, major."

"Of course, Mr Montgomery, and I did not expect gentle conversation, however pleasant that might be."

The major had been in London more than eight years. It suited him and his role to carry a low rank, to float just below the surface, to have a reputation for competence and for access. He would have known of Denys Montgomery as an officer opposing him, credited with insight and expertise. Two good men – with clever minds and wearing backpacks loaded with suspicions – who would have enjoyed each other's company over a drink, except that a rather troublesome frontier of allegiance divided them.

"You have a situation of embarrassment, I believe, major. You in a general sense. I am thin on detail."

"I know nothing of any embarrassment."

"Sometimes a brief opportunity arises where we can be of help to each other. In this case me to you."

"Where mutual interests apply, of course."

Sitting on his bench, and appearing to be no part of the discussion, Jonas imagined them as boxers and appreciated that initially they would spar, dance around each other, but not for long. The bare-knuckle fight would begin soon enough: no place left in the ring for the Queensberry Rules, but to each other there would be a display of old-world politeness. Jonas would hear the exchanges but Montgomery had insisted that he would not be briefed. "I will stand on my own two feet, Jonas, and don't want or need any distraction in my ear." And on to the quick, because the luxury of time was denied them. Jonas had to thank the gardener. Those three benches had been cleared by him, the reason given for turfing people off them that was no doubt fraudulent, and across the paths from them a derelict slept off his alcohol consumption, a couple provocatively embraced, others devoured sandwiches – and amongst them, a power game was being played out.

"I am informed, major – on that awful treadmill that powers the gossip industry – that you have lost an Albanian boy, from inside the principal family of a criminal clan."

"You have to excuse me, Mr Montgomery, but issues of criminality rarely fall inside my bailiwick."

Jonas allowed himself a flickered smile. Good word, *bailiwick*, and demonstrating the level at which the major was bedded down in the United Kingdom.

"You are looking for this Albanian boy. We know it because of enquiries being made in Geneva. The Swiss are so loose-tongued, make an industry of indiscretion, and there are reports dripping out of Belgrade of this disappearance."

"Which has not crossed my desk."

"It will, I assure you, and with trumpets and alarms, major. Assuredly, it will. To the point . . ."

"Thank you." And the Russian lit a cigarette and inhaled deeply.

"We know of him through time he spent in the UK – running drugs and women. The family has a serious criminal footprint in our country, make much of their money here. We track him where possible. We will deal in given names – Skender. We believe that for a few hours, a very limited period, we might – *might* – be able to lift him off the street. A limited period, I emphasise. We would – if we could locate him – then, and within that limited period, return him to his home in the north Albanian mountains."

"I would have to consult. See if anyone has heard of this Skender, this juvenile criminal, and is interested in him."

"We hear there is great interest."

"Why might that be, the interest?"

"No idea – it's just what we heard."

"And where are we travelling? Is this merely from the goodness of the heart of the UK's government that it looks for an act of generosity to my administration, involving one minor criminal that we may not have a note of?"

And Jonas assumed this would be the moment when push came to shove, when the representatives of two powers that spent most of their time flexing towards a collision course, eventually made their positions clear. As a piece of choreography he found it a tedious performance but supposed it necessary. All about a side-show, but with a guillotine blade due to come down if a timeframe was not met, and another cigarette lit which Jonas believed was always an indication that concentration heightened.

"So that we understand each other . . . we would expect you to recognise our good offices should we be able to locate and transfer this felon back to his home where other matters might take their course."

"How?"

As if it were not a matter of any significant importance, Denys Montgomery replied, "We would *hugely* appreciate a reciproca-tion of goodwill – if that were possible – the release of two prisoners from your custody. An American citizen who wandered into your sovereign territory of Kaliningrad, apparently researching the battles on the eastern front in the Great Patriotic War – and some wretched woman making an exhibition of herself by crossing into the Murmansk *oblast* with the misguided aim of highlighting false claims of nickel pollution at a factory.

Two idiots, and our American friends, yours and mine, would be very grateful."

"That is it, that is what you would want – a gift for a gift?"

A pause, smoke wreathing them, and the sun shining through the bare branches of the trees and making trellis shadows on the two men and an atmosphere of collaboration and even friendship, both of which would be utterly false in Jonas' mind.

"Yes, and one other thing, always that way. We had a junior clerical worker at VBX, Frank somebody, made a complete mess of her life, fled to your place when under suspicion of minor espionage, panic, all that stuff . . . You have her at the moment in a prison colony in Mordovia, IK-2 Yavas, and we want her back. A matter of duty of care, which is the new bible in these parts, and anxiety about her wellbeing. We'd want her tacked on."

"I say it immediately, Mr Montgomery. Matters involving prisoners are subject to the bureaucracy of the Prisons Department which answers to the Ministry of Justice, and if matters of security are involved then FSB would expect to be consulted, and perhaps SVR, which is not quick. Could not be done in a hurry."

Jonas could only see half of Denys Montgomery's face, and therefore only caught half of the smile that represented true understanding, and sympathy for a predicament.

The Sixer shrugged and said, "Always look on the bright side, major, always that way. My suggestion, put the matter of the Albanian boy, the one that is missing, into message form and have it within thirty minutes on the desk of your organisation's commanding officer, and if he is uncertain as to how he should react then, please, get him to copy to Viktor . . . A moment, major."

Denys produced a small notepad, took off a sheet and passed it to the major, who pocketed it. Clever, Jonas, thought – the name would not be recorded on the tapes.

"I hold out very little chance of this – even should we wish to – being effective quickly."

"There is a time schedule."

"I have warned you."

"Upon which everything is dependent."

"Again, I emphasise my warning."

"I give you until midnight Moscow time. No compliance, no deal. By your midnight, I would wish to know you agree to the movement of these prisoners from gaol. Your guarantee is required. And by midday tomorrow, Thursday, they would be across a Federation frontier. And we similarly guarantee that the boy would be again with his family in Albania. A simultaneous swap. In the event that the deal is honoured then I also give a pledge that the exchange will not in any way be publicised by either party."

Dryly put, "Anything else?"

"I think not." They stood.

"A pleasure to meet with you."

"And when this has happened, major, and I am very certain it will, once you have informed a higher authority, I hope we can enjoy a pleasant drink together. Perhaps the Barley Mow which does fine cask beers. My card, the number you should call me on."

A firm handshake. Two tape recorders switched off, and the boy with the high cheekbone hurrying away in the direction of Victoria station, a taxi and his embassy. Jonas and Denys Montgomery left St John's Gardens and turned towards the river.

"What matters now, Jonas, is who is at his desk and not on top of somebody else's mistress. If it reaches the right people, it will happen. If it doesn't then . . . That's where we are."

Jonas said, "Throwing our weight about a bit, Denys, aren't we? Heavy stuff for a sideshow. Fortunately I am not risk averse."

No handshakes, no slapped backs, and both aware that they now hazarded all that had been planned . . . and a countdown was in motion.

What Jonas Merrick had not done, not even considered it, was share the problem of a missing, a "delayed", surveillance expert. Not anyone else's problem, only his.

It was hard for the *shef* to see the detail of the descent.

Old eyes handicapped him, along with old ears and the onset of deafness, and aching limbs if he went too far and too fast. He was approaching the end of his reign, knew it, acknowledged it, and had felt confident that his future, the family's and the clan's, were assured.

One of the most trusted of the villagers was at his side, a pistol loaded and lodged in his belt and a snub-barrelled sub-machine gun dangling on a strap from his shoulder. The *shef* understood the scale of the crisis and what he saw – faintly and indistinctly – confirmed it. The column was spread out on a track that was narrow and presented a challenging descent. Years since he, himself, had been up there. His granddaughter came down easily, as sure-footed as the goats that trailed her, and the dog that was one-eyed, wretched and utterly loyal. He thought he had seen Klea skipping alongside the man who carried the burden, seen her punch the dangling head, then had leaned towards it, near enough to spit on the face, then she had hurried on, leading the way.

It would be, he reflected, a moment of triumph for the troubled child. Her achievement, justified by her certainty . . . The man beside him was a lowly *mik* but devoted to the family, had been one of the most trusted of the villagers since he was a teenage boy, had been a bodyguard of the *shef's* when both were younger, and he knew the secrets of the household and the problems of the grand-daughter's damaged mind, and knew also of the tensions that grew around his grandson . . . but that was not for now. A man being brought down from the mountainside was both immediate and chilling for the *shef*. He tried to stand tall because stature gave him a greater presence in the village, and his life, his wealth, his power, depended on stature, that seeming ring of confidence and authority on which he survived. There was no "retirement" for a man such as himself unless he had the commitment of his grandson to protect the family's assets. He had distant family in Milwaukee and New York, in Lima and La Paz, in the Australian city of Adelaide, in Hamburg and Rotterdam, and relatives and their kids in England, but the heart of his existence was where he now stood, in this village that lay at the end of an unmade road that went no further down the narrowing valley. His place, his theatre of operations that dragged in pallets loaded with sacks of cash, and his investments around Europe were all controlled from here, where a sliver of low sunshine fell and where the cloud cleared and where high peaks were still snow clad – and an enemy had penetrated the heart of his place for a second time: a Frenchman killed and disposed of, and then this ... he watched as the column disappeared into the tree line. He had listened to her, to Klea, had given her what she wanted and his grand-daughter had sat all night on the hillside and, at the first trace of dawn, a group of his most reliable, most physically fit, villagers had gone up the mountainside by a roundabout route and a difficult climb and had formed a blocking line across the only route out: Klea had identified it. He had heard the explosions, had seen the puffs of dispersing gas, and had known then that the child's instincts were proven – and she had spoken to him about her brother, about his own heir, been equally insistent, and he had not cared to believe her, but that was for another hour that day. This was the immediate. He took a cigarette from his packet and the attentive *mik* lit it for him – he had also to consider his Russian "friends" and the money paid for services, and his head shook with a nagging pain.

They came out of the tree line, the goats and the dog and the child. He thought it almost obscene that she wore that patched-up dress where the inserts were obvious and which she would not discard. She walked easily when off the scree and reached the football pitch, and he heard her voice, and that awful tuneless song that was her anthem. He had no idea of how to control and manage her, and had hoped it would be done by his grandson, by Skender. The men followed. The prisoner was trussed at the ankles and the wrists and was draped over a big man's shoulders, his head by the man's arse, his feet dangling by his groin, and his head lolled and the *shef* thought he would be regaining consciousness by now. The column came closer.

Klea's face was lit up. She skipped along and that fucking ugly dog bounced beside her, and the goats were playful. His mind was grey with the degree of his crisis, but the child was wrapped in pleasure. She went past him and towards the pen where the goats were kept. The men reached him and ducked their heads in respect ... every aspect of his authority was governed by respect and if he lost it his life was over. The big man came towards him and dropped a shoulder. The figure fell to the ground.

The head was at a strange angle but the breathing was regular. He saw a tanned and weathered face, a countryman's. A camouflage suit was hooked round his ankles, had been stripped back from his arms and legs, showing ordinary clothes underneath. A man came forward and upturned a rucksack and out tumbled a night sight or image intensifier, binoculars coated in protective rubber of military colour, and food, and foil-wrapped parcels and bottles of yellow liquid, and a notebook and pencils. And then came the grenades – and he had sufficient intelligence to realise they were incapacitating gas and those that flashed bright and let loose a thunderclap of disorienting noise and were likely government issue.

He thought his world collapsed.

He pointed to that building across the square, where steps led down to a cellar, and told his *mik*, Bresnik, as faithful in his service as any, to supervise the move and to have him kept secure. And another should collect the material deployed against him . . .

He heard the clattering, recognised the sound, and Klea had come back, carrying in both hands the rusted garden shears. She stood close to the prisoner's head and opened and closed the blades sharply a few centimetres from his nose, and the *shef* believed the man would have been aware of her and what she did. She came to her grandfather, and love beamed up at him, and he knew what she wished for. His arm was on her shoulder and he led her to the villa where she could dry herself, and he recognised it would be hard to reject her demand.

All collapsing around him under the weight of crisis – and added to it was the burden of his grandson's disappearance – and anger shafted in him.

The woman had taken the phone call. Skender had strained to hear the exchange but had failed.

The three of them talked among themselves for a few minutes, then coffee was made. From the last time his bindings had been checked, and when he had been given water, he had realised they all now wore plastic gloves all the time.

The gloves told him that decisions were made. "What is going to happen to me?" was near to getting an answer. There was a phrase Skender remembered from his time in England: *Be careful what you wish for*. He sensed they had now received instructions.

Were not going to kill him, then dispose of him.

Were going to send him back.

Why not kill him, one shot in the back of the neck, a shallow grave or remote ditch down towards the river? Because they wore gloves and had cleared the apartment and because they kept him hooded.

The woman had crossed the room, knelt in front of him.

A honeyed voice: "You're going home, Skender. It's a swap. You go home and somebody that we want gets to come home at the same time. You cooperate and all goes well. You don't cooperate and it goes badly. Simple enough, Skender. Cooperate and you spin a good line when you are home, and tell them you are just needing a few days away, invent what you need to, and off you go with that pretty girl in Chamonix. Don't factor her into the story . . . and remember all the things we did to you and remember to tell them that you gave nothing away, nothing at all. What happened to the package? You left it in the car and the car was given to gypsies, and they stripped it down and burned it. The documents were never found . . . Run that for twenty-four hours and then be on the road, and the family will still love you. That is how to cooperate . . . Now the other side of the coin, don't cooperate. You stay in the family and you are named on the Europol and Interpol Ten Most Wanted lists. You spend your time running and looking over your shoulder, and you don't get to see the girl. She is now staked out. We'd lift her anytime we want. You don't cooperate and you never see her again. That's a mistake, sorry. You do see her again but on the front page of a trash tabloid, and a photograph of her with bare boobs in a photo, which we fake, and she's dead, strangled or something. You do see her again but in a photograph and you can read what was done to her because you didn't want to cooperate. I like to explain everything slowly and simply, Skender, so there are no misunderstandings. Always best when everyone understands the consequences. Is that good, Skender?"

He nodded.

"You're a hard old cow, Cress," Sword whispered.

"I'll not argue."

"Hate to be on the receiving end if you were in poor humour."

"You'd have cause to."

"What's his manoeuvre room? What have you left him?"

"Left him nothing. He's shafted . . . We're not running a kindergarten."

Sword said, "Don't suppose we are."

Tank said, "He has to trust us. More fool him if he does."

Cress said, "Perhaps that needs a bit more explaining, the trust bit."

Skender felt her fingers on his knees.

She said, "Just do as you are told, Skender. Don't argue and don't second guess. Believe in us and we'll see you through. Guaranteed . . . Imagine it, you reckon you've covered your tracks and are far away, a little bar on the corner of a street in Helsinki or Bremen, or in Cape Town, could be Ho Chi Minh, and you've told her where to come. You go up to the bar and order a drink, and the bar staff say *That's okay, Skender, it's looked after, and there's fizz in a bucket.* We can do that . . . that's an up-side. You don't need the down-side, Skender. Too smart to need it spelled out again. Actually, Skender, you are lucky that it was us that are handling you because it could have been some real bastards. Just say when you want to piss and I'll send one of the boys off with you."

Heard her clearly.

What he did not hear was Sword say to Tank, "He'll be certifiable if he puts his trust in us."

Or Tank's reply, "Better he believes in us and trips back to his beloved family because he's not exactly loaded with alternatives."

In her grandfather's office, Klea still held her garden shears. He was with three of the more trusted villagers, all of whom held rank in his clan and formed the *bajrak* which was his leadership council, loose and not binding but from which he took advice, and all had a ranking of *krye* and went abroad in his name, and had authority over the sub-groups in distant continents and across Europe. Each would have taken an oath of loyalty to him, a *besa*, as was laid down in the *kanun*. Each was nominally excessively rich but still lived in the homes in which they had been born, scattered around the village, and where their fathers had been born and had died. They had been called to the villa to examine what the child had led them to. She danced around them, and the blades hung open and the men flinched from her. Each would have, in his own home and with his own child, clipped her ear. She was allowed to interrupt them, and to dance among them, and to gain the pleasure that came with praise. There had been praise, loads of it, and justified. Her face was a picture of jubilation, theirs mirrored concern, and justified anxiety.

"When? When do I go in there? When?"

A grimness in the old man's voice and a wheeze in his throat. "Soon . . ."

A shrug towards his men. What could he do? And their thanks to her was owed.

In turn they fingered the items that had been retrieved from the hide. He was interested, of course, in the sophistication of the equipment . . . As he understood what had happened, and it was vague, the prisoner had realised he was watched and had tried to break out. Had thrown gas and the canisters that made a blinding light and a considerable explosion, had hoped to escape while confusion ruled, but would not have allowed for the guts, courage, determination – or handicap – of his beloved Klea. She had clung to him, refused to free him. Perhaps the prisoner had shown weakness is not killing her immediately: whatever . . . One of the men in line had crushed his resistance, a blow from a pick-axe handle across the shoulders and knocked unconscious. Without her suspicion, the prisoner would have hid in safety for days, weeks . . .

As interesting to them as the image intensifier and camera and binoculars was the rubbish. Bottles of urine, tinfoil packages of crap, spare meals and enough to show he had been there for some days, could have stayed another week – looked like a government operation, and he reckoned not his own administration working from Tirana because he paid enough to have that information delivered on a salver.

Dominating the *shef's* thoughts was a question as yet not asked. Where was Skender, the heir to the empire? And he kept the question close, passed nothing to the men in his office. For every hour that he kept from them the news of his grandson's disappearance their eventual anger would increase and his excuses seem ever more deceitful . . . he walked on a dangerous mountain ridge. Where was the boy? And the conspiracies played in his mind as he handled the prisoner's powerful binoculars. A watcher on the hillside, his grandson gone, contacts not kept and no shows at meetings – and money at risk, and his reputation . . . without his reputation he was a dead man. Those in the office with him were all poorly educated, but all loaded with cunning and deceit and ambition or they would not have climbed so high in the *fis*, held such authority inside the clan, and he feared showing weakness.

He thought he knew of the potential forces arranged against him. They would be from Europol in the Netherlands and Interpol in France and a spider's web of connections, but the words in the notebook were English and he assumed the prisoner was British. He assumed also, since he was targeted in his own village, that at the very highest levels of the UK government his name was flipped around a table and a determination was reached that he be brought down. The very highest and ablest men would have been awarded that job – bring down this humble creature with his small resources, merely making a living and keeping food on the plates of a village community. Almost, he saw himself as a victim of a grand and powerful conspiracy.

What to do? Fight.

For centuries, the priests reminded their congregations every Sunday that the Albanian people fought back, never bent a knee.

The Greek invaders had regarded the people of Albania as barbarians and had limped away from battlefields. The Roman legions had built roads better to garrison the country. Ostrogoths and Visigoths, an Austrian army, a German army and Italian troops – none had crushed the people of the north, with their dialect of Gheg. Those aiming to bring him down now would be versions of those "aristocrats" parachuted in during the the Second World War, and then running for their fucking lives because they were not wanted, were unable to divide and rule. He pictured them, and saw the chaos now around him, and the blackness of clouds over the valley, and the scale of crisis and felt a fury, and had not a trace of mercy in his mind . . . Would let his granddaughter loose on their prisoner, might even go himself and stand at the top of the cellar steps and hear the screams. He imagined what they looked like, effete and drawling and so utterly superior – chaos and crisis, bedfellows he barely knew. And amongst the bastards would be one, a top man – no face – aiming to destroy him.

She danced some more, then shouted at him. "When? When am I allowed?"

"Very soon, my angel. That is my promise."

His chauffeur drove Viktor in the armoured Mercedes along a traffic lane that was available only to men and women of a certain status.

A week before, his sole source of agony was the inability of the garage to locate the irritating rattle somewhere at the rear end of the car. Today the sources of pain multiplied at spectacular pace . . .

"What the fuck do I do now?"

Easy enough to voice the query, and Viktor was an intelligent man and would not have risen so high and so fast had he not been, but an answer to the question *What the fuck do I do now?* eluded him.

He had received the phone call from GRU. Had been informed of a meeting in London where those supercilious and arrogant bastards, English special service authorities and lying through their polished teeth, had laid out an answer relevant to his agonies.

One aspect of the situation he faced was now alive and present in the Aquarium, in the GRU offices . . . a message from a major in the British capital and sent to a duty major in the depths of Ulitsa Grizodubovoy, meaning nothing to him so passed up the chain to a colonel, who had taken advice from a brigadier and still making no sense so travelling upwards and landing on the desk of a general, and a call made to him, to Viktor. *So good to speak to you, excellency, and I hope you are well, and your family. Of course I know little of affairs to which this may refer but the UK people seem willing to arrest an Albanian boy and have an eyeball on him – apologies, that is a visual in close surveillance – and are prepared to send him home, presumably some pigsty in that God-forsaken country where his family run a successful crime syndicate. As a reward for their "kind" actions they would want the freedom from our justice system of two American citizens, both stupid and unimportant, and an Englishwoman, and they want an answer very soon. I am inclined to ignore, but I am first running it past you, and* . . . At that point he had been interrupted.

"Do the swap, arrange it. Meet the conditions."

He, of course, had no rights under the statutes of the state to instruct a man as powerful in his own right as a general in GRU as to how he should behave, what he should do. But he was Viktor and he had access to extreme power, more access than the general. It was the way things worked. Power was about access, and access depended on an ability to deliver – ultimate access was to the man, the spider at the centre of the web, with protected quarters in the Kremlin.

As yet that man did not know that a simple courier operation had stalled. As yet that man did not realise that there was potential grief for a considerable basket of assets owned by him. As, others in the group of *siloviki* – all with that precious access – did not know that a courier was missing, and along with the spider they had all had lodged huge sums with Viktor.

"What the fuck do I do now?"

It churned in his mind. Go to each of them whose money he ingratiated himself by handling – like he was some low-life domestic manager who jumped at their instructions – and cough up the details of what he knew and skate over the flimsy ice of what he did not know? Go to the Kremlin, request an appointment in person from the chief of staff to the President, and perhaps be given an audience, and scrape and bow his way into a room and see a welcoming smile turn acid with annoyance, and confess? Do nothing, and sort it, and hope?

A message came up on his phone screen. By midnight, the swap was to be guaranteed. By noon, the next day, Thursday, the release would take place, a bridge from Ivangorod in Russian territory to Narva inside Estonia, and at the same hour the UK authorities gave their word that the boy would be returned to his village. Did he accept? He did.

It was now a matter of record for the general of GRU that he had been told what to do, had done it . . . Viktor felt he was climbing the fire escape staircase, floor after floor, step after step, would get to the top and would look down and see tiny vehicles moving and ant-sized people, and consider what was better – throw himself in free fall. Or end up crouched in a concrete cell, wondering when they would poison him?

He went home to talk to his wife.

"There is a bigger picture," said Jonas

Sarah stiffened, suppressed the words in her throat. She turned away from him.

"I have a wider scene, and a schedule to maintain. His situation is one corner of that scene, one part of the picture . . . which does not mean I am not working on the problem of the delay. Not at all. Time for me to leave. I wish to be copied in on all relevant messages. So, I'll see you in the morning."

He stood. Only then did Jonas realise that the AssDepDG stood outside the cubicle door and had that infuriating expression on his face – part amusement, part bogus concern. He packed his brief-case. His empty sandwich box, his empty flask, a notepad, a map of a mountain region in the north of Albania. He might as well have told the girl to stand up and face him, raise her arms, and then have punched her hard in the stomach. He realised it. Did not know what else he might have said.

He went past her. She seemed crushed, and knew so little which was how it would remain. He had no doubt that she would manoeuvre her own chair and his to the side of the cubicle and make herself a bed of sorts, and she'd have her own phone and one that was linked to his mobile: two ears for two earpieces and for two phones . . .

He made a brisk exit, relieved that his tears earlier in the day had not been witnessed. He crossed Aggie Burns' territory and the AssDepDG followed him and his iron toecapped shoes beat a rhythm alongside the clatter of Jonas' brogues.

From the corridor they headed, mutual agreement, for that staircase rather than be trapped in a crowded elevator.

"Do we stand well, Jonas, or stand poorly?"

"Fingers on the keyboards, entry points into accounts. They call themselves the Mustangs, which I believe is a wild horse. They are ready to go."

"And what is holding them?"

"The need to deliver to those I am indebted. Montgomery wants his woman. Kravnic wants two bodies jerked out of gaol. Montgomery came with the courier information and Kravnic has bankrolled us . . . We are into the last hours . . . and we are offering to send an Albanian hood, sounds a vicious little creature, back home, and are trying to appear as an innocent and good-natured party."

"Of course, what else would we appear to be?"

"Except . . ."

"Always one, isn't there? An 'except'? An *except* that takes off the gilt."

"They will not know, till I am ready, that I am actually a deceitful little man, but there is an 'except'. Regretfully."

"Spit it."

They were outside the door on to Horseferry Road. The traffic had thickened, headlights and street lights burned bright, the bridge ahead was clogged. The AssDepDG would have known that he'd need to keep up with Jonas, that a train would not be missed.

"I'm missing one of my people. Rather a special young man. The surveillance lad, and good at his job. Missing or delayed, uncertain. Causing some anxiety."

"Have to be prepared to take casualties, Jonas, if a job is worth doing."

"I don't require a lecture on command responsibilities."

"The loneliness of the boss man. Heard that before, my friend. Getting squeamish? What are you going to do?"

"Think about it."

And he was gone, lengthening his stride and out into the traffic and his raincoat flapped at his knees, and he held tight to his trilby and traffic parted to allow him to cross safely. He thought the AssDepDG might overnight at Thames House, might bring a mug of cocoa down to 3/S/12 in the small hours, might have laced it with a splash of 12-year-old. He thought it all stood, the big picture and the sideshow, on a knife edge.

Before he was off the bridge he had slapped his phone to his ear.

In a soft voice he said, "Sorry to disturb you. My name is Jonas Merrick and I understand, Matt, that you have been of help in earlier parts of this operation, and I think I may need some more of that help from you . . ."

Most parts of his body hurt. Where the child had hung on to his legs with her arms wrapped round and the grip not weakening, where the dog had bitten hard, and where he had been battered on the shoulder as he had steadied himself to strike her. He had been dumped onto the ground, and then dragged to the cellar steps and that had scraped his stomach and knees, left them raw. They had dropped him down the flight of stone steps and he had wedged halfway, and they had taken his arms and dragged him down the last flight and that had battered his spine. Everywhere hurt.

It hurt worst in Croppy's mind.

A child had outwitted him. He had lain in the hide and had watched her for many days, had felt sorry for her misfortune. Had

not realised that she stalked him, had closed in on his hide, then
sat herself down so that he could not move. All planned, and timed
to perfection, building the pressure, then forcing him to break out,
use the flash-bangs and the gas, then pulling him down and
holding him fast.

He was not hooded, which told him something.

Had a chain around his throat, tight enough to have made a raw
weal on the skin, and the end of it was hooked to a ring with a
padlock.

Croppy thought of the humiliation – done over by a peasant girl
in a mountain village . . . and thought of himself. Not of his girl,
nor his parents in the bungalow Kilchoan. He was in silence, with
a faint light fron a small and guttering candle.

He was not blindfolded, not hooded. He took that as a sign of
a bleak future. Before being tipped down the steps and pulled
into the cellar he had seen a jumble of faces, and knew them
from the magnification of the binoculars. The old man and the
child and some of the men who ambled around the village and
had no obvious work and would drive 400 yards in a Mercedes
rather than walk. The guard must have sat very still, until the
tickle was irresistible and he coughed hard. Croppy could see
that he was sitting against a far wall, beside the door into the
cellar.

It would be bad for him, painful. Had a degree of fatalism, and
supposed that was the way for a big stag, one that was doomed
and would want to get it over. Croppy did not know how he would
be if they made it bad for him, or whether it mattered if he spilled
it up.

He heard footsteps outside the heavy door. Heard a man spit,
then cough, and heard the child's voice, shrill and demanding, and
heard a clattering noise like metal closed on metal.

They came inside and the man carried a flashlight and the child
held a pair of old garden shears. The man went to a stool by the
far wall and Croppy noticed the automatic pistol wedged under
his belt, and saw the child sitting on the floor with her skirt hitched
awkwardly high; and she was humming and clattered the shears . . .

He tried to think of Sarah, but her face was a confusion and misted and he took no comfort from it.

The car reached the gated compound and the private security company allowed the Mercedes to enter.

Viktor needed to be home, to feel the safety of what was familiarity and safe. His phone had started to vibrate – three messages.

Hi, Viktor. A nasty little rumour in a high place that all may not be well in Swiss matters. I assume untrue. Call me . . .

Viktor. Reports from a confidential source that a problem may exist regarding mutual matters. Good if you call me . . .

Viktor. What the fuck is going on? Something or nothing? Is the boss copied in? Don't fuck me about. Call.

A daughter was at home, his wife was out.

He poured himself a drink, and slumped. The daughter asked why he was at home so early. He shrugged. Waited until she had gone and then rang Belgrade to hear what was known – perhaps even to take advice – from that village in the mountains, populated by savages and where what had seemed an excellent ruse against the sanctions now seemed dangerous, perhaps lethal – but would not know until the releases he had authorised had been completed. He shivered, and did not know the future, and could not imagine how it would be, late at night behind the fences, the arc lights and watchtowers of a corrective labour colony.

The dormitory was in silence.

A hundred women were housed there – some convicted of murder, some of persistent store theft, some of fraud scams, some of street muggings. They were the majority, 96 of them. None of them coughed, wriggled in their bunk beds on the thin mattresses issued in IK-2, and none made a sound: They listened, strained to hear – and knew.

They were witches and bitches, that striking majority, not stupid. An atmosphere was registered. Meals eaten, last cigarettes smoked, and lights turned down in the dormitory. All that was usual was absent. No hacking coughs from chests suffering from the cold and the damp and the dreadful food. No movement in their bunks as they tried to get warmer, find a position where the cold cutting through ill-fitting windows was less keen. No weeping, the sign of self-pity and regret, no calling out the names of lovers and children. They were street-wise and aware, knew an event was in the final moments of preparation, that it would be dramatic, vicious and beyond anything any of them had experienced in IK-2 before. Detail was short, death was inevitable. How it was to be managed they were unsure of.

Would any of them intervene? They would not.

It had been passed on earlier, along the bunk beds, that the rebels – as the four were known, the *povstantsy*, the four of them halfway down the aisle – were close to acting out a cataclysmic event, even by the standards of the camp and the despair that it bred. It was known that sheets had been taken from two of the bunks and they might be used for a hanging, or a strangulation, or might be taken out into the night and the women sprinting as fast as under-nourished legs were able, towards the fence and slinging the sheets over and climbing, and shredding their bodies on the barbed wire. It was known also that the four had collected dead light bulbs, old screws and bent nails which might be used as weapons. Possible that the four, would attempt to attack members of staff – stab them, skewer them – and be shot dead in retaliation.

There were older women in the dormitory who might have felt a calling to intervene – but none spoke up.

And the younger women? Not one sidled close to the four and demanded a place in whatever plan was hatched. An owl was out beyond the wire and the arc lights and the watchtowers where near-frozen guards carried firearms, and it shrieked, but no sound came from inside the dormitory.

Nor any sound from the four women. No need for speech because decisions had been taken and doubt erased. They lay, two of them in each bed, and eked out what they believed to be the last moments of the greatest friendship of their lives, about to be curtailed and not done prettily. It was their private world of summer fruit, and what could be turned into the *confitures* that bound them, the JAMs, and the English language slogan *just about managing*. Decisions had been made ... methods chosen. Blueberry said she would crunch up the light bulbs and swallow; Currant would take a single sheet and loop it over one bar in an upper window and would hang herself; and Apple would swallow all the nails and screws and needles from the sewing machines, gulp them down. And Apricot would go for the wire, out of the main door to the dormitory and past the dozing "trusted" prisoner, and run barefoot for the perimeter wall and the coils of the wire, and launch herself. She had chosen a place where the lights were brightest, the best chance that the man in the tower would shoot her with certainty; get it done. All decided, and the time that it would happen ... eleven minutes more, and a high clock on a far wall at the end of the building showed each of them, if they cared to look, how long was left.

No one slept in the dormitory, and no one spoke. The hands on the clock moved and the 96 women were on their backs, staring at the ceiling and wondering, minds churning, whether it would all happen in synchronised form, or whether one would be weaker – or whether courage bound them together.

That dead time in the administration block of IK-2 when a shift was nearing its end and when the relief had not yet arrived. A screen pinged, demanding attention. An official swore, rubbed her eyes and swayed forward in her chair. A message appeared.

For fuck's sake ... eight minutes before going off duty, getting to the mess before the bar closed. A demand for "Immediate Action". Bad because it meant the timeline was monitored. The official knew the prisoner who was the subject of the instruction. They all knew her. The foreigner, a woman who had attached herself to the core of rabble-rousers, activists, parasites – and was going home. The instruction, with the full authority of the Ministry of Justice, said this woman, and gave her correct gaol number, was to be isolated from her dormitory now, fucking *now*, dressed in presentable clothes, and a plane would be arriving in two hours to collect her – and she was going home, wherever the fuck that was. *Take me with you, and I'll carry your fucking bag,* the official murmured. But she was disciplined and conscientious, and heaved on her thick quilted coat, and headed out into the darkness and slithered on the icy ground and was guided towards the dormitory by the arc lights illuminating the fence and the coils of wire topping it, and walked briskly but not so fast that she risked falling.

Bedlam in a dormitory in the corrective colony designated as IK-2.

The commandant sent for; further staff had already arrived.

Four prisoners handcuffed. A cache of light bulbs, a glass pane, bent nails and rusted screws and needles from the sewing machines discovered. One prisoner already separated from the remaining three and bawling in a mixture of Russian and English, and the other three shouting but unable to cling on to her.

Full lights on, and the clock hands had passed the hour.

The Englishwoman was to be removed, issued with new clothes because her own were long lost, and a plane was coming to collect her – and she would not go. Would not. Would not clap her hands over her head, say, *Cheerio, girls, great to have known you, and when I get to Piccadilly I'll raise a glass to you, here in IK-2, and won't forget you for at least an hour. Stay safe, girls.* Didn't. Shouted that she wasn't going, wasn't leaving. Shouted. "Take me from here and all the way back to UK I will tell whoever will listen of the brutality in this camp, the abuse, the cruelty especially of the commandant . . . or they come with me, these three. Then, if, we pledge that we will never criticise the Russian state, the camp, any aspect of the administration, a vow of silence . . ." Might have been Apricot's finest hour.

A telephone connection made. A call patched through from the mobile of the commandant and through the duty officer of the Ministry and into the private apartment of a man whose name was known to those who followed the fortunes of the hierarchy running the Federation, and parade ground attention, and a situation explained. A denunciation and a fight in a red corner. In a blue corner, a guarantee that the camp and the past are closed areas and not discussed, not ever. The cold ripping down the length of the dormitory, and the hand of the clock steadily moving.

A shrug – *what does it matter to me* – a grimace. The commandant said to Apricot, "You make a deal, you stay with the deal. You break the deal and you pay a consequence. Big consequence ... you piss with Russia and we can inflict a difficult time for you – do not doubt that ... the four of you go. Why? I am not told. In an hour you will be gone, all of you. We have a phrase that is appropriate, *skatert'yu doroga,* which I think for you is good riddance."

They would be taken out of the dormitory, would be clothed, would be gone.

The knotted sheet, the light bulbs, the nails and the screws were in a plastic bag.

Blueberry asked, "How is it that you are so important?"

Currant asked, "Why do your people do this for you?"

Apple asked, "What is your value?"

Apricot answered, "I have no idea why I am so important. No idea."

They were led out of the dormitory, crossed the yard under escort and walked past the fence and the wire and beneath a watchtower and saw the barrel of the machine gun and the light glittering on the belt of bullets. Would she actually have done it? Apricot asked herself. Jumped and climbed and kept going when she heard the weapon cocked ... did not know. They were brought to the administration block.

He lay on his back, the cat spread-eagled across his stomach.

Beside him, Vera slept.

He knew of nothing else he could do. A question bubbled in his mind and it must be asked, and he hoped it would be answered.

Midnight approached. Raynes Park's streets and avenues were quiet. People were at home, in their beds, asleep preparing for the traipse to the station the next morning, and those silent, uncommunicative journeys to work. He would be amongst them. Quite an important day awaited him – and a fair assumption that most of those who'd be squashed around him on the train, and those who speed-walked from Waterloo and off along the south embankment and past the brick wall of the Archbishop's Palace, and the stampede over the bridge, all of them would have thought their next day to be fulfilling, worthwhile – and himself? He should have felt excited, but instead was gripped by a sense of inadequacy.

He thought he had done what he could . . . some would probably believe that the outcome was both profitable and served a purpose. Not Jonas Merrick . . . The outcome was, he believed, stained with failure. Faces and figures came in a kaleidoscope of images in his mind and he made little effort to block them. Having them in his mind highlighted the guilt he felt, and with it an impression that his thinking had been second rate. There was the girl, Sarah, a crushed face and beaten eyes, and him unable to offer any comfort; there was the AssDepDG who he had walked away from in order to catch his train, and there was the man who burned him out of dark corners. Had an impression from the voice of Matt, who would have shifted mountains to help his friend and whose, anxiety had rung clear in Jonas' ear, and a dog was spoken of, with the name *Tricikle*, missing a leg and beloved, and of the young man himself.

Remembered a hero of the last war, a scientist who had developed a weapon of massive destructive power, had been in a command post when the air raid was launched and was congratulated on its success but had stayed in place while the survivors limped back to their base, numbers reduced. He had said, it was reported, *If I had known how many would be lost I might not have started this.* Thought again of the girl, of his mentor, of young Matt, of Croppy, of what he had authorised . . . Jonas reached across the bed. Was he equal to what he hoped to achieve? He gripped Vera's shoulder, and the cat moaned at him. Was it vanity that undid him? He shook her shoulder.

She might have complained, but did not. He supposed there were some amongst the Sixers and the Fivers who could cope with the burdens, might have enjoyed playing God, flicking pieces off the board that were expendable, not him – and thought the image of indifference was a theatrical fraud.

"Is it that bad, Jonas?"

"Pretty bad."

"Do you want to tell me – and stuff 'need to know' – that bad?"

"I have to ask a question."

"I'll answer it, then go down and make a pot of tea."

"The truth and only the truth . . . am I boring?"

"What?"

"Am I boring?"

She climbed out of bed, sighed, grabbed her dressing-gown, put on her slippers. The cat followed her to the door.

"Not boring, Jonas, just predictable. 'Predictable' is allowing a subject to take control of you. It is infuriating but I offer no criticism. I'll get the tea."

His phone rang. Sarah. An exchange would take place on an Estonian bridge, one shared with Russia, at midday Thursday, all in place . . . He asked of Croppy? She told him there was no news – like a prize was snatched from his grasp.

12

In "predictable" mode, Jonas Merrick crossed the bridge.

Same clothes, same briefcase, same plastic box and thermos. Like a great truth had dawned on him, and a "predictable" target lying ahead of him in a few hours. About the only thing not predictable, or "boring", were the contents of his plastic box and he had not liked to ask Vera what filling she had put in his sandwich.

He saw that Kev and Leroy were on the steps of Thames House, traversed glances, always suspicious, up and down the street as pedestrians and cyclists poured into work. It would have been predictable for Jonas to have slowed his stride as he came off the bridge, giving time for the pair of armed policemen to drift off the pavement and arrive in the centre of the traffic flow. The presence of officers with machine guns in the middle of the road brought vehicles to a standstill, even the limousine carrying the Deputy Director General, who was on a similar timetable to Jonas. That morning he increased his speed, was almost at a lumbering jog, and was on the kerb taking a deep breath, before they were out in the centre to do the Red Sea moment. He stepped off and had just about closed his eyes and walked. A cacophony of horns erupted around him, and he heard brakes shriek and windows were coming down for people to gun at him . . . He rather enjoyed it, a moment of pleasure. Cars and vans surged past him, but by a strange alchemy his own safety was preserved. The DDG's car overtook him, and he saw the face inside the privacy window, and raised his trilby in acknowledgement.

What was predictable lay in the reactions from Moscow; from an Albanian boy who was part of an organised crime group; from a team he had put together; from a young woman with a dose of romance that now blighted her work; from Denys Montgomery and Solly Kravnic on different sides of the ocean . . . what had been utterly predictable was that Croppy would go back. Would return to his hide because of the equipment he had left there, and that was about training and the disciplines taught him, and Jonas remembered that he had suggested – without a moment's thought – that to leave gear in place was equivalent to providing a clear footprint. He had no evidence of it as fact, but the situation for Croppy was now dire.

Jonas Merrick held a lowly grade on the staff register of the Security Service, and had been granted minimal authority. To most who knew him inside Thames House he was either derided for his clothing and "predictability" of timekeeping, or was a dangerous and unrepentant loose cannon, without a vestige of discipline. He was a man who suffered self-inflicted wounds, was punished for it, and who had brought stunningly successful coups to the front doors of MI5 . . .

At the café he ordered his cappuccino and his Danish, paid as usual in cash – and asked a favour of the manager. He requested that a member of the staff there, perhaps the Polish girl who wiped the tables down or perhaps the Lebanese boy who filled the rolls, should go on his behalf to the nearest pet shop, off Victoria Street, and said what he wanted purchased. His visits to the café were predictable, five days a week as long as any staff could recall: "Not a problem. For you, a pleasure."

He took his coffee and his pastry into St John's Gardens.

He sat on a bench still wet from the overnight rain. The wheel-barrow was pushed along the path towards him, and an edge was swept with a stiff brush, and cigarette ends were carefully picked up and binned, and leaves gathered. He lingered on his coffee, and ate sparingly of his pastry, which frustrated the cabal of chaf-finches that clustered round him.

"May I please steal a few moments of your time?"

The request furrowed a frown in the man's forehead, it would be an interruption to his routine. Jonas knew him to have been a lowly ranking soldier, and suffering from the exposure to danger in a meaningless Mid-East skirmish years before, and then recruited for a temporary Fiver job that had frazzled his mind further, and traumatic stress dominated him. But Jonas knew of the man's innate common sense, which seemed an undervalued attribute, and usually took comfort in what the gardener told him.

"If it's only a few, yes."

An unenthusiastic answer. The man did not stop his work, did not lean on his broom, but carried on working around Jonas' feet and left unswept only the small area where the crumbs had fallen for the birds.

"A question, only one. In combat, what scared you most?"

A pause. Jonas knew he would not receive a flip answer. It would be considered. A cigarette was rolled, the diameter of a knitting needle. It was lit, inhaled and a waft of smoke floated away.

"Letting people down."

"You were not an officer, not a senior NCO. You did not have a weight of responsibility for others."

"Letting down anyone who was up close to you, dependent on you . . . excuse me."

The barrow was wheeled away and the birds left to their feast. Jonas finished his coffee and shook the last crumbs from his coat. It was a decision, of course, already made but now confirmed in his mind. It should have been a day of triumph but was not.

There were mice in the cellar, could also have been rats.

Neither would bother Croppy.

There had been nights when he had slept on the slopes of the mountain with stars as a ceiling when he had wanted to see the first taint of a summer dawn, and there had been a minimal frost in the heather, and mice had come to him because he had warmth to share. And another night he had slept in a bag inside the ruin that would be his home, on earth where thin grass had grown through the sheep shit, as if that was a way of acknowledging the place was now his, and a pair of young rats had tried to burrow under his clothing, and he had gently removed them, sent them on their way. Neither rats nor mice were his enemy. Nor were eagles, nor five point stags, nor the winds that whipped the waves on to the cliffs at Rubha Ailein or Sgeir Fhada, nor cold, nor darkness.

An enemy that he acknowledged came several times in what he thought was the night and shone a torch down at him and did not speak nor offer him water, or bread. A man came with a flashlight but not close enough for Croppy to be able to swing a kick at him . . . and how would that have helped him? A man on his back and yelling, and Croppy still fastened to the manacle on the wall behind him and his hands trussed behind his back and his ankles tied. He was an older man and tucked into his waist, fastened by the belt, was an automatic pistol. The man did not come close enough to examine the bindings that held Croppy but took them in faith, but would go out through the door and the steps would be revealed before the door was slammed and Croppy heard a key turning. They had drilled into Croppy when he was with the Regiment that the "golden hour" was all important – not just for getting medical help to a battlefield casualty, but also to seize the chance of escape or of rescue. The hour was long gone . . . he was on the floor, needed to pee and needed to squat and could do neither. He did not know whether they had the sophistication to leave him – sweating, stewing, the vermin running over him – to soften him before they began an interrogation. There would be one, and with it would be a beating and a kicking, and worse. Those thoughts he tried to remove from his mind, fat chance. He had seen a man executed after torture in Syria, had seen a man executed here – had seen a child with garden shears that dripped in blood and the blades wiped on her dress. They would question him first, then would play with him, and when their time was exhausted or they wished to go for their lunch, they would kill him. He would like to have thought of Sarah at that moment, waiting . . . but felt that somehow the memory of her would be dirtied, as if he positioned himself behind her and used as protection.

Nor did he think with anger of those who had packed him off to this place, had fashioned a conversation that had seemed so casual, so matter of fact, and that had pitched him off his own

territory and brought him here. Nor did he consider the responsibility for his position of the soft-voiced old man who employed
Sarah and who had never seemed to entertain the possibility
that Croppy would say, *Really sorry, but I've left all that stuff
behind me, and don't think I want to go back into that type of business. I'm sure if you pop down to Hereford you can find a gang of
guys only too pleased to be of assistance. I'm not one of them.* He
was alone, beyond help. Was not a hero, and hoped it would be
soon, and quick.

"There is an understanding."

Not a question from the commandant but a statement of fact.

Frank answered her, "We have given our word, ma'am, that
none of the four of us shall make any statement of criticism of the
Russian penal service. We will abide by that assurance. Good
night."

The commandant had dressed in full uniform and the tags
showed up well on her shoulders, and the medal ribbons on an
ample chest. She would have been roused from her quarters by
the flurry of late-night calls. She had ordered that the four women
be given food in the staff canteen: sausage, eggs, new bread – and
jam. She would have been pleased to see them go and anticipated
a quieter life with them no longer under her – almost – control.
There was a strip suitable for light aircraft close to IK-2 and they
had been driven there from the camp. None of them had cheered
or yelled as they had walked from the canteen, dressed in new
clothing, past their own block and then to the main gate and then
invited to board a minibus. There had seemed to be a flatness as if
the waging of the war had been more exciting than the victory
parade ... a deputy, to the commander, or an assistant to the
deputy, accompanied them to the airfield, and carried the necessary paperwork. The aircraft was waiting, an American-built
Cessna 172, one that had been sneaked into the country before
the sanctions knife had dropped. They were treated – from the
minibus driver to the camp staff and senior official and the aircraft
crew – with a studied politeness. They had boarded, fastened their

seatbelts, had taken off into the night and the winds against them, would dictate a turbulent ride. They were not told their destination and enough of Russia remained in them for none of them to ask. What would have seemed obvious was that enormous stresses had influenced the authority's decision – when challenged – to roll on its back, expose themselves and submit to their demand: what the stresses were, and why their freedom from IK-2 was considered, they had no idea. They flew west. No refreshment was served. No information given them about toilet opportunities, so each sat, *legs crossed, girls*, and beneath them was a countryside that was barren of lights except for occasional pinpricks. The engines strained against the wind and to speak in the hope of being heard it was necessary to shout.

Frank's question, still Apricot but only for a few hours more, "So, guys, were we all prepared to do it? Myself I was going to run at the wire, a few more minutes, then out of the bunk, kiss you and gone. Maybe you would have heard the shots, maybe not."

Blueberry said, "I might have, might not have. Easier to talk of it."

Currant said, "Would have needed one of you to push me, help me. Could have funked."

Apple said, "All be dead now, in the morgue. For what?"

Apricot said, "Never to be spoken of again. Past history. Done, dusted, forgotten. Only a future, whatever that is, wherever. Remember, girls, we beat the bastards. No matter they haven't offered us a drink . . . A man said, 'I don't drink water. Fish fuck in it.' When we get to 'wherever' it won't be water we drink, and it'll lift our heads off."

They were all laughing, and the pilot's hand slipped on the joystick as he turned to see what was so ridiculous and the aircraft shuddered.

The senior pilot of the Gulfstream executive aircraft was rarely overworked. He was that day – and more was about to be piled on him and his colleague, and his phone was alive with further schedules. He was up from Geneva with a filed flight plan.

It was bizarre work, different to where he had been. He was 37 years old, married with kids, lived by the Washington beltway, an Air Force veteran and had the skills to fly the F-16 Fighting Falcon in combat missions over Afghanistan and Iraq. He now did the equivalent of Uber driving, but at 30,000 feet and at 500-plus klicks. When he would get back from this leg of his European mystery tour was unknown, but he doubted Beth and the kids would have noticed that he was away. He had brought over the hack boys. Easy enough to register their occupation because they talked it non-stop from boarding to disembarking. He was now in the territory of spooks, black arts, with three guys – and one girl, who was harder to read. In fact was shifting a prisoner: but not one who was bound or handcuffed, gagged or hooded. They had odd names – Tank and Sword and Cress, but their prisoner was not given a name. His usual trade was with politicians and government – sponsored lawyers, rich list names who could afford the fees charged by the company employing him, musicians and a smattering of celebrity sports stars. He kept a small black notebook in his case and sometimes would quietly ask a passenger for an autograph, but not that day.

The one he suspected of being a prisoner was a good-looking boy, a suntanned face, dark hair that was not cut short as if he had been institutionalised, decent clothes that had been washed but not ironed, a couple of days' growth on his face, and nervous, flickering eyes, dark and deep. He reckoned the other three were scumbags, and he had made up his mind on that from a quirky piece of equipment in the aircraft. There were a couple of microphones in the cabin, fitted into ceiling lights that could play the sound they dredged up through his earphones, or those of the co-pilot. It might have been an add-on to protect them from hijack threat if they were uncertain as to the character or motivation of passengers. They had good fun using it, including what a British co-pilot had called a soundtrack of "rumpy-pumpy", but it was not fun that he heard that morning, up above the clouds in clear blue skies, and such obvious falsehoods spoken.

"... just be confident, Skender, and stick with your story ... hijacked, a packet hidden in your car – you lifted ... the car set on fire, burned out. You gave them nothing ..."

"... don't deviate from that line, Skender, hold tight to it ... that is the route back to your girl. Your courage and resistance to the white noise and the sleep deprivation and hooding and wall-standing saw you through, and you played dumb about your appointments ... they wasted their journey, and you get to go home ..."

"... not my business, Skender, how you turn your life round, but the girl offers your best, could be last, chance. Sort the family out, then slip away, and just lose yourself. What is important is that you convince the family that you are one twenty per cent honest and reliable, and you will have nothing to fear, nothing ..."

But just like the Uber drivers in DC, the pilot and his colleague would keep their mouths shut, would not blow whistles, and the little facility that enabled them to hear lies so bare-faced as to be naked was not spoken of, off limits. He reckoned it would go bad for the kid, Skender ... not his business.

Tank was in the aisle seat beside Skender.

Two rows behind were Sword and Cress. The message came up on their phones, and would have also dropped on Tank's.

She said, soft, "That's another good day's work ahead."

He murmured into her ear and the stud diamond there, "And might require a bonus dollop."

"I need a new fridge and the washer's playing up – that level of bonus?"

"Enough for a week on a Greek island, plenty decently heeled widows."

"Fell on our goddamn feet, didn't we?"

"No such thing as *luck*. It has to be earned, doesn't drop off trees."

"The fridge and the washing machine, not cheap stuff, German made – that degree of bonus."

"I reckon we'd be on for that, with the extra hours ... Don't mind my asking, might you be in the mood then?"

Cress did not blush. "No, not in the mood, not yet."

"Fair enough." Sword raised him eyebrows, blew her a little kiss, eased back in his seat like this was the good life. "Let me know, about the mood . . . You're the clever one, Cress. How long do you give him when he's back in the family's bosom? How long?"

"Nothing good about him, is there? Are we talking *moral fibre*, or rather a lack of it? If he spouts the shit we've given him . . . maybe twenty-four hours. Has to keep to the text, bluff them, chuck it back at them. Might, *might*, pull it off. A day and a night, not more."

They came down at Levashovo. An airbase. Had taxied past rows of transport aircraft and ranks of military helicopters, and dawn was coming up behind them, and must have been at the near limit of their fuel because the pilot turned to them and shrugged and raised his eyebrows, but the gesture was for their escort. He told her the base had not yet woken and the minibus not yet assigned to them. He was yawning, and pointing at a dashboard dial that seemed to show a needle embedded in a red section and then he was grinning. The official grimaced, like nothing was as bad as working in IK-2 Yavas, even being at 6000 metres altitude and running out of gas – preferable to a normal day in a corrective colony in the wasteland that was Mordovia.

One said, "Why is all this happening to us? Why?"

Another said, "God alone knows . . . if he knows I'm not on his mailing list."

Frank said, "We are very small, pygmies. Out of our league."

"It is a sideshow, Denys."

"Important to me, Jonas."

They were back in St John's Gardens. Might have been a second office for him. Sitting on a bench, Denys Montgomery beside him. The man was not standing up well and had already confessed to spending half the night in his attic, worrying about the next stage of the Somerset and Dorset line, on to Cannard's Grave and

Binnegar and Evercreech, but not concentrating, and hearing updates. The women were between St Petersburg and the Federation border town of Ivangarod. The gangster boy was in the air and five minutes out from Podgorica. They had staff from the UK embassy in Tallinn who were at the border crossing on the Estonian side of the bridge that crossed the frontier, and a young man, Matt, was at the border of Montenegro and Albania, where the other side of the swap would take place . . . all on schedule, ready in less than an hour. Nothing more that Jonas could do, nor Denys Montgomery.

"A sideshow and no more," Jonas said, his voice distant as if his attention was far away.

"They are all sideshows, Jonas. They appear important at the time – you know, the 'salvation of the Free World and triumph of democracy over dictatorship'. The sort of stuff that keeps the troops happy. In my juvenile days I used to go to Berlin for an exchange, and they had a good bridge for it, on the road to Potsdam. I was a mere infant with Sixer-life. It was drilled into me that a swap is not a swap until both parties are one pace from the line. Our people scanning their people with power binoculars, and their people doing the same. Our snipers in position, and theirs. Traffic halted on both sides. An agreed time, and to the second, and the two Persons of Interest start walking. What could possibly go wrong? Plenty. Would I trust you, Jonas? *No.* Would you trust me even if my word had been given? *No.* Would you trust them, Jonas, the other lot? *No,* of course not. Doesn't matter whether it's a big top circus, or only a sideshow it is only done when the line in the road is crossed."

Jonas said he was going back to his office in Thames House. He abandoned Denys Montgomery, having suggested it was time for him to get buried in some work, which was impertinent of him. On his way to the side door he called at the café and there was a paper bag waiting for him, and a receipt from a pet shop.

One slept, snored and grunted.

One read a soft porn magazine, wrapped in a computer kit cover.

One watched horse racing on his phone.

The laptops were on the work table, and loaded on to all of them were the accounts – investments, property, cash – that had been routed via obscure Caribbean islands, after a thorough rinsing, back to the Swiss and German banks well represented in the City of London. They were waiting for the phone to ring, for the accounts to be killed, the screens cleared.

The women allowed the two Americans to go ahead of them.

They had linked arms, Currant and Apple on either side and Apricot and Blueberry in the centre.

The American eco-fighter had complained about the lack of food on the transport bringing them to the crossing point, and had looked down the length of the bridge and had further complained that she saw no camera crews waiting for them. "I mean, no TV, what sort of shitstorm is this."

The American WW2 historian, always a decent cover, had criticised the absence of any comfort in the truck bringing him from gaol. He too had looked down the bridge, scanned it, seen one anoraked woman and a couple of uniforms, and had bitched. "No sign of our fucking ambassador – what sort of fuck country is it, if the ambassador isn't here after what I've been through?"

A mark of the women's importance was that they were kept out of the main performance. Nobody stopped them and their raised voices faded as they set off over the deserted bridge. In the centre, the measured halfway point on the Narva river below, was a faint white line. Either side of the bridge was the evidence of the fault line that divided two cultures, proof of their long mutual enmity. On the Russian side was the immense fortress of Ivangorod, the first stones in the walls laid 600 years before – and with good cause. Across the river was the Narva fortress in present-day Estonia, and three centuries older.

An official, a pleasant-faced young man, in a decent suit and tie, orchestrated the women's pace, a mobile clamped to his ear. The three Russians, the political activists, whispered in each other's ears behind her. The official spoke only to the English woman; she had removed the usual level of tedium in his working life, and he spoke good enough English. Talked to her about the weather and the chance of snow later, and the poor climate of the *oblast* and the height of the river proved it, and said she must be pleased she had been released from gaol, and spoke of the charity of the authorities in permitting her early release. A smile broke on his face ... he had not himself been to London but knew many who had and hoped that night she would give his best regards to Piccadilly Circus and Leicester Square. They should walk forward. It was, perhaps, fifty paces to the white line and the bar was raised at the start of the bridge.

Best foot forward, Frank. The others had let go of her arms and seemed to have dropped back and she heard the murmur of Russian behind her, and the official's voice. She walked. She did not know to what she would return. Thoughts gambolled in her mind. She thought about Jonas Merrick, saving his life and going to IK-2 Yavas, thinking she was forgotten, not knowing why she was pitched from her bunk within minutes of trying to take her own life, and now being carted with her "sisters" to a bridge and a walk into the unknown. No love waiting for her, and no family, and nothing she knew but the "sisters" would be there, and ... Her name was called softly.

She stopped, turned.

Arms around each others' shoulders, not seeking to embrace her.

Currant said, "We changed our minds. It is fucking awful here, but it is our fucking awful. To us, where you live is a Disney Park. We stay here because here we can fight. You are, Frank, never forgotten."

Apple said, "We think, to have killed ourselves would have been cowardice. We think to have walked across this bridge would also have been cowardice. We doubt we are important enough for you ever to hear of us again – but remember us."

Blueberry said, "You showed us how to laugh there which made us rich. Always, whether together or not we will Just About Manage. You have our love."

As if on a parade ground the three of them spun on their heels, turned around and walked back towards the checkpoint on the Ivangorod side of the river.

The official ducked his head to her as if she had an importance that Frank had not recognised. She walked towards the line, a little frightened, but tried to keep her spine straight and her shoulders back and her head high – and an old world closed down and she could not fathom who had worked to achieve it.

Two cars, both black Mercedes saloons, waited at the far side of the frontier post.

He had been allowed to drive his own car from the parking area of Podgorica. The woman beside him, and the two men behind him – and a young man called Matt had been squashed between them on the back seat and he had his phone against his ear. A taxi from the airport followed them, empty but for the driver. The ones who had held him talked in Skender's ear.

The big man, the muscle, said, "Don't change the story, don't add to it and don't take away from it. Just keep with the story and you'll be fine. Don't fuck around with the detail."

The one who acted like an officer, said, "Don't ever forget, Skender, that we can find you. Can find you and can find your girl. Don't mess with us – because that is not clever. It has been a pleasure working with you, and we appreciate cooperation."

The woman, the one who he thought did the slicing with the boxcutter, said, "You got off light, Skender, and you should realise that. You were wrong place at wrong time – where it's dangerous to be, anytime. Just a little boy and out of your depth and recognise it, and you might just survive."

They had reached the control point. They lifted their coat collars and lowered the peaks of their baseball caps and she wore a scarf that covered most of her face. The one he did not know, who was Matt, had caught hold of his coat, held it grimly. Had spoken in the Montenegran language that was dual with Albanian in that region. Only time he'd spoken, and with intensity.

"We are missing my friend, Croppy. Croppy is surveillance. He followed you out, fingered you. Went back into his hide above your village to collect his gear – and is missing. Listen very carefully, Skender . . . if your family have him, and if a hair on his head is harmed, we hold you, responsible. *You.* We will come after you. Believe it, it would be unwise not to."

Skender asked, "Because of this man, I failed? What did he do?"

"A hair on his head is harmed."

He was told they would be in the taxi. When the horn sounded he was to go forward to the passport check.

He switched on the radio, music, went over the story. Tried hard not to let confusion overwhelm him. Tried also to imagine the face and the feel, the scent and touch, of his girl, and failed. Realised the scale of the business confronting him, the status of the managers and brokers and lawyers in the Swiss city, and the organisation that brought the Serb couriers to his village, and the depth of the purse paid to his grandfather for the family's services.

He heard the horn, one blast.

He drove forward. He knew all of the men standing beside the Mercedes cars on the far side of the control point, and principal among them were two with the rank of *krye* and trusted by his grandfather, and he saw no welcoming smiles on their faces as they dragged on their cigarettes. He turned the story of his experience over and over in his mind, clung to it . . .

He had known the men by the cars all his life. No love, no friendship, no respect were on display. He looked back once but the taxi had disappeared. His passport was checked, handed back and he drove on and reached them. He wasn't asked whether it suited him but was waved out of his own car and ushered to one of the Mercedes, was hemmed in for the drive to his village.

A phone call was received in a cubicle on the third floor of Thames House, and told of a delivery across the bridge between Russia and Estonia, at the city of Narva. A second call, this time from the Montenegran side of the border with Albania, and that also spoke of a delivery. Then a call was made to the premises of an independent bank, linked into its boardroom and indicated that the Mustangs were free to go to work.

The list of names on the table, representing the cream of the *siloviki*, as if it were an honours board of achievement in the cabal around the Leader, indeed included that great man. The three hacks might have registered a degree of surprise at the scale of holdings in investments and properties, the wealth it represented, and realised that it was a demonstration of naked theft. In the world of "ordinary" people, there was always a rider attached to advertisements issued by money managers that values of investment could go up and could go down . . . The geeks were at work and when those men had shifted their funds into the hands of their trusted friend they would not have contemplated that a loss could be registered as blank screen, as if a print-eating caterpillar had chewed the contents, eviscerated them. Some went to government funds, some to international charities, some had ownership transferred to men and women by an unsophisticated programme of choice, names taken at random, some quite simply disappeared. The Trojan Mustangs worked at speed, gobbled at sandwiches and smoked, had music at volume and showed no signs of pleasure or elation. Did what they were asked to do and did not consider the consequences that might accrue. That was a formal interpretation . . . in fact, none of the three gave a flying fuck for what might happen as a result of their tunnelling under, above, around and through so many firewalls.

And the man who had planned this act of computerised mayhem, the "everlasting flame" secure in his cubicle, would not have understood a word of the tactics that had been deployed – no idea. He would have felt challenged if Vera had demanded that he change the light bulb in their snug, would be rudderless if South Western Railway changed their timetable and cancelled the 17.37 that daily carried Jonas Merrick home. His value to those he served was his ability to focus attention on the few who did know, were the best at knowing.

Viktor and Natalya were regarded by contemporaries of similar affluence as being a golden couple. They had money, enough to fill vaults, they believed, but did not flaunt it. Their lives were lived in extreme comfort, but with taste. They were at the top of the pyramid . . . or had been.

"It's gone," said Viktor, "It has disappeared. Other than in extreme emergency I would not check accounts. Activity leaves a footfall. But I did just now. Actually saw it disappear, black fade to grey and grey to white, gone. Figures, balance sheets, all removed. We breathed the fresh clean air from a position of height and advantage – and now we have fallen. We are now amongst shit and weeds and violence and are without protection. I had an arrangement with others. They brought their money to me for safekeeping. They do not know of the crisis, I have not told them . . . and he, the new czar, Peter the Great in his opinion and Ivan the Terrible among the rest of us, I had his money."

"What do we have to do?"

"We can run for the border – which is not easy, not intended to be easy. Can go to the airport and try to board a plane for Belgrade. We can go together, to the top of the Federation Tower, hold hands, close our eyes, start to walk to a window, then swing a leg over, then . . ."

"Without the girls?"

"Or I can take my car and go to the Kremlin, and ask for an audience, and tell him this has happened because of his fucking stupid war, and without his fucking stupid war all that he had stolen would be safe. Could do that."

They were both crying, and his phone had rung but he did not take the calls. Then his home line, and then Natalya's number. And the dark settled around them and they sat close, and beyond the window were the "ordinary" people who struggled with their lives and did not look up at the darkened room above because that might breed acute envy. They would sit like that until their daughters came home.

"Do you know how it happened, Viktor, who did this?"

"I have no idea."

"Do you know what I can do to you?"

Croppy did not answer. The question put to him by the translator, an old man speaking for his boss.

"Do you know how much pain I can give you?"

Did not see the point in an answer.

"I ask you again, what have you done?"

Had been brought up to respect truth. To lie would be difficult and he doubted he could lie with conviction.

"You spy on us, come like vermin in the night, find a place on the hillside and watch us . . . to what purpose?"

And Croppy wondered if there were such a thing as "a good death". In the Regiment there was no hesitation in stating that no "good death" was possible if the ISIS had their hands on you, or Al-Qaeda, or anyone who an Albanian clan disliked. He sensed also the puzzlement of the man not used to being ignored, familiar only with men who begged for their lives.

"You have watched us. You know us. Your camera shows our pictures. My granddaughter, not a happy child, but has an animal's instincts. She identified you. Knew where you hid. You remember her?"

Remembered her.

"You know her and you remember her. Perhaps you also remember that she often carries garden shears, and many times the blades are dry and rusted, and a few times they glisten as if fresh paint is settled on them. Not paint . . . blood.

"Many years ago, I chose UK to begin to expand. I am a businessman and I look always for opportunities, and where there is a void I try to fill it. The men in UK want women, clean and not too expensive. They want cocaine and marijuana, and that too I provided. UK was kind to me, and I respect your society, but only if it does not fuck with me. If it fucks with me, then I will give a freedom to my granddaughter, and she will use her shears. You understand?"

He had seen men killed in Syria and seen a man killed here – brought up the steps he had been taken down. Brought out of the darkness and into the light and the mountain air, and bleeding and so wounded that a numbness would have settled on him.

"My granddaughter is a persistent child. She demands to be satisfied. Her satisfaction is to use her garden shears. I tell you, every man in the village – with due cause – has a fear of her. It would be your fingers and then your toes and your testicles and you would bleed but not enough to kill you. You understand that?"

A stag had a good death, one shot and the legs sinking beneath its body, and a shock wave of confusion, then helplessness, then darkness. Only had a bad death if the marksman was useless, or if the estate workers were more interested in tea and hot food than in the animal, and that behaviour might be tolerated elsewhere but not on Ardnamurchan. Did it matter, the quality of death, good or bad?

"You are merely a small part of an organisation. The people in charge of it, they would not know your name. One screw, one cog, one nut. But I am suffering, and so is my grandson. But, my stranger, I have to know who has chosen to fight me. You must tell me. It is a necessity. Who is against me? You are from UK, you write in that language in your book, your clothes have UK labels. At what level in your country are the men against me? What departments of government? I have to know . . . do not make the mistake of not believing me."

The old man held a torch and its beam was shone straight into Croppy's face. Another man stood behind him, and seemed to rock on the balls of his feet, as if ready to spring if Croppy were able to jump forward. There was a sadness, a tiredness, in the old man's voice and sometimes his speech slurred, and sometimes it was hard to hear and then he would shout.

"You have something to say?"

What might Croppy have said? Could not think of anything that he wished to say – other than a request to "get the show on the road", finish it. Didn't think of his girl. Nor did he think of the rude and patronising people who had taken over from him at Chamonix. Tried to picture the hills and feel the wind on his face, and . . .

"I do not admire men who believe themselves brave, and see that as a virtue ... it is stupidity. I tell you, I have experience, I would not be in this position – me standing and you below and in your own piss and shit – if I could not read men. Honour, your feeling for it, will not help you when my Klea comes close to you. The shears are blunt and she has to snap hard to take a finger or a toe or your private pieces. I have tried to help you, have tried hard, and you have not returned my kindness. You tell me nothing ... my answer, you will say something, will say much, when you are with my granddaughter. It is my promise, and ..."

He did not finish. Light flooded the cellar. The door at the top of the steps was opened. A man was in the doorway and hissed for the old man to come to him. The guard with the pistol at his belt took a pace forward. The one who was chief of the clan spat in annoyance, turned and headed for the steps.

More Serbs came, and Russians with them, and the parking space in front of the villa was filled.

The *shef* was outside his gate and men in suits were gathered around him, and voices were raised and fingers jabbed.

One question above all, "What the fuck is going on?"

Immaterial to Skender now, as they approached his home, his village, as to the moment he had realised the depths of the betrayal, the scale of the deception.

His grandfather had the funds to have had the road turned into a three-lane highway, with a reservation and crash barrier in the centre, and high-quality tarmac used for every metre: it would have been like clearing loose change from his trouser pocket. It was the view of his grandfather that no visitor should imagine the community to which it led was in any way remarkable, different from any other village.

They lurched along the rutted road, the driver knew each of the potholes. Not a word had been addressed to him. When he had left the village at the start of the week, the men who were now around him had wished him well and had slapped his back, but had kept the necessary distance of respect because he was the future: they would depend on his patronage. *Did you have, Skender, a good journey?* Not asked. *Did it go well, Skender, your trip to Switzerland?* Not asked. *How was it, Skender, that you fucked up so big?* Not asked. The man next to him, on the back seat, smoked incessantly but did not offer him a cigarette, and had not a word to say, and once he had shifted and his coat had slipped open and his shoulder holster was visible.

He could see the mountain peaks that were still coated in snow, high above the football pitch – where he was always a winner, always scored. He saw the bright red of the English telephone box, transported back to the village after a power drill had been used to free it from its concrete base and a lorry had brought it as a reminder to the village of how much money the community had made from that part of the UK. Passed the small houses and common to them was the presence of high-quality German cars parked haphazardly outside. Saw old men standing in groups, hands in pockets, cigarette hanging from lower lips, silently watching the convoy come closer. Saw young men in knots, and girls, gazing at the cars and the spray the wheels threw up, and the kids on the way to school ushered by their mothers to the side of the road. No smiles, no waving, none of the little ones sprinting cheekily towards the cars and shouting a greeting ... He was Skender, had been the future. No longer.

They approached the square and he saw the gates to the villa on the far side, and parked cars in a line and the protection with them. His grandfather's shock of white hair made him easy to see. The old man was hemmed in. At least half a dozen people were around him, agitated and angry. His grandfather's arms were gesturing for calm, for cool heads, and he was ignored. His grandfather turned. Skender saw his face, and the cars pulled to a stop, and a door was opened and the cold and the damp of the air buffeted Skender's cheeks. He was shocked. A few days and his grandfather had changed. He had thought of him as indestructible – virile and strong, in control – and those few days had ravaged him. Sunken eyes, thin lips, straggling hair, and the buttons of his outer coat were slotted out of order, and his spectacles were askew. The journey had warned him of an altered atmosphere; there was confirmation. They had told him in the safe house to spin a line, stay with his story, use his affection for the family, and had not told him of how the information he provided would be used. Did not know that detail, only that he had brought catastrophe to the family, the village, and the clan.

He stepped out of the car. Every eye was on him.

He started to walk towards the group – hatchet-faced men, dark suits, shirts and ties, quilted coats, shoes smeared with mud – and was watched. He set out with a brisk step, but his arms were caught. A couple of paces and he was restrained. A man on each side of him, and his sleeves gripped. Instinctively, he shook his arms to free himself, but they were held. Skender lashed with his fists and the reaction was instant. An ankle was kicked, hard, and pain ran up his leg . . . He thought of his dignity, allowed the men to hold his arms. He was brought to his grandfather.

He smiled because that was what he had been told to do. Appeared confident, because that too was necessary. Looked into the old man's eyes, searched for warmth.

A jerk of his grandfather's head in the direction of the villa. Skender was taken through the gates and to the door which was ajar, and it was awkward going through because neither of the men who held him would loosen their grip. Went across the hall towards his grandfather's office. Sitting outside it, on an ornate chair, was his sister and across her lap were the garden shears, and she was laughing as if the world treated her well.

"That's not very predictable, Jonas," Vera said.

He had rung her at work, at the gallery where they sold water-colours from the previous century, most of them featuring landscapes with hills in the background, water in the medium view, and sheep in the foreground.

"And unlikely to be boring."

"You'll be sensible?"

"Of course. Must get on."

He ended the call. Rare for him to feel emotion, but this marked a change of direction, and an area of work that he was unfamiliar with. He was grateful to his wife for not spouting a string of questions, and had decided hours back that the less said the happier he would be. The AssDepDG knew, had raised an eyebrow, pursed his lips, nodded as though surprised, flattered, to be on an inner loop. His calls were done, and he reckoned little remained that was left unsaid. He had done what he could . . . and taken the other calls.

A bizarre response from a trio of Russian girls on the approach to the Narva bridge, but understandable and perhaps a crash course in martyrdom suited them best, and Denys Montgomery was on his way to meet a flight from the Estonian capital of Tallinn. Two Americans, idiots who had caused difficulties, were in the air and heading for a USAF base in Germany. So the sideshow was pretty much played out. Three hackers – now under some degree of curfew in St Peter Port on the island of Guernsey – would be lifted back to their home base, but not until the work planned for the Gulfstream had been completed. Matters had that "end of term" feeling, all packed up except for a few loose ends that needed tidying. He took a last call, checked his watch and realised he had only a couple of minutes before he should be on his way. He had sent Sarah home, thought the girl was near dead from anxiety. Jonas Merrick could never be accused of presenting a sympathetic image – he had sent her home to collect some more clothes, and a sleeping bag, then come back in. That call was predictable, should have heaped satisfaction on him but that was not his mood.

Solly Kravnic: *Kravnic calling you. Was told, Merrick, that you had a magic touch and should be elevated to genius status, but was sceptical. Your effort is perfect . . . Their screens are dead, the cat fight round the Krem is gathering pace. You are a star and your praises will be sung. Best, Solly.*

Jonas Merrick: *More to do, Speak soon, Sincerely, Merrick.*

The car would be waiting for him. Would be under the watchful eyes of Security and no doubt half on the Horseferry Road pavement and masking a double yellow. He tore a Post-It from his desk drawer, took out his pen, and wrote his message. Had poor handwriting but thought she would be able to decipher it. He stuck the note to the centre of her desk.

"Thank you for minding the phones. Have gone to bring Croppy home."

13

Jonas used the basement to leave the building.

Had taken a staircase down, only used in fire drills, went past the corridor leading to the Post Room, paused for a nostalgic glimpse of what had been happy and productive days for him, then went by the open door to the police rest area.

Both Kev and Leroy were there, one with a magazine and one with a crossword book. It was noted that Jonas Merrick seldom exited at the back on to Thorney Street, also noted that it was a full two hours before his scheduled march to Waterloo, and noted that he carried a small grip bag as well as his briefcase.

A rare moment of humour from Leroy: "Afternoon, Mr Merrick – need *something* for the weekend?"

More serious from Kevin; "You all right, Mr Merrick? Can we be of help with *anything*?"

He paused, bit at his lower lip. Did not say, "What I need is for you two, full kit, to come with me", and the best help they could give would be one of them in front of him and one behind, and . . . He nodded dismissively, needed nothing, required no help. Perhaps they would have realised that his features were drawn, perhaps even a little haggard, that his eyelids drooped, that his cheeks were pale and his forehead set in a frown. He had reached the top of the internal fire exit staircase, had paused and sent a text to his wife, economic with detail. *Away for a night – or two – have my overnight bag. Hope we catch up on our holiday at the weekend, Alfred's travels etc and cake burning. With affection to you and Olaf, J.* Had sent it, had not reached the last flight when his phone had wriggled in his jacket's inside pocket. He had paused, read the answer. *Jonas, Stay boring and predictable, stay safe, stay*

SENSIBLE, Love, Vera xxx and Olaf. He shook his head as if to dismiss the nervousness . . . had said nothing to Kevin and Leroy. If he had, the chances were above high that they would have loaded the big bags they humped around with them, and added an extra few magazines for the H&Ks and would have been on their way to the garage where their car was parked, and . . . he would have given much to have had them close with him in the coming hours. He walked out into the street and pre-empted the man on the barrier and who controlled the ramp by giving him a savage glance. No clever remarks about an early start to the weekend, and was it Brighton he'd chosen? Down the street, headlights flashed.

He walked to a black Jaguar. It was the vehicle with the tailbar . . . Harry had the door open for him. Lolling against a lamp-post was the AssDepDG.

"In good shape, Jonas?"

"Why would I not be?"

"Death warmed up, my pertinent description of your appearance."

Jonas said, "Don't have a chance to bug out."

"Others are well capable of doing the job."

"I doubt it," and Jonas managed a sheepish grin.

"On your way then – if there's a main battle tank with a spare berth, Jonas, grab the place and don't shift off it."

Jonas settled on the back seat. "And, assuming I'm back in time, I hope to resume my holiday from which I was dragged, screaming and . . ."

"As I remember, you could not wait to be released from it. If it is needed, Harry will do the necessary. Have a good trip, Jonas, and don't forget to put your towel poolside . . . Oh, nearly forgot. The Yankees have booked a secure call to the DDG tomorrow morning which will all come as quite a surprise to His Eminence. Keep your head down, you daft old thing, and bring him back."

"Will do, but can't say in what state of health."

Jonas slammed the door.

Harry pulled away, turned into the traffic and put the blue lights on behind the ventilator grille. Jonas slumped back in the comfort of the seat. The delight of the AssDepDG's driver was that he never ventured into conversation himself. Jonas pondered . . . His phone told him that the Trojan Mustangs were clear to go home, their job completed, and they had done the computerised equivalent of pulling the pin on it and then rolling the hand grenade into a room where the privileged and the richest stood shoulder to shoulder in central Moscow. The Americans had been well served and would likely gush down the line in the morning. The sideshow, Frank, was in the air out of Tallinn and Denys Montgomery was on his way to meet the flight, and . . . awkward that a loose end needed tidying and the responsibility for it was in Jonas' lap, and Vera had urged him to be sensible, and he did not know whether that was achievable. Much depended on whether an ambassador had the clout to rake in a powerful crowd of men from a distant capital city: he had been promised by Jonas that a knighthood would wing his way if he managed it, but perhaps should have considered whether this "daft old thing" had the necessary status to chuck gongs around . . .? He did not.

Harry said, "Fifteen miles, and at this time it'll take about an hour."

They headed for RAF Northolt – something of an adventure because Jonas Merrick had never flown in an aircraft before . . . but then "never before" had such a weight of personal responsibility weighed on him. Would he be in time? Did not know.

His mouth bled, a trickle on his chin.

He was unsure whether his nose was broken or severely bruised.

On his side, awake and in pain, Croppy was on the flagstones of the cellar. No water given him and no food.

He shared the space.

The mice, or they might have been rats, had disappeared. One had been kicked away and the rest had taken note. The guard, Croppy thought, was the same who had escorted the boss, old and with good English, who had cajoled him and had threatened him

– and had seemed to have strained his tether to breaking point – as if Croppy were now of mere minor importance compared to a new burden of trouble. A pair of men had come down the steps and into the cellar and had kicked and beaten Croppy. Could barely speak English, might have picked up some basic phrases from DVDs or TV, but did not have the language to interrogate him. Beaten him for no other purpose than to cause hurt to a guy on the other side of whatever fence they sheltered behind.

The guard sat there and barely moved. Held a torch which was switched off. The only light in the cellar came from a candle. . . . All his working life, Croppy had practised his own version of Need to Know, and had it practised on him: he would not tell a client on the slopes of Ben Hiant what alternative stags were up high in the early mist of the day and with a better set of antlers than the one Croppy had chosen for killing. His officer and the unit Intelligence guy would not tell Croppy what the position was for life and death of an individual he was tasked to watch . . . he did not know why he was supposed to have the community under surveillance, what they were accused of, when they would be hit. Just did his part of the job. And had decided that the job meant coming back, clearing the hide, collecting the gear – doing all the right things, like he was a Boy Scout and had a sleeve covered in little badges.

The guard occasionally smoked. Croppy had seen his face the last time his lighter had flashed, and noted the loaded gun. Nothing that Croppy knew that was worth saying, and time slipped, and he could not estimate how long his time would run.

He lay still, and saw his mountains and the bare slopes and the curl in flight of an eagle, and heard the sea crash on the rocks, and heard the gulls' yelling and saw his girl.

"Can somebody not shut that fucking kid up . . ." a Serb said to a Russian.

There was a glance from the Russian to the Serb, and the *shef* would have heard and glanced at the Serb, a criminal lawyer from Belgrade and capable of pulling in powerful, influential friends, and the *shef's* glance was withering.

"Seems not," the Russian said, and he was a fixer, who worked out of the Serbian capital at the GRU station. "Should have been drowned at birth."

Skender heard the remarks, and saw his grandfather's reaction.

A second Serb said, "Can we not get on with this fucking show?"

Skender had been given a chair. He sat in the centre of his grandfather's office. The carpet under the chair was Persian, an antique, probably worth 100,000 euro, had been a gift from a grateful heroin trafficker for a favour done. The chair given him was canvas on a tubular steel frame. He understood. They put him in a servant's chair, brought from the kitchen, sent a message.

He was asked by the second Serb who he thought was an accountant, "You were coming from Chamonix, your story . . . you had no business in Chamonix . . . you were intercepted, your story, on the way to Geneva . . . why did you go to Chamonix?"

Skender answered, "To look at property, to look for investment."

"Why Chamonix?"

"We already have investment in Chamonix, I think we need a wider portfolio."

"You were there for a night. Where did you stay for that night?"

Skender said, "I slept in my car."

"Slept in a car, washed and showered in the parking lot? Clean clothes and changed into them in the open air, then checked over property to buy, and not shaved and not washed and smelling . . . you think us idiots."

Skender said, "I did not see any properties, but I checked windows in agencies, and took in the atmosphere because it is years since we bought the first investment there, then I left and was heading to Geneva, and . . ."

The question put and a smile to go with it, ice cold. ". . . and from nowhere a car or a van or a lorry arrives with police lights on it and stops you, and you then realise you have been car-jacked, captured, and are a prisoner – and the package you are taking to Geneva has been hidden in your vehicle."

"That is what I said."

"It is what you said, and expect us to believe. Why? Because you think we are idiots."

His grandfather sat slumped at his desk, had lost his posture of power and sometimes his head was in his hands, and sometimes his head shook as if he too, Skender's own flesh and own blood, saw holes in the story . . . He faced his grandfather. The two Serbs and the Russian were sitting to one side. One in a single armchair and two on a settee, and had fresh coffee in bone china cups, and Skender had been offered nothing. The room marked the success of the dynasty. A portrait in oil of his grandfather's own grandfather, in a heavy frame, hung on the wall behind the desk, and above the settee was a faded sepia-tinted photograph of his grandfather's father, wearing combat gear and carrying a German machine pistol, and another frame holding another oil – his grandfather on his wedding day, in traditional costume, and another that was a newspaper picture of the wrecked Range Rover in which Skender's mother and father had died . . . And behind Skender, by the door, sitting cross-legged on the floor, was his sister and all the time she hummed her song, and kept pace with the blades of the shears.

"You say you did not tell these people, who kidnapped you, anything about the location of the package you were to deliver in Geneva, which you had been given here."

"I did not."

"Did you know what information was inside the package?"

"I imagined, I did not know."

"What did you imagine?"

"Details of secret accounts. The accounts of rich people, people from Russia. Accounts that were secret inside Russia, and outside, and . . ."

"Enough that it is about confidential bank accounts, but you say you did not share that information with the people who had taken your freedom?"

"I did not."

"How did they attempt to persuade you to share such information?"

"By noise coming through earphones. No sleep, no food, no water. Stress position on the wall. No chance to pee or shit. I was hooded. I told them nothing."

More sarcasm: "Heroic of you. The people sent to Guantanamo they would have admired you. You resisted them, yes? Resisted, frustrated them, annoyed them, then they let you go."

"They let me go. They had gone back to where my hire car was – but it had been taken to a gypsy camp. Had been stripped and burned. They let me go."

"You told them nothing?"

"Nothing."

"You gave them no help?"

"No help."

"Were prepared to go to your grave rather than give details of the package to these people."

"Would not betray my family, my clan, my own honour."

There was a pause, quiet settled on the room. Skender scratched his armpit – realised he had not needed to all the time he had been away from the village and assumed it was because of the stress of the interrogation. Thought he had done well, thought also that his grandfather showed increasing frustration at the tone of the questioning, its lack of respect for their name and their status. Even his sister had stopped the monotony of the opening and closing of the blades, and the humming. He thought the time was right to attack. He was confident that he had the protection of his grandfather. It would have hurt the old man to see him sneered at, and threatened. His grandfather had told him, after the death of his parents, "The time you are protected is finished because you do not have your own father to watch over you. I do my best, and I hope, but you are responsible and you do not take one step back. Be resolute." That lesson had stayed with him.

Skender challenged: "We are business people. We do not steal. We provide a service. Guns, girls, 'phets, coke. We sell. We do not thieve. I understand that the monies dealt within the package is cash generated inside Russia by a most influential group, and at the expense of the people of that country. It is stolen money. We are only a taxi service. We make a journey, are paid to do that. I could say we are honest people. We do not cheat."

He heard the door into his grandfather's office open and close behind him. He saw his grandfather nod agreement, realised he spoke as the old man would have wished him to, and saw that the men who had met him at the border, who had the rank of *krye* in the code of the *fis* and owed their influence in that clan to his grandfather, and had no love for him because he was the future, were still impassive. He went further – too far but did not recognise it.

"I serve only my village, only my people. You treat me like shit on the pavement, a dog's shit. You come here and argue about a communication dealing with the disposal of *stolen* money, and you no doubt consider us to be peasants, barbarians . . . I tell you, we have honour. We have a code, a *kanun*, by which we live. Do you? Is your code dictated by greed?"

He heard the door again open and close behind him.

"We have enough of this game . . . I told them nothing. I endured torture but honoured my family with my silence and obeyed our code. I serve my grandfather and believe him a man without equal, an example to be treasured."

He saw the enmity on the faces, and in the eyes of the two Serbs and the Russian.

"I have work to do – do you?"

He heard the refrain of the song come closer and the sound of the blades clattering together, then squealing as they were dragged apart. He swung his head. He looked from the settee to the armchair and then to his grandfather – and their eyes met and he believed he had brought the old man with him through flattery, had massaged his vanity – then on to the henchmen at the side and if . . . *if* . . . big word, if he came through, then their faces would be remembered – never forgotten until punished, and . . . his sister held the shears in one hand and from the other she trailed a shirt, held it by the collar. He had bought it on a Geneva visit two months before. A businessman's casual shirt but smart and costing 150 euro. Had worn it when travelling that unexplained day earlier than his schedule required, and diverting to Chamonix, and kissing her and holding her before they had gone into her apartment in the block, and before it had dropped to the floor as he had stripped, he had realised that her lips had smeared a collar, a coral stain on a light check of beige and green on cream. Klea stood behind their grandfather and she carefully laid the shirt across his desk, and her smile was pure happiness and she pointed to the mark left by the lips, and Skender could feel Birgitte and see her and taste her. And then she lifted his shirt and held it under the nose of their grandfather and sniffed noisily as if to guide him.

The old man did as she directed and pain creased his face.

His sister, as if in conversation, said, "He lies. My brother lies. All he says is lies. If he lies once then everything he says is lies."

His grandfather looked at him, at first with a trace of sadness, then with confusion, then a degree of agony, then anger. The girl now sat in triumph on the old man's lap. To his own people, a croak in his voice . . .

"Find it, find where there are lies. What is the level of his deceit? Find that."

Following Skender out of the office, a Serb bent his neck and had his mouth close to the Russian's ear, and was grinning,

"Embarrassing, a mess to be cleared, a painful one, but with discretion."

"The lie is obvious – the screens are dead, money is gone, hacked out."

"They have a phrase, the British – 'What is done is done, cannot be undone'. Yes?"

"The codes were broken and the cash is gone, like it never existed."

The park was one favoured by families for summer picnics – then there would have been ample shade from the canopies of the trees against the season's heat.

The Park Berozovaya Roshcha was the place chosen by Viktor for the meeting. He had told the general that he would be on a bench on the central path that ran north to south across this haven of quiet and calm, and discretion. For Viktor, who had until the past few hours rather relished the unofficial title of "oligarch" and who had regarded the sanctions imposed on him by American, European and British agencies as badges of honour, the dilemma was to identify who, if anyone, he might now trust . . . or, to turn the question on its head, who might trust *him* in his hour of need. Like a hundred million dollars, and that was only his own loss and not the debit to the fortunes of those who had called him a "friend".

Viktor was alone. The general came with his chief of staff, who would hold back and not join the conversation, and further behind him were personal protection officers. The general, who commanded GRU, was a survivor, had come through various purges of military intelligence. He needed advice. To an impassive face, he explained details of arrangements made at a lower level in the organisation of GRU – ditched those who had trusted him and cared not a damn, chucked them into the furnaces . . . perhaps the general knew that his subordinates were liable to accept free-lancing assignments if they paid well, perhaps he did not: the man gave no indication of ignorance nor of being privy to illicit, illegal financial transfers. Viktor claimed – of course – that others in the *siloviki* loop of the most favoured had pressured him into acting as their banking link, twisted his arm, and had shrugged as if to explain that he was a partially innocent party – even the Leader had requested his services.

The answer came, and the wind was sharp between the bare trees, and no mothers pushed buggies and prams, and no dogs were urged to defecate quickly so that owners could go home quickly. No kids on bicycles eyed them, The general smoked incessantly, tossed away his cigarette half finished, and the chief of staff crouched and picked up the ends and binned them. The evening was coming fast, and sleet might fall.

"People claim 'you can run . . .' True, it is possible. People state '. . . but you cannot hide.' True, a certainty. Where is a welcoming country in which you might accept the status of exile for a few years? Iran, and the clerics? North Korea, and the little man? China, where they despise us? Defection is an option. The United States, I promise it, where you would be found? Only one option in my opinion."

"Which is?"

It was said of this general that he might be the sole man in the inner cabal who did *not* have investments in Switzerland, the Caymans, the British Virgins, or in Panama, and nothing in the City of London. Did *not* go down that route and who lived with his family in a modest three-bedroom apartment supplied by GRU.

"My advice, your best option, take a change of underwear and a change of socks. Ring *his* gatekeeper. Request an audience as a matter of urgency, and stop by on the way there and light a candle, or two or three, for St Olga. Explain fully and frankly – and hope. Good evening to you."

The anger lived with him – sadness and confusion and annoyance, all ditched. Only fury stayed with the *shef*.

It would be done and the whole village would watch. Perhaps the place for it was the square in front of the villa, or on the football pitch. The degree of his anger was measured by his determination to allow his granddaughter her chance: not so that either of them had the release of death, but only that losing fingers and toes would ensure neither found the release of death.

It was necessary for an example to be made. The regime of the *shef* of the village, the clan, the network stretching across the world, depended on his authority being maintained. It was not possible for him to roll his eyes, shrug, demand actions were not repeated, placate his granddaughter and deny her the opportunity to use her shears, and all the time maintain power. If he spared the boy he would be gone within a week. If his grandson lived then he, himself, would be a walking dead. The vultures and the eagles that sat high on the crags or cruised in the thermals could spot the approach of a meal thousands of feet below them – and the men from Tirana and Shkodra, Durresi or Lura would have those eyes, that ability. He would be dead, his village torched. His own grandson had weakened him, and the future was fogged ... he could see no further forward than putting to death his own blood, and spilling that of the man sent to spy on them. It was necessary, could not be argued. There was a ditch that ran from the English telephone box beside the road that led away from the village. However warm the sun in high summer there was always water in that ditch, and village dogs went to it to drink or to bathe in the mud. If the *shef* failed to clinch his authority that section of ditch was where he'd be thrown ... after treachery the next most grievous crime in the *kanun* was weakness.

He thought it were best done by himself, with the whole village there to watch, to demonstrate his authority, but after the girl child, his beloved Klea who had his trust, had been permitted her moment.

Saw himself reflected many times, as he made his way through reception, departures, the lounge, the exit to the apron. As usual he wore his trilby, his raincoat, his jacket of Harris tweed, and his flannels and his brogues, his Tattersall shirt and his quiet tie, and carried his briefcase and the overnight bag with pants and socks and a plastic razor, and his toothbrush and toothpaste.

Out on the tarmac was a glistening small aircraft. The first time that Jonas had been up close to an executive jet. Two pilots waited for him by the steps.

Behind him, Jonas heard Harry say, "Good luck, Mr Merrick, but hope you don't need it. We'll take care of this end."

The pilots were young, wore white shirts with pilots' epaulettes and black trousers with a sharp crease, and managed welcoming smiles. Americans, with the accent of the south and showing warmth, genuine or not.

"When you are, Mr Merrick, we're all ready to go."

"Who else is on board? Am I late ...?"

"It is only you, Mr Merrick. It is you we have come to collect."

A degree of astonishment. "Just me?"

They went up the steps. He followed, and sat in an aisle seat at the front. Light music played. At least twelve passengers could have been carried. The air smelled of some sort of deodoriser. His seatbelt was fastened for him and he was told the flying time and the ETA, and they'd serve sandwiches ... Did he want a drink: gin, beer, a Scotch? A cup of tea would do very nicely.

The doors were closed, the engines kicked in. They went off down the runway, then lifted. There were many places Jonas Merrick would rather have been than climbing over London's lights, but that degree of responsibility dictated where he was, and where he went.

Walking off the plane, she saw a pair of uniformed police, and a couple of suits who would have been Branch. She had sat alone on the flight, had declined food and drink, had kept her eyes closed and had tried to numb her mind into oblivion. She had no handbag, no luggage, no spare clothing, and IK-2 was already a lifetime away and unreal. The hardest cut of all had been on the road that crossed the Narva river, and the turning back of her only friends. Had never been so alone ... embassy people, cool and aloof, had met her off the bridge, had put her into the back of an embassy Range Rover and had driven her to the airport at Tallinn. No conversation other than the offer of a "comfort stop", which she had not needed. She had not initiated a conversation, nor had they. The skirt returned to her at the prison camp would have been too small by a couple of sizes before she had been shipped there, now fitted quite well, and the blouse was too large, and her hair was unmanaged and grotesque, and her bones protruded under her skin and she had the pallor of vitamin deficiency.

One of the suits took a step towards her. She wondered if they would produce handcuffs. A brusque, "This way, ma'am, the formalities are all in place." She was directed out of the line of other passengers through an unmarked door and into a corridor. She realised that she was no longer Apricot, and supposed that Currant and Apple and Blueberry were on their way back to whichever part of the *gulag* archipelago had been chosen for them, and it had been merely an episode and she was no longer a part of them. Down a long corridor which no one else seemed to be using, then through another door, and light and noise there. One of the Branch produced a clutch of papers, bearing her name. Up to a desk, and they were handed to a woman who looked languidly at them, whacked a stamp on each page and handed them back, never glancing at Frank. Off into a queue, eased to the front and the papers inspected again and a shrug, and then to Customs and Nothing to Declare, and opaque doors slid open.

It took her a moment to recognise him.

One of the uniforms said, "All yours, Mr Montgomery."

And one of the Branch said, "A bit of a miracle, Mr Montgomery, but all worked out. Good evening, ma'am."

He shook her hand rather formally, she thought, and rather nervously, and she realised that both the uniforms and the Branch had peeled off. She was in Arrivals, and the great movement of the airport cascaded around her, and announcements blasted her ears.

Stumbling over his words, he said, "Welcome home, Frank. You have been released into my care. Some of us have worked hard for this moment, but actually it was Jonas Merrick who made it all happen. He called getting you out of there a sideshow in a bigger picture of what he is involved in. An excellent conclusion, his sideshow. If you have no objection, I'm going to look after you for a bit. You are quite safe now. Let's go."

He steered her through the crowds and out into the evening, and he wore a path for them through the cars and taxis, and his own modest vehicle was parked illegally and had a ticket under the windscreen wiper, and he lifted it clear, tore it in half and then into quarters, and went to a bin and dropped them, and opened a door for her, and they drove away.

She asked, "Did the sideshow matter?"

"Some of us thought it did, considerably, and was integral in something huge. Was a big part of it, and it's not yet complete."

Skender had seen many men taken to the top of the cellar steps. Most times they'd had their arms pinioned at their backs, unable to break the fall when they were pitched forward. They bounced off each of the stone levels, might break a shoulder, or fracture a knee or split open their head ... In the cellar, men who had offended his grandfather were "softened up" and questioned if any more answers were required of them. Some died down there and that was usually because the violence inflicted on them was beyond what was required, and either physically or mentally they passed on – and that was always a disappointment to his grandfather and harsh words would be said to those responsible for too eager a beating – and there was hesitancy about permitting his sister into the cellar with those fucking garden shears because she had quite literally terrorised a French agent to death before the questions had even started. She would be allowed into the cellar, but not immediately. The majority survived the steps and the cellar ... they were then, later, dragged back up into the light. Some could walk, some needed to be supported. The village always turned out when a man, a wretch at the end of a tether, was brought up from the cellar and there would be an opportunity for him, in his death throes, to fight and struggle and attempt to humiliate those holding him, and have the chance to scream at the *shef*, the man who led the clan, and his family. If they did not fight and did not yell obscenities then the final act of the play was done quickly. That was the deal and was understood.

It was all as Skender had seen it before, except for the considerable difference that he was the focal point.

His arms were tied at the base of his spine. His face showed bruises and the breaks in his skin and puffed lips and the near-closed eyes, and caked blood. He sucked for air to take into his lungs. He was now the one at the top of the steps.

Three men surrounded him ... It had been the Serbs who had hurt him most, and the "professional" among them had been vicious: not a street fighter, not a gutter-kid, but with an education and qualifications, a lawyer's or an accountant's, and worst had been near the end when a kick had gone direct to his undefended groin, and a level of pain that Skender had not known before ... and much of the time his sister had watched and listened as the questions were flung at him, those fucking shears hanging in her hand, and an angelic smile on her face. None of the men holding him, steering him towards the cellar entrance, showed him any of the old subservience that was required only a week before . . . his authority was stripped. What did the villagers who gathered around the square think? An aberration, a mistake, an error that should be reversed? That his power was gone, never to return? That his situation marked the end of the dynasty, and his grandfather was old and succession would be bloody and their future uncertain. No one called his name. No one applauded, neither did they jeer . . . He had been the heir and men and women and children had ducked their heads in respect as he passed, and he was worth limitless money. Now he would spend a few hours in the darkness and then suffer death by shooting.

He tripped and his weight fell forward. The men around him could have stopped his fall but let him slip from their hands and he crashed down on his face, already bloodied. He was lifted up, dragged to the top of the cellar steps, and was pitched forward, as helpless as any other prisoner.

Torchlight flooded into the cellar.

He had heard a sob, as if breath were squeezed out from a ball, along with an impact.

Croppy had stiffened, as alert as he could have been but had failed to sleep. The guard pushed himself up

A man was lifted at his armpits, then thrown forward and hit the slabs and rolled which was the moment Croppy saw his face. Disfigured, bloodied, but he knew him. Knew it because of the hours he had studied it. Now saw up close the target's features.

Had seen the face, each expression magnified in the lenses of the powered binoculars; had seen it in the driver's mirror of a car ahead of him that he had tracked towards Podgorica airport; and at the desk for a hire car in Geneva; and in a parking bay close to the entrance of an apartment block in Chamonix – and with a girl . . .

Not now.

Croppy's hip was kicked. Not done to cause pain, but to shift him. He wriggled on his backside and a pool of urine was left behind him, and that space was occupied by the guy who had been the prince, the heir apparent. Another length of rope was found from a corner and knotted to the arms pinioned behind his back and then to the same manacle that held Croppy.

The guard who watched over them, showed his prisoners that his fag packet had only two smokes left . . . then made a production of finding more packets, enough cigarettes to last him many hours . . .

Croppy supposed he owed this man and knew his name and the extent of his authority, and how much he had lost. Had handed him over to the team, had been dismissed after clinging to Skender's tail, and been told, *suggest you go get a bit of sleep, a big burger, crash for an hour, and then a bar and a few, and a few more, then bugger off home. Job done, over and out and we'll get on with it.* And had not "buggered off home" but had gone back for his kit.

"Skender . . .?" Seemed important for him to speak first.

No response.

"You speak English, my briefing said you'd been in the UK. People call me Croppy."

No answer.

"It was me. I put you here."

Matt had brought the people carrier, plenty of seats and plenty of room behind. The bags, heavy canvas with strong straps, were stowed there. Tank said he'd drive it, and brooked no argument. Sword opened the largest bag. They were at the back of the main Podgorica airport parking area and far from prying eyes but – one of those knee-weakening moments – the bag had been heavy with the weight of automatic weapons, and bullet proof vests, and combat helmets.

Fastening the bag, Sword said, "Don't seem to remember signing up for that sort of shit. Sort of thing I would have expected to have recall of if I had done."

Matt answered him, "My military attaché was unhappy. Quote, 'I want nothing to do with this – not my business. Make sure you bring the bloody stuff back,' end quote."

Sword said, "I had reason to believe that my days clutching an SA80, the world's worst infantry rifle, and squeezed into a BPV, and with a chamber pot on my head, were over . . . Jesus, what sort of place are we going to?"

Matt said, "There will be others, Mr Merrick told me. We'll be at the back."

"Too bloody right."

A distant rumble in the depth of the night. A lone flight on approach. Matt had said that there was a protocol here about night-time landings, but that *Mister* Merrick had managed to get an exemption, didn't know how he'd worked it. Tank and Sword left Matt with the wheels and the firepower to start a minor war, and crossed the car park and climbed an internal staircase, and found them looking out over the apron from behind plate glass. All of them would have thought the same – the boss travelled in style. An executive jet, transport for a man who did not answer to a budget restriction. And they would have remembered conversations with a quietly spoken voice, not one over-endowed with dynamism or authority.

Half-awake, or less, ground crew wheeled steps up to the aircraft when it had come to a stop. A door was opened by a guy in a crew outfit. There seemed to be a handshake in the shadows of the interior of the cabin, then a single figure in the hatch.

Coming carefully down the steps, one hand on the rail, and the other carrying a briefcase and a small grip bag.

"God Almighty, is that real?" asked Tank.

"It is Methusaleh and his costumier is Oxfam in the High Street," contributed Sword.

"And we have to credit that guy has put all this together," said Cress.

Had to believe it because that was the one contact they had and no one else followed him down the steps, and he looked relieved as hell to have made it to the apron. He rammed a trilby on his head, and carried a raincoat and wind whipped his trousers. He set off for the terminal building, like he knew why he was there, where he was going.

It was a few minutes after midnight, local time. The most important day in Jonas Merrick's life was beckoning. He felt intimidated . . . had reason to because he trod the sort of ground where it was usual for him to send young men and women. New for him to stride – not strut – towards an unknown. A brief conversation with the pilots before he'd disembarked.

"You'll be here and waiting for me?"

"Of course, Mr Merrick. Here. Fuelled, Ready to go."

"Thank you."

"Your call, Mr Merrick – whatever time it suits you – and more passengers?"

"My intention."

"And a UK destination?"

"Also my intention."

"Hope your day goes well, Mr Merrick."

"As I do."

He had supposed it the sort of mutual encouragement practised by fighting men on the edge of combat, and found it unmatured and did not believe himself part of that world. He must have smiled then, but weakly, and the pilot tapped Jonas' arm as if a small gesture of reassurance was called for – Enough of that. Work to be done.

Had negotiated the steps, down into the cool of the night, and had headed for the lights and the main doors and a uniformed official came to meet him. And at that time, at home in Raynes Park, he would already have called the cat in and would have locked the back door, and his sandwiches would have been in the plastic box ready for loading into his briefcase in the morning, and he would have been upstairs and undressed and settling into his side of the bed and Olaf would have scowled at him because he disturbed the place the cat had already taken on the eiderdown between them . . . But he was not there, and had work to do, and carried a ball and chain of responsibility, laughingly known as a duty of care, manacled to his ankle.

He was enjoying his new status. Already in the bank was the chauffeured ride to Northolt, the flight in a Gulfstream G550 and seeing the landscape of Europe laid out below him. Now, he was met by a Customs official. He seemed to be the only passenger inside the glass and chrome building. Not asked his business, not asked the reason for his visit, and his passport was stamped without being examined. He followed the official past the carousel that awaited the next day's baggage and past the booths and kiosks not yet staffed. He assumed that a combination of the rank of the AssDepDG and the endeavour of the young man, Matt, had achieved it . . . but this was just the trappings, and the work of the day was not yet kicked into action. Whether that ambassador had succeeded in fashioning the near impossible remained to be seen, and whether he would be deserving of that spurious promise of a knighthood was as yet unsettled. Jonas tapped his jacket pocket, satisfied himself. He had done so in the car, several times throughout the flight, and again when he had unfastened his seat-belt and been ready to leave the aircraft: and each time, which was "predictable", the packet from the pet shop had been in place. Little else was predictable that he would face that day, and not much would be "sensible", and all was unavoidable. The official left him at the outer door, gave no sign as to whether he regarded Jonas as a guest or an hostile intruder.

They were waiting for him. He knew them by the names they had given themselves.

He made the judgements: Tank would be the muscle, loyal but not a leader. Sword would be intelligent, oily, untrustworthy and ruthless. Cress would be for herself, and then for herself, and herself after that. He reckoned them better than average and they had done well and his faith in them justified . . . They greeted him with a cocktail of complaints and questions. Where were they going? What their mission? When was their bonus going to be paid? Why was an arsenal of firearms waiting in their transport? Recalled an apt quote from the Iron Duke, *I don't know what effect these men will have upon the enemy, but, by God, they frighten me.* They'd bitch, but they would not run. He always enjoyed making the more pithy character portraits. They led him to a people carrier, and he met Matt . . . and the back seat had been cleared for him. He took off his raincoat, folded it into a pillow and settled himself . . . and did not know what the coming day would bring.

He spoke firmly, rather surprised himself. "All of that is for the morning. Nothing worth saying before dawn. I've had a long day and would appreciate a nap, the back seat of a vehicle will be very satisfactory, and we move off at 06.30."

14

The smell of socks was in Jonas' nostrils, and then a different smell, as strange to him.

He was lying on the back seat, woke slowly and without fanfare. He registered the time, a minute after 06.00. They were awake in the front and his team were lounging on the bench seat in front of him and outside a few paces away from the people carrier, was young, Matt. He was the source of the smell that competed with that of socks.

Jonas listened. Wanted to pee, but could wait. He felt he bristle on his face. He had omitted to loosen his tie before settling for the night, but had removed his brogues. They talked, he listened.

From Matt, crouched by a portable gas cooker, and with a crackling pan. "I tell you for nothing, this boy, this Croppy, he's a great kid. Really good at what he does . . . too good. Of course he shouldn't have gone anywhere near that bloody place after what'd happened, but he's got that rather naive sense of obligation. The boss, him in there, should have vetoed it. I mean who gives a damn about a pair of bins and a few fancy gadgets. He's a brilliant guy, Croppy, and takes everything he does seriously, wants to do it with no short cuts, and . . ."

From Sword. "That's not naive, it's fucking idiocy."

From Cress, "Maybe he was told to go back and get it . . . we only saw him once, when he fingered the target, and we suggested he was best employed pissing off home. Maybe he was ordered to get back in and clear out the hide."

Matt said, "Any experience I have, albeit limited, of the system means they are really tight-arsed about money – anything that goes on a budget they have to answer for. It was probably the cost of what was left. You know what they call him, Merrick, in his place? 'Everlasting Flame'. Why? 'Never goes out' ... Reckon that's why he's here. Guilty as charged. Knows what he did. Though what he's going to bring to the party I have no idea ... I mean, comes here looking like an escapee from a museum ..."

Tank said, "If he reckons I'm going in there, a mafia village, with an SA80 that'll probably jam on the first round – and him hiding a mile behind me – he's got a rude fucking awakening, and ..."

Jonas yawned loudly. "Morning, gentlemen, morning my dear. I've had an excellent night's sleep."

And Cress rescued the moment from embarrassment. "A cup of tea, Mr Merrick? Sugar and milk?"

He said that he liked it with just milk, no sugar. He was then asked whether he wanted his bacon fried to a crisp and if his egg should be turned over. Sitting upright he saw a camping stove adjacent to the back wheel with a sizzling frying pan that Matt tended. Vera always served cornflakes and yoghurt for breakfast. On the plate was bacon and an egg turned over, and a plastic knife and fork, and a tin mug for his tea that came from a thermos. The others had more to eat than him. Even on holiday he would have expected breakfast in the van, and nicely prepared sandwiches for lunch. Not to eat like a boy scout. Not that Jonas had ever been a cub or a scout – not that he had ever slept stretched out on the back seat of a people carrier. He ate what was given him, enjoyed it, grunted an indistinct thanks – and made a decision that he would not attempt to persuade them of the merits of his plan unless quizzed, would let it roll out. He drank his tea, warm, refreshing, felt ready to face what ever brickbats would be loosed off against him during the coming day, and the sun was up. He was escorted to the terminal building by Cress, and had taken clean socks and a razor and a miniature tube of shaving gel from his bag.

In the toilets he joined other men about their business, and surprised himself after using a stall by coming out to the bank of basins and taking off his socks, replacing them, and putting his shoes back on and knotting the laces, then folding his jacket and taking off his shirt and running enough hot water for his shave, and did it carefully because he thought it important he looked smart that day, and was at pains not to cut his upper lip or his chin. When he came out he was clutching the worn pair of socks, and Cress was waiting there for him. She took them from him and dumped them in a bin, then looked at him and, raised an eyebrow.

"Don't think we need to take them home, Mr Merrick. You can always bang a new pair on expenses. Considering what this caper is costing, I'd say that won't break the bank."

He had never charged anything on expenses before. Not the train journey down to Canterbury where he had captured the ISIS boy, not for the dry cleaning of his jacket after his dunking in the Thames, nor to get the bloodstains off the same jacket in a Liverpool street, nor for the chemist's repair kit after an assassin had failed to slit his throat. He said he would think about it. They walked back towards the people carrier and the time was advancing and the car park was filling. He asked her a question.

"The other boy, the village boy, the one you broke – tell me about him."

She said, "Two answers and you can pick the one that suits you best. For quoting, 'Typical low-life, over-indulged clan kid from the upper reaches of a family and with entitlement and we had to work hard on extracting the necessary dope from him, heavy and unpleasant work for which we are all expecting a decent bonus' . . . Not for quoting, 'Quite a pleasant lad, well-spoken and well-mannered and fitted none of the stereotypes I see when I'm doing interpreter stuff with the Flying Squad. Had a decent looking girlfriend in Chamonix, and he gave us all we needed and we don't know why. We did some white noise on him, stress-standing at a wall, hunger and thirst, a bit of threatening, but wasn't needed. I doubt we'd admit it, but the three of us felt sorry he was so screwed up.' "

Back at the people carrier he told them what time he wanted to be at the border, then settled back and worked his phone. Questions about the next steps were ignored.

It was me. I put you here.

They had slept as best they could, squashed against each other, and sometimes peeing down their legs, their hands swollen because the fastening on their wrists behind their backs had seemed to tighten. The guard had changed an hour back. The replacement was equally silent, but spat from time to time as if wanting to demonstrate his feelings for his prisoners. Each time he spat, Croppy felt that Skender winced. Time might be short and perhaps things needed saying. He was confident the guard spoke no English.

"They call me Croppy. That comes from Covert Rural Observation Post. It's what I do, because of where I come from. I was in the military on surveillance . . . but I'm from a mountain area and I stalked deer for shooting. In the army it was about surveillance of targets."

"I was a target?"

"Sort of, but not for killing, but for watching. See where you would lead us."

The little candle threw up faint light, but had created an intensity on the new, and frantic, working of a spider: he watched its industry.

"Because of where I came from?"

"For where you went, what you carried."

Ironic, almost a laugh, but hollow. "Not personal then, but what I took to Geneva?"

"Not personal. They brought me because of my understanding of terrain, especially mountains."

"The wildlife here? The flowers?"

"All of those . . . they thought I would be well hidden up there."

"We have eagles and we have bears, boar and wolves, and wild cats. You do not have them where you come from."

"Only eagles. You were the target and I followed you from the village, and went after you over the border, and scraped on to the plane – was in Geneva, was with you to Chamonix . . . then the other people came because I had called them in. It is my fault."

He saw it clearly. A small fly went into the web. The spider itself had barely moved but would have been aware of the prey that thrashed slight wings. Perhaps would wait, perhaps anticipated a second fly being trapped and a better meal.

"For you it was a job of work."

"A job of work, for which I am paid . . . I have a love of the mountains."

"Paid much money?"

"Not much . . ."

"You do this and are not paid well?"

"I was made an offer, didn't argue. I've little interest in money, and . . ."

"But you came back. Why? I think I know. Came back to collect the gear. Me, I would have left it."

"It would not have been professional to have left it."

He said it flatly, as if he realised the ridiculous position he had taken. The spider was on the move and advancing on the fly that had now ceased to struggle, was exhausted or ready to be eaten.

"You live simply, Croppy. May I call you that?"

"Thank you. Yes. Call me Croppy."

"You may call me Skender, my name."

His voice tailed. And Croppy thought it mutual, enough said for that time . . . The spider had begun to devour the small fly, kill it and swallow it. Maybe beyond the cellar steps a gust of wind came with a new strength, and tunnelled close to them and around them, and the candle flame shook and shadows bounced, and with the wind was the cold. He shivered, could not help himself.

The man who guarded them, sitting on the far side of the candle, shifted.

Skender hissed at him, "For fuck's sake, Bresnik, move yourself. Free us, forget this fucking game . . . I am telling you, Bresnik, do it . . . without me, you are nothing, nothing – are nothing."

He was not answered.

The light came through thin curtains. Frank woke, stretched, was warm, then jack-knifed in the bed – and was awake.

The pattern on the curtains was of overblown red roses. For months, through winter, she had been driven from a bunk bed in darkness with lights hanging from the angled ceiling above the dormitory and around her would have been the noise of protest and of coughing and sometimes screams. If it were daylight then somehow she had missed the compulsory evacuation from the dormitory, the physical exercise in the yard, the breakfast and worst, the ultimate crime, was late at her workplace and firing up her sewing machine – and was not with her friends, and . . . She heard a low-pitched droning sound, irregular, above her. Heard a single vehicle pass. And birds cheeping.

She opened a wardrobe built of heavy, old wood. It was empty. On the back of the door was a dressing gown which she slipped into. She had not wanted to sit up late the night before and could not be bothered to discuss whatever "terms and conditions" she'd be obliged to observe. She had beem given a sandwich of tomato and ham and pickle to take upstairs which was still on the bedside table along with a mug of cocoa, untouched, and had been shown where the bathroom was. There had been no talk in the car because she had closed her eyes and slept. Now she followed the droning noise, climbed a narrow staircase from the landing and her head poked through what was little more than a hatch.

He was there. Denys Montgomery, senior figure on Russia Desk at VBX, was bent over a table, and the noise she had heard came from the rushing sounds of small electric trains . . . He said it was the reconstruction of the Somerset and Dorset line, of a section between Bath, Green Park, and Radstock (North) – the Shoscombe and Single Hill Halt – and his model engine was a replica of the BR Class 5. It had been gabbled and she realised his shyness in her presence. He had told her his mother had died, told her vaguely about his new position at work, told her that he lived alone, told her that she was not about to be arrested and that no charges lay on file, told her that her freedom was gained by a side-show alongside a major operation. Told her there was a shopping mall within easy walking distance, that he had taken a day off from work, and that a few edibles for breakfast were in the fridge.

She went back down the stairs. With the time difference she imagined that Blueberry and Currant and Apple would be well into their day and might already have forgotten her.

Viktor made a phone call, using a restricted number, one known to very few, and reluctantly shared. He was connected to a private switchboard and patched through to an aide. He was not fluent in his request although what he would say had been repeatedly rehearsed. The aide listened to his brief explanation – a matter had arisen that required the attention of His Excellency – and he was respectfully requested to wait on the line which was then connected to the gatekeeper, the sweeper-up of earthquakes and trifles.

He explained some more. "A matter of finance" needed to be discussed. Urgently? He suggested that the need for discussion was indeed urgent. He was given a time later that morning, awarded a fifteen-minute slot. He grovelled his gratitude and the call was terminated.

It had taken him a full hour to prepare for the request and he had needed the encouragement of Natalya – *For the love of God, Viktor, get on with it* – before steeling himself. He had not bothered to telephone the others involved. The previous evening his daughters had waltzed in from a party in the Arbat district, now gentrified and patronised by the kids of Viktor's and Natalya's friends: it was their playground, where money ruled. Neither parent had thought fit to settle them down, tell then the now home truths and their implications.

Much frightened Viktor that morning, not least the matter of his own trustworthiness. What if he were not believed? Critical. What if it were imagined that he, Viktor, had siphoned off the funds now missing and lost from view? *What if* it were thought he had fucking ripped them off, stolen from the Leader, thieved from the inner circle? *What if* that were believed? He went to prepare himself for the journey to a side door of the Kremlin Palace.

Skender spoke softly, broke a long silence.

"Do you understand, Croppy, what it is to break away?"

"A little – not easy."

Across the cellar, sitting on a hard chair, a pistol tucked in his belt, was Bresnik. Skender had known him all his life. Taught to ride a bicycle by him, and taught to drive by him, taught to shoot and to fight by him . . . and Bresnik was a favourite of his grandfather.

"To leave the village and the family – and to leave the life."

"Difficult."

"My father was killed in a car, RPG-7, and my mother. And my sister was with them but in the back and somehow survived, not even hurt, but was psychologically affected. I became my grandfather's heir. Everything was prepared for me to control the clan of our family. The continuation of the clan depended on me, and the village, and the network that my grandfather and his father created. I was not asked. Of course not. I would not have been asked where I wanted to live, the business of the clan would dictate it. Nor was I asked with whom I wished to spend my life. A wife would have been found for me, but that would involve a strategic alliance or the joining together of our clan with that of a family who handled matters we did not – heroin, migrants, mercenaries in Africa. It was assumed."

"I was put in the army because a client I took out to kill a stag praised my stalking. Impossible to refuse. I was in Iraq and Syria, and men were killed, and their families, because of me. I wanted out, not easy. But not like you would have."

"An ordinary life, what I wanted."

"For me a very ordinary life."

When Skender had gone to London, for the first week he was there, Bresnik had been with him, which showed those he met there, from his own village, that he had the protection of the *shef*, the master of the clan. Bresnik had not enjoyed his time in Essex and east London, and would have been relieved to get on the flight back to Albania and his wife and her cooking – but the big man had asked him to travel, which would have been enough. Of all the men in the village, Bresnik was the one Skender had valued most, would have been a bullet catcher for him.

"And the money is not necessary. You need one meal a day."

"You need money to pay the bills."

"Do not need money for gold taps, when taps can be made of chrome."

"But just talk, Skender, and talk is cheap."

"Talk is cheap and life is cheap."

"You have the right to hate me, Skender."

"And does that help me?"

"I don't know what does help you, me – us. Now . . . what, if anything, helps us?"

"There is no reason for me to hate you, Croppy. It was business, it was money, it was about the way I live."

At the end of any day. It would be the *shef* grandfather who would tell Bresnik what was wanted from him, by a gun or by a knife. Never speaking, allowing the quiet of the cellar to nestle round him, but with the sharp tip of the barrel end and the foresight gouging his waist, and never considering that an order would not be obeyed.

"When will they do it, Skender?"

"Today. They will do it today. I do not know at what time, but today. They will make a show of it. Do it to you because you came on to the territory of the clan . . . Do it to me because I was a failure and by failing I showed the weakness of the clan. I do not know at what time, but today."

He had thought of appealing to Bresnik, asking for the wrist ties to be cut but had not done so. Had thought it would have degraded him, and also thought that the chance of success was nil – fucking nil. The name of Bresnik meant "faithful" which he would be, faithful to Skender's grandfather.

Jonas felt surprisingly good.

Was almost relaxed. Had enjoyed his "unpredictable" breakfast, had shaved closely, had absorbed his phone messages, and taken some exercise.

Timing was important. He did not wish to be hanging around at the rendezvous point, nor would those he was meeting be happy parked up in a lay-by, not in that area. He had indicated a point on the map to Matt, and had asked at what time they should go through the border formalities to be there at 10.30 hours, local time. Who they were meeting, and what the result of it would be he had not told the team. They were a couple of hundred metres on the Montenegran side of the frontier. The weather was dry and Jonas had abandoned the back seat of the people carrier and had gone walkabout, a full twenty minutes. Had pushed the blood round and, bar a couple of times when he might have been unwisely close to being run over by a heavy duty lorry and trailer, had enjoyed it. That was his way of playing out the two weekday legs of stamping his way to and from Raynes Park station and then on from the London terminus and over the river and to Thames House.

He was uncertain what was ahead of him.

The team had done firearms drills, Sword sorting himself out, and Tank showing Cress how the SA80 infantrymen's weapon worked. Had done it in the shelter of a lay-by and where they could not be seen by traffic passing either way. Did he, also, wish for a lesson or did he already have full firearms experience, Jonas had been asked. With some dignity, he thought, he had declined the offer. He had never held a loaded weapon of war, let alone fired one. What role were they supposed to fulfil, Cress had asked of him, but he had shrugged, reckoned that the enigmatic response was better than shoving together a whole bucket of potentials. What remained constant was his commitment, whatever the obstacles, to bringing Croppy home or in the process . . . better not explored.

He checked his watch, had done it too many times.

Had received one message from the AssDepDG. *Still have your bum on the towel poolside?* Had not replied. Another message arrived: *Your bucket of tin and gonic holding out?* Had not replied to that either . . . and rated it as a bit late for turning back.

Jonas said, "That moment when any faint hearts are allowed to step out . . . None? Thank you. Can we go, please?"

He saw that Tank, now in the driver's seat, lightly punched Matt's shoulder. Saw beside him that Cress, on the bench seat in front of him had lifted Sword's hand and held it tight enough to turn the knuckles white ... He was alone on the back bench, preferred it that way, and did not know how it would be. They headed for the Customs check, a formality, then drove into Albania and to the crossroads he had pointed out to Matt – and switched off his phone.

Might be in time, might not. Perhaps could influence events, perhaps not.

"I don't," Croppy said.

"You might as well," Skender answered him, and nodded to his man.

The guard had come forward, had produced his packet of cigarettes, had put one between Skender's lips and had been about to give one to Croppy. He'd turned his head away ... he hated cigarettes, a little bit because of the health factor, a big bit because the smell had a lasting life and hung in the air and was a giveaway of his presence. He allowed it to be lodged in his lips. A lighter flashed twice.

Croppy retched, then coughed. Skender inhaled deep then blew smoke. Croppy thought it pretty damned stupid to refuse a fag given his situation. The face of the man, Bresnik, was mostly in shadow but Croppy reckoned he saw genuine pain, and the man probably risked trouble for himself if it were known what he did, made that gesture of kindness.

Skender asked, as ash drooped on his fag, "You have a girl, Croppy? You have a girl who does not smoke?"

"I have a girl."

"You live together – what in England they call an item?"

"No ... I am in the far north-west, in Scotland. She is in London."

"It is the big love?"

"For me, yes. For her, I think so. We are going to ... am I stupid? ... We *were* going to rebuild a ruin up on a peninsula that goes out into the ocean. New roof, new floor, new plumbing, new everything, and have a life there. It is remote, wild ..."

"Like here."

The man, Bresnik, was up from his chair, and removed their cigarettes, flicked the ash off, replaced them.

"Like here and not like here. And very few people have much money." He coughed again. "They would talk in the village for a week if a local drove a new Mercedes and wonder how he could afford it."

And laughed a little as if that were truly funny.

"Every man in this village can have a Mercedes car . . . Tell me, Croppy, about your girl."

Could picture Sarah in his mind. He did not think it important what colour eyes she had, or the shape of her nose or the width of her mouth, or the cut and colour of her hair – nor what she wore other than jeans and trainers and sweaters and anoraks. Thought a smile was all that mattered to him, and she smiled mostly when she did something that surprised her – talking to him about the sort of digger they would need on site, or the type of cesspit they would dig in a gap between buried granite stone, and where roofing beams could be most cheaply bought and then transported on the long road from Fort William to Kilchoan, 52 miles, more than two and a half hours for a lorry. He'd say, dour, that she had done well, and she would smile – then they'd hug, then the shyness would gather round them, and maybe she'd blush and maybe he would hold her some more and hug her closer, and . . . and it hurt to think of her, but he needed to share.

"She's a lovely girl, from a city but wants to be up there where it rains and the wind blows and the wild creatures are around you, and people have simple needs but are not stupid. The village looks after itself where it can, mucks in and helps. We are going to be married . . . haven't told her yet, but I've already lined up a best man, and I'd imagine she has looked at a dress she might want. We'll live in a caravan on the site while we're getting a roof on this cottage, while we're getting a well dug and linking in with the power. We'll have a dog, likely one of those crazy spaniels, and I hope we have some babies. I haven't told her all this, and she hasn't told me that's what she'll want. But it is obvious. What I had already decided is that I would never again go on a trip like this – that snared you, Skender – never again. But a bit late for that, isn't it? A whole lot late."

And Bresnik was back again, his features wreathed in sadness, and he took the fags from their mouths, and killed the embers under his boot on a flagstone, and sat again.

"And her name is?"

"Sarah."

"A nice name."

"She has no money, and I have no money. People will help if they can – not many can . . . I'll take clients out in the season and we'll cull the stags that need taking down. We don't say kill but use a silly word, *cull*, and then feel better about it. I like to kill the stags that can't live properly, put them beyond misery. Sarah would understand that. Once we've the roof and the basics, and we live in this croft, what they call a cottage there, then we'll have fires and play board games, or maybe just watch the flames . . . I'd reckoned we'd spend the rest of our lives there."

"They haven't come to look for you, Croppy, your people."

"Not the way it works."

"How does it work, your side of the fence?"

"They chose me. Chose me because I am deniable. Not a soldier, not a policeman, not a spook. Means they don't have to start a search for me. Between me and you, the two of us and together, we gave them what they needed, enough for a big prize, and we'll be written off as casualties. That's the price, Skender, of deniability . . . God, did I make that speech? Was I that pompous? Forgive me, Skender."

"The truth is always forgiven, which is my speech. Not pompous, Croppy. I apologise, apologise for much. Can I tell you about my girl?"

"I'd like that."

Skender grimaced.

"She is clean."

"Of course."

"She has no criminal record."

"Of course."

"No criminal record, has never been arrested. She is not an offender. She does not launder money, does not procure girls, does not courier narcotics. She sells real estate. She is a normal girl and the women I meet in my life are not normal. She has a business education, she had a full schooling. Nobody looked to shoot her parents with a Russian anti-tank missile and they live in a small house with a dog and with her younger sister, somewhere in the south of Germany. She could not bring me home, could not say that she has met up with an Albanian boy, from organised crime, who is worth many millions, who is – *was* – the heir to a clan that is watched – but without success – by Interpol, by Europol, by FBI, by your Crime Agency. They would be horrified. But I love her, and I believe that she loves me, and that our future is – *was* – together. You have seen her, Croppy."

"I have seen her, a very pretty girl."

"You saw us together."

"Was skulking, using my training which is to be seen but not noticed, was watching. That is the guilt I have."

"We would have gone away, perhaps to the north of Germany, up by the Danish border. It was the intention. I don't know if it is possible, today and in this world, to disappear. Leave no trace – without an identity card, without a tax number, a social security number, a health number, a driving licence. I do not know how it would have been possible. If I have those things then there was a probable outcome . . . I would be shot, and a possible outcome is that Birgitte would be shot with me. If not shot, then in a car with a bomb underneath the driver's seat. If I walk away then they come to find me – they hunt me. What sort of life is that? Always looking over a shoulder. Always wondering who is the stranger at the end of the street. Always concerned about a car, about a crowded street, about a hedgerow high enough to hide a man. She understood, said she accepted that. Would it have been a life worth living, Croppy?"

"But you came back here."

"Listened to your people. Believed what they said. In and out and before the catastrophe exploded on us. Russians here, Serbs here. It seems, Croppy, that the idea was to remove big monies from the accounts of prominent Russians, take them off the screens, hack them. They have lost millions, many millions, enough millions to make them angry. Which is why I am here, why you are here . . . My girl, could we have had a life if we were running and were hiding?"

"I don't know."

"I have been given everything I have ever wanted. Everything . . . except for her. I cannot be with her. We used sit in that church close to her apartment. The church of Saint Michel. It was a good place to go . . . Were you with us, Croppy? In the church?"

"Saw you go in, then handed over to the other people."

Skender said, "You had a real possibility of a life after this place, my village. I did not. You would have had a good life with your girl. For me, just a dream – and a dream ends when I wake, and you do, and find myself here, in this fucking place."

He thought he had talked enough, or talked too much, and closed his eyes, and heard Croppy's breathing, and wondered how long was left – hours or minutes, did not know.

The AssDepDG had been called up to the fifth floor.

He detected a tension in the air. Had been welcomed by aides but coolly had been asked to wait in the lobby, had seen favoured staffers hurrying in and out and crossing the lobby from the DDG's room to the DG's suite.

As well they might . . . might well ponder why at six o'clock in the morning, Washington US time, a senior man from the Agency was wanting to have a call – one on one – with Brian. He would be being briefed as if in deep dark shadow over what crisis was currently bothering the favoured friend in the mythology of the 'special relationship'. The AssDepDG was called in. Had an idea, a well sourced one but kept it close. He had not been asked to sit, but leaned against a wall on which hung the usual photos, framed in gilt-painted wood, of Brian meeting the great and good, and more influential, of the counter-intelligence global community, and a smattering of presidents and chancellors, and in a queue waiting to shake a royal hand. A young woman staffer lifted the handset when the phone rang, did the formalities, passed it to Brian, and handed a remote to the AssDepDG.

The AssDepDG listened, and worked rather frantically at the "excuses" that might need deployment.

"Brian here, good to speak, Larry. A ghastly hour for you, so assume it's pressing."

"My pleasure in touching base with you, Brian – the matter is indeed pressing and well worth my getting my socks on at this accursed time of the morning."

The AssDepDG would not at that stage have read the voice, determined if it would deliver the usual faint and rather sarcastic praise dripped out by the Agency, or whether it presaged an utterly polite and utterly savage bollocking for a UK failure.

"What is pressing?"

"Are you hearing me okay, Brian?"

"Very well, all ears."

"Wanted to say this, and it is a viewpoint widely held in this building since the events of last evening became apparent ... Wanted to say that your ship, so well managed and run, has the admiration of all who know about Safety Deposit. An excellent codename, and further shovels shit in their faces. We loved that, what a sense of humour, Brian. Anyway, our investment in this operation seems minimal compared to the rewards and we would like to offer our heartfelt congratulations. Over there, on the Moskva River, they are well and truly skewered. Which means they will further turn on each other, savage in-fighting which we really like to see, and the big boy will be further weakened. It is so good to have a grandstand view of the chaos inflicted on them. And, I sincerely admire the way, Brian, you have given the prime role in this operation to that excellent operative, your Jonas Merrick. Wish we had a few with that man's capabilities, and his balls, and his ability – uncanny – to look far into the future. You might consider, Brian, letting us send some of our brighter younger people to the UK for a long weekend, have some lectures from Merrick. He is amazing, but so are you, Brian, for giving him free rein. To finish, what we can see so far is the destruction of the core wealth of a number of very unpleasant individuals, and we rejoice at that, and we will be analysing this for weeks. God speed, Brian, and I am now off to get myself a worthwhile breakfast, but wanted first to offer those congratulations in person. Thank you for your help and cooperation."

The AssDepDG looked across the room and saw a face that was well flushed, had gone beyond pillar-box, had taken on a deeper red, that of a Merlot.

"What's he done, that bloody little man – and where is he?"

"Not too sure, but something to do with Albanian gangsters, but not sure." The AssDepDG lied frequently in Jonas's defence, and had made the untruths about him into an art form. "Where is he? I seem to think he's on holiday, abroad."

"I'll not fucking take it."

"Agreed, Brian, and that degree of ego-massage from the 'cousins' is not really welcome – though good to have for future needs, secure in a Safety Deposit box."

The AssDepDG went to the third floor, to S/3/12, and interrupted an Aggie Burns briefing, found the girl in Jonas's cubicle, alone and seeming to be short of sleep and food and coffee, and of hope, and was told that Mr Merrick's phone was switched off.

He left, paused in the corridor, muttered, "You silly old beggar, what have you gone and got yourself into?" and went in search of the refreshment trolley, and would take her back a large coffee, at least three sugar sachets, two pastries and a bar of chocolate – and imagined a situation, away in a mountain valley on the far side of Europe that was worse than fraught, far worse.

"Where's Poppa going?"

A question to Natalya from their younger daughter. The girl wore a gossamer-thin nightdress and wandered barefoot in the apartment, and the central heating was turned up as high as she was used to.

"He's going to the Kremlin," her mother answered.

"In that suit – really?"

"Yes, in that suit."

In the hall, Viktor had heard the exchange, and the girl would have noted the way Natalya had clung to her husband in the moments before he had glanced at his watch, known it was time to leave. The matter of which clothes Viktor should wear had been discussed. Not an Armani suit but something ordinary. They agreed that he should not travel in his chauffeur-driver limousine, but use her car which was more modest, ordinary.

He drove from their underground garage out on to the street and took the lane reserved for men and women of importance and their wives and husbands. The city was going to work and he sped past the usual traffic queues. Twice motorcycle police eased up alongside him, then noticed the badge at the side of the windscreen, saluted him and veered away. At a side gate he was stopped by the Presidential Guard and his identity document checked against the list of those with appointments. At another guarded door he left his car and was led inside an area with a double gate, a metal detector arch, and an X-ray machine with a tray into which he was requested to place his wristwatch, valued at perhaps $100,000, his spectacles, his wallet, his phone – and his belt. He went through the arch holding up his trousers. His belongings were returned to him, but at the end of a corridor he had swabs taken from his mouth which were then tested for the disease of which the big boy was so fearful. And resumed his journey, until he reached the outer office of the Chief of Staff, and had counted that he had already passed a minimum of ten armed and uniformed people, and wondered, with a sprinkling of mischief at such a heretical thought, who guaranteed the loyalty of the men closest to *him*, who checked *their* trustworthiness. When previously he had met with the Leader it had been at informal parties at the *dacha* villas in the forest, before the paranoia bred by the war. He met an aide, a young woman with a tight uniform who asked him what was his business, but he declined to answer, and she shrugged as if such a reply had been expected, then on again, and another door, and more guns protecting it, and the faces of the men holding them seemed lifeless to Viktor. He met the Chief of Staff, was asked curtly what was his business. He started to explain, hesitantly. A chair was then given him, and sheets of Presidential Office headed paper, and a corner of a desk was cleared, and it was suggested he write down his concerns about the investments he had handled, and briefly. He was then offered a seat at the back of the room, and there were unopened newspapers in a pile, and he was told he should wait, and a glass of water was brought him.

A rather stammered question, how was His Excellency today?

A sharp answer that declined further explanation, "Concerned with military matters, those from the front line."

"That is more like what I wanted to see," Sword said.

Behind him, Jonas Merrick had his phone out and called the directions to Tank. They were driving along switchbacks and were high up and could look down on a single-track road below them.

"Like Christmas come early," Tank said over his shoulder. What there was of the sun shone on plate metal.

More cigarettes lit which was a sure sign in the world of the two army men and the woman who went out on "lifts" with the Flying Squad that it was closer and more real and that they would have serious company approaching a "sharp end".

"This is beyond incredible, having them on board. My martyrdom is going back on the shelf," said Cress.

What they saw was a lay-by filled with the awkward and ugly shapes of three Hummer H1 offroad vehicles, what had come from Humvees, maybe secondhand or third, but heavy from armoured plate, and Tank did the honours of describing their specifications.

The vehicles were visible for less than half a minute before they were again on the sharp bends and closing in. In that time, all of them turned to stare at Jonas Merrick but he gave them no acknowledgement.

It would be done in the afternoon, and the village would watch it done. He had given the order. The *krye* would ensure it, and the bosses of the sub-groups would ensure that each home in the village was emptied, except for the few people who were bedridden. No excuses accepted. And it would be done on the square in front of his villa. The stranger first who had come to spy on them . . . a seemingly decent enough young man but he would follow to his God the Frenchman who had also watched and deceived the village. He was reminded of the story told him by his own father: in the last days of the Patriotic War, a German junior officer had been captured and was about to be shot and had calmly gone with a smile on his face to each of the men who would form the firing squad and wanted to shake each hand, but the *shef's* own father had spat in the German's face and prevented it so his own people would not feel any sympathy for an enemy, would not remember him well.

The *shef* was alone in his office. His wife had locked herself in her bedroom at the front of the villa. The Russians or the Serbs, whatever they were, had left, would not witness the private grief of a man who considered himself betrayed, betrayed by failure, his grandson's failure. He had the curtain almost closed and little light filtered into the room which was designed to show the magnificence of the mountains behind his desk. He had no interest in views or the opulence of his villa, or the wealth harboured in his accounts, and the power he possessed. None would help him achieve the impossible. His grandson was to be killed. He had decreed it. He smoked slowly, steadily, and was on his third cigar and a fog hung in the room like a mist on the valley fields at dawn. It was the burden of power. He would have lost all authority had he gone to the cellar, freed his grandson, brought him up the steps, shaken his hand, watched as Skender walked away from the village and down the rough road that would take him to Shkodra and beyond – and then shoot the spy. Impossible to show such weakness . . . The *shef* was 74 years old, and it would have been the right time for the coronation of his grandson, something as symbolic as once had been the rise of Zog to the Albanian throne.

He would have settled for a lounger in the summer overlooking the far end of the valley, where the geese came in summer and where the eagles swooped to feed, and in the winter he would have gathered with other old men and played cards and drunk coffee from thimble cups, and talked of the old days and know his dynasty was safe.

It could not happen . . . he thought himself a surgeon who had found a cancer and cut it out, had no hesitation. Without his grandson, but with his power still intact, he would live for a few more years, and then . . . ? A headache that consumed him. Outside the door to his office sat his granddaughter: he heard the rhythmic clatter of her opening and closing the blades of the garden shears. Perhaps another family had an idiot boy – the boy and his grand-daughter could be taken to a church and a ceremony performed, and the two dumped together, and the other family would assume control of his own clan. Otherwise the future was as bleak as the winter's storms that surged over the village. Otherwise, the future was one of argument and dissension and murder and collapse, and likely his own grave would be trampled over and the head-stone bulldozed. Soon, before the afternoon came, he would permit Klea to go down the steps and into the cellar, felt it was owed her. It would be a bad afternoon but the *shef* knew no other way.

The door to the cellar opened.

Her dress was freshly ironed, and she skipped inside, and her song grated and echoed inside the cellar walls.

He felt Skender flinch. Saw that the guard, rose from his chair and backed away to a darkened corner where the light of the candle barely reached.

She took the chair. She said how long her grandfather had given her. Said she had no need to hurry because two hours had been given her . . . and between each verse of the wretched song, Klea laughed out loud. And the shears' rusted blades crashed together, and the candle flickered.

Croppy's head was an inch from Skender's.

"What do we do?"

"Something – when we can ... but do not know what
– something."

Jonas straightened his tie.

He smoothed his hair then slapped on his trilby. He took his
handkerchief out of a trouser pocket and flicked it loosely over the
brogues – then fastened a single button on his jacket of Harris
tweed. There was a cutting wind but no sign of rain. He told them
to wait, and Cress eased across the seat in front so that he could
get past her. Jonas stepped down from the back door of the people
carrier.

He looked ahead. Twenty men had been sent, and a woman
who he assumed was the resident interpreter with the RENEA
force, literally the Albanian Department of Neutralisation of
Armed Elements. Their motto: *Tueri vitam cum nostrum ipsorum
vitam*, "Protect life with our own life". Also given them was the
title of Unit 88. They bulged with weapons, with kit, with bags
slung from belts and harnesses, had BPVs, and a uniform of drab
olive. He was separated from them by 25 yards of tarmac. He
straightened, attempted to increase his height, then raised one
hand to his mouth and let out a piercing whistle, sucked air into
his lungs and called.

"Tricikle, come ... Tricikle, biscuit."

Bedlam in the second Humvee. Barking and scratching. A heavy-
weight door was opened. A dog came out, looked around and
seemed confused, and rocked a little because it missed a front leg,
amputated at the elbow. He had read of their mascot, he had told
the ambassador that he would grateful if the animal attended. It
located him. Not a handsome beast, small and thin but with a carefully groomed coat, mixed white and brown fur, short ears, a docked
tail. It charged, made amazing speed. He had wanted the dog,
thought he needed it. After a fashion, as if remembering his manners
late, the dog sat. The plastic bag in Jonas' pocket was torn open, and
a treat biscuit, bone-shaped and gravy-tasting, produced and
gobbled ... The men would have been suspicious of him, as they
should be, and he had reckoned this a way to fracture ice, create

initial warmth. They might die, might suffer from violence inflicted, might have the life-changing bit, and so had the right to trust him.

There was a round of scattered applause. An officer walked forward ... Jonas was always suspicious of any fighting man belonging to what was loosely called an *elite* force. These boys were supposedly trained to Hereford standards, and the officer would have spent time there. The dog, Tricikle, hobbled back to its people. Brutal looking men; he could not read their faces as all wore balaclavas but they were laughing. Not raucous, but little titters, then more handclapping. The officer had a hand out, and pushed up his face cover, and still laughing, said he had the rank of "Major Kapiten" and explained.

"The friend of our dog, our mascot, is our friend. They like your appearance, sir. They call you Milord Wooster. The programme is very popular on the TV. For the duration of the operation you will be Milord on the radio communications. I am addressed as Kapiten because we do not deal in names. You have to understand, Milord Wooster, that my men have a difficult life in today's Albania. We are, only sometimes, deployed against organised crime, which – as in Italy – is an octopus, your word, an *oktapod* in our language. It feeds off corruption, its tentacles reach in all corners. Had you gone through correct channels then the whole world would have known what you intended. For our co-operation your ambassador has promised us – sent directly to our barracks – a minimum of twenty-five sniper rifles from the factory of Accuracy International, and the offer is appreciated, and accepted. All of this, whatever it is, it never happened. We understand each other. We are indebted to you because it is very rare that we have the chance to be deployed against a clan as serious in criminality as this. They are protected. Very rare, and we savour a chance to hit them. You will ride with me ... you have experience of combat?"

"Some," Jonas answered, airily.

"I like that, a modest man and one of few words, like it much."

Abruptly, the captain lifted Jonas's arm, held it high. He shouted in English then in Albanian, "He likes his name, Milord Wooster, likes it well. And I have his word that the unit will receive thirty-five of the Accuracy International rifles . . . We go to work, and we fuck them big time."

Jonas was put in the second wagon and the dog sat on his lap and sniffed at the bag in his pocket, and his own people made up the back marker, and the convoy went at speed as if time was short and the chance of surprise limited.

15

Jonas sat quietly and the dog slobbered on him.

The captain used a radio and also his mobile. Cigarettes did the rounds and the windows were shut and the ventilation was insufficient. And the captain talked frequently with a man who Jonas assumed was his senior NCO figure, and there was a map open across his lap.

A flock of sheep with a sense of survival ... the convoy met them, perhaps a hundred, and they filled the road and were followed by a shepherd and his dogs. Nothing romantic or biblical about the scene as the Humvees kept moving and the sheep scattered. Had to fill the ditch on one side or go off on the other and risk tumbling down an escarpment. The convoy's speed did not slacken. Did not slow when a tractor appeared and had to go off the verge. There were lights on the roofs but no sirens, and a pricey saloon was left nudging a treetrunk. Jonas thought he understood, and supposed there were times in the UK when a police operation was compromised because it moved too slowly to generate surprise. He was able to follow where they were because the captain's finger pointed on the map to their location. He was not included and the talk was in their own language: there would be a time when the debate became inclusive and then he would *insist* on a certain procedure – or try to.

The sun was out. A cold and wintry one, with a full month before the start of springtime. The shafts of light came low through the bare and bent trees, and sometimes was blinding, but there were places where the sun did not reach and the road seemed to plunge into a tunnel of darkness. It mattered not to their driver, nor to those in front or behind, who continued at the same speed.

Water came off the slope, fell and frothed, then was diverted into culvert drains, then tumbled out, and in places their wheels sent up walls of spray. Jonas thought he had bonded with the dog, and reckoned that would see him in a good place when he needed to assert himself.

A moment's quandary: was he, Jonas Merrick with the lowly rank of analyst and on temporary attachment to the Post Room of Thames House, behaving in a "sensible" manner, was he acting out a "predictable" role? Was he still in "strutting" mode? Just a moment, and then the doubts were wiped. Sitting with a three-legged mongrel attempting to chew a hole in his pocket, accepting that a weight of obligation had brought him to this mountain road, travelling too fast and weaving round the potholes, a smell of gun oil in his nostrils, feeling a sense of nakedness because he did not wear a bullet proof vest, and wondering whether the whole charade was too late and would be greeted by a curtain and end titles . . . He felt no bravura, was quite frightened.

They reached a T junction. Brakes on, dirt spat from under the tyres. All agreed before they had met him. No explanation needed. He could see on the map that the main road swung sharp to the right, and that a lesser route went left, not much more than a track but with a sign in characters he could not read, and anyway it was indented with bullet holes. Business to be done here. Weapons armed. The ritual scrape of metal on metal as they were cocked, safety levers checked. Aggie Burns would have said it was "the time when the bullshit stops being legal tender", and at home Vera would have said "sadly this indicated a serious turn in events". A stop that lasted a minute, no more, and more fags lit and with an urgency as if they might be the last ones smoked. A black thought that Jonas could not escape. And off they went again, and all the nonsense talk, the joshing, had stopped.

There were two resolutions in his mind. Firstly, the ambassador in Tirana would get a flat sword tapping his shoulder, win or lose or score draw, and might get on to the shortlist for Beijing or Paris or Washington. Secondly, out of that sniper rifle factory, the cottage industry of Accuracy International, a generous load would be donated to the RENEA unit by HMG, for services rendered.

They were thrown forwards and sideways, jerked and jolted, and the finger moved on the map, and he saw a valley, and a cluster of buildings and the close wavering lines of the surrounding steep slopes, and knew they were close.

And remembered where it had all begun.

Scurrying from south to north on Lambeth Bridge, slapping down his brogues in the usual pattern, and hearing his name called. *Jonas Merrick. Please, Jonas. A moment.* And sourly turning and seeing Denys Montgomery, a Sixer off their Russia Desk, and the man hurrying to catch him, and himself complaining that he was on a schedule and hadn't the time for tittle-tattle, and rebuked. *She saved your life, Jonas, once from drowning and the next time from assassination, did her best – more times, I venture, than most would have. To get her out of their wretched gulag we need leverage. I have it. I'm giving it to you because you alone in our Special Services might have the bloody-minded and obdurate mindset to get things moving. The oligarchs' wealth is serviced by a courier system. To interrupt the flow and then hack big at it would be a promising venture. And they – those bastards – would want him back if – always the "if" – he was ours, would badly want their courier back ... We'd shaft them, goes without saying, but we'd also demand Frank's return ... For God's sake, Jonas, can you not be late for your coffee and your damned pastry and listen to what I am waving in front of your nose.* He had listened, had thought it appropriate to name it as a sideshow, and now it was done and dusted, all finished except for this little bit of a loose end ... Had felt quite proud of the handling of the sideshow, and hoped they'd make something of a life – up in the attic with the train set.

He closed the front door behind him. She dumped the bags on the hall carpet.

He supposed that the visit to the shopping mall had been a success, but Denys Montgomery was short of retail experience. Over breakfast, before they had gone out, he had explained – with hesitations – his intentions, and his hopes, and had seen a gradually deepening frown gouge her forehead. He had spent, he estimated, £1000 . . . they had paused at the window of an outdoor clothing shop, and she had gone inside, with him following, and had searched for a quilted topcoat, and he had thought they were a month away from official springtime, but he had dutifully paid for it.

They sat at the kitchen table. Frank took a deep breath, and spoke slowly as if in a foreign language.

She said, "No way of saying this nicely after what you have done for me, Mr Montgomery, and I am sincerely grateful for your contribution to my freedom . . . *But*, I won't be staying here. Only one person that I want to be with. You see, I am Apricot and she is Pear. You don't have to understand that. Pear is in Iceland, and I want to be there, live there. Apologies, Mr Montgomery, and I believe this will be easier for everybody. Thank you for what you have done."

He replied, "Jonas called you a sideshow. Important but secondary to the main event – yes, a sideshow."

For Skender, some minutes were slow to exhaust themselves and some raced.

The candle was low and guttered when sufficient wind blew in under the heavy door down the steps.

His sister sat in the vacated chair and was an automaton with her garden shears, slapped the blades together, and opened them slowly and allowed the screeching sound to echo in the cellar. He was confident that his grandfather had told her what she could do and when she could do it. He had once been fond of her and protective.

He said softly, "It is important, Croppy, that you make your peace. You have someone to make your peace with? Do it because time is against us. You will go first, Croppy, because that is better for you. Not right that you should be left waiting and watching when they take me. But I tell you something else, and that is a contradiction to what I said to you just now. You are hearing me, Croppy?"

"Hearing you."

"You may say, Get it over with, go with dignity, not me. Fuck doing the right thing. Fuck leaving people to say He went well, showed some balls, not me. My aim, get you done, and then lift the roof. Fight, kick, bite, scream. Won't help me win, but it is what I'll do. That's me. And what is you?"

"How?"

"When the bitch, my sister, comes close. They've not seen us move. Reckon we're done for. Kick the shit out of her. I feel nothing for her, she is as bad as it comes. Feel nothing. I take a chance."

"What chance?"

"The guard is called Bresnik. He is loyal to my grandfather, but loyal also to me. I take the chance that he will not shoot me. I do not believe it. Not me . . ."

"And then?"

"Cut ourselves free. Take his weapon. Go up the steps."

"Then . . .?"

"Don't know what we find. Run – run like fuck."

"And . . .?"

"Don't know, Croppy. Don't know. So I said to you that you should make your peace. Do that."

"I tried. Not good at it. Just my girl, not anyone else – and don't really have too much to say to her . . ."

"You are not alone, Croppy. I am with you, and . . . I am alone like you are, but if the chance comes . . ."

Skender thought he had no more to say and he did not know whether he had spoken gibberish. Their situation, shared, meant they had much in common, too much, enough for a true and genuine friendship . . . they were together, shoulder to shoulder, the smells of their bodies linked, and neither could clearly see the man who guarded them, who might not shoot, and the girl who clattered her shears and would relish cutting off their fingers, their toes . . . and nothing left to say.

With a loud voice, the *shef* of the clan organised. It was his way, had been drilled at him by his father and grandfather: if he wanted something done to his liking then he did it himself. And to his liking, that late morning, were the arrangements for the public killing of his grandson and of a foreign spy. The whole village would be a witness. He knew every family who lived in the village. Had been to their weddings, had attended the parties to celebrate the birth of their kids, went to the funerals of the old people and held the hands of their children. It was about power, authority and the cementing of loyalty . . . Without that loyalty he was as weak as a dog that had lost the agility of its hind legs, or could not eat because its teeth were rotten.

A hundred metres from the dark hole where the steps to the cellar were, he had supervised the laying down of a wide sheet of plastic, where their lives would be finished. The villagers would be in three lines, in front and to the sides, leaving open the side with the steps. He had chosen the men who would go down to the cellar and would extract his grandson and the foreigner, and likely by then they would have fainted from the pain and would need dragging to the plastic sheeting. Had chosen the man who would, when he signalled it, go down those steps and tell his grand-daughter that she was free to use her garden shears. In the villa, before coming outside into a low sunshine that threw lingering shadows on the square, the boy who helped with the household jobs had polished his black lace-up shoes so that they shone grati-fyingly, and the housekeeper had pressed his trousers, and he had chosen a discreet tie, and he had squirted lacquer on his hair so that it would stay in place regardless of the wind that blew down the length of the valley. The villagers would watch, would denounce his grandson and the stranger, would be permitted to abuse them. Would applaud when they were dead. Would cheer him . . . he had no alternative if he were to hold on to his power, his authority and be able to rely on the community's loyalty. By that evening he was confident that throughout Albania word would spread – to Tirana and Durresi and Elbasan and Vlore, from north to south, in the mountains and the coastal plains – that the *shef* of that clan had the strength of purpose to root out weakness and betrayal wher-ever it showed itself, that he was a man of an iron will.

It would be a good message, and when the day came that he could parcel off his granddaughter, with assurance of maintaing her honour and dignity, then – only then – he might find rest from the burden of leadership. The alternative was to die in the ditch that ran beside the track out of the village and towards the road that linked his home to the town of Shkodra and the Montenegran border. Tomorrow he had much to sort through including the relationship with the fucking Russians and the fucking Serbs and their fucking money. It would be necessary to go down into the basement under his own villa and draw out some of the heavier weapons that were stored in his personal armoury, RPG-7s, heavy machine guns, 81mm mortars, and issue them to his principal *krye* lieutenants for the defence of their community if the fucking Russians and fucking Serbs sent their gangs. He was confident. He walked along the lines that he had formed and stopped to speak to women and their husbands, and kissed some babies, and smiled and made a pretence that his mood was one of steely dertermination.

A man came to him, touched his arm.

He turned, annoyed at the interruption.

A man, almost cringing at being the messenger, told him of a call from a farmer up the track, several kilometres towards the mouth of the valley, who had seen three police vehicles speeding towards the village and . . .

The warning was not heeded. The *shef* snapped, "The police will not be a problem. I own all the police. If I had needed to be worried, I would have been warned. They are all mine."

All eyes were on him because it was close to the schedule he had set for mutilations by his granddaughter, then the killings.

"We could have been friends, Croppy."

"Might have been, Skender."

Been quiet for too long and maybe both felt their isolation.

"Dealt a different hand of cards."

"From opposite sides of a line."

"But we are mountain people, the contact point."

"See the sun come up over a mountain, and sink over one."

"Where I come from it is usually rain that hides the mountains."

"Or snow, here . . ."

And both laughed, which Croppy thought ridiculous, and Skender's sister kept up the rhythm of the opening and shutting of the shears, and Bresnik, on whom their lives might now depend made no sound, no movement, hardly breathed, and the candle threw even less light.

Skender murmured, "Would have been good if our girls had met."

Croppy said, "Both wanting to rescue us, whether we wanted it or not."

"Change us and take us away."

"Simple places. No drugs, no women for sale."

"And no wars to fight on another continent."

"Good one, Skender, and you were entitled to it . . . But not our business, fighting far from home. Not for either of us."

"You know what?"

"What do I know, or not know?"

"We are going to fight, fight like fucking she-cats."

"If the chance comes . . ."

"Wrong, Croppy, *when* the chance comes – when."

Croppy said, "Now we go quiet, like we've given up, put the towel in the ring. Go quiet."

He nurtured an image. A table on the grass outside the hotel in Kilchoan and his Sarah and Skender's Birgitte with filled glasses and feeling their way towards a mutual place – and the two men not speaking, but with amusement in their eyes . . . Or the place might be on a picnic site on the Kiel Canal. Just an image, a dream.

They waited. A bit of him, remembering the Regiment days, would have expected the Chinooks to come in with the battering noise of their rotors, but he didn't hear them, and was no longer a part of the Regiment, and supposed himself not important enough to warrant being rescued. Obvious that the sister had the patience to soak up time, until given her freedom. He could not fight. Had never fought with his fists, his teeth, his boots; his training was about slinking away from combat. Skender would know about fighting, and would know about winning.

Jonas tapped the captain's arm, interrupted his talk to his NCO, and they had slowed and the map was folded away, and ahead of them little spirals of smoke rose from chimneys.

He said, "So we understand each other. I am here because of my responsibility for the British boy. I will take him home. I am grateful for the necessary support you offer, but I cannot shelter behind you. That is understood?"

"Understood, milord, but I doubt it is acceptable."

And a shrug from the captain, and a rueful grin from Jonas.

"You want a vest, milord?"

An answer, of sorts, "Do you hear of many complaints to the manufacturers?"

In a jumble of words which Jonas could not understand, the question and his answer were repeated, and the inside of the Humvee filled with raucous laughter. He was aware that these men were volunteers, were on his side of any fence, would put their lives at risk. Doors were opened. He stepped out into the crisp morning and felt the wind on his face and the freshness of the air and saw a ditch beside them where water flowed. He held out his arms and a BPV was threaded over them and allowed to fall across his chest, and a helping hand did the fastening. It seemed to Jonas to be pretty damn small and to leave quite a bit of his body unprotected. Did he want a helmet? He did not. He did what he usually did when he was nervous: straightened his tie, hitched his trousers a little higher, straightened his back. And felt the additional weight of the vest. His team – a little "green at the gills", Vera would have said – were behind him.

Jonas turned to the captain. "He is my boy, it is my job."

His own team did not wear protective clothing or helmets, which settled the matter. Tank did it for him, freed the fastening at the chest, lifted it off Jonas' shoulders, handed it back. Jonas flicked his fingers, made a little cracking noise, dipped a hand in a pocket of his tweed jacket, produced a treat and started to walk. The dog scurried along at his heel, seemed to manage well enough with three legs, and seemed satisfied. Jonas thought he walked well too, was scared half to death . . .

They reached a twist in the track and the ditch bent too, and ahead was the village and dominating it was the villa. He saw the bright colour of a telephone box, a souvenir of status, and saw a crowd of people in a horseshoe shape and standing in front of them an elderly man with a shock of white hair and wearing a suit. It seemed inappropriate to Jonas to hang back. The idea was lodged in his head that it *might* just be possible to extract his boy and turn smartly on his heel and get shot of the place. Proven to be of a short gestation – a man ran out of the line around the square, and carried a snub-nosed weapon to the village leader. He turned, saw his team, and approved. Tank and Sword carried coats folded over their arms and hanging down far enough to conceal the infantry rifles they carried: Jonas had noted the reservations as to their weapons' efficiency. Cress had her coat draped on her shoulders and her SA-80 was also hidden.

Jonas said, "For better or worse, here we go. If I catch a bullet, it will be unfortunate. If my friend the dog is hit, let alone killed, then I imagine a retaliatory massacre. Best foot forward."

He walked. His legs were leaden, but weak.

He imagined that, by now, the captain would have had his men fan out, and they would have chosen targets. Principal among them would have been the old man, and two or three of the telescopic sights would have had crossed hairs on his chest, on the laundered shirt and the smart tie, and on the men closest to him. The dog seemed comfortable, kept close. Very soon, Jonas would be near enough to make his statement, and hoped that business could be conducted, and speedily.

From behind him, Cress's voice. "Steady as she goes, Mr Merrick, no sudden movements. Keep it calm."

Around him was silence. The villagers were assembled with the one purpose of seeing a demonstration of his authority. The *shef* held the weapon loosely, an Ingham sub-machine gun. Most weeks he went with a few of the men closest to him and fired at rocks, and sometimes a man-sized target was rigged up. They had competitions and bet money – but he always won. He did not know whether he was as good a shot as he had been half a century before. He looked with astonishment at the figure who came towards him. He knew about the dog. Most months, the animal figured in a government newspaper photograph being paraded with the RENEA group and he regretted that he had not made a greater effort to win their loyalty.

It would have been possible for him to have bargained with a hugely superior force – a battalion of the regular army, or double the number of the police unit that advanced in a wide line towards the village. That prestige depended on him showing no loss of authority and he knew the importance of his appearance. The man walking towards him was a joke, was dressed in a style that would have disappeared at about the time he had taken over control of the clan – and had two men and a woman behind him who concealed firearms. The man was English, could not have been anything else. Stony-faced and coming forward with determination. He glanced at the steps leading down to the cellar, and men were clustered there. Prestige, as defined by the *shef*, was something hard to gain, easy to lose. He did not speak English beyond a few trite phrases, and it would have been Skender who would have interpreted for him, but Skender was . . . and the woman behind him was now at the man's shoulder and the other two men seemed military but old for it and he knew they had weapons. The group stopped, some thirty paces from him, at the end of the track and where the ditch started. He dangled the Ingham, and the whole village watched to see what he would do.

Sword said softly, "What you are wearing, Mr Merrick, will have completely fucked them. Won't know what circus we're out of.

Best not to taunt them. He and his principals are very confused, and need to know what we want. So you tell them, and we hope they can give it us. Slow and clear, and using Cress."

Tank's contribution: "Them being confused is part good, part dangerous. Means they're unpredictable. They're looking for certainties, the way they will operate – but don't have them. Be simple when you tell them what you're looking for. No threats beyond the obvious of the firepower behind us which they can see for themselves."

Cress said, "Short sentences, Mr Merrick, so I can translate. If he is already dead we demand his body. If he is still alive we want him now – no debate, no delay. I can't see a way they can come out of this with their reputation intact, but that's their problem. Go for it."

Jonas stared at the man. Imagined him to be worth, if his bank stayed open and his investments stayed good, a billion American dollars. But now unsure of himself. A near obscene sum . . . Jonas and Vera lived in a three-bed semi-detached home with 100 feet of garden at the back, and lived off a medium-grade civil servant's salary. He had been told to hustle towards a business conclusion – and did so.

"I am Jonas Merrick. An official of the UK government . . ."

Allowed Cress to interpret, and thought she had a decent voice, and, did not mutter or stumble.

"You are holding a young man sent on a mission of surveillance . . ."

He had decided that he would not indulge the usual spook procedures of no names and no honesty. Spoke briskly and with authority – man to man, that sort of nonsense, but apt.

"I am here to collect him. He is to be given into my care . . ."

With each sentence of Cress' translation he sensed the growing astonishment of the clan leader, and saw the first blink of the eyes, and heard a growl among the villagers, and he could see a sheet of plastic spread out behind him, held at the corners with heavy stones.

"That is not tomorrow, not some date in the future, but *now*. I want him now, and I do not have to explain to you the consequences of a refusal . . ."

The man spat, did it with bravado, but the phlegm did not reach Jonas. It was a gesture, not intelligent but expected. The dog sat quietly at his left foot and he thought the animal with its three legs was a useful theatrical prop, showing up the bombast of the key man in an empire that defied law enforcement.

"I said now. If we kick into consequences you will be destroyed, and your village, and your people, and there will be a scramble of enemies to take what once was yours. Not any longer – so, may we please get our business done? Give me my boy and I will leave with him. Now."

All bluff, of course. He waited, sensing an explosion. The face reddened and veins seemed to protrude on his cheeks and above his ears, and the growl continued behind him and perhaps the cancer of doubt had started to grow. His arms had been folded, but now Jonas felt in his pocket and fed the dog a bone-shaped treat. He waited to see if his bluff had been called. Cress's translation went full frontal. The explosion came, a torrent.

The *shef* gesticulated with the Ingham machine gun.

"Who are you? Who is Jonas fucking Merrick? Who does he represent? Why is he here? Who is he and what right does he have to come here to *my* village? Dressed like an old man, walking like an old man, hiding behind their guns. You think I am frightened? I will show you, Jonas fucking Merrick, what is power – what I have, what you do not have. I show you."

The *shef* took his phone from an inner pocket of his suit jacket, his fingers flicked keys as he yelled at the intruder and the intruder's escort.

"You send a man to spy on us. You think him clever enough to remain hidden. I tell you very frankly, Jonas fucking Merrick, that it was my granddaughter who found him. She is eleven years old and she saw him. You sent an incompetent useless man, and now you want him back . . . you can *want*, can want until tomorrow, until next week, next month. You have no power over me . . . so just go, get the fuck out. Go . . ."

The *shef* had called the number of a phone that always nestled in the pocket of a senior official in the Justice Ministry, with links to the Interior, with more links to Police HQ in the capital. The *shef* paid half a million American dollars a year for that number always to be answered. This was the man who had the authority to cancel any operation by the police against him, and to silence a court's search or arrest warrant. It never went to a recorded message. It had never not been answered. It meant word was already abroad that the Russian upper echelon in their society had trusted him and the trust had not been merited. The *shef* tried two more calls to lesser men, but neither was answered. He felt doubt, like a shiver on his spine. But had warmed to his rant.

"We have your man. He was useless. If that is the best you can find then you have only a fraction of my power. You want him, then beg. Plead. You are on your knees, Jonas Merrick, and you crawl to my feet, begging for me to show mercy to your boy. He is like some pervert who watches lit windows in the night to see if people undress, bare themselves. You sent him? You want him back? You must beg for him."

A new experience for the *shef* . . . and unsettling. No one ever stared back at him, made eye contact, did not try to look away. The eyes stared back at him, did not waver, were bright even in the shadow of the brim of his hat. The *shef* recoiled and had raised his voice – and had started to wonder at the loyalty of his village, his audience. How impressed were they? He had demanded the begging and the pleading, but the man did not respond.

"I tell you something, I tell you who I am. I am a businessman. People want something and I provide it, they pay and they receive it. That is business. If you are an official then you would not know what is business. People demand and I supply . . . This village has wealth, because of me. We are comfortable people, but you come to persecute me because I do business in your country. Many other countries, and good business. You piss in the wind if you think I give you your boy when you have not even started to plead or beg."

Jonas' stayed locked on the *shef's* head, but he had managed to extract another biscuit from his pocket and dropped his hand and the dog reached up and took it gently.

Barely moving his lips, Sword said, "High octane stuff. But our old beggar is doing well."

Tank whispered, "And has to keep doing well."

"It's an Oscar performance."

"Needs to be."

"In your country, Jonas Merrick, if people want an aspirin then I provide it for them. If they want a line of cocaine then I provide it. Will send them a kilo if that is what they ask for, the best cut, the cleanest, and discreet. In your famous City of London, I have a fine reputation for prompt delivery, for the best product. Why do your people need to buy cocaine from me? Are their lives so depressed that they need cocaine to get through the day? I tell you, if there was cocaine in my village then I would personally kill the provider and I would expel the whole family of the user . . . But in your society it is acceptable, desirable, and so I provide it – that is business."

He knew his granddaughter waited for the signal, would have her shears in her hand, would have sight of the fingers and the toes of his grandson, of the man dragged down from the mountain above the village. Behind Jonas Merrick were the two with draped coats, and 200 metres back were the men of the tactical police unit. Men he had not bought, had not thought he needed to. And raised his voice further and felt the pain in his throat.

"I tell you more about business. What are your women like? Like dogs? Fat and ugly dogs? Why do your own men reject your own women and demand that they go to a bed with the girls that I bring in from eastern Europe? Pretty girls and expert, and your men queue at the door to be let in, given a chance to screw these girls. Am I to be blamed because your own men reject your own women, and ask me to provide what they want? That is my fault,

that your own women cannot satisfy your own men? Is that what
you tell me? They want heroin, and I will sell them heroin. They
do not want to pay tax, so I will give them the lawyers and investment men who can wash their money and keep it clean and far
from your Revenue. Are you ready to beg? If you want your boy
then you need to crawl to me. Or do you want to hear his scream?
I am not a man of patience. What is your answer?"

The *shef* sensed that his authority waned. Saw there was now a
light machine gun mounted on the roof of one of the Humvees,
saw also two places where the sun – low and fierce and without a
building or a tree to block it – caught the forward aperture of a
sniper sight, one man on the track, one on the far side of the ditch,
and the barrels aimed at him. Saw that the hands of the guys
behind the translator woman hidden under their coats and would
have weapons there, the catches probably off, and rounds in the
breech. Saw that there was the confusion amongst his own
villagers, and knew all of them, knew their names, knew their
weaknesses. Saw the huddle of men at the cellar steps, and saw to
the side of where he stood the sheet of plastic that was pinioned
down by stones and which the wind flapped at . . . and he waved
the hand that held the Ingham.

Tank said, "Near break point."

Sword said, "Right up tight against it. About to hit the fan."

It seemed to Jonas that the self-control of the old man was almost
lost. *What was his answer?* Did not really have one, need one. Had
said what he had come for. Anything else would put him into the
area of debate, where he had no intention of going. He had seen
the gathering of men at the void where it was likely that steps led
down to a cellar below a storage building, and thought it reasonable to assume that was where Croppy was, possibly alive and
possibly not.

The anger in front of him frothed unchecked, and he thought
they were near a moment of danger. Sometimes, the old man
waved the barrel square at Jonas' chest, and sometimes to either

side. Increasingly irrational, and gurgling in his throat, and coherence lost. Playing out well, Jonas thought, and the aim of the barrel swinging back towards him, and a flash and a recoil and the hand holding the weapon flying up, and an impact.

Jonas felt a great weight hit him and he was pitched sideways. The dog went with him. They said you could never dodge a bullet once it was fired, pretty damn obvious . . . He went down into the ditch and could not move, could not see, could not hear. His life passed fast in front of him, as it had when Frank had dragged him off the bridge and the Thames swallowed him. When the girl in Liverpool had loomed over him with a knife raised, and when the assassin sent to saw off his head had pinioned him to the grass beside the caravan steps . . . Saw Olaf who was his cat, and Vera who was his wife, and . . . nothing more.

The captain called his order to his snipers, and his machine gun man, and to anyone else with a decent shot possible.

"Do not return fire. I want the scum taken, cuffed, not a martyr in a fucking bag."

Cress said, "He will stink. So will I. So will the dog."

Tank said, "A good arse pucker moment. The big man lost it."

Sword said, "Went about half a mile over his head and frightened the beggar half to death. You good, Cress?"

"As I'll ever be."

At the moment she slammed the blades shut, annoyed because the message had not yet come to her, Klea heard the shot and winced.

And Bresnik did, and dragged the pistol from his waist, and cocked it.

And Skender did, and Croppy too.

The dog struggled beneath him.

Jones felt hands gripping his jacket.

He opened his eyes, and the wind still blew and the sun still shone, and columns of smoke rose from the chimneys and the crowd was still there but the lines were less regimented as if the villagers had shifted and were wary. Saw the big man, his shoulders hunched and his chin on his chest, and trying to use his phone Jonas had, truth be told, thought he was dead – at the very least unconscious. Had assumed that a bullet had struck him, that the pain, a throbbing ache was a better description, in the small of his back was the source of the wound.

Cress had a hold of him, hauled him from the ditch and started to drag him, no ceremony, back up the track, far enough to have brought him behind Sword and Tank, who knelt and aimed. The realisation came slowly that it was Cress who had whacked him in the back with her knee and levered him into the ditch, and he had been on top of the dog and then she on top of him. Would have been a reflex action on her part to cover him. Jonas was now back in a world where realities, truths, were exposed. She had put herself in harm's way in order to provide better protection for him, and he had never bothered to have even embarked on a conversation with her. He understood some more about those with whose safety he played God. His back was sore. Mud, slime, water ran off him. The dog stood close to him, looked with pleasure into Jonas' face, then shook vigorously and the filth spattered out.

She said, "You all right, Mr Merrick?"

"Why might I not be?"

Tank asked, not averting his eye from the man who was now crumpled, like the sense of survival had left him, "From your experience, Mr Merrick, was that the village sewer?"

He supposed they joshed him, more familiarity than even Kev and Leroy would have shown him, and felt rather proud, like he was accepted. Then reminded himself: they were nowhere, had achieved nothing.

He stood, and a pool of dirty water slowly collected beneath him. He looked at the steps that led down into darkness, and felt the cold on his back. A portion of the crowd had drifted away and the lines were broken, but not the men who stood at the head of the steps. Had Vera been there, and fortunately she was not, she would have described them as the clan's Praetorian Guard, and told him how many cohorts they'd be, and then might have suggested to him what he do next – thank the Lord she was not.

Just a loose end or two to be tied up, which was Croppy and the last duties of his obligation. He took the first step towards the presumed cellar entrance, and the team were close around him . . . from the smell in his nostrils he might well have been in the village's sewer.

16

Jonas heard the scream. Felt the rigours of age and tiredness and hunger, and yearned for a drink of clean water. Realised his work was far from finished.

Not the scream of a rabbit when Olaf had a hold of its throat in a hedgerow, not a scream of pain as if a man might be in terror. It was the scream of a child who was denied. The scream of a wilful, wanton, spoilt child. He had heard it often enough on the train, confirming all the worst fears he might have harboured of parenthood relieved that the state had never visited him. A child howling, yelling, shrieking because it had been thwarted. It seemed to come from beneath the ground. In front of him, the guard had stiffened and made a cordon on the upper step.

Behind Jonas came the voice of the man he had faced down. Calmer than it had been when delivering his rant, but louder, as if he had remembered who he was and his need for proven dignity. Not a clue what he said until Cress was against him, an arm around his shoulder and a fist in his armpit.

"My angel, my child, take them down. Do it, the foreigner first, then my own blood. Kill them, my angel."

The old man was clubbed. Tank had done it. A short blow with the stock of the pint-sized rifle. He tottered, staggered, then needed a hand to prevent himself falling. The police swarmed around him and the low sun lit the metal of handcuffs. And no reaction from those villagers still gathered in the horseshoe shape around the plastic sheeting.

Indecision at the top of the steps, and weapons reached for. And the police team stalking closer with their rifles raised and sub-machine guns aimed. Like the moment when the dawn has not yet arrived and the night has not yet gone. A stand-off while the guards and the RENEA people evaluated each other. Jonas did not know what he should do, did nothing. And the dog had gone back to its own people.

And again the scream came as if from the bowels of the earth. Not just Jonas who did not know how to react: and the guards did not, nor the captain, and Sword and Tank frozen. He had thought himself capable of sensible behaviour, and no longer knew how to be, and looked around him and saw only hesitation, and . . .

The old man shouted. On his knees, an empire of money and influence slipping like sand between his fingers, perhaps his last gesture of power.

"Do it, hurry, my angel, and . . ."

He was hit by a gloved fist. The blow was hard enough to dislodge a set of teeth. Jonas thought that the ultimate humiliation – a dental plate.

Jonas called behind him, felt small and pitiful, "I don't know what to do, but somebody should do something."

Sword said, "Not in my pay grade to go down there."

Tank said, "Best left to them, their shout."

Cress said, "Have to know what something is before you can do it."

The screams filled the cellar. The candle was failing. Skender had heard his grandfather, and the appeal to his sister. Would she? She fucking would . . . He was rigid against the English boy, his friend.

"One chance . . ."

"Take it."

"She yelled because Bresnik would not allow her to get at us with her shears, said she had to wait. She's free now, is coming."

His sister was up and out of the chair, and opened the shears and closed them, and opened them again, and enough of the candle's light showed her face, wet with tears of frustration. But that was done with and she was up and rocking on her feet and a trace of the candle flame showed the happiness on her face.

She had heard her grandfather's second shout, and that was enough confirmation for her. Skender knew that in abattoirs some went docilely and would have known what awaited them, and some were frenzied and kicked and bucked and had to be forced in to the narrowing rails that would hold them tight enough to be killed. He would not be docile.

His sister relished each step as she approached and her face was wreathed in a smile: they had been inseparable until the day that she had been taken with their father and their mother to Durresi and he had been left behind in the village, and she had clung to him . . . all changed when she had come back and been returned wearing the same dress she wore now. Had shown happiness when she had the shears and had a trussed victim, but had never laughed since driving into the village behind the hearse that had carried two coffins, and both light to lift because not much of the corpses had survived the impact of the RPG-2 weapon, and all who had an opinion had said it was a miracle she had lived. She had, but changed, and not recognised, and had become the "angel" of her grandfather.

His legs were not tied. His legs would have to act as his hands. If he were to move then the English boy must move with him, as if they were a pair of dancers.

His sister looked down at him, and the blades clattered, and her voice was a shambles of tuneless music, and his body was coiled. Had to choose the moment; too early and they were fucked, too late and they were fucked, and did not know how to choose.

She said nothing to him.

He said nothing to her.

Eyes locked.

Skender estimated she was so familiar with her own power and influence that she was unhinged by being held back by Bresnik, but had obeyed him because he spoke with authority given him by the old man.

She was close enough . . . Skender swung his legs out, tried to make the movement as sudden as he was capable of, except that his shins and feet were cramped, and his effort was laboured and

he thought she almost laughed as his legs swung heavily towards
her and she skipped sideways, and he missed and the moment was
lost . . . because now she would have to work at outwitting him,
she was down.

Croppy had scythed with his own legs and had hit her at the
back of her knees, and the shock spread on her face and she was
on the ground.

And one of her hands was on a handle of the shears, the other
protecting her face, and the fucking song had died in her gut.
Skender kicked her.

Croppy had never used violence on a woman.

Croppy had been caught out on the mountainside, should have
belted her. But teaching and instinct had held him back. Then, not
now.

Had seen the opportunity, had realised that Skender had missed
the chance. Had lashed out with his legs, the only weapons he had,
and had caught her hard. A moment when her face, a child's had
shown utter confusion, as if a new script was written, and the
happiness gone, and the cold gone, and the disbelief that she was
flattened and control taken.

The next blow came from her brother.

No mercy shown – why should there have been?

And all of it pointless unless the child was first disarmed and
then disabled, and might be killed and might have a limb broken,
and might have blood running on her sweet and smooth-skinned
face. Croppy went next, using his heels to hit her head. Saw
Sarah's face, and the shock and the pain and the surprise that his
own girl would have shown . . . and all of this was without value
unless the man standing in deep shadow was prepared to come
forward and disregard what his boss had told him, free them and
let them go up the steps – to what?

In the classes on Escape and Evasion, all the troops were told of
the need for total ruthlessness when a breakout was attempted.
Very few would get the chance to prove the truth of that. Croppy
was in a cellar in an Albanian mountain village with a deluded

child, a guard who carried a handgun, and the son of the local *shef*. He could only kick, and did it harder, and felt himself a changed man and shame coursed through him. Everyone he knew in the village of Kilchoan would have turned away, as if they did not want to recognise him, if they had seen what he did. He and Skender were both trying to extend their legs far enough to be able to trap her between their thighs, get them around the child's waist and drag her towards them, pull her over the slabs and then roll their weight over her so that she lost the power of movement. She was a tough kid. Had seen her in foul weather tracking up the hillside with her dog and her goats, and in his ignorance had felt sympathy for her and had misread the danger she brought him.

He whacked her again, and so did her brother, and her fingers were still tight on a handle of the shears.

A question put with urgency by Skender to the man he called Bresnik, who had his pistol raised, but had not moved from his corner.

Of course, Croppy, did not understand the words, but sensed their meaning.

Bresnik, the faithful Bresnik, the dutiful Bresnik, had heard what the *shef* had instructed.

My angel, my child, take them down. Do it, the foreigner first, then my own blood. Kill them, my angel.

Had heard it and believed it. He had never disobeyed an order given by his *shef*, would not have considered such a possibility.

He cocked the pistol.

Bresnik had hoped that when Skender became leader of the clan, perhaps in a year's time, he would be honoured with the position of principal protection to him . . . not with all the paperwork of visas when they went abroad, but the main man, anywhere they visited in Albania. He would travel alongside him, speak when spoken to, show full deference, but be on hand to give advice when his opinion was called for. He had no doubt that over the years he had accumulated sufficient wisdom to make his contribution, rather excelled, he thought, in the judgement of character . . .

except that he had failed in this crucial test of the new man, and it had been – which savagely hurt him – the child, Klea, who had identified the hide where the foreigner spied on them, then had denounced her brother. He had wondered then whether any future existed for himself when the old order fell away.

Skender spoke, breathless from the exertion of what they had done to the leader's "angel". His voice was not one suited to the leadership role, Bresnik's opinion. They had fooled the girl, which had surprised him, but would not fool him, and he heard the honeyed words.

"My good friend, Bresnik, my best friend. For my love and eternal gratitude, would you cut these ties on my wrists, and on the foreigner's. Thank you . . ."

Men in the village who were higher ranked in the clan than himself, those with greater authority, said that Skender had lied about a woman he slept with in Chamonix, a German woman, which was a double insult to his family after what had been done in the Nazi war. Had lied to his grandfather, and had allowed himself to be – as his story went – "kidnapped", taken into Geneva and held somewhere but he did not know where. Said that documents had been "lost" by him and that, as a result, huge sums of money had been stolen from Russians who had paid the clan well for the security of the courier run. It was a betrayal. There could be no licence given to those who betrayed the clan. Simple and understood by everyone in the village and understood by him.

"Come, Bresnik, come and do it. Remember all the good times, remember when we . . . Bresnik, hurry."

He considered what he was asked to do. He had never believed himself patronised by the family. There had been, not denying it, alcohol binges in European cities when he was being introduced to other organised groups, and he had been the one who had dragged Skender out and carted him back to their hotel, had eased off his shoes, and undressed him, and twice he had needed to work around the shape of a naked girl already in the bed. He had maintained the family's reputation for staying tight-lipped. He thought it insulting that he was now told what to do, when to do it, but not *why*. The assumption was that he would renounce the loyalty he had shown for his whole life, would piss on the kindnesses shown him by the *shef*, would turn his back on all that . . . and afterwards? He understood it, the two men would take his pistol, leave him to pretend he had been overpowered, and they would run up the steps, burst through the cordon, and would charge off down the track. Then the loyalties of others would be tested, his own having failed. He doubted he would get as far as his own home, and would also have to explain Klea's battered body. He thought Skender sold him short.

. . . *Do it, the foreigner first, then my own blood* . . .

He was always careful with his pistol. It had been his father's. German, taken from an officer in a transport unit, and maintained with care. Bresnik had given it the same attention as his father had. It would not jam, there was no question of a malfunction. He had looked after it so well because he had always believed that if he were tested, if the threat was real, he would be able to confront any man aiming to harm his *shef*. It had not happened. If God remained kind to him, it would not happen. But he took good care of the pistol.

And went forward.

. . . *the foreigner first* . . .

For a moment he was in front of the candle and his shadow covered them as they huddled on the stone floor. He could hear voices above, like orders were given, and he believed little time remained for him to carry out the instruction given him. The girl was now twitching on the ground and her dress was rucked up and he could see the line of her pants, and it disgusted him that he had seen it. And more than disgusted him, it hurt him.

"For fuck's sake, Bresnik, free us. How many more fucking times do I have to . . ."

Skender was writhing, pulling the foreigner with him but could not free himself, and the more he tried it seemed that the ties at his wrists were tighter.

His hands shook. Had never been a quality shot, but good enough on the practice range.

. . . the foreigner . . .

He aimed as best he could. It would have helped if Skender had not wriggled so much – then a realisation had hit him, might have been a punch on Skender's face, and a look of bafflement. And Bresnik thought it was about fucking time that the boy who would never be leader, whose friendship was without value, learned a truth.

Skender was wide-eyed and disbelieving, and Bresnik could see the torso of the foreigner and his head. Klea was to the side and would not be harmed. His hands wavered and it was difficult for him to still then.

He fired the first shot, and heard the impact on the base of the wall, then the sing of the ricochet, and his pistol pointed, swaying in aim, at Skender's back. The foreigner's head and chest were lost, he had no sight of them. He fired again. Bullets struck Skender, seemed to lift him before he sagged. He writhed as if a great pain gripped him and he bled. Bresnik could not loosen his finger from the trigger and it had squeezed until the soft metallic click told him that the magazine was emptied. He took a step forward, did not know why because the death below him was so obvious, so he did not see . . . Klea launching her shears at him – but knew when a rusted blade pierced his back, went deep, chipped bones, perforated his stomach wall, sliced into veins . . . and would not have understood.

Sword said, emerging from the celler, "Don't let the old man go down there – don't."

Tank said, blinking in the daylight, "Never seen anything so bad. Makes you want to heave."

Cress said, "It's like a charnel house. The cops'll have bags, and we can get the fuck out. Can't be soon enough, not after that."

He had travelled in the Humvee. Had said little to the captain, and the quiet suited Jonas.

They had reached the lay-by where, only a few hours ago, he had come in the people carrier and met up with the police, and the dog, Tricikle, back again on his lap, and nuzzling at his pocket. Best that he had not talked because he still felt the rawness in his throat and mouth.

Never one to listen to advice, Jonas had insisted on going into the cellar. Had ignored the suggestions from his team that it would be better if he missed out on that experience. He had shrugged them off and they had stepped aside. He had paused a moment at the top, and had noted that the square behind him had now emptied, and the old man had been carted off to a Humvee, and the men who had stood at the top of the steps had slunk away. He had gone carefully down the steps. They were steep and unforgiving and he could see footprints on them that were highlighted because the tread of the boots, those elaborate patterns, had stepped in blood pools in the cellar and transferred the stains to the steps. He had started to look around him, and had felt the pain grab at his stomach, and then had vomited. Hardly the dignified entry of the all-supreme defender of society after a victory of immense importance against the forces of organised crime and international state-sponsored money laundering, and creating a meltdown of chaos and confusion in the upper echelon of oligarch society. Torches had shown him the scene, and he had turned and had known he would not be in time to reach the steps and put it behind him. None of the choice phrases would ever again pass his lips or be tolerated in his presence if spoken by others: *Don't you know, you can't make an omelette without breaking eggs?* Not that there was much in his stomach for him to heave up, but that had compounded his suffering. He had retched, retched again, and now felt queasy and his stomach was loose. Felt, in fact, pretty damned awful. A medic – a cop with a Red Cross armband – with a fairly brutal disregard for his sensitivities was checking the guard from the cellar, and underneath the body was the barrel of a handgun, and prominent in his back was the upright set of garden shears that had been thrown with such force that one blade was still embedded. He had seen the body of a child, and was uncertain whether he heard whimpering, but there were men around him and movement and torches roving. He had not seen Croppy, but against a far wall were shapes and that was where the blood still flowed. He had been coughing, shaking, and arms had grabbed him and had pushed him unceremoniously towards the door and the flight of steps. He had stood at the top, had been sick again. The team had not responded, did not remind him that he had been "unwise" to risk the sights of the cellar.

Ten minutes later, they had left the village.

Jonas felt as if he were now surplus weight and of little use in the back of the captain's vehicle. He had pulled rank, might have to do it once or twice more, but others had taken up the burden. They had driven on the winding roads at speed, and he had lurched forwards, backwards, sideways on the bench seat and had clung to the dog.

It would be a tight fit in the people carrier, with all of them heading for the UK with their kit, and his eyes were misting and his vision slewed, then the time came for farewells.

The captain said, "It has been a pleasure, Milord Wooster, for us to meet with you. A pleasure to be a part of an operation controlled by your enterprise. We would claim that today has brought us a significant victory over the criminal shit, and the unit may again be awarded the Golden Medal of the Eagle ... and I want to assure you that the fifty Accuracy International rifles, for sniping, that the RENEA force receives will be put to best use in our hands. We will not forget you, Milord, you will be forever in our thoughts."

He had been incapable of making a speech of thanks.

He was lifted, his backside planted on the warm metal of the Humvee bonnet, his feet hanging over the radiator grille and between the headlights. The dog was placed on his lap. With precision, the unit formed up around him, some kneeling, some standing, some behind him. A team photograph. Inappropriate? Of course. In poor taste? Of course. Fists were raised, and weapons. His face was probably still smeared in the ditch's mud, his trilby was battered, and his jacket hung wet and filthy and shapeless on him – and the name was shouted to the bright sunshine cupping the heavens. *Milord ... Milord ... Milord ...*

And what remained of the treats were left for the dog, and he was helped down and went slowly to the people carrier, and was given a push to get him inside.

Tank was at the wheel. Jonas looked around him. The satnav showed the route over the frontier and to Podgorica airport. He realised that he understood little of what had happened inside the cellar. And registered that the clothes Cress wore were as messed as his own, and her face as dirty, and saw that the coats that Tank and Sword had on, tightly zipped, were dark with the stains of blood not yet dried.

Cress asked him, "You good now, Mr Merrick?"

"Never been better. Wake me when we're down the road."

And his eyes closed, and darkness came ... and he doubted it had been real – a dog under him, a ditch of rainwater and probably sewage, and quite a handsome woman straddling him.

Viktor had read about his situation.

It was an Erwin Rommel one. A deal of a sort had been agreed.

He had two men with him and they crossed the foyer of the hotel and paused briefly at reception where a sheet of paper was given to him to sign. The room he had "booked into" was prepaid, and the key passed to him. He held the card for a moment but then the man on his left took it from him, smiled at the girl and twisted sharply, as did his companion. Viktor was taken to the bank of elevators.

The Rommel option was supposed to look after the survivors in the family – in Viktor's case that was his wife, his two daughters, and her parents. Such an option depended on trust. A promise had been given which he needed, in the next crucial minutes of his life, to believe in.

The room chosen for him was on the 14th floor, so it was a long journey and, as if to exacerbate his distress, he had had to wait until an empty lift arrived as it was regarded necessary by his minders that they travel alone.

The field marshal, with a reputation for competence and charisma – neither of which Viktor enjoyed – was believed to have been associated with the failed bomb plot against the Fuhrer's life. Known as the Desert Fox, the *wustenfuchs*, and idolised by the troops of the Afrikakorps, he was given a choice. A public tribunal and a certain sentence of death and his family going to gaol for complicity in fraud, or a staged suicide and the promise that his family would not be harassed, would face no charges. But his death sentence was inevitable.

He had to trust the small man who he had seen down the length of a long table. His eight-minute account of the situation, as best he knew it, in the Swiss city of Geneva, and how much money had disappeared from the screens and could not be found because hackers had mined into the listed holdings managed by bankers, accountants, lawyers, had been heard out. He had named the fellow investors who had encouraged him to handle their wealth when the criminal sanctions of Western governments had become so oppressive. The face of the man slouched at the far end of the table was for the most part impassive. Viktor had not, of course, suggested that the reason for the sanctions, the need for secrecy, the need for such convoluted protection of funds, was the crazy war in Ukraine. Lastly, he had declared the amount of money owned by the man he addressed that had gone into this seemingly bottomless pit. The man had shrugged, as if it were a small matter, had given a little flick of his hand to indicate the meeting was terminated. He had been escorted from the Kremlin, and out to the car park where he had left his wife's vehicle, and there the proposition was put to him.

He had spoken briefly on the phone to his wife, told her he loved her, told her he loved his kids, and the phone had been taken from him. Her car had been driven to the hotel and he assumed that the cameras in the lobby, the elevator, and the corridor on the 14th floor would be switched off for a short window of time. In some ways the Rommel deal seemed generous, certainly preferable to awaiting the verdict handed down on one man's whim.

He went into the room. It had a balcony and an excellent view over the city.

The balcony door was slid open.

One of his escorts, a hand on Viktor's shoulder, said, "You know that story in the Western movie, about the man who jumped from a ten-storey building, and people on the lower floors heard him say as he went past, 'So far so good'? Know it?"

They did it expertly, as if they had done it before.

The doors opened and Frank went through, and they closed and she was gone.

For a full minute Denys Montgomery gazed at them. When they opened again to allow more passengers to go into departures, he could no longer see her. They were calling flights and the Reykjavik plane was waiting for the last passengers to hurry along. It hadn't actually been much of a conversation after lunch.

"Grateful for what you've done, but no way am I going to stay around in London. The place I am headed for is out there, north and up close to the Arctic Circle. Staying here, living in this house, is not in the equation."

It had been the hope of his life since the day his mother had died, and was dashed.

"Did I get this wrong? Was it your plan to instal me in some bedsit, like I was on call, available any time you wanted it? You didn't think that, did you?"

He turned, went off as he supposed a lovelorn teenager would have, headed for his car.

"Is that what this whole business was about, Mr Montgomery? Destabilising the big bad bears, interrupting the flows of sanction-busting cash, bringing down a top-ranked OCG? All to get me out and tucked up in your mum's old bed? Bringing the tea up to the attic and watching you with the train set? That it?"

He would go home, leave the car, would then be on a train back into the office.

"Well, apologies, if that is what it was all about. Getting me under your roof, and me sat there all day and us pretending that I was still part of the set-up, not a security risk, not a spy. And office bashes, when the wives and partners are allowed an appearance, and who is going to talk to me? Have you any idea what it was like in that gaol – any . . .?"

His phone might have told him the events of the day, how the last bits of the sideshow had turned out, but he had the machine on silent and had left it in his jacket pocket. He had waved courteously at the woman next door who was having an early chop at her roses, and knew it would have travelled up the street that Mr Montgomery, something in Whitehall, rather dominated in her lifetime by his mother, had entertained a woman at home, rather gaunt, then had taken her off that afternoon and had come back and seemed rather depressed. At the end she had softened.

"I'd be your friend, Mr Montgomery, but you'd have to come to me – where I'll be Apricot and she'll be Pear. That's a promise, but not here."

He came off the train at Vauxhall and crossed the road and went over the section of pavement where Jonas Merrick had sat down in the rain until the necessary entry-permission was provided for a humble Fiver, and had walked all over them, and had denounced Frank as a traitor. He showed his pass, and was respected by security as a man of importance.

"Come and see the puffins and the whales in Iceland," she'd said, and laughed, like there was no chance he would abandon his train set.

He went to his office. There was an open area and his glass door was on the far side. He went in and the room stood, all the young Turks who worked for him on the Russia Desk, and the applause seemed both spontaneous and genuine, and a couple of bottles of fizz were on the table, and he was invited upstairs for 5.00pm. He read a note, managed it before his eyes misted.

So utterly worthwhile, Denys, because Safety Deposit has kicked them in the short and curlies and understood that you are the progenitor of the operation. Fantastic, congratulations – we are most proud of you.

He sat at his desk and began to read the cables and messages, the papers and analyses, all necessary if he were to have even a slight hope of regaining some purpose in his life.

The AssDepDG waited for the incoming call. He was irritated, frustrated, but swallowed it.

He had sent one message. To Harry, his driver, a man of enduring patience, reliable and uncomplaining. *Harry, Pls have the big beast fuelled and oiled, whatever else it needs. Don't know where we're going because Mister M has not yet told me. It will be somewhere as inconvenient as it gets – fuel, oil and sandwiches, and gin. Thanks.* Just the one message but more would follow when the wretched little toad of a man, Jonas Merrick, came back from the moon's far side.

He had no love for Jonas; actually more harboured a deep-rooted dislike. There were some in Thames House, with experience of dealing with the "toad", who quizzed him as to why, how, he put up with the snubs and slights handed to him. He could answer them that affection hardly helped get the job done. He did not work with Merrick in order to have a more convivial drinking partner. Did not know how Vera, a decent woman, put up with him, a man as disagreeable as the bloody cat idolised in the Raynes Park home – but his feelings for Merrick were of trivial import. Rudeness was an acceptable counterweight to the results that accumulated, and the rewards of success outweighed those irritations, frustrations. There had been times when he had reached home in the evenings and had thrown tonic tins round the kitchen because calls were not returned. He would not have known how to explain, in words of one syllable, the sheer excitement that the miserable man ferried to his lap. And it was a mark of the full rein given Merrick that he never, almost never, chivvied for the commentary, running or static, good news or apocalyptic bad.

He called the Post Room, told the girl he would let her know news when it reached him.

Jonas had woken. Had started to work his phone.
Bringing Croppy home ...
Matt had given him a peppermint, and Sword had passed him a bottle of water.
... all a bit of a mess, but wrapped ...

Not as lucid as he would like to have been.

... we'll need a dug grave and a priest ...

All plain enough to Jonas, and he went on to list other transport elements that he would be requiring, and a schedule for when and where, and how he intended to resume his holiday after being pulled off Glastonbury Tor a week earlier, and involving Vera and his cat – and Sarah, his assistant. Had he been able to make the arrangements himself then he would willingly have done so, but his position, on the move, and the day slipping along, precluded him making his own calls while outside the jurisdiction of the UK ... and an ambassador should be considered for a gong – as an afterthought he informed the AssDepDG that he had committed HMG to a gift of sniper rifles for the Department of Neutralisation of Armed Elements, the detachment based in the Albanian city of Shkodra.

Not the way of Jonas Merrick to allow others the chance to query his demands and so he had switched off his phone, and made a request to that effect to the others in the people carrier. Matt had told them when they would hit the frontier checks, and knew when shifts changed, when considerations of sovereignty mattered least. It had meant travelling at slow speed, and pulling off the main drag for half an hour. Matt would have work at the airport, at the Customs and Emigration desks, but Jonas had confidence. He was pleased that the vehicle was quiet, just the sounds of breathing, some of it heavy, and was relieved that useless chatter was suppressed.

He stank. Cress stank, all of them were filthy. He imagined he left chaos behind him, and ahead, and was out of contact, and others could fret and snarl insults – the thought of which lifted his spirits.

17

Jonas had asked, diffidently, "Do I smell very bad?"

The pilot had said, "Compared to some we have had on our taxi service, Mr Merrick, you're quite fragrant."

"Thank you."

"Were told one of your fares is from the Regiment – that's good enough."

The jet had put them down in darkness at an airfield north of the Scottish coastal town of Oban. There had been a roar of reverse thrust and Jonas had clung to the seat in front of him as they had juddered to a stop, would have been on the extremity of the runway. First light was peeping over hills to the east as the helicopter had flown in. They had had to wait until it was refuelled, then had boarded. Obvious that it was military, a pilot and co-pilot, neither with rank insignia on their shoulders or with their names on their flying suits, but they did have the emblem of the Union flag on their upper arms, the size of a matchbox. It was pretty much what he had asked for, and the AssDepDG had grunted in the way that indicated that he'd promise nothing, do what he could. He was told it was an SA 365 Dauphin 2, would have come up from Hereford, likely take three, three and a half hours. That it was here was because of Croppy and his link with the Special Reconnaissance Regiment. He assumed it would go down in their flight plans as an "exercise" and the control tower and officialdom would have been told to go and make a cup of tea. The pilots had watched as Jonas's people dutifully filed off the jet and across the apron and then clambered on board, and brought their load with them, into the chopper's cabin. Some of them filthy, one rather well dressed, all yawning and all sombre, and Jonas had followed and been offered a foldaway seat up front.

"Don't mind me asking – aren't you a bit old for mucking about in the mud?"

He'd answered, "Actually a village sewer, someone shot at me and it was thought right by my colleagues to put me in a ditch."

"Sensible."

"Usually try to be sensible."

They would have known a great deal about him. Had they not – in spite of the best efforts of the AssDepDG, and Croppy's connection – they would still have been asleep in their homes within spitting distance of the camp at Stirling Lines. The first cars of the day were arriving at the airfield when they switched on the engines. He had been given a headset. Two engines, each with a payload of 830 plus horsepower. Was told the route and the flying time. He had noticed their chopper carried the usual call sign letters and digits, but they were painted pretty much the same colour as the fuselage – so protocol was adhered to but identity minimised. They went up and out over the sea, the mainland on the right and an island on the left. He was told they had a mobile phone link with "a guy from the spooks" at their destination and assumed it to be the AssDepDG, and that preparations for their arrival were "pretty much in place". He did not like running commentaries, never had, and so eased the headset off and put it carefully between his feet. There was a mat of dog hair across the lap of his trousers, most of it embedded in caked mud. Where he had been, what he had seen, seemed an ice-age ago. Hard for him to believe that a village still existed, 2000 miles away, and a huge villa as proof of the way crime paid, and an English telephone box, and steps down to a cellar where there would be stains on the slabs and a burned out candle, and a scattering of cartridge cases, and probably a legacy of his own vomit . . .

They flew up a narrow strip of water where a fishing boat made slack speed and pushed out a bow wave, and he saw the peace of fields and low cliffs and water with white caps. They went low over the surface, a hundred feet he estimated. The wind was funnelled over the water and the helicopter bounced a bit, and he imagined their usual passengers would have been Special Forces, the men and women Jonas sent off into dark corners without too much thought of what was involved, what right he had to do so. He reckoned from the dials in front of him that they might be touching 150 miles per hour, and a farmer on the mainland side, out with cattle and a dog, did a desultory wave with his cap.

His arm was tugged respectfully. An arm pointed ahead.

Jonas saw the village, Croppy's home. Saw a jetty and cars waiting, and a ferry nearing a mooring, saw a pair of sailing boats, a mountain towering over them on the right side, and they went low over a ribbon of homes facing the sea, and saw the sun reflecting off a line of windscreens away to the north. They flew over a small walled cemetery, and faces peered up at them, and backing away was a yellow-hulled digger leaving a fresh rectangular hole. The robes of a priest blustered in the draught from the blades. And further along a single carriage road, with a grass strip on it, and more cattle and a restless horse, he saw an awkwardly parked caravan that near as dammit blocked it, and saw his wife, and thought of the fusillade of questioning he would face, and they turned back, and the AssDepDG was gesticulating and waving them towards a field, to the east of the cemetery, and wondered how Olaf was after such a long journey.

She had scoured the horizon of bare hillsides. She had heard their cat, yowling in its cage. Had carried it to the caravan door, opened it and, with scant dignity and foul-tempered, it had scampered clear and had headed for a mix of rocks and fallen bracken and traces of flowering heather. Its high vantage point, on a thermal, and the power of its eyesight, would have identified prey to the eagle. The bird saw a mess of body fur and a tail which added to a decent meal, enough to fill its crop for a full day, and dived – and the sense of survival came late to Olaf and he ran, and Vera was screaming, and trying to run towards him and the helicopter swept by, and the bird veered. The cat found refuge under the caravan. She sagged with relief, and went to meet her husband,

and doubted she would ask whether or not he had been sensible, wherever he had been.

They landed, the engine killed. The rotors swung lazily. It was a pleasant morning, the sun just above a mountain and throwing long shadows. The hatch door was yanked open, and the co-pilot jumped down easily.

Of the passengers, Jonas was first out.

He rocked on his feet. The AssDepDG was coming towards him.

"God, Jonas, you look a bloody mess. Have you no sense of time and place?"

Jonas supposed that Aggie Burns would have had a suitable, vulgar response. He did not, so turned his back on the one man at Thames House on whom he depended for survival.

"Well done, you old bugger, a hell of a show – the sun shines from your bum."

But he was not at Thames House. He was here among the quiet beauty of the hillside and above a seashore where waves played patterns of spray on rocks and where the skyline was smoothed by the implosions and convulsions of long-ago volcanoes and where the winds cleaned the ground, and smoke from a farm chimney came near to horizontal and he felt the raw freshness on his face. He was a changed man, knew it – but was concerned he might regret it.

His team followed him, Tank and Sword and Cress.

He spoke laconically to the AssDepDG as if that were the necessary tone to forestall the prospect of interrogation. "That's my team. They broke the target, that's how it all came together. She's Cress, did the interpreting and put me in a ditch yesterday afternoon to protect me from what Sword called 'incoming'. They are rogues and are brilliant. I smell a bit because the ditch doubled as the village sewer."

It was difficult, in the confined space, to manoeuvre the bag. The cockpit boys had the forward corners and Sword and Tank had the rear ones. They lifted together, then waited. Next out was the tall, blonde woman whom Jonas had spoken to briefly when the jet had put down at Geneva's airport and she had joined them, and they had stayed only long enough on the ground for more gasoline.

He said, "In the bag is Skender, grandson of the clan boss, and our target. I killed him as surely as if I'd put a garrote around his throat and tightened it on his windpipe. She is a German citizen and Skender and she were lovers, and were planning to flee, and try to start a new life. His family, what remains of it, regards him as a traitor. We thought it right to bring her with us . . . don't often hang about waiting to do what is 'right', but did this time – for a change. He's to be buried here, with an absence of paperwork, but I expect you'll sort it out."

Jonas thought the AssDepDG gazed at him as if he had lost some marbles, or just exhausted and therefore emotional. It was hard work for them to carry the bag. Men at the cemetery gate took off their caps and beanies, and women had brought bunches of flowers, and he saw that Vera was there and had found time to collect a posy of the first of the spring blooms, small and fragile. The woman walked alongside the bag and her hand rested on the canvas. He had not known what to say to her. They went to the cemetery gate . . . he wondered what inducement had been offered the parish priest for a discreet performance, and would not ask.

He saw Croppy jump down . . . He had barely spoken to the boy, would have found words hard to conjure. Really only two sentences that were relevant to Croppy's own life; one was a biblical paraphrase along the lines of *greater love hath no man* and the other would have probably been dinned into the boy's head by a master teaching English Literature *it is a far, far better thing that I do than I have ever done, a far, far better rest that . . .* Two aspects of sacrifice and Jonas did not know whether either would ever have been appropriate to himself.

The target had covered Croppy so that low velocity bullets hit his own body, not Croppy's. He choked at the sight of the boy he had brought home. Croppy reached back, stretched out his arms and the child eased into them. She was white-faced, and wore a military style tunic, far too big for her. Cress had said to him that, her opinion, what had happened in the cellar had jolted her back from the trauma of the killing of her parents. She seemed vulnerable and frightened of everyone around her. Cress had said that the child had nothing to stay in that village for because it would be a site of conflict . . . Croppy let her feet down onto the grass. He held her hand and walked slowly with her and followed the column.

Jonas let them pass him, and followed.

Like the survivors from a disaster, natural or manmade, all of them headed for the gate into the cemetery and the open grave. He saw Sarah. She did not push forward, fling her arms round Croppy's neck, claim him, but stood back. It would be explained to her when the time was appropriate, who was this child, why she was important . . . And he had had enough of it.

He reached the gate and Vera was waiting for him. The villagers and the helicopter crew and the passengers were all at the graveside, and the priest was intoning, and a snatch of the words carried to Jonas, . . . *a stranger who came to us and who needed our care, and was welcomed* . . . which was probably the right thing to say.

Vera touched his hand. "You in one piece, Jonas?"

"Of course."

"Do you want to hang around a bit longer?"

"I don't think I do."

She hooked her hand in the crook of his arm. They walked together away from the cemetery. A cloud had come in, scurrying to intercept the rising sun, and he felt the cold search for his bones. He thought he had learned enough of the foot soldiers for whom he took a degree of responsibility – did not like it and felt that it would suffocate him. They reached the caravan and the cat was asleep in its cage. Jonas would drive, needed to.

He said, "I think if I stay here any longer it will destroy me. If you worry about who lives and who dies, who is harmed and who comes through, what is the end game and who has benefitted, then you will never get anything done. They will say, Vera, that I have no morality and a heart of stone. That I am not prepared to give up, am too selfish to care for others . . . other than you, other than Olaf. Because I am a seriously unpleasant person I am able to do my job. But, I suppose that is what any lowly functionary would claim."

She did not argue with him, which was a relief.

The flowers she had carried were left on the verge. She told him they were hyacinths and harebells, a few of the earliest blue-bells, ragged robin and marsh thistle, the best she could find. He drove a hundred yards up the road, found a gateway into a farm yard, and did rather a good reverse, and a successful turn, and he drove back down the road and had to pass the phalanx of parked vehicles carefully because of the caravan's width. Slowed almost to walking pace, and allowed himself a last look at the cemetery and was in time to see the bag being lowered and flowers thrown after it, and the girl close against Croppy's leg, and Sarah, and the German girl and his own team, and the helicopter crew were staring down purposefully, maintaining a level of dignity. At the first junction he swung the wheel and took the car and the caravan east and on to the main road that would eventually lead him off the peninsula.

It was done.

"Jonas, why did you drag me all the way up here?"

A job finished.

"I was frightened they might capture me, corrupt me with all this duty of care and responsibility stuff, don't want it. Needed you here, with me, to stamp on it."

A slate wiped clean.

"Where are we going, Jonas?"

He laughed. "Just want to show you a couple of places which gave me a bit of fun. Worth remembering before I get too boring."

Two hours after leaving the village of Kilchoan on the Ardnamurchan peninsula they stopped by the sea and waited for a small ferry to take them across Loch Linnhe. While Vera bounced with excitement at seeing a distant splash and swirl as an otter ploughed through a strait, Jonas took himself across the seaweed marooned after a high tide and peeled off his jacket and shirt, and washed his body in the chilly water, and slapped himself and would have astonished those familiar with him. Dunked the jacket and scrubbed at the muck with his hands. Thought he had purged himself of the smell and stain of where he had been – and heard a drone of a high engine, or pair of them and with God alone knew how much horsepower, and the "boys" must have seen the caravan, recognised it or perhaps it was spotted by the passengers, and its fuselage wobbled, like that was a gesture of salute. He would not see them again, did not care to and he was no "sharp end man", and reckoned he had brought little to the table, and had *cared* too greatly.

Two days after leaving the cemetery, the Jonas Merrick memorial tour had reached a small village south of the English Lake District and the caravan, inexpertly parked, was outside the car park of an old and weathered church. The village was Over Kellet, the church was St Cuthbert's. He was again asked, inevitable, as he left the car and stretched, and wondered where Olaf could be given space for a short roam, "What's the relevance of this place?" She was well justified in her question. He said that it was because of a situation that had brought him pride and pleasure, and he had reached out and held Vera's hand, and the "grumpy old fucker" image so often bestowed on him was replaced with that rather nervous smile: as if he gave away too much of himself. He had launched into his monologue about the value of "small" people, little people like himself – not the academics, not the "brains" of counter-intelligence, and not the blighters slumped in the leather chairs of London clubland who made no fuss, just rolled up their sleeves, and had the dogged determination to sift and sort and filter . . . He was about to tell Vera the merits of those keeping the trains running on time, the functionaries, when he was interrupted.

"This is not a picnic site. Overnight stays are strictly forbidden."

Jonas had not heard the cyclist's approach.

"And keep your cat away from our song birds, and their nests. Murderous brute."

An elderly man's face was contorted in suspicion and hostility.

"And the church is locked. So you had best be up and on your way."

It fell into place. Suspicion and hostility and noticing Chinese newspaper on a car seat, its driver gone to visit a grandparent's grave, and a long retired security guard from the factory nearby, which built the Eurofighter Typhoon, and making a phone call with the indignation of expecting an immediate search and destroy mission because of what he had seen – and hearing nothing, and never being thanked. The information had come to land, dog-eared, on Jonas Merrick's desk, and perhaps the greatest coup of the UK's agencies against Chinese espionage had followed. Did he congratulate the man? No. Did he explain anything of his own role in the triumph? Of course not. He said, meekly, that they would be on their way, and from the caravan door Olaf scowled.

"This is not a tourist place, but a house of worship."

Jonas drove away and his caravan lurched behind him, and he was chortling by the time they were back on the motorway.

Their next stop, reached by early afternoon, would be a quiet residential area in the city of Liverpool where Jonas wanted to check whether a pothole in a particular road had yet been filled by the City Council, and to see if there was still a small pencil-sized hole in the tarmacadam made by the second bullet of a police marksman's double tap. He might tell Vera on the way about the bravery of a stooge, working as an asset of the Drug Enforcement Administration in an area fed by an Amazon tributary. Might even tell her of the supreme courage of an undercover officer who had succeeded in bringing to court criminal clans from that city and in northern Spain . . . and might not. Might just stand on his own at the place where the pothole had been, likely still was.

And a few stops, a few days later, would be the hedgerow on the narrow lane, where he would pull in, below the cruelly steep incline of Glastonbury Tor, and a powerful bishop had met a bad end on the summit, and there resume his interrupted holiday, and hope to see the harriers beating up the helpless ducks.

Two weeks after a burial on a peninsula that had taken place without the appropriate paperwork, a light aircraft had landed on the north Icelandic coast.

Denys Montgomery could not claim that the welcome was enthusiastic. He told them, "It was just a sideshow getting Frank out of that place, and could have been the rest of the women, and we burned boats to do it, and tricked the GRU folks. It won't play out again like that. But a sideshow matters because it sends a message."

He had little idea where he was. A car had collected him at the airstrip and had driven him through a couple of bare mountain passes, and had set him down in a parking lot – shared with half a dozen cruise ship buses – and they had approached him warily. There was a waterfall as a backdrop, but his map told him that a waterfall seemed obligatory for every National Park on the island. He was the new Station Chief for Iceland, and the previous occupant had had a nervous breakdown, gone "stir crazy", and the switch had been welcomed in Human Resources, and his house was to be let and the hatch to the attic and the Somerset and Dorset, Shoscombe and Single Hill Halt, was padlocked.

"I saw Jonas a couple of days back, and he sends good wishes. He went to the limit to bring you home, Frank, beyond the limit – like a debt had to be cleared. And in the process he damaged their power structure to a huge degree. The government there is now holed below the waterline because of the money that was lost. Battles don't matter, nor the casualties in their trenches, but losing money is more than they can tolerate, turns them against each other . . . down to Jonas Merrick. End of speech."

Rather gravely, Denys Montgomery shook their hands. The one who called herself Pear kissed him lightly on the cheek, but Frank did not.

He said, "I'll be there in Reykjavik so come by and see me, please. Don't leave it too long. As a sideshow it packed a hell of a punch."

Nothing more to be said, he walked back to his car. Above him an endless stream of water plunged down the millennia-old layers of volcanic rock. Worth it? He supposed so, a level of policy achieved, and at low cost, as any useful sideshow should be.

Two weeks later, a section of a cemetery was closed off.

The Novodevichy burial place was much sought after, and was the resting place of many who had illustriously served the Kremlin in Soviet days, Yeltsin times and now in a twilight rule, also musicians and sculptors and artists who had been approved. It was an irony that a small plot had been found for Viktor inside the walls and railings. The coffin could not be open for the last rites as repairing the damage to his head was beyond the skills of the morticians. Good things were said about him. He was a loyal friend, a dedicated servant of the state, many had much to be grateful for through experiencing his company. All of those except one, who had lost money through his enterprises, were present, but the Leader sent a personal wreath of sombre flowers . . . There were smiles and hugs, and mutual hatreds abounded in the blame game because of the damage done to the leaders of an elite, and a clock could not be turned back.

Strangers came to a village, cursed the state of a track on the suspension of their Mercedes cars, and drove past a cemetery where they might easily have missed the mound of earth and mud that marked a newly filled grave. They would have had more urgent business in their minds than wondering about the death of Bresnik, a loyal and faithful servant of another regime. New faces, a new authority, ruled in the village – and they would be accepted because that was the route to survival, well practised over many centuries. The price of cocaine across Europe would not dip, and the price of girls, by the hour or the night, would rise. A bonfire at the back of the villa burned the former occupant's possessions and among the ashes would be the remains of a pair of garden shears.

Two months after Jonas had driven away from the bare hillsides of Ardnamurchan, the DepDG had "requested" that the AssDepDG accompany him on a tour of various areas of Thames House seldom visited.

Why? Because of Merrick.

There had been, as yet, no disciplinary courtroom drama in the building, but the kangeroos were still available and the AssDepDG thought they must have been champing at the bit. It was considered, in the view of the outstanding praise heaped on the Fivers by the Agency across the ocean, that Merrick had been allowed some safety slack . . . not to be relied upon because the criticism of freelancing ran deep in the suites of the fifth floor. They had met at the elevator bank on the third floor on the south side. There were various offices they might have visited first except that the DepDG had set off with a powerful stride until reaching the closed door, number 12. Had paused, had rapped on it, and without waiting for a reply had opened it . . . Aggie Burns was briefing. A brief pause, and she had kept going. Her audience of A section watchers, the cream of the surveillance teams, glanced up, noted the visitor, went back to listening. The AssDepDG hung back and permitted the Deputy Director General a clear run at the closed cubicle door in the corner with a view over the Thames, and of Lambeth Bridge across which Jonas Merrick tramped twice every weekday – and he was now past 70 and had the right to claim retirement on full pension. The door was opened. The DepDG, Brian to his friends – if there were any other than the ambitious – went inside. The AssDepDG knew, because he had checked, that he would find only the cleaners' kit, mops and brooms and dusters and squirters for polishing and window cleaning, and the racks of clothing that the A section needed depending on where they were working and the computer was gone and the walls were bare. Behind him the AssDepDG heard a snort, a demand for his attention . . . Aggie Burns caught his eye and gestured with her head at the wall behind her desk . . . her new and prized photograph, framed in gilt. There was the mounted vest from the pothole section of the Liverpool City Council, high visibility except for the dark bloodstain, never washed off, when it had been worn by Jonas Merrick, and an attacker shot dead by armed police. There was a new image – and he was responsible for her having it.

He had been shown it on a phone screen in a hotel bar, by as disreputable a creature as only Jonas Merrick could have employed, name of Sword and rated as a shagger and crawling all over a woman on the team. He had copied it, damn sure he had, and his sides had been close to splitting.

Aggie Burns had said, when Jonas had shown it to her, "I'd give my right tit to have a copy of that."

And here it was. The AssDepDG would not have wanted Brian to see his face. A wonderful picture. A group of men best described as ruffians, or hunter-killers and formed up around a fighting vehicle's bonnet for a team snap, loaded with lethal kit, and a three-legged mongrel dog, looked as if it might once have been a good ratter, sat on the lap of Jonas Merrick in the place of honour. Merrick's bloody lap. The grumpy old fucker covered in filth and mud, clothes and face, his hat askew, and adoration on their faces, and the dog's, and him almost managing a smile, and, Aggie told him, apparently named Milord by his new best friends.

He abruptly shepherded the Dep DG out. "Where now, Brian?"

"I think the Post Room."

"Yes, of course, why not."

Down in the lift, then a flight of stairs, then past the garage area where the AssDepDG's driver would be waiting – Harry who seemed most years to have to pull a caravan from one end of the kingdom to another, and who seemed always to have time to do some electrical or mechanical repairs for Vera Merrick which her husband was incapable of. Past the armed police rest area where Kev and Leroy were taking a tea break but hurried to avert their faces because twice the week before they had managed to hold up the DepDG's transport while getting Jonas off Lambeth Bridge and across the traffic lanes. And on, and into the Post Room.

The AssDepDG said, "You will remember, Brian, the plaudits we received in this building from our American allies, our colleagues? Remember the blood-letting in Kremlinville? The kicking of the Swiss government that meant a clutch of lawyers and accountants having to leave town? And the moaning from the City about our interference and things best left alone? Remember all that? I've put Jonas into a sort of hibernation. His current job, no surprises forecast, is to reduce waste in the building, cut it down, save money, preserve resources."

"Excellent, and . . .?"

He said, straight-faced – which was hard, "He's after paper clips. Metal paper clips. Touring sections, going floor by floor, hunting for them. Doing well, I hear."

To what extent the DepDG was aware of having his pecker tugged was unclear. They went inside. The Post Room had not been visited by a Deputy Director General for the best part of a decade, other than for layout familiarisation, before Jonas had come to join them. Work stopped. The man flushed. He was not greeted. Gazed around him, raked his eyes over racks and file holders and stationery stores, tables and desks and screens and keyboards, and secure metal cabinets, and located his target. Half-hidden in a corner with a barrier of cabinets guarding him was Jonas. Still in that bloody jacket of Harris tweed and it must have been sterling work by dry cleaners to get it back in play. They headed in his direction.

The AssDepDG said quietly, "What I would also feel worth reminding ourselves of . . . Merrick is the sort of chap you want around in case of a rainy day – or when an event – capital E – falls from nowhere, no warning. Whatever triggers it, an event or the heavens tipping down, we have a use for him. With me, Brian?"

Not that a reply was expected.

The DepDG stood behind the chair occupied by the hunched figure. Olaf, the Norwegian Forest cat, had been demoted . . . The screen saver on Jonas' computer showed a ruined croft on a hill-side with a mud-streaked digger sunk in a rutted bog and a girl in shorts and a T shirt and wellington boots, her hair tied back in a scarf, manoeuvring a roof beam towards a ladder at the top of which was balanced a wiry young man. Behind her was a pile of similar beams and the work seemed awesome, and all against a backdrop of gunmetal grey clouds.

With a tone he might have used visiting a care home, the AssDepDG asked, "How is it going, Jonas, the search for unwanted surplus paper clips?"

He was glowered at. On the desk were transparent plastic bags each containing paper clips, and on the floor beside a briefcase was a black plastic bucket half filled with paper clips. There was on Jonas Merrick's face, as the AssDep DG read it, "dumb insolence", but the war on waste was a totem of good management, a sacred icon, and could not be mocked.

"Surprised how much over-purchasing there's been – even up on the fifth floor. You'd be amazed."

"I am sure I would be, amazed . . . Keep up the good work."

It was a protocol in Thames House that staff were not permitted to put up personal pictures, use sellotape or blu tack, because that would damage the expensive colour schemes called for by interior design consultants. Close to the screen, on the wall, was a montage of photographs: a cheerful looking spaniel, just out of a mud bath; an otter dismembering a giant crab; and two pictures of a teenage girl, dressed in a white blouse and a black hoodie, and a black skirt, and clutching an armful of books.

The AssDepDG said as they left the Port Room, "I'd like to share this with you, Brian. About Merrick. I'm glad, very glad, he's on our side, not on theirs. Yes, very glad about that."

And Jonas Merrick was left at peace, and would not have to go out again to a stationery shop and buy another gross of paper clips, and could get on with what he liked best, working at his screen and keyboard, receiving tips and leaks and snippets and making sense of them, and finding something on which to lock a lowly analyst's concentration.